To Flash and Rapunzel, we will go to Japan!

Acknowledgements

Massive thanks to Cheryl, Angela, Auntie Lill and Eddie for being my guinea pig readers and giving me the courage go forward and publish. Huge thanks to Jamie for your editing and suggestions.
To my three children, thank you for being so patient whilst I worked all day, then completed this book on nights and weekends. You are truly the most amazing children a Mother could have. Yet the biggest thanks to my Davey, not one single part of my dream and this book would have been possible without you and your support. Over the years, you have created a world full of joy, laughter and security for me and my children, all whilst encouraging us all to reach for our dreams. Cannot put into words how amazing the world would be with more people like you in it.

And to all that read this book, thank you, and remember, this is fiction!

Chapter 1
Joshua - The Alternate Future

The building rocked as another explosion was heard outside. The full city was in utter turmoil, with the financial district their main target.

Wistern Tower, 1120 Down Street, hosted only the most prestige financial institutions. The once upmarket foyer was strewn with broken chairs and smashed glass. Dust, debris and now meaningless papers scattered the once highly polished pale marble floor; an unwelcome residue of the riot that had happened only hours earlier. Chunks of plaster lay at the foot of the walls from the continuous explosions that shook the building, revealing the brick and metal work underneath. The lights flickered, signalling the electricity had been cut and the generator had kicked in. The six lifts, three either side of the long foyer, now dented and sprayed with the blood of the dead that lay at their floors, remained open.

An eerie silence adorned the foyer, instead of the bustling financial tower block it once was. The stairs to the left of the lifts, partially blocked by a couple of bodies and a large amount of wall that had contributed to their death, led up to the other 33 floors. The explosions, gun fire and screams of people from outside, running from their imminent death, started to echo inside the office block, trying to inform the occupants there had been a breach into the building.

On the twenty-eighth floor, a group of five people slowly emerged from the panic room they had been hidden in. Walking out to the untouched office that had once served a senior member of the bank, they nervously smiled at each other.

A mid-twenties, athletic male with dark, short hair, dressed in old, worn clothing, walked across to the window and looked through the glass at the destruction below.

The once protected area of Rylitte, owned by the leader of the Matriats, Lamia Rylitte, had fallen. The streets were littered with the dead, Matriats and Servians alike. Squinting at the carnage, he could easily tell the Matriats from the Servians by their stance and weapons. The Matriats staying in formation, rigid, skilled, and in sync, robotic in their duty. The Servians fearless, resembling old age warriors, pushing forward with no regard, little in protection. Their muscular, sweating bodies, glinting in the morning sun. Organised chaos between them.

The world's history was steeped in the separation of the Matriats and Servians, two different worlds on one planet. The Matriats, made up of the rich and powerful, ruled with fear, most gleaning joy from twisted torment. The Servians, poor and weak, were made to breed to keep the stock high for the Matriats entertainment. The Matriats raided the Servians towns daily, raping and killing anyone they wanted to, pillaging the little they had, leaving the children scavenging for food. Blowing up their tiny shacks while the occupants were asleep inside, the Matriats laughed as the blood and gore, splattered the faces of Servian men, women and children. Screams echoed through the villages as the Servians awoke to flames licking the walls of their simple mud and wooden huts, crying in anguish as they watched their children consumed in the fire. Whilst the Matriats sat back and watched with wicked smiles on their faces, the carnage they had caused from afar.

It was only a matter of time before the Servians had rebelled. A growing underground opposition had been planning the overturn for many years, secretly building an army and weapons, keeping them hidden in villages that had just been attacked by the Matriats, knowing they would only come back when it had been rebuilt. Children that showed strength, intelligence or beauty within the Servians, where taken from their Mothers and trained for the Matriats use. A 'taken' was used for their talents, then tossed back into the Servian world or killed when their gifts faded with age or illness.

'Be careful Joshua!' A well-dressed woman shouted across to him.

'They won't see us up here Liz.' Joshua replied throwing her a cheeky smile.

He loved Liz like a Mother, she looked younger than her 60 years, with her long red curls and voluptuous stature. Always immaculately dressed in a sharp business suit, though she had sold her business and retired 10 years ago to take up her hobby of Physics. Extremely intelligent, savvy business woman and a long standing family friend, Joshua was incredibly lucky to have her as an influential person in his life.

'No one is watching the CCTV, Joshua, the drones are looking for anyone out of place. If one of them captures you in Servian dress, they'll storm this building.' Her tone warned him to get away from the window.

He moved out of view and looked around the room that was once his Fathers. He touched the large mahogany desk and leather chair as he passed, knowing he wouldn't be seeing it again. His Father's office was always timeless. The dark bookcases, highly polished wooden flooring, with a carpeted area near the expensive leather couches. The bookshelves neatly packed with the usual accounting hardbacks and encyclopaedias, yet at the far end corner, housed his Fathers guilty pleasure, medical and physic journals.

The coffee machine was fully stocked, as if to host its next meeting, and the next generation of tablet, which automatically downloaded the new Financial Times and archived the old ones for reference, still laid on the coffee table, as if his Father were about to walk through the door.

His childhood was littered with memories of visiting his Father here, and even now as an adult, he still felt small in comparison to the vast room. A huge digital frame featured in between the couches, above the coffee table, sequenced through family photos, his Father, a well fed, jolly man, thin greying hair showcased in them with Joshua.

A slim brunette walked up to Joshua and reached out to touch his face. She looked into his blue eyes with concern. 'Are you ready?' She asked, her voice shaking with emotion. She knew this day would come, although, she was not ready. She looked down not wanting him to see her cry. A piece of her wavy long hair fell in front of her face. Joshua reached under her chin and pulled her face up to look at him, brushing the loose hair behind her ear.

'I know you are worried Jess, but we have no choice.'

'I know' she whispered. 'If I had known today would be the last day …..' She trailed off.

'Me too' Joshua answered her unspoken words. Sighing, he kissed the top of her head and wrapped his arms around her. He would miss her smile, her smell, her comfort. No-one knew Joshua like Jess did. Childhood best friends that turned into a love story. A love story that was about to end.

Another explosion reverberated outside and a howl of the newly injured echoed in the room.

'Shit, we need to get a move on.' Richard shouted.

Joshua nodded at Richard, a solid muscular 6-foot-tall genius. His curly brown hair was all that gave note to his 'geek' side. Dressed in trousers and a casual t-shirt that was made to measure, Richard was clearly a taken. Not a total fit into the Matriats, yet too well dressed and educated to be a Servian.

Joshua walked to the right of one of the couches and opened the cupboard next to the en suite bathroom with the key from around his neck. He reached inside and pulled out his full protective suit. Stroking the fabric, he smiled as he remembered the first time he saw the shimmering material.

He was fifteen years old and upon returning home from visiting his Fathers office early, he noticed the door to the private study was slightly open. Peeking through the open crack, Joshua saw his Mother bent over a shiny metallic machine, waist height. Curious, he had watched as she took different materials from his Fathers desk and carefully fed them into the top of the machine. A soft, elastic fabric slowly folded itself midway out of the polished appliance. The machine had jammed and his Mother had cursed, causing Joshua to inhale sharply. He had never heard that language from his Mother before. Upon hearing Joshua, his Mother had looked up quickly, fear of who was watching her etched across her face. Seeing Joshua, the fear soon reset itself to a smile, yet her eyes still showed the worry inside.

'Joshua, my son, how was your Father? You are home early, is everything OK?'

'Father had to attend an emergency meeting, so I came home. What are you doing?' Joshua asked walking further into the room.

'Just a little hobby of mine, I like to experiment with fabrics as much as your Father loves to gaze at the stars. I am hoping to make him something that is light weight and warm so he can still watch the stars outside in winter. Come, you must be hungry. Sarah has made some excellent Goulash.'

His Mother had guided him out of the room and locked the door upon exit. The housekeepers Goulash had indeed been delicious, yet he could always tell when his Mother was lying. Finding out years later, she had been working on designing a light weight bullet proof suit for his safety, yet had never been successful. Although she may never know, she had completed a perfect suit for the journey he was about to take.

The building rocked again, the wailing of the wounded growing louder.
'We have to go NOW' Richard shouted.
His protective suit on, Joshua made his way to the bookcases. Reaching under the second shelf, he felt around for the button. Pressing it, a thin horizontal blue light shone out and moved down his face. The others waited behind him as the face scanner authorised him entry. The bookcase moved, revealing a metal door that slid open.
'Welcome Mr East' A robotic female voice addressed Joshua as he entered the lift.
'Are you sure this is safe with the electricity out?' Jess enquired as she followed him inside.
'It runs on a secondary generator, powered by the river that runs through the city, my Father designed it himself, I hope this reassures you.' Joshua gravely replied.
With all of them inside the lift, Joshua pressed his thumb against the finger scanner. Authenticating him, the lift doors shut and started to descend. Reaching inside his protective suit he located his pocket, checking to see if his Fathers letter was still there.
His Father knew this was coming. He knew it before he was murdered by the Matriats, before they cowardly laced his drink with poison.
In his last minutes, he had sent an encrypted message by email to Joshua, which deleted two minutes after being opened. It gave Joshua instructions of the hand written letters location, and to only open when the war broke out.
Mixed emotions ran through Joshua when he read the letter, however now it all made sense.

Chapter 2
Rachel - Present Day

The irritating screams of party goers echoed out of the club. The thudding bass of the dance music vibrated down the street. Music blasted out each time the bouncers opened and shut the door for the punters. Venture Club was crawling with the most obnoxious of Stanis Town. Snaking around the corner, the queue was impossible, unless you were scarcely dressed or had the money for a quick entrance.

Rachel sat on the cold pavement opposite the club, not caring it was still wet from the rain earlier. Taking a long drag from her menthol cigarette, Rachel blew it up into the night sky and leant back against the cold, damp wall. The streets were awash with festive lights, discarded bottles and bits of fancy dress, which had long since lost its owner. Party goers shouting unintelligible Christmas lyrics as they staggered across the cobbled paths, made Rachel shake her head.

A fight broke out in the queue, a Santa and a reindeer going hell for leather at each other. A crowd emerged, shouting and jeering at the two drunken men rolling around on the floor. The Santa stood up and staggered backwards slightly. With his fist held high, he swayed awkwardly, trying to focus on the reindeer. Surging forward towards his target, the Santa punched the air, missing the reindeer, leaving the crowd screaming with laughter.

Rolling her eyes, Rachel wondered to herself again why she agreed to attend the works Christmas party, the night was bound to end in trouble. Not wanting to appear a complete bore, she'd agreed, however, the promise of a VIP Booth and fast track passes into the club made it slightly more bearable. Having to queue on a cold winters evening, playing photographer and best friend to the strangers next to her, was not Rachel. Never the social type, she preferred to be at home with a cup of tea, or even a meal with close friends, than out on the town, fake smiling and complimenting people she normally tried to avoid.

Rachel hated the month of December, why people turned a religious holiday into a month's alcohol fuelled, coke taking party bemused her. She did not believe in religion, the beginning of her life involved far too much misery to believe in God. Then as she grew older, learning about the wars that ravaged over 'sacred' ground, reading the men, women and children that had died for their religion, cemented her opinion.

Rachel could understand why people celebrated, yet did not understand their mentality when they took it too far. Watching them at a supermarket made her stomach turn. Their trolleys overflowing with food, only to be thrown out a few days later, it was glutinous and pointless.

It was even harder seeing a small thin child stood outside the shop, desperately looking at every full trolley, wishing they could be part of that household for one day, yet knowing their parent will come out with just a packet of cigarettes and bottle of vodka. Rachel knew it was wrong on so many levels.

Many had tried to get her to participate in a bit of Christmas cheer, whether it be secret Santa or some illicit drug to loosen her up, yet Rachel had always declined, not one to crack under peer pressure. She was misread as straight laced, yet Rachel had fought far too hard to be where she was today. She would not lose what she had accomplished to date, for one night of illicit pleasure.

She wasn't looking forward to tomorrow morning either, work nights out always ended in drama. She didn't mind when Steph, her admin, relayed her latest conquest, in fact it was quite funny the situations she ended up in, but the Christmas night out was guaranteed to end messy with Rachel the one clearing it up. Dismissing an employee based on allegations from the works night out was not her idea of fun.

Rachel heard the sound of footsteps coming towards her, turning her head she saw Nick approaching. Nodding to acknowledge she'd seen him, Nick sat down on the floor next to her.

He shot up. 'Bloody hell Rach, its frigging wet! Look at my jeans.'

Rachel couldn't help but smile, a large wet patch had formed on the back of his faded denim jeans.

You wouldn't think Nick was her boss, MD of the firm. In his late 40's, he looked good, his floppy light brown hair, blue eyes and

clean-shaven face made him look younger than his years. His wicked sense of humour complimented his confidence well, yet his accent and mannerisms indicated he came from a wealthy background, though he never mentioned his home life.
Spotting her fake leather jacket underneath her, he chortled to himself
'Why are you always so sensible' he asked.
Rachel shrugged her shoulders and took another drag on her cigarette, hoping Nick had not noticed her sullen mood. They had a friendly work relationship, yet he was still her boss and effectively, this was a work occasion.
'Fancy getting out of here and going for a coffee?' Nick questioned, raising an eyebrow at Rachel.
'Immensely' Rachel replied, her mood lifting instantly. She got up and walked towards the cigarette bin.
Extinguishing her cigarette into it, she raised her eyebrows at Nick. 'Always so sensible.' She mocked looking at the cigarette ends littering around them.
Nick laughed and led her to the 24-hour Fast Food outlet which was conveniently around the corner of the club.
Lighting another cigarette, Rachel stayed outside while Nick went and ordered the coffees. The place was bustling with drunken scoundrels and a few homeless begging for money. The security on the front doors, stood gossiping to each other, only stopping to gawp when young females entered the place wearing scarcely any clothes. Looking at her cigarette, Rachel made a mental note to buy some nicotine patches for the New Year, she may not believe in Christmas and its madness, but she believed in fresh starts and it was time she gave these up.
Nick walked out with their coffees and a bag with a couple of cheeseburgers. He offered her one and suggested waiting in their office, which was a 10-minute walk from the fast food place, for a taxi home. Rachel nodded and bit into her Cheeseburger, not realising how hungry she was.
They bantered as they walked towards their office, Rachel grateful she could trust Nick. More like an older brother or Father figure, she felt reassured no harm would come to her if they were alone together. Though occasionally, her childhood memories would creep in, replaying parts of her childhood she had hidden deep, making her doubt anyone's credibility. Rachel shuddered as the memories tried to sneak in when she realised she would be alone

with Nick. Closing her eyes, willing them to go back in the buried box in her head, she reasoned with herself, she was just tired, she had known Nick far too long for him to be like that.

The office was located in a large seven-story building. Situated on the corner of an intersection, the drab, murky structure, jutted out like a sore thumb next to the stylish, newly built office blocks adjacent to it.

Smiling at Nick as she ate her cheese burger, Nick pulled a face at her and asked what she was doing.

'Thanking you through the art of face mime for the burger.' She answered.

'What is face mime?' Nick asked laughing pulling another face. 'You look deranged!'

'Ok, I'll use the art of speech, thank you for the burger, you are an angel for buying me it!' Rachel muffled through her last bite as they reached the entrance.

'One, don't ever show me the contents of your mouth again.' He laughed. 'And two, I thought you didn't believe in angels? What kind of compliment is that?' He quipped.

Rachel stuck her tongue out at him as he punched in his code and opened the door for her.

The inside of the building did not pay homage to the interior. Immaculate white walls and bronzed sculptures adorned the entrance. Abstract Art hung on the walls with soft lighting above, highlighting its features. To the left of the entrance area, pale gold couches, chairs and small glass tables with fanned out literature, dotted around the seating area, giving a warm feel on entry. The in-house coffee shop closed for the evening featured on the right of the entrance, normally offering an array of drinks, snacks and food.

The marble floor clicked beneath their feet as they walked towards the high-tech security desk. A large board displaying names and numbers for the companies that were located in the building hung above the desk alongside a TV showing the news. Volume muted, subtitles on.

'Hands out!' The night security barked, pulling back his jacket and placing one hand on the gun that was holstered at his waist.

Rachel's eyes widen with shock, their normal security guard Adam was never armed. Nervously she placed her now slightly sweating hand in the scanner until it beeped, bringing up her name, occupation and company she worked for.

'Proceed.' The night security guard waved his hand towards the full body scanner. Confused, Rachel stood, hands up as the scanning machine whirled around her. Throughout the time Rachel had worked there, she had never noticed a full body scanner. It was a huge machine, she would have seen it within the buildings entrance.

It beeped, Rachel held her breath unsure what to do next. The security guard waved her through and motioned Nick to enter. Rachel exhaled slowly, her heart beating out of her chest as she waited for Nick.

'What the hell!' she mouthed at Nick when he'd finished. Nick just smiled calmly, not fazed by the added security measures.

After checking their authenticity, the security man relaxed his stature and moved his hand away from his gun. 'I hope I didn't scare you Miss?' he asked, aiming his apology at Rachel 'It's not that often anyone comes here after midnight.'

'No problems Glen, better to be safe than sorry.' Nick answered for her, leaving Rachel lost for words.

Nick never took the lift, therefore Rachel followed him in silence, as he walked up the stairs, unsure how to broach the subject of the added security.

She had started at S.U.S. Industries over 14 years ago, gaining an apprenticeship as an office junior and had never noticed the body scanner at the entrance. Unlike her to be unobservant, she realised she had never visited the office after hours. S.U.S. Industries were employee focused, if the work was not completed by 5pm, it needed to wait until the next day. Emily, the long standing receptionist, rounded everyone up at the end of the day, ensuring the work force left no later than 5.30pm. It was common knowledge if you worked for S.U.S. and worked hard, you had a job for life. Gaining the apprenticeship was a chance to leave the past behind her. Grabbing it with both hands, Rachel worked hard, went above and beyond on every project or piece of work she was given, never took a day off sick and ensured her work was head and shoulders above everyone else's. Nick, spotting her enthusiasm, coached her into what she was now, S.U.S.'s head materials buyer. Giving her the opportunity to learn different languages, he fully supported and paid for her courses to become multi-lingual. She often wondered what would have happened if she had not won the sought-after apprenticeship at S.U.S.

Industries. Most probably on the street, with her crack head mother.

Breathing heavily when she reached the seventh floor, Rachel lent against the wall, swearing she would never take the stairs again.

Nick raised his eyebrow. She knew Nick was referring to her smoking habits contributing to the breathlessness. He had never approved of smoking with anyone, yet she convinced herself she deserved to smoke as it was her only vice. She rarely drank alcohol, never took drugs and had a clean police record.

They reached the entrance to S.U.S. Industries reception and to Rachel's surprise, a heavy wooden door was closed where she normally just breezed into work. It had 4 glass panes towards the top half of the door and intricate carvings decorated the rest. Stopping in her tracks, Rachel bent down to take a closer look at the bottom half of the dark oak door in front of her. She ran her hand over the first carving, a tribute to a very beautiful woman.

Nick moved in between her and the door, blocking her view before she got chance to inspect the carvings further. About to protest, when, for the second time that night, Rachel's eyes widened. Nick raised his hand and pressed on the lower right pane of the glass; a blue glow emitted from the pane as it scanned his palm.

'Welcome Mr Jenson.' A robotic female voice boomed out as the door automatically opened. 'I see you have a guest with you tonight.'

Opened mouthed Rachel looked at Nick. He gave a brief, reassuring smile.

'This is Rachel, V.E.L.U.S.' Nick spoke as he walked across the plush light grey carpet, towards the unmanned reception. 'She is the head buyer of S.U.S. Industries, steel works.' Moving behind the white pristine desk, Nick stood still and looked up. A blue horizontal light, slowly moved up and down, beeping after every 5 centimetres.

'Welcome Miss Nichols.' the female robotic voice boomed. 'The others are waiting, please proceed to the meeting room when ready, we have been expecting your arrival.'

Chapter 3
Joshua - The Alternate Future

Moving down in the lift, the silence between them all was deafening. Joshua could hear his heart pounding and was sure the others could hear it too. The lift was spacious enough to fit all five comfortably, yet they stood close together.

Jess was by his side, her hand around his waist and head resting lightly on his shoulder. He looked down at her innocent face. Gazing at her petite features, his heart swelled with love and pride, knowing that this renowned surgeon was his. She was well sought after; her knowledge and quick thinking had gained her a fantastic reputation, her tough attitude and no nonsense approach is what gained her consultancy.

Joshua scanned the stainless-steel surrounding and wished his Father was with them. Designing and building it all to withstand any type of attack, he was a technical genius to them all, Joshua hoped by the end of the day, he still was.

His eyes stopped on the left-hand side of the lift displaying eight different screens, six giving a 360 vision of the interior of the shaft as they went further down, the other two displaying the carnage outside. As he watched the bloodbath occurring out there, Joshua was distracted by Caelan clearing his throat.

Caelan, a mid-50's stocky man, with light brown hair, normally of very few words, took a deep breath and addressed them all.

'When we get down there, I need you to wait while I check the area.' Pausing, he checked they were all listening. 'On my word, you need to go straight to your stations. Any doubts we may have, any tweaks we need to make, it's too late.' His voice faltered and his grey eyes began to fill. Joshua felt Jess's hand tightened around his waist. 'It is time to honour everything Stephen East fought for, it is time to honour your Father Joshua.'

Joshua nodded towards Caelan, his Dad's best friend and security guard, acknowledging the love and loyalty Caelan had for his Father.

Caelan was a taken. Removed from his mother at the age of three.
The small village Caelan resided in before he was taken, was situated miles away from the Matriats domain.
An evil Matriat by the name of Avali, renowned for her hours of torture on her chosen victims, was leading a section of the army to retrieve weapons on the current leader of the Matriats, Lamashtu's orders. Stumbling across the village on their travels, the troop could not believe their luck. A night of entertainment had been bestowed upon them. Avali rubbed her hands together with glee as she barked orders of the raid to her troops. Delegating to her second in command to document the unknown village and report it back to Lamashtu, she stood up ready to give the signal.
Avali, extremely tall and muscular, was feared by all, including her fellow male Matriats. Twisted beyond belief, she sought out young children, only leaving the youngest alive to watch their own families bleed to death.
Giving the signal, the troops ran ahead whooping as they went to pillage, rape and kill the Servians.
Followed by two guards, Avali walked slowly, looking around the huts, hunting for the ultimate prey. Her sharp eyes spotted a little boy playing with his two older sisters through a hut window. Seeing his big grey eyes, small stature and sweet nature, a slow wide smile spread across Avali's lips. She did not care for riches or possessions, she only cared for the way she felt when she watched the innocence drain from a child's eyes.
Removing her knife out of its sheath at her waist, she signalled to the two guards accompanying her to stand watch at the door. Avali had no time for guns, a coward's choice she would often roar at the other soldiers. She had been shot previously, but only her pride wounded when she had been stabbed. Avali did not feel pain like others, often tending to her wounds herself, no need for pain relief.
Checking the two Matriats were standing guard, she smiled, she would enjoy this without any disruptions.
As she opened the wooden door, she was greeted by screams from the mother.

Avali scanned the small shack. Two beds, a table with four chairs and a little store cupboard was all that furnished the one roomed hut. Avali realised the Father of the family was not there, a favourite situation of hers. Drawing out the pain and anguish. The boy would watch as Avali tortured his sisters. She would make him stare into his Mothers eyes while the life left them. She would relish watching the child in anguish as the people he loved bled to death in front of him. To merely repeat this again when she had hunted down the Father, leaving the boy alone with only a corpse for company. Twice the pain for him and twice the pleasure for Avali.

The mother tried to guard her children behind her, yet one of them attempted to escape through the window. However, Avali practised in this situation, caught her immediately, and tied her up with thin cable wraps. The little boy reached for his sister. 'Caelan No.' The mother sobbed pulling him back. Avali sneered at Caelan and tied the rest of them up.

Kneeling down, Avali moved her head to whisper in Caelan's ear. 'You will watch. If you do as you are told, I may spare you and your Mother.' She lied, grinning at Caelan as she moved away, her black teeth barely visible in the shadows.

The little boy did not flinch, instead she saw his eyes grow angry, but no sound came from his mouth. Avali threw her head back and laughed, strange little boy, he would soon be crying and pleading with her when he watched the life die from his family's eyes. She stood up and grabbed one of the sisters, a quick flick of the knife on both her heels to cut the tendon. A trick Avali used to stop them escaping. They would not escape if they could no longer walk. The sister screamed in pain. The little boy watching, did not react, not even a tear shed, just merely stared. Those intent grey eyes, getting darker with anger, not blinking, simply staring straight at Avali, slowly rocking from side to side, not taking his eyes off her for a second. Avali looked at him moving about.

'Stop fidgeting' she ordered. The little boy carried on swaying.

'I said stop fidgeting!' She screamed over the howls of his sisters' agony.

Caelan kept moving, his eyes not leaving Avali. Dropping the sister, Avali marched across to back hand the boy, a warning to keep still. However, Caelan had anticipated the giant's actions. Watching as she raised her hand ready to strike, he jumped up, free from his restraints and leapt onto the table. Avali saw the glint of the knife in the corner of her eye as Caelan plunged the blade into her neck. Twisting it as he jumped down. Caelan kept his eyes trained on Avali. Blood pumped from her neck, spraying the room and its occupants. Caelan remained still, observing the wet warm blood oozing down the giants body. Putting her hand to her neck, Avali's eyes widened with disbelief as she felt the helm of the blade poking out of her. Dislodging the knife, the blood flowed more freely. The pale blue fabric from her uniform, now awash with red, soaking little of the liquid that continued to pulse from her neck, whilst the excess pooled at her feet.

Caelan's Mother and sisters screamed in the background at Caelan to run, find his Father, screamed at the blood running from the ogre in their little shack.

Caelan's eyes stayed on Avali until she fell face down on the floor, dead.

The Matriat from outside the window, had seen it all. Secretly relieved Avali was killed, he called for the taken team. Caelan was taken from his Mother and sisters to be trained as a protector to the highest bidder, never to see his family again.

The lift ground to a halt and the doors slowly opened.

Caelan pulled out a gun and pointed it at the slowly opening doors, expecting anything or anyone could be in the well-hidden laboratory at a time like this. The Matriats were dedicated to knowing all that happened within their cities, yet so far the lab had not been discovered.

'You all ready?' Caelan shouted.

'Yes' they all replied in unison.

The doors opened, Caelan walked out slowly and checked the room.

'GO!' he shouted, signalling the room was clear.

The laboratory was vast and white. A colossal semi-circle control panel, mirrored half of the round room, and featured a variation of different buttons whilst housing five black leather office chairs. Blue projections floated above the console, showing intricate diagrams of machinery and maps. The dome shaped roof was padded out for sound proofing and a round metal trap door featured on the ceiling.

Jess ran to a door positioned halfway around the room. Pulling out a heavy box and a first aid kit, she carried them back to the lift where Joshua and Caelan still stood monitoring the screen that displayed the carnage still occurring in the outside world.

Holding a small metallic object in his hand, Caelan waited. No sound was heard, but he spotted the ideal moment, an explosion lit up the monitor and Caelan pressed the metal object.

'Brace yourselves' he shouted.

The sound of the bomb going off in the lift echoed around the laboratory, rocking the room slightly. Caelan let out a long sigh. Against all odds they had made it this far, and he had secured the lab.

The guilt of Stephen Easts murder still ate away at him, he was his protector, yet had failed. He had not slept since his death, keeping watch over Joshua, ensuring when the time came, Joshua would be safe to carry out the mission and complete Stephens work. It was the least he could do.

He looked around, marvelling at the craftsmanship of the laboratory. If it could withhold that bomb, the rest of what Stephen had constructed would certainly work.

His eyes rested on Joshua still stood next to him. 'No going back, its time.' He said as he slapped him on the back.

Turning away, they walked together towards the circular white metal contraption in the middle of the room. A door opened from halfway up, slowly lowering and fashioning itself into stairs, revealing a comfortable padded white interior. A large white chair that could be reclined into a small bed featured in the middle, with two IV drips hanging just above the chair. An oxygen mask dangling slightly below the IV drip, still rocked from the earlier blast. Two monitors embedded in the interior switched on, and the buttons below lit up.

Caelan led Joshua to the huge machine, at least three times taller than his stocky frame. He touched the white coated metal exterior as he climbed up the steps. Motioning Joshua to follow him, Caelan explained they had made a few adjustments. Talking through the modifications, Caelan could tell Joshua was not listening. Patting him on the shoulder, he left, to give him a few minutes on his own.

Joshua had been listening to Caelan, yet his mind was wandering. He looked around, registering the small changes that had been made.

His Father and Liz had commissioned the full build. Buying the building next to his Fathers office block, they had not only built the laboratory and hidden lift, but also designed and built the huge machine he sat in.

Requiring assistance to quicken the build, they found Richard. Richard had been placed for sale at auction, his owner having died and the family members having no requirements for his ability. Richards's reputation as a gifted taken in computer science had intrigued Liz and Stephen. Snapping him up, Richard had not disappointed. Methodical and confident, he became an asset to their cause overnight.

Richard admired Stephen, from how he treated him as an equal, to the reason he had been brought in. Stephen had safeguarded Richard, ensuring he had the freedom of a Matriat, thus Richard had proved his loyalty by working harder than he ever had before, pushing the boundaries of coding and progressing the build vastly. Designing all the security measures, including the face recognition, Richard proudly presented him with V.E.L.U.S., the first of its kind. A programme that thought like a human, yet had the brains of a computer. Stephen was overjoyed and promptly invited Joshua to try it out. Feeling exceedingly awkward talking to thin air at first, Joshua soon marvelled at the never-ending abilities V.E.L.U.S. had.

Seeing Richard working away on the console through the door of the capsule, he knew this would not be happening without him.

As he sat on the edge of the chair, the new carpet caught Joshua's eye. Smiling to himself as he realised his initials J.E. and S.U.S. Industries was emblazed across the floor.

S.U.S. Industries was his Fathers 'company' he and Liz had set up. As to not arouse suspicion, their joint venture also included buying two factories, providing steel for building contractors. Joshua had been heavily involved in both factories, providing good working conditions and a safe place for Servians. His Father, a thorough man, had ensured full control of the accounts prior to being issued to the auditors, safeguarding the expenditure for the laboratory was hidden well.

Joshua laid back into the chair, arms outstretched, ready, as he saw Jess entering the pod. Jess hooked him up to the IV's, one for fluid and one for nutrients.

'Remember, the gas that will be released to put you to sleep will smell slightly strange, however this will not compare to the worst hangover you will wake up with.' She laughed, yet it did not reach her eyes. Motioning to the bottle of water in a holder just below the monitors, she continued. 'I have had this put at eye level, so when you awake you have water. Please sip it.' A little bag hung next to it with the words *open me* embroidered into it. 'This has a combination of pills for the pain and to help your memory. You'll be confused when you awake.'

'I love Dr Jess' Joshua smiled and pulled her in for a kiss.

'Come on Jase, I need to attach you.' Jess pushed him off, her eyes brimming with tears. She didn't know what was going to happen next, no one knew what was going to happen next. The only certainty was the pain she felt knowing she would never see him again. Placing the oxygen mask over his face, she kissed his forehead. 'Don't forget me.' she whispered.

'I won't.' he whispered back, his voice thick with emotion.

Jess blew him one last kiss and left to make way for Caelan to finish the checks.

Clicking the restraints into position, a sad smile crossed Caelan's face. 'We'll track you as far as we can, however we will know if you have been successful. It's been an honour serving you and your family.' Caelan saluted Joshua and climbed out the pod.

Liz and Richard were fervently working away on the console, sliding this way and that on their chairs, shouting check every few seconds.

The door on the huge machine started to close.

'Ready in 30 seconds' Liz shouted.

Jess sat in the seat next to Liz, the screen was on Joshua's face. A single tear ran down her cheek.

'25 seconds'

The metal hatch in the ceiling was moving sideways revealing a long metallic tube that pointed towards the sky.

'20 seconds'

The colossal white metal ball, slowly started moving higher, pushed up from underneath by a mechanical arm. The capsule rotated, placing it in position for departure. A protective glass shield moved up from behind the console, enclosing the four that was left into a safe environment.

'15 seconds'

The flash from beneath the ball showed the engines where working and ready.

'10, 9, 8...' Jess put her hand on the screen trying to absorb every last memory of Joshua.

'5, 4.' She felt Caelan's steady hand on her shoulder as he watched the screen with her.

'3, 2, 1'

The thrusters ignited, throwing anything loose in the laboratory to the side, however in the glass box, they heard, nor felt anything. The magnificent white shiny ball shot up in the air and through the tunnel, with the four below catching a glimpse of the lettering on the underside of the capsule.

J.E.
S.U.S.
INDUSTRIES

Joshua and the machine gone, they all looked at each other.

'Caelan......' Jess started to say as she reached out to his face that was fading into dust. Her outreached hand, also started to fade away. She looked around at the others, they were all fading. Joshua's mission had been successful.

Chapter 4
Rachel - Present Day

Rachel looked at Nick, at the door and back at Nick again. Not the foggiest idea of what she should do. A million thoughts and scenarios ran through her mind. It did not feel real, it felt like a dream, it felt, surreal.
Nick walked around the desk and put his hands on Rachel's shoulders. 'If I told you, you wouldn't believe me, I have to show you.'
Using his hand on her shoulder, Nick guided Rachel to behind the reception desk.
'Stand here and stand still.' He pointed to where he had just been stood. 'V.E.L.U.S. is scanning your full body to project later. Think of it as a photo.'
'Who is V.E.L.U.S.?' She whispered to Nick.
'V.E.L.U.S. is our Virtual Expert Link Up Server. She organises, records and protects all what we do. She will make more sense once you have met the others.'
Rachel, too scared to move let the blue line move up and down her body. Not daring to breath, she glanced over the reception area. Nothing seemed out of the ordinary, the leafy potted plants in the corners looked real. The two corridors that led off to either side of the reception area, were dark and still. Nothing seemed different, yet she knew there was more to come.
One corridor led to the offices where she was stationed most of the day. The other headed towards two small meeting rooms, a training room and a large board room. The blue line disappeared and Nick motioned to follow him. Her heart pounding out of her

chest, she followed him down the corridor to the right, away from her office.

'Nick, how did V.E.L.U.S. know I would be coming here?' Rachel asked.

Nick stopped and turned to face Rachel. 'Please accept my apologies for not mentioning any of this previously. It must all be extremely strange. V.E.L.U.S. is part of our company and only revealed to the ones that have clearance. I anticipated you exiting early from the Christmas night out due to your loathing to partake in such activities, planning this meeting in the case I was correct. I understand you will have a lot of questions. Please be patient and soon you will understand the importance of the security and why this was not just dropped in to casual conversation.'

Nick turned around and continued walking. Rachel shook her head, even more confused and slightly nervous.

They walked passed the two meetings rooms that she used for conference calls. The corridor usually a hype of activity, eerily quiet, with their shoes silenced by the plush grey carpet. Passing the training room, this was the farthest Rachel had ever ventured down this corridor. Never requiring to visit the board room previously, she had not realised how far away the entrance was. Not being part of her daily routine, most of the time Rachel forgot they had one, only recalling when Nick had arranged meetings with 'high profile clients'. She had seen him escorting them occasionally to the board room, mostly military types or influential people, ones that had an air of authority surrounding them. Rachel's position kept her extremely busy, dealing with their overseas suppliers, negotiating and occasionally travelling to meet with them at the production factories. She never needed or had interest in the board room and Nick's clientele.

Rachel enjoyed her role at S.U.S. Industries, earning respect by focusing on her work, keeping out of the office gossip circle and keeping all private and confidential matters to herself. This had not gone unnoticed by Nick, mentioning it to her in her last performance review, she was one of a select few he trusted.

Hearing her heart beat in her chest, she carried on following Nick as he walked towards the heavy dark brown door, at the end of the corridor. The motion sensor lights switching on just a few steps ahead of them made Rachel catch her breath nervously, wondering what awaited her. The walk to the board room seemed to go on forever and was a lot farther away than she initially thought.

Half way between the training room and the boardroom entrance, gilded gold frames with portraits of people she did not know started to appear. As if sunken into the wall, they had not been visible from further away. Names of the people featured in the portraits were engraved on gold plaques' underneath. Only Nick's was the portrait Rachel recognised, although his name differed on the inscription beneath the painting.

They reached the end of the corridor and from close up, Rachel could see carvings, similar to the ones at the reception entrance. Anticipation rose inside Rachel, not knowing who was behind the door and what these carvings were, a lump formed in her throat.

'What's happening Nick?' she pleaded.

Images started to conjure up in Rachel's head of her childhood for the second time that evening. Dark memories suppressed from a lifetime ago. The feelings transported her back to that scared little kid, no control over what was about to happen to her, feeling like a lamb being brought to slaughter.

Seeing the fearful look in her eyes, Nick held her shoulders and looked straight at her.

'Rach, to be invited to this meeting is an honour, there are very few people in this world that will be part of something as special as this. I cannot talk freely until we are inside. I trust you implicitly, none of this would be happening if I did not. If you want to leave at any point, just walk out, there is nothing in this room that will bring you harm, yet you may come out with more questions than you have now.'

Still not understanding what Nick was saying, she at least registered she had the option to leave if she wanted to.

Putting her trust into Nick she nodded to allow him to continue.

He pushed the door and it glided open effortlessly, slowly stopping when it reached a perfect 90 degree angle.

The board room was as you would expect. The same plush grey carpet, a large oval mahogany table sat centre of the room surround by twelve high quality black leather chairs. A drinks cabinet and coffee machine stood near the back of the room. In the same mahogany, a small table displayed a mix of crystal champagne glasses and tumblers, with a large decanter half full of whiskey.

The room had no windows and strangely no people.

Rachel's stomach turned over with a mixture of emotions, disbelieving everything Nick had just said. A little voice inside, reminded her no-one could hurt her anymore, she was an adult, she did not have to stay if she felt in danger. Taking a deep breath to compose herself, Rachel remembered she had the control. She was an adult now, she was no longer the prostitute's daughter Chantelle Shaw, she was Rachel Nichols and she would never let anyone sell or abuse her again.

'Where is everyone? Why am I here', she demanded.

'Please sit, you are safe here.' Nick pointed to a mid-way seat at the table.

Nick was aware of Rachel's past, had been long before he arranged her apprenticeship and changed her name, yet she had never mentioned it. Nick found this commendable, he saw too many people blame others for their life of crime, yet here stood a perfect example of what could be achieved, irrespective of their start in life. Nick's protective nature arose in him, knowing this could awake her dark past, he offered her a drink to try and normalise the situation.

'What I need is a cigarette Nick, I'm really not comfortable with all this.'

'Here' he passed her what looked like a vape. 'I had a feeling this is how you would react, it is not often we bring someone of your age into our close knit community, however it has been discussed as length and we all agreed, you would be a great asset.'

'Who's we?' Rachel was on the verge of screaming. 'Look around, no one is here! How do you seem to know how I am feeling, what I am about to do? You bring me alone into a room to meet the people you trust, beam me with a weird blue light and expect me to stay calm?' Rachel was panting now, adrenalin pumping through her body as she thought about darting from the board room and running all the way home.

As if it could read Rachel's mind, the boardroom door began to slowly shut of its own accord. Watching Nick carefully as he walked around the table, Rachel fumbled in her jacket pocket for anything she could use as a weapon. Sitting on a chair adjacent to her Nick, pointed at the midway chair again. 'Please, sit, they are about to arrive'

Rachel could feel her adrenalin subside and be replaced by the lump in her throat again.

She moved the chair slightly in case she needed to escape and sat down.

The lights dimmed.

'Caroline Bennett, here.' Rachel jumped and faced the way the voice was coming from. A blue outline of a mid-fifties woman started to form in the seat next to her. She recognised her as the owner of Brodells, the high profiled gun makers and arms dealer.

'Field Marshal Sanderson, here.' A voice to the right of Nick rang out. Another outline started to form of a man, in full military uniform, decorated with high ranking medals.

'Sandra Callaghan, representative of her Majesty, Here.' Rachel's jaw dropped. The outline of Sandra Callaghan, the well renowned and trusted advisor of the Queen of England was forming in the mysterious blue light right next to her.

Seven more prominent figures appeared around the table, including the Archbishop of Canterbury and the Minister of Defence, advising they were present, projected by this mysterious blue light. Rachel tried to figure where it was coming from, but the source was unknown.

'Stefan East, here with Rachel Nichols' Nick said. Rachel looked at Nick, mouth wide open, who on earth was Stefan East?

Sandra turned to Rachel.

'We understand you must be currently in a state of shock and please appreciate this is not how we conduct ourselves normally. Upon the time the committee is required to incorporate another to ensure we always have twelve members, we usually already have our member prepped, chosen at, or just after birth, being taught the knowledge throughout the beginning of their life, consequently not knowing anything different. Generations have passed this information to their offspring, ensuring maximum protection. The world is changing rapidly, and our current method, unfortunately has met some challenges just recently. The one that was chosen is not secure. We have all followed your progress Rachel, within your personal and work life and would like the opportunity to go through our expectations. Our only request is this knowledge is taken to your death bed. Please do not ask how or what happens when we find out you have passed the knowledge on, as we will. Before we proceed, I need an answer immediately. There is no turning back and no magic wand that can erase from your memory what you are about to learn. Do you wish to proceed? '

Rachel, looked at Nick who signalled to her to say yes and looked back at Sandra.

Stuttering slightly, Rachel replied. 'Ms Callaghan, I am honoured I have been invited to sit at this table with the most prestigious figures in England, yet I feel you have made a grave mistake. I am not who I portray to be. I was brought up by a drug addict Mother on an estate that breeds prostitutes, criminals and paedophiles. I do not have any financial offering to give nor social or business influence.' Rachel gulped, as she gathered the confidence to express the next part. 'I was sold, abused and tortured as a child. This has left its impact, and on occasion, can consume me. I am not the right calibre of person to deliver what you require. I apologise if I have wasted your time.'

'Miss Nichols. It is commendable you brought all this to light, yet we already know your history. Your intelligence and loyalty to S.U.S. Industries have shown us your value, we have no need for monetary aid. You are indeed the calibre of person this committee needs. It is admirable that you have doubted your integrity, yet you are the most courageous person in this room. To fight through life and achieve what you have, display's strength and determination. You are the most worthy person at this table.' Sandra smiled warmly at Rachel. 'I hope this shows we do not choose members lightly and we do need you more than you need us. I will not lie, a lot will be required of you Rachel, this is a commitment that will last a lifetime, yet you will be part of a remarkable organisation and will have access to information you could only dream about. I appreciate this is a lot to take in, however we do need to move on. Can you confirm if your answer is yes or no, as if it is a yes, we have a lot to cover this evening?'

Rachel looked around the table. The blue 3D projections all had their eyes on her, some encouraging, others unreadable.

Taking a deep breath she replied. 'It is a yes.'

Chapter 5
Joshua - In the Airs Atmosphere

Joshua's head was pounding, he felt sick. Opening his eyes slowly, the white interior of the pod started to come into focus.
His neck felt stiff as he tried to move and his mouth was unbelievable dry. He stretched his arms out in front of him and noticed the IV drips snaking their way into the shimmery white suit he was wearing. Nothing looked familiar. The stark white bubble he was in, reminded him of a hospital room. Confused, he raised his hands in front of him, checking for any clues that could relay if he had been in an accident or not.
Trying to ignore the waves of sickness, he looked around and noticed a little black bag dangling below two monitors with the instructions, ***open me***. A bottle of water suspiciously placed next to the bag. Realising he was not in a hospital, Joshua tried to sit up. A wave of sickness came across him and he laid back down. Waiting a few moments for the sickness to pass, he slowly eased up into a sitting position.
Leaning forward to grab the small black bag, his now shoulder length hair fell in front of his face partially obscuring his vision. Puzzled, Joshua lifted his hand to his head and felt how long his hair was. Feeling his face, he realised, he also now had a beard. His head still pounding, he brushed his hair behind his ears and lent forward to the black bag. Inside was a note and some pills.
'To ease the pain and confusion.' He read. He knew that writing, it was Jess' writing. Trusting her implicitly, he poured the pills into his hand.
Grabbing the bottle, he threw them into his mouth and swallowed the pills down with a gulp of water. His dry mouth instantly craved more, and he drank the rest of the water in one go.

Laying back down to let his headache subside slightly, Joshua began looking around in more detail. He was dressed in an all-in-one protective outfit. Shiny white, he could make out his initials that were embroidered on the left arm of the suit just above the small openings that let the IV's pass through. Inspecting the IV's entrance into his arms, trying to work out how he could remove them, he was alerted by a serious of beeps coming from the monitors to the right of him. Jerking his head up to look, a female robotic voice echoed around the pod.

'Hello Mr East. I am glad you have awoken. You are approximately 60 minutes from your destination, please instruct when you wish me to activate the information.'

'Erm, hello, who are you? Where am I?' Joshua asked, looking around to see where the voice was coming from.

'I am V.E.L.U.S., Mr East, your on-board companion. We are in the TT Pod. Do you wish me to activate the awake message from home?'

'Yes please.' Joshua anxiously replied.

The screens that were black, now flickered and turned on. The buttons beneath them, shinning different colours in sequence as if to test they were working. Joshua pushed himself up staring at the screens, unsure if to be cautious or not.

Both screens came alive with colour, Richard and Caelan were on one monitor and Jess and Liz on the other.

'Hello sleepy head!' Jess cried out. 'Sorry, I should have said that a bit quieter, your head will still be in pain right now. I hope you have found the bag of pills and the water. Try to sip the water, your stomach will not be used to any fluids or solids inside it just yet.' Joshua looked at the empty water bottle, oops! 'The first aid kit is located under your chair, there are instructions on how to remove your IV's. V.E.L.U.S. should have already removed your oxygen mask.

Richard's serious voice interjected Jess. 'You will be wondering where you are right now and I would suspect you are around 60 minutes from your destination. Therefore, if you still have memory loss, you will need to familiarise yourself with the plan.'

A tablet slowly revealed itself from the console and moved towards Joshua on an outstretched metal arm.

'Also use V.E.L.U.S., she will have access to a lot of information. It will be quicker than reading for an answer to any question you have. V.E.L.U.S. has also been programmed into the tablet, take her with you but keep her hidden. You have been in a deep sleep for nearly a year. The chair you have been sleeping in has been providing you with muscle building massages, although you will still feel stiff, sore and slightly uncoordinated until your memory and body recovers. If you look to your left, you will have the map of your travel and where you will land.'

Two blue 3D images projected themselves from beside the console, one showing the galaxy and one showing a detailed image of what looked like a desert.

'Upon landing, YOU MUST hide the TT Pod as best you can. The technology is far too advanced for the time. Keep it safe. If they discover you and the TT pod, they will capture the TT pod and you for data analysis and unfortunately, you will be at the mercy of excited scientists of this time. The experiments they will conduct will not be pleasant.'

'Remember your training and remember why you are doing this.' Caelan added.

Lastly Liz took her turn to speak. 'As all best laid plans can go wrong, do not beat yourself up if the mission is unsuccessful, you are a clever boy, always have been and always been able to talk your way out of any situation. Use your natural abilities.'

A chorus of Goodbyes and love you's followed and the faces disappeared. The pounding in Joshua's head had started to subside and he reached for the white tablet.

Caelan's few words had stuck with him and were repeating in his head, yet Joshua wondered why his Father had not been in the message.

Joshua had a great childhood. Brought up by Stephen and Mary East, a wealthy reputable couple. Stephen's parents before him had been extremely affluent and though Stephen had no need to work, he chose to. Secretly donating his monthly salary in food and clothing to the Servians.

Joshua, an only child, had been their focus in life. Dedicated to his upbringing and ensuring a well-balanced, kind, but fearful man emerged. His childhood full of lessons surrounding finance and science with the compulsory assassin programme set by Lamia.

Lamia, the leader of the Matriats imposed assassin training on all Matriats to teach the young that had recently come of age, the Matriat way and show loyalty to her. Hunting for Servians made

Joshua sick to his stomach, yet to lead an uncomplicated life going forward, he attended the mandatory lectures.

The final lesson for all that attended the assassin course, regrettably came as a field trip. Joshua and his fellow Matriat students had to participate in a raid on a sleepy Servian village. The village had been chosen for its weakened state, ensuring the trainees had no resistance on their first invasion. The easier the first kill, the quicker the trainees felt the euphoria of assassinating a Servian.

The glints of enjoyment that lit up on the most of the Matriats faces when they arrived at the sleepy village, made Joshua wished he was not part of the human race.

The most successful trainees would prove they had no feelings or obligations to any Servian. Instead they would demonstrate that the Servians were only a source of entertainment and in turn validate loyalty to their almighty leader, Lamia.

The ones that failed, were nailed naked to trees lining the street that led to Lamia's mansion when they returned, giving them a slow and painful death for the shame they had brought upon the Leader.

Joshua and his Father had many discussions regarding the field trip. Joshua argued he could feign illness or go undercover, yet his Father sadly made Joshua realise this was one fight he could not win without repercussions. Although, they could utilise the field trip to their advantage and explained his plan to Joshua.

The day came for the field trip and once the troop commander had bellowed 'GO', Joshua ran away from the crowd and ensured he was out of sight. Unhooking a bag that was hidden within a secret pocket on the inside of his left trouser leg, Joshua dowsed himself with the contents.

The stench from the cows' blood was unbearable, retching at the sight and smell of it, it baffled him how the more blood Matriats were covered in, the more they celebrated.

After carefully ensuring he had splashed enough, but not too much to arouse suspicion, Joshua ran to a hut and pounded on the door.

The screams inside from young children turned his stomach. No child, no human, should have to live in fear like the Servians.

Shoulder barging the door open, he tumbled into the middle of the shack. Looking around, Joshua realised it only housed one room. A bed was the only piece of furniture that featured inside. Wooden handmade toys laid on the dirt floor and two ruck sacks containing the family's little belongings, were placed next to the bed.

Three children huddled together, on the far side of the small hut. The eldest, who looked around twelve, placed himself in front of the younger two. Joshua smiled at the heroic nature of the boy.

'I promise I have not come to harm you.' Joshua held out his hands to show he was free from weapons. 'Where are your parents?'

The eldest tried to hush his siblings but the youngest, a sweet five year old girl spoke up 'Dada never came home and Mama went to get water.'

Hearing a crackling sound, Joshua turned to investigate the noise. Seeing the nearby huts engulfed in flames through the small doorway, he knew he needed to act fast.

He spoke softly, yet with authority while reaching inside his jacket pocket.

'You need to listen carefully as we do not have much time. Do you know where your Mother would have gone to collect water?'

The children nodded in unison.

'I need you to run to her, do not stop and do not look back. I will do what I can to protect you out of the village, but you must not tell anyone of our conversation. You escaped when you heard us coming. Agreed?'

All three of them nodded their heads again. Joshua pulled out three bars of chocolate and offered it to the children. Their eyes lit up.

'Is that real?' The middle child around seven asked.

'It is, now take them and when I say run, you run. Do not run until I tell you to. Understood?'

Snatching the bars, a serious expression crossed their faces. The eldest looked at his younger siblings and then at Joshua. 'We are ready when you are Mister.'

Joshua quickly poked his head out of the hut to check the coast was clear. His stomach dropped and his heart started beating hard as he noticed the troop commander walking through the flames towards him.

This was the only exit; the hut was built out of mud and clay with no windows. Smashing through the flimsy wall would only bury them alive, yet if the commander saw the children alive and well, she would cut their throats herself and ensure he was nailed to a tree for crimes against the Leader.

Joshua stood tall and walked out of the hut towards the commander, hoping she would stop and wait for him to join her. The commander carried on marching towards him. Pausing, Joshua quickly looked back at the hut. The sun was shining behind the hut, casting the inside into darkness, showing no signs of life. The children were still safe, for now.

Marching up to meet the commander, he noticed she had a wry smile on her face.

'Well, well, well Private East. That is exactly what I like to see, straight in there, job done and on to the next. These Servians are nothing but vermin. Now go find Private Sutherland and show him how it is done. He seems to be cracking under the pressure.'

The commander carried on walking to the hut which was now scarcely one hundred metres away. Joshua's heart fell when he realised why she was heading towards the hut. A portion of kills were photographed and documented to prove to Lamia the trainees were worthy Matriats.

Joshua had picked this hut on the outskirts for the precise reason the commanders liked to be in the thick of it.

'Commander Cooper, do you know which way Private Sutherland is? I would hate to waste time looking for him that could be spent exterminating' Joshua asked trying to distract her.

'Straight ahead, seven huts to the right.' Answered the Commander still walking towards the hut.

Barely fifty metres away now, Joshua knew he had to stop her.

He withdrew a small oval shaped piece of glass from his top pocket. Given to him by his Father, he was under strict instructions to use in only extreme circumstances. On impact, the glass like grenade would break into a thousand shards, shooting in all directions, sacrificing innocent Servians and slaying Matriats. Rubbing his thumb over the smooth surface, tears sprang into his eyes. Releasing this grenade would save the three innocent children, yet he would be sacrificing others. Servians and Matriats would perish at his hands, yet three children would live on.

In turmoil, he raised his arm with the oval glass grenade firmly in his grasp, ready to make his decision at the last second. The tears that had formed, made their way down his face as he realised he would be responsible for innocent people killed in both options. He shut his eyes, prepared to live with whatever decision he made, when screams and gunfire made him freeze. Opening his eyes, he could see shots being fired from the other side of the village.

'Commander Cooper, what happening?' Joshua cried running for cover behind one of the huts.

'We're under attack Private East, those vermin have weapons! Fall back! Fall BACK' the commander yelled as she ran towards the commotion.

The coast now clear, Joshua stealthily manoeuvred his way back to the children. Checking they were all unhurt, he guided them around the outside of the village until it was safe for them to run to find their mother.

'Thank you, sir,' the eldest saluted Joshua. 'We will never forget you, nor tell anyone about this.' Joshua watched them run into the distance before he went to find the rest of his troop.

He often thought about them children and hoped they were still safe.

His confusion starting to slowly lift, he realised this was not the training Caelan had meant in the fare well message, and sadly also the reason his Father was not in it.

He started to read the tablet and hoped when this was all over, no Servian would ever have to live in fear again.

His mission would soon land him back to the exact spot he launched from.

Then this is when the real work would start as it would be one hundred years before he was even born.

Chapter 6
Joshua - The Landing

'No, No, No – this cannot be happening! Richard said One year! One year not seven!' Joshua checked and rechecked the dates and times on the tablet. 'V.E.L.U.S. What is happening?'
A projection from the console showed a 3D earth with a replica of Joshua's pod circling it.
'Mr East, the TT pod left S.U.S. Industries base with no complications as predicted. Once the TT pod had reached the required speed, you were indeed transported back one hundred years. After arriving at the specific time period, the weather was not as anticipated. You arrived in an unforeseen electrical storm and the TT pod was struck by lightning. An unfortunate event that no one could have foretold. The TT pod malfunctioned and accelerated again, taking you further back in time. We have orbited the earth two times to slow your speed and after my observations of the tectonic plates and atmosphere, I have determined we have gone back approximately two thousand years. I have taken to transfer information you will require to your tablet. If you require any further information regarding this time period, please advise.'
Joshua watched the projection of the TT pod rotate around the earth disappear and reappear. The land and seas on the blue projected earth moving with each time lapse. Viewing the projection on repeat, panic rose in Joshua's chest, he was not prepared for this. They had not prepared him for this. There was always a chance the times may not be exact and had prepared for a fifty year buffer but not two thousand! They had spoken about atmosphere, weather and the moon's gravitational force, yet none of these had been an issue.
Joshua laid back on his chair, his mind in overdrive, all they had prepared for, only for the mission to fail before he even landed.

Grabbing the tablet, Joshua read the information V.E.L.U.S had provided. He would be landing in a different country to where he set off in Rylitte. After reading the local dialect was Aramaic, Joshua was relieved Richard had insisted the V.A.I. be on board.

'V.E.L.U.S. does the V.A.I. have Aramaic installed?'

'Yes, I had already premediated the usage of the Voice Activated Interpreter and installed Aramaic in preparation. Would you like it now?'

'Yes.' Joshua replied.

A small white tray slowly made its way from the area the tablet had been produced, with a white metal arm pushing it towards Joshua. On the tray stood a black velvet box and a small bottle with orange liquid. Opening the box, Joshua saw it contained a transparent capsule and a small metallic disc. Picking up the transparent capsule first, he moved it towards his mouth and then stopped.

'V.E.L.U.S., please confirm the V.A.I. is one hundred percent programmed with the dialect of this time. Once this is swallowed, I cannot get it back out.'

'According to the dates and location, yes it has been programmed with the correct dialect of Aramaic.'

'OK, here goes.' Joshua swallowed nervously before putting the transparent capsule on the end of his tongue. Unscrewing the bottle, he raised it in the air. 'Cheers' he muffled before swallowing the entire contents of the vile orange liquid.

The burn on his throat was instant, he had seen, but not experienced using the V.A.I. before. Finding it hard to breath, Joshua clutched his neck, coughing. He could feel the electronics moving up and down his throat, feeling its way to the precise position. Falling to the floor still clutching his neck, Joshua gasped for breath. His throat felt like it was closing, becoming smaller and smaller, preventing the air getting into his lungs. Sharp pains reverberated through his throat, informing Joshua, the wires were piercing his vocal cords. The pain was excruciating, and Joshua tried to scream out in agony, yet no sound came out. The pain seemed never ending. The burning sensation seemed to be growing hotter and hotter. He could feel tiny needles crawling and piercing. Feeling faint, Joshua was unsure how much more of this pain he could take. His hand still clutched around his neck, he felt the hotness penetrating through his skin. The pain was beginning to take over, and Joshua flopped to the floor. His vision began to blur as the lack of oxygen registered in his brain. Feeling dizzy and sick, his eyes began to droop slowly. Joshua tried fighting to keep awake, his breathing now a small hiccup intake and just as Joshua thought the end was near, the pain stopped, he could breathe again. Sweating and shaking he pulled himself up and sat back on the chair. Seeing the ear piece in the box out of the corner of his eye, he pleaded inwardly, hoping it would not be as painful. Not giving himself the time to back out, he quickly grabbed the small metallic disc and pressed the middle. Small spindly legs appeared out of the ear piece. Quickly pushing it into his ear before he changed his mind, Joshua felt as it crawled down his ear. Putting his head in his hands, he prepared for the pain to come.

'Installation complete' V.E.L.U.S.'s voice broke the silence in the pod. 'Mr East, I will now speak some different words, please confirm with a simple Yes or No if you understand.'

Lifting his head up in surprise, Joshua was relieved the ear piece was so simple. 'Yes V.E.L.U.S.' He replied with a smile on his face.

After completing the word test, V.E.L.U.S. made some slight alterations to the V.A.I. and now all was working perfectly.

Looking at himself in the camera of the tablet, Joshua did not recognise the aged man he now was. He was shocked at the slivers of blonde that ran through his long hair, when all he had known, was it to be short and dark. The fine lines around his eyes told the story of how he had missed the last seven years of his life in a deep sleep. Inspecting his beard, he decided he quite liked it. It was a new look for his new life.

Getting ready for the landing into an unknown world, Joshua wished he had someone else with him. Nervously he had looked at diagrams V.E.L.U.S. had uploaded to the tablet of the clothes worn. Joshua had tried and failed to fashion himself a robe with the clothes on the TT pod. Surrendering himself to the fact he would not blend in when first landed, he decided to put his mind to use on the other issues he was about to face.

'V.E.L.U.S. when we land is there somewhere you will be safe? Somewhere for me to hide you from discovery?'

'Mr East, we will be landing in what you would call Prastona, yet is locally known as Northern Israel.'

'Isn't that Servian land.' Joshua interjected.

'Yes Mr East.' V.E.L.U.S. answered. 'Although this is two thousand years ago, they are not known as Servians. We will be landing in mountains in a place called Capernaum, near the Sea of Galilee. The people in Capernaum are intelligent and can, on occasion, be hostile. I will try and direct the landing towards the mountains were fewer people dwell. Yet, the people that reside there will not understand the sound that the TT pod will create upon landing. It may cause a lot of interest. The people of this time cannot be predicted. Friend or foe, be prepared for both.'

'Be prepared for both?' Joshua muttered. 'How can I prepare for both?'

'Mr East, gauge how they react when you come out of the TT pod. We have fifteen minutes until landing. I suggest you get ready and read the information regarding the Israeli people on your tablet.'

Joshua sat in his chair and let the restraints ready for landing wrap around him.

He tried to focus on the tablet but his mind wandered elsewhere, to Jess, his family and to the events that occurred prior to receiving Darias' handwritten letter, warning the war had begun.

The leader of the Servians army had awoke to find one of his own nailed to a tree opposite his shack the morning before the launch of the TT pod. He was still alive but slowly bleeding to death, a note stapled to his chest.

The leader, Demitrius was young in age, a rare mix of strength and intelligence, yet one of the few that had not been found and taken by the Matriats. He had gained respect from his peers with his ingenious, fearless nature and his determination and development on the upcoming rebellion. It was him that designed, sourced and hid the weapons. He was the one that rallied around, secretly organising his army with recruits that had the same burning desire for the rebellion as he did.

Aged eight he had witnessed his Mothers rape and brother burnt alive. Their screams still haunted his dreams, thus dedicating his life to the overturn of the Matriats. Not short of female adoration, he shunned marriage and children to focus on the revolt and justice for his murdered family.

His army was ready, and the plan of attack was to commence in five days' time. His second in command, Darias lived on the other side of the village, married to the cause as much as he was, and the only one he trusted.

Wary, Demitrius exited his shack. His muscular body rippled under the thin, dirty fabric as he walked towards the tree.

Snatching the note, Demitrius' face fell as he realised the Servian had spilled details of the rebellion to the mortal enemy.

'Why?' The leader asked 'Why would you betray your own for these murderers?'

'I needed medicine for my wife, she's dying, and I cannot live life without her.' The traitor cried as his tears mixed with dirt and blood ran down his face.

Raising his hand, Demitrius back handed the traitor. 'You do not have a wife.' He spat at him. Demitrius furiously turned around, intending to go straight to Darias with the note and inform him the war had started, yet ten Matriats surrounded him.

Spread out in a semi-circle, their guns all pointed at Demetrius. The tallest Matriat dressed in a red uniform and not the customary black, took one step towards Demitrius.

'For crimes against Lamia Rylitte, we have your village surrounded. Take us to your weaponry and commanders.' He shouted at Demitrius.

Demitrius spat at the Matriat and started to walk away.

'The village will perish because of your insolence.' The Matriat sneered at Demitrius.

'The village will perish anyway, because of you beasts!' He snarled back.

Opening fire, the Matriats gunned down Demetrius and any Servian villager in their sight before searching Demitrius' shack, yet they found nothing relating to the rebellion. In a rage, the chief Matriat stormed out of the hut and ordered his soldiers to burn the full village down, leaving the traitor to watch it burn.

On the other side of the village, Darias had heard the gun fire. Seeing the villagers running passed him, screaming about Demetrius and the traitor, his heart fell. Time slowed, as he heard the chaos erupting to where Demetrius lived, his Demetrius. Turning to face the area, tears pooled in his eyes. Demetrius was more than his friend, he was his everything.

Leaning against his shack to compose himself, Darias knew it was time.

Demitrius had prepared instructions in the possibility of his death, knowing they needed to be prepared for every eventuality. He had commanded Darias to swear an oath, that on his passing, Darias would lead the rebellion in honour for his family and fellow

Servians. Darias had taken the oath without hesitation, at the time confident in the knowledge Demetrius would not perish before the rebellion began, yet, he had, and now Darias was prepared to fight to the death in Demitrius' honour.

Feeling the determination in him, Darias dashed to his bag inside the hut and quickly penned a letter, only a few could decipher. Checking to ensure the Matriats were not nearby, he ran the fifteen miles to the next village through the forest.

'Rarft' he shouted to his nephew when he arrived, half bent over and panting.

'Uncle, what happened?' Rarft asked him concerned.

'Rarft you need to get your horse and ride to the S.U.S. factory. Do not leave until you have given this to Joshua East.' Darias shoved the letter to him still gasping for breath. Rarft started to protest but Darias cut him off. 'Rarft, there is no time, we are all in danger do it now!' Rarft ran to his horse and Darias walked to a water well.

Gulping down the water with this hands, Darias prepared himself for his next journey. The journey to the hidden Servian army. To lead them to victory, for Demitrius

When Joshua received the letter from the young Servian, it took him by surprise. Giving the boy payment for his letter, he grabbed his phone and called Liz.

'The rebellion is starting early, the Servians have been found out. We need to get to the shelter.'

'No Joshua we can't. It is time. Lamia has ordered the NESRE to be deployed at 12noon tomorrow.'

Pausing as Liz's words registered, Joshua took in a deep breath. 'Alright. Get everyone to bring their overnight bags you know where to meet.'

Changing into Servian clothing, Joshua entered the factory floor and mingled in with the workers. He had formed a committee of high ranking Servians that trusted him to pass information and help when required. Locating Nessa, who was part of the committee, he stood next to her as she packed boxes. Checking to ensure the Matriat guards, that were required in all factories by law, were not watching he whispered the news to her.

Nodding her head, a serious look on her face as she continued to pack she whispered back. 'I shall inform the others. Now you must leave, before we take down the guards.'

The NESRE was a unique cluster bomb designed by Lamia's daughter Sophia. Once fired, the NESRE would split itself into ten different parts and deploy itself to ten positions around the world, then detonate at precisely the same time. Commissioning the build of the NESRE for her little pumpkin, Lamia was immensely proud of her daughter and held a party in her honour, displaying the NESRE for all to see and labelling it as a work of art. Lamia delighted with her daughters abilities, had not thoroughly checked the plans of the NESRE. Nor had she had it verified by anyone other than her daughter.

Sophia was the most dangerous kind of human, spoilt and intelligent, with arrogance brought on by her prestigious childhood.

Showing an interest in missiles, Lamia had been delighted with Sophia's academic choice and had sourced the best teacher, Prof. Grodanl.

Prof. Grodanl had painstakingly taught Sophia the chemistry and engineering behind weaponry, yet Sophia only listened to what she wanted to.

She was tasked by her Mother to design a weapon that could wipe a few Servian villages out at once, Sophia had taken Lamia's words literally and designed the NESRE. Proudly presenting her design to Prof. Grodanl, he had been horrified by the huge miscalculations within the cluster bomb. Over compensating his excitement on her design, he tried help Sophia understand the mistakes within the NESRE plans, yet Sophia dismissed his claims. He then gently tried to coax her into changing it. Sophia ignored him. Finally he pleaded with Sophia to relook at her design and refused to help with any part of the build unless she modified it.

This angered Sophia. Who did this man think he was? Daring to question her, Sophia, daughter of Lamia, the Leader of the Matriats, about the NESRE? Furious at the old man for daring to challenge her, Sophia enlisted other engineers and craftsmen to help build the NESRE without any modifications.

Even with the build taking place, Sophia was still angry with Prof. Grodanl's defiance, therefore hatched a plan to teach him a lesson. Crying to her mother that Prof Grodanl had touched her, Lamia ordered the hit on Prof. Grondanl immediately.

Knowing his fate was sealed the moment the build of the NESRE began to take place without him, Prof. Grondanl had made a copy of the designs and anonymously sent them to a few acquaintances that he knew. One of them Stephen East.

Intrigued at these anonymous plans on his desk, Stephen immediately called Liz.

Only a few minutes of studying was needed for them to come to the same conclusion. The NESRE would not just wipe out a few Servian villages, it would wipe out the entire world. The explosion would be violent enough to trigger the earth's core to explode, ripping the world apart, causing the earth and all its inhabitants, to cease to exist. They needed to prevent this from happening, yet knew they would not get anywhere near Sophia's NESRE, nor would Lamia hear criticism about her precious daughter. Forming a plan, they knew it was outlandish, yet they it needed to be completed to prevent the end of mankind.

Joshua's mission was to go back approximately 100 years and intervene Lamia's parents meeting. Cajoling Lamia's mother to fall in love with him, ensuring she was never born. It was a risky mission and Jess was not happy about it, yet Joshua would be able to turn the tables and free the Servians from torture, along with securing the worlds future.

When he first heard it, he called his Father insane, he would be meddling with the future.

'A war is coming son. A war I hoped would never happen.' Stephen reasoned with Joshua. 'I had hoped we could live together in this vast world as equals, yet Lamia is driving that wedge further and further apart. There will be a rebellion and it will not be pretty. As soon as the NESRE is ordered, I need you to do this. For the sake of human kind. Promise me!'

Not totally convinced his Father could pull it off, Joshua had promised him.

Building the Time Travel Pod with Liz and Richards help, they had initially tested it with different household objects, the first starting with a small piece of tissue. Analysing the fibres in the tissue, confirming they had not been altered by the time travel, they moved to different household objects getting larger and larger with each test.

Some objects came back differently to how they were sent. Liz, Stephen and Richard worked tirelessly, rectifying the faults, then testing all the objects again in sequence, until finally they were ready for 'live' testing.

Sending a potted plant, then a mouse, then a pig, when finally it was time for Joshua to test the machine. Sitting in the time machine, excitement rippled through Joshua. He was ready to be part of history. The first human to be transported in time.
'I am not sure we should be sending Joshua.' Stephen worriedly said to Liz.
'Me either, Stephen, yet we have tailored the mission around Joshua. He needs to know what to expect, what it feels like. We need to ensure Joshua is the right person when the time comes.'
Stephen sighed heavily knowing Liz was right. He had been so engrossed in getting to this point, he had not anticipated how it would feel sending his only son into the unknown.

Joshua went back five, then ten, then twenty years and managed to come back successfully. Not taking it seriously, he had never thought he would have to carry out the mission. When the time came, he would not be coming back to his life, he would have to create another, knowing everyone he loved would have ceased to exist.

V.E.L.U.S's voice cut through Joshua's thoughts 'Mr East, we are approaching the airs atmosphere. The landing equipment along with the boosters have failed, the landing will be a tricky one. Please brace yourself. I am going to try and aim us more towards a softer landing. You may not be able to hide me before being seen.'
Joshua laid back on his chair, a new lease of life entering him. He could still change the world, he just needed a new plan.

Chapter 7
Rachel - The Plane Journey

Laying in her bed, staring blankly at the wall, Rachel turned around and reached for her phone on the bedside table. 7AM. Only five minutes since she had last looked.
Pulling the bed covers over her head, she was still unable to sleep. Unsure if it was due to the events from last night or the drive home.
Nick, had ordered a taxi for her after the meeting. Although she was unsure if it was an actual taxi and not a driver owned by the company. The car arrived too quickly and the driver asked too many questions regarding her work life. His constant questioning irritated Rachel. Too tired and emotionally worn out, she snapped at him to shut up. The driver got the hint and the journey continued in silence.
Yet, Rachel could not shake the frustration the company was already testing her. Even if she did blurt out what she had been told, it wasn't as if anyone would believe her, she was still finding it hard to understand herself.
Concluding the driver was indeed an employee of the company, she turned the tables and asked the driver how he could afford the brand new Lexus he was travelling in. The look in his eye was all confirmation Rachel needed, and she sat back in her seat smiling.
Arriving at her address, she offered payment, however the driver just waved his hand, dismissing her money, giving her a 'you found me out' look.
Chuckling to herself as she manoeuvred out of the car she looked up and down the street, still on high alert after the events of the night so far.

Opening her door, she walked in, mentally exhausted. A quick teeth brush and make up removal, she flopped into bed at 5AM, yet sleep evaded her.

Against her protests, Nick had been firm and instructed her to take today off and rest before her trip. 'There is a lot to take in Rach, you need the day off to make sure you are well rested and ready for the information you will be given. Trust me.' He had instructed. Too tired to argue, she had agreed.

Although Callaghan had been more relaxed when asking Rachel her willingness to go S.U.S. Industries Head Offices. Explaining the easiest way to learn is to start from the beginning, which will include an excursion to where it all began.

The head offices for S.U.S. Industries were located in Cyprus and before giving an answer, she needed to check her passport was in date. As if reading her mind, Callaghan declared all checks, including her passport had already been verified by V.E.L.U.S. and if she felt ready, she was good to go. A heavy feeling settled over Rachel; Callaghan, V.E.L.U.S. and S.U.S. Industries, probably knew more about Rachel than she did about herself.

Trusting they knew what was best, she agreed it would be beneficial for her to start at the beginning.

Laying there, thinking about what awaited her in Cyprus, her alarm went off, 7.15AM. Yawning, she admitted defeat and sat up.

Deciding she would try and have a nap later she stretched up, wound her hair in a messy bun and fastened it with a hair tie from her wrist.

Pulling on her tracksuit bottoms and a T-shirt, Rachel made her way downstairs to the kitchen.

Waiting for the kettle to boil, Rachel grabbed her organiser, then thought better of it. She would need a separate book for her notes on this matter. Too many people accessed her organiser at work, she had purposely encouraged it to ensure messages where never missed.

Rummaging through her draw, she grabbed a diary she had been given as a joke last Christmas. As she never celebrated Christmas, yet could not bear to throw anything away, it had been lurking in her kitchen drawer, ready for her to take to a charity shop. Looking at it properly for the first time, the diary was encased with a metal border, only to be opened with a key and a three digit code. It was perfect.

The kettle switched off, indicating it had boiled. Grabbing a white mug from her kitchen cupboards, she sloshed the boiling water into it with a tea bag. After adding milk, Rachel grabbed her tea, her new diary and walked into her living room.

She sat on her pale blue couch and read the instructions to the diary. Setting a new code, she opened it and was relieved to find it was just lined paper and not a calendar.

Sitting back on her couch, cup of tea in hand, she began to piece together the events of last night. Still unsure if she had interpreted it correct, she wrote down what she could remember to refer back to at a later date.

Looking at the scribbles in her new diary, she knew anyone would think she was crazy if they read it. Callaghan had drilled into her, discretion and secrecy is required on all that had been discussed that evening and all that will come to light in the next few days, yet Rachel could not help but write in big bold letters, Stefan East. The meeting had only lasted a couple of hours, yet it felt like longer. Sandra gave her a brief outline of S.U.S. Industries and how they came to be, then it was on to an interrogation. Question after question had been fired at Rachel, asking what she knew about religion, the effects of companionship, her thoughts on the hierarchy system, did she agree with war if it created a better world? Looking round at the table, Rachel could see the blue projections taking notes after her answers, yet Nick just sat there, a proud smile on his face.

Finally Sandra had finished and ended the meeting. A swift bye from them all and Rachel was left alone with Nick.

She opened her mouth to speak but Nick held his hand up to stop her. 'Part of the learning process will involve my name, keep calling me Nick for now.' He said reading her mind.

'How did you ...'

'I know you Rach, after everything you have been told this evening, I knew that would be the one thing you would pick up on.' He said chuckling as he grabbed a water. 'You want one?' he offered.

Rachel nodded. Sitting back down across from Rachel, Nick gave a brief summary of what lay before her at the head office in Cyprus. Her mind swirling with questions, Nick again put a halt on her queries.

'Any answer given, will make way for another question. Start from the beginning and all will be revealed.' He said like a magician.

'How can I take this seriously when you act like this?' Rachel grinned at him.

'It's the only time I get to see you smile.' He replied.

She smiled as she recollected Nick, he acted like a proud parent with her, yet there was still a part that stopped her from 100% trusting him.

Her childhood in Trinity Estate had paid tribute to that.

Distracting herself from the childhood images popping up, she looked around her living room, which she was most proud of.

Her house had been incredibly cheap for the area, yet upon viewing she saw why. Floor boards missing, holes in the walls, animal faeces everywhere, yet Rachel liked a challenge.

Spending her nights and weekends learning DIY from online tutorials, Rachel had transformed the full house on a small budget. The wood burning stove was her favourite purchase, cosy and warm on a winters evening, she relished the feeling of safety as the winds howled outside.

Blood, sweat and tears had gone into this place and whilst she was proud of her accomplishment, she had never invited anyone to see it. It was her safe haven and a million miles away from the shit hole she grew up in.

Feeling far too bright eyed for not having a wink of sleep, Rachel decided to pack. Knowing she would only be there for a few days, she located her small carry on case and neatly arranged her work clothes inside. She may be in Cyprus, yet she would still be working.

Excitement rippled through her as she zipped up the bag. Rachel had a feeling she was about to become part of something big.

'Remove everything from your pockets. Coats, bags, shoes onto the trays. Remove all electrical items from your bags. Phones, tablets, laptops and straighteners need to be put in a tray, separate.' The security guard at the airport barked.

Removing her belt, Rachel cursed herself for not wearing socks with her slip-ons. Walking through the scanner where thousands had already been in her bare feet made her shudder. She walked on through, and was directed to the full on body scanner.

Standing in the machine with her hands up in the air, took Rachel back to two nights ago. Was it really only two nights ago? She felt like so much had happened between then and now. Nodding, the security guard motioned her through, to collect her belongings.

She was glad she was travelling on her own. It gave her time to go through her notes she had taken prior to falling asleep on the sofa.

She was awoken from her 12 hour nap yesterday by a knock at the door. Checking the time, she grew suspicious of who would be calling on her at 11pm in the evening.

Blearily eyed, she answered the door to a man in a sharp black suit asking for Rachel Nichols. Advising it was her he pulled out a white plastic gun and asked Rachel to stare straight ahead. Squeezing her eyes shut, wondering if she was about to die, he had laughed and asked her to open her eyes. Explaining the gun was an eye scanner, he apologised she had not been informed of their security measures. Scanning her eye, he passed her the package he had in his hand and left.

Bewildered and slightly embarrassed, she locked her front door behind her and walked back into her living room. The plain brown box was blank. No indication of who sent it and in her surprised sleepy state, Rachel had not thought to ask the man when he passed it to her.

Opening the box carefully, half expecting something to jump out, she found it contained her boarding card, a brand new ipad and the name of her driver that would be taking her to the airport.

A letter had also been enclosed, explaining the ipad was encrypted with face recognition software installed. Her face had already been authenticated and she would be the only person able to access the information. Once read, the information would auto delete.

The phone rang, interrupting Rachel's thoughts towards the company's ability to programme the ipad with her face, without her being there.

'Good Afternoon Nick.'

'Hi Rach, all ready for Cyprus?'

'As I can be.'

'Everything you need to know will be on the ipad, I will be joining you in a couple of days. Andreas will take great care of you until I get there. Oh and Rach?

'Yeah'

'Don't doubt yourself, you're made for this'
'Made for what?' Rachel asked, but Nick had already put the phone down,

Boarding the plane, Rachel wondered how she would watch the tablet without anyone seeing. Normally used to the squashed economy class seats, she had slightly hoped she would have been promoted to first class or even business, to comfortably digest what was on the tablet, yet her boarding card did not have an allocated seat, nor was she escorted to the first class lounges. Hoping there was enough room for her to place her carryon luggage above where she was sat, Rachel showed the air hostess her ticket.
'Please follow me.' The stewardess said in a thick accent and picked up Rachel's bag.
This is new, thought Rachel as she watched the airhostess manoeuvre her luggage through the seats leading her towards the front of the plane.
Making their way through first class, Rachel noticed all seats were empty barring one, which seated a well-dressed lady. Her nose buried into a book, Rachel could only see the top half of her face. Wearing glasses with a gold chain attached and her grey hair styled into a sleek bob, the woman radiated class and elegance that could only be associated with a rich, privileged upbringing. As Rachel passed her, she acknowledge Rachel with a little nod and carried on reading her book. An open laptop on the tray at the side of her displayed the S.U.S. Industries screen saver. A peculiar feeling came over Rachel, as if this flight were not for just your average traveller.
The airhostess walked towards the cockpit and just as she thought the airhostess was taking her to meet the pilot, she turned right and motioned her to follow her into a small room. Curiously, Rachel followed her realising once inside, it was a lift. The floor was covered in a thick red carpet and the walls imitation shiny gold. The doors closed behind them revealing a mirror, reflecting the airhostess and Rachel.
Rachel looked at the reflection of them both, staring straight ahead, serious yet slightly nervous. Rachel's apprehension gave way to a fit of the giggles. The airhostess looked at her in surprise.

'I am sorry.' Rachel giggled. 'We just looked so serious in the mirror. I am not even sure why I am laughing.' She tried to explain, wondering if she was having some sort of breakdown.

The airhostess broke out into a smile. 'Many people that fly with us are too nervous to talk. I welcome your laughter.'

The doors to the lift opened and leaving the luxurious lift, Rachel found herself standing in a small thin corridor with two doors either side. The pale blue interior reminded Rachel of train toilets, yet luckily without the smell. The air hostess opened the first door on the right and motioned Rachel to follow her.

'My name is Eleni and I will be your personal assistant today.' The air hostess said in her thick accent.

The room was small, but comfortably furnished, featuring a single bed, a large arm chair and wooden desk. Eleni showed Rachel the retractable tray attached to the arm chair, citing most preferred this, than sitting at the desk.

Opposite the arm chair was a TV attached to the wall with a cabinet underneath it. Eleni presented to Rachel the mini fridge and snacks that were inside. On the right of the room was another door. Pulling it open, Rachel was surprised to find Eleni showcasing her own private bathroom.

'This is your bathroom, shower, toilet and wash basin.' Eleni instructed. 'All requirements should be stocked, if you need anything else, please let me know.'

Eleni opened the cabinet underneath the washbasin to show where the toiletries were kept.

Exiting the ensuite bathroom, Eleni addressed Rachel. 'I will be along in 10 minutes, just before take-off to bring your infight meal. If there are any drinks and snacks you require, please inform me and I can bring them. After I bring your meal, your room will be set to Do Not Disturb. If you need anything at all, please call me on this.' Eleni showed Rachel the call button on the side of the arm chair. 'No one should enter your room but me. If anyone tries to enter your room. Please press any of these buttons.' Eleni showed Rachel different panic buttons scattered around the room, one always easily accessible, no matter where she was.

'Thank you very much Eleni, I am Rachel.'

'I know who you are Miss Nichols, it is an honour to be your assistant today.' Eleni did a little bow and walked out shutting the door behind her.

Rachel's face flushed red with embarrassment after Eleni's little bow. Rachel was not royalty nor should Eleni be honoured to serve her, it was almost relic. Deliberating if Nick had a hand in this, she decided to shrug it off, knowing she had a lot to get through before landing.

Grabbing a water and some crisps, Rachel sat in the comfy arm chair ready for her five hour flight to Paphos. Looking across at the bed, she almost wished it were a night flight so she could take advantage of the soft pillows.

A knock on the door interrupted Rachel mid note taking. Not sure what she should do she shouted 'Enter.'

Eleni popped her head around the door. 'Sorry to interrupt Miss Nichols but we are ready for landing.

What already? Rachel looked at her watch, not realising how quick the flight had passed. 'Thanks Eleni.'

Rachel put the ipad down and rubbed her eyes. She was on information overload, learning about how one company monopolised the world, shocked her. She found it unethical, yet excitement rippled through her.

Stretching her legs out, she was ready to discover what brought this one company to control most of the earth's assets, and what part they thought she should have in it.

Chapter 8
Joshua - Joshua's Name

Joshua squeezed his eyes shut as he felt the TT pod coming to land. Bracing himself for impact, his body instinctively became rigid. Jolting upwards, only the restraints keeping him safe, he felt the thuds as the TT pod bounced once, twice and then a third time. Feeling the capsule hurtling along ground, Joshua could hear the sound of metal scraping as it plunged through the unknown.
Coming to a complete stop, Joshua physically relaxed, he had survived. The restraints keeping him safe through the bumpy arrival.
Opening his eyes warily, Joshua glanced around the TT pod. Relieved to see it was still intact and nothing had managed to penetrate inside, he let out a sigh of relief.
V.E.L.U.S. announced they had arrived and released Joshua from the restraints. Gathering his bearings, he sat up, noticing the floor was on a slight angle.
As if reading his mind, V.E.L.U.S.'s voice boomed out. 'Mr East, due to the landing, the TT pod gathered debris, causing a 23% level difference. Do you wish me to rectify?'
'Not just yet V.E.L.U.S.' Joshua replied. Needing a few moments to prepare himself for what may be outside.
Wiping the sweat that had formed on his brow, he could feel the inside of the pod growing increasingly warm. Immediately fearing the TT pod was on fire, he started to panic.
'V.E.L.U.S. why is it so warm inside here?'
'The midday sun from outside is heating the pod up. Would you like me to switch on the cooling stat?'
'Yes please.' Joshua replied, relived it was not anything more sinister. 'V.E.L.U.S., could you also show me where we are?'
The monitors flickered and slowly the screens came to life, giving a 360 view of outside. A long indentation into the ground showed

where the pod had scrapped to stop. Dusty mud and vegetation was piled up on one side of the pod, partially blocking the view. Fields of crops surrounded the pod with a house not too far away.

'The weather is a mild 14 degree Celsius, 15mph winds from the east. 10% chance of rain. Excellent air quality. Once outside the pod, you will not require breathing apparatus.' V.E.L.U.S.'s robotic voice echoed around the pod.

Joshua moved to look at the projection above the console. A 3D map was displayed with the capsule situated in the middle, blinking to show its position.

'We have landed in Capernaum, within farm land, slightly off course of the mountains. Would you like me to commence reconstruction of the land?'

Just as he was about to approve, Joshua stopped himself. Something was moving in the distance.

'V.E.L.U.S., camera 3, 2C, zoom 20%.' He instructed. Seeing two people in the distance running towards the TT pod, Joshua focused on them, making out one man and one woman.

'Pause reconstruction for the moment V.E.L.U.S. We have company. Do you think they are a threat?' Joshua enquired.

The screen zoomed in further on the two people running. 'No, they are not carrying weapons.'

Examining the other angles outside, Joshua felt relieved there were no other signs of life. V.E.L.U.S. had managed to land in a pretty rural location which was reassuring.

The man and woman slowed down as they neared the TT pod. Moving slowly, as if approaching with caution, Joshua could see them, talking between themselves. Getting closer, Joshua noted the man was dressed in extremely dirty red rags, his face weathered with the sun making him appear to look in his early fifties. His shoulder length dark hair, softly blowing in the wind. His face etched with concern, he put his hands to his mouth and began shouting.

'V.E.L.U.S. what is he saying?'

'Mr East. The male is asking if you have come to invade. I shall initiate your ear piece and voice interpreter, please wait one moment for it to activate.'

A high pitched noise reverberated through Joshua's head. As quickly as it was heard, it disappeared.

'Mr East, the translating ear piece should now be working.'

'Hello.' He heard from the man outside. 'What are you? Are you here to claim our land?'

The woman had moved away from the man and was wandering around, inspecting the TT pod more closely. Dressed in the same coloured red rags as the man, hers were covered slightly with a make shift apron. Up close, Joshua could see her dark wavy hair, which was kept away from her face by a head wrap, was peppered with grey. Same age range as the man with a friendly motherly face, she motioned to the man to come nearer to show him something on the TT pod.

'I think it is time I introduced myself V.E.L.U.S.' Joshua said. 'Please open the door.'

Joshua struggled to stand upright in the pod as it was still on a slight angle. The door slowly creaked open, revealing the TT pod had sustained damage upon landing. At the noise of the door opening, the man and woman ran around to the entrance of the TT pod.

Joshua still wearing his protective suit, stood near the entrance. 'Do not be afraid.' He addressed the man and woman. 'Please accept my apologies for the damage to your land. I will repair it.'

The man and woman looked at each other, bewildered.

'V.E.L.U.S., what's happening?' Joshua whispered out of the corner of his mouth. 'Can they understand me?'

V.E.L.U.S's voice sounded out inside Joshua's head. 'All is working and correct Mr East. Do not be alarmed, I can remotely connect to the V.A.I. ear piece, they cannot hear this conversation. Maybe try and smile at them. Human interaction responds positively to warmth and kindness.'

Joshua held his hands out and smiled at the man and woman. Feeling awkward, stood there smiling at them both with his hands out, he was unsure what his next action would be.

'They may be in shock, Mr East. Offer them anything that contains sugar.' V.E.L.U.S. informed Joshua.

Feeling grateful he had V.E.L.U.S. to help him he started to move back inside, when he stopped as he noticed the woman move closer to the TT pod.

'Are you a Roman?' The woman meekly asked.

'No I am not' Joshua replied 'I am from a country far away from here and mean you no harm. I am extremely sorry about the damage to your land and will start to repair it this evening.'

Leaving the snacks, Joshua started to make his way down the TT pod. The stairs had not fully extended due to the odd angle it had landed on and Joshua was finding it a struggle.

'Let me help you.' The man replied. Fashioning some steps from nearby sticks and mud, Joshua marvelled at his swift craftsmanship. Reaching his hand up to Joshua, the man offered to help him down, the steps holding Joshua's weight effectively.

Reaching the ground, Joshua could feel the wind blowing in his hair and inhaled deeply. Turning around he thanked the man and complimented him on his craftsmanship.

'You are very welcome traveller. I am a carpenter by trade, yet we were gifted these lands by my wife's family. Now working with wood is a hobby I enjoy. Motioning towards the woman, Joseph continued. 'This is my wife, Mary.'

'My mother was called Mary.' Joshua exclaimed.

'We must meet her.' The woman warmly smiled at Joshua. 'And this is …' she pointed to the lettering on the pod. 'What are these symbols?' Looking at the letters on the base of the pod, Joshua could see that the industries was hidden beneath the mounds of mud that had amassed when he slid to a stop.

'The letters are J.E.S.U.S but the ind ….'

Mary cut off Joshua. 'Jesus, is that your name? Does this belong to you?'

Joshua paused, unsure what to reply. 'You are under instructions to not reveal your true identity.' V.E.L.U.S's voice entered his head.

Sighing Joshua put one hand on the TT pod and replied.

'This is my Fathers, and yes, that is my name, Jesus.

Chapter 9
Rachel - Cyprus

Travelling light was an advantage, Rachel thought to herself as she breezed through passport control and out into the hot sun of Cyprus with just her small carryon case.
Trying her hardest to use the vape that Nick had given here, she had cracked and bought duty free cigarettes in the airport on the way there.
Deciding to sneak in a quick cigarette, she loitered near the other smokers before checking the instructions to find her driver.
She had dressed in her office attire, expecting the weather to be warm, yet the afternoon Cypriot sunshine in December was scorching.
Removing her suit jacket and shirt, Rachel looked like other holiday makers in her vest top and skirt. Making the decision to redress upon arrival at S.U.S. Industries Head Office, she folded the jacket and shirt and placed them in her case.
Following the directions, Rachel walked towards JPE Hire as instructed. A young man dressed in a full black three piece suit was leaning against a sleek silver car, playing on his phone.
Seeing Rachel approach, he quickly stood up straight and put his phone in his pocket.
'Good Afternoon. Can I help?' The young Cypriot man asked with an accent as his black, unruly curly hair, moved in the warm breeze. He was tall and slim with a cheeky smile and Rachel liked him instantly.
'Hello, I am Rachel Nichols, I have been advised you are expecting me.'
'Yes, Yes!' The young man cried. 'Sorry, you are not dressed like a Miss Nichols.' Rachel cocked her head to a side, wondering what a Miss Nichols looked like.

'Please, let me take your luggage.' He continued and took Rachel's small carry-on bag. Looking behind her, his face creased in confusion. 'Anymore?' he enquired.

'No, just that one case.' Rachel replied.

'Ha! I like it! A woman with no luggage!' Rachel smiled at his infectious happiness. Opening the rear door, he motioned to Rachel to get inside the black sleek car. The leather interior squeaked as she sat in the back seat, and the young man closed the door behind her. Getting into the front of the vehicle, he slapped the top of his head with his hand.

'I am sorry, I forgot.' Awkwardly turning around, he offered his hand to Rachel. 'I am Yuri. I will be your driver for your stay. Anything you ask, I can get.' He said winking as Rachel shook his hand.

'Thank you Yuri.'

'Did you have a nice flight? Would you like a water? Have you been to Cyprus before? Lovely day today, 20 degrees Celsius! Is it cold in England? Please tell me if you want me to shut up. I do talk too much!'

Rachel laughed at Yuri's chatter. He was a welcome relief after the serious information she had been absorbing for the last five hours.

It was nice to hear how passionate he was about his home country. Pointing out different landmarks and where they grow salads, the journey passed exceptionally quickly. Pulling up outside a reception surrounded by villas, Rachel asked Yuri if this was S.U.S. Industries head offices?

'Ahh no.' Yuri laughed. 'You will not be going to the Head offices until tomorrow. Now you relax.'

A man with light ginger hair, dressed in jeans and a t-shirt, looking anything but Cypriot, opened Rachel's car door. Walking to get her bag out of the boot, Yuri passed her a business card. 'This is my number; I am available 24/7. I will be here this evening at 7pm to collect you.'

'Collect me for what?' Rachel asked, but Yuri was already walking back to the front of the car. The ginger haired man picked up her bag and guided her towards the steps leading to the reception area.

Placing her bag at the side of the counter, the man walked behind the desk. 'Hello Ms Nichols. It is an honour to have you with us.' He bowed slightly to Rachel as he spoke.

'Erm, Thank you' hesitated Rachel as the man pushed a brown A4 envelope across the reception desk towards her.

'I am Constantine, or Tan as people call me. This is your itinerary provided.' He said tapping the envelope. 'I will show you to your place.'

Tan grabbed some keys and walked out of the reception carrying Rachel's bag. The reception led out to a vast swimming pool with a Jacuzzi attached. A quaint walkway ran over the top of the pool, leading to an array of sun loungers, yet not one was in use.

Seeing her staring at the desolate area, Tan spoke. 'It gets busier after work hours.' He smiled.

Following Tan in silence, Rachel took in the area. The reception looked like it was attached to the hotel, yet Tan was leading her away towards a road dotted with little single story houses going down a hill.

Leading her to some stairs, Tan descended down them making small talk about the area. Guiding her to another deserted road, he crossed and walked towards a house which had a silver car parked in the drive way. Opening the door, he motioned Rachel to follow him inside.

'This is your villa.' He said to Rachel. 'There are three bedrooms two bathrooms, a small kitchen area and your own pool outside. The cupboards have been fully stocked, but anything else you require, please call reception and they will bring it right to you.'

Rachel walked into the open planned living room. A leather couch featured opposite her, a six seater table was to the right, with a breakfast bar opposite, indicating the start of the kitchen. The kitchen counter had a basket which contained, tea, coffee, fruit and snacks.

Opening the patio doors behind the table, Tan led her out to the rear of the house. A wide patio led onto its own swimming pool, yet the most impressive thing was the view.

The villa was set on a hill, giving an expansive view that stretched all the way down to the Marina. The sun sparkled on the sea, and in the distance she could just make out people frolicking on jet skis. Confused, Rachel turned to Tan.

'Will anyone else be joining me here?'

'This is for you, and for you only. If you have colleagues that need to stay, you have the extra bedrooms.' Placing a black fob with four buttons displayed on it, into her hand, Tan continued. 'This is yours. It will tell us when we are allowed to come and clean, restock your food items and such. The instructions to use are in here.' He said pointing towards a binder placed near the huge TV. 'Now I leave, everything you need is either in here.' He tapped the brown envelope. 'Or here.' He pointed again at the binder. Passing her another key, he continued. 'This if for the car outside. You have Yuri, yet if you need to go and cannot wait for Yuri. You have the car. I hope you enjoy your stay with us.'

He smiled as he left, leaving Rachel in the middle of the living room wondering why she would need to make a quick exit. Checking the time, she realised she only had a couple of hours before she had to meet with Yuri again.

Deciding she would leave her unpacking until later, Rachel grabbed a water from the fridge and sat on the two seater black leather couch with the binder and the brown envelope.

Placing the water and binder on the coffee table she laid the envelope across her lap. Her name was handwritten on the front in loopy large lettering. Taking a deep breath, she opened the envelope to reveal a detailed schedule for the next 6 weeks. Exclaiming out loud, Rachel quickly thumbed through the papers. Details of where she should be at what time, along with an option of what she should wear featured across each page! Throwing the pages on to the leather sofa, she quickly got up and ran into the each bedroom. On the third and final bedroom, the wardrobe and draws were filled with clothes. Everything in her size.

Her stomach turned over as she opened the draw beside her bed and found it filled with underwear in her precise measurements. The thought of Tan or Yuri purchasing her underwear made her skin crawl. Storming back into the living room, Rachel grabbed her phone.

Ringing Nick she was furious, she had been told it would a few days, not six weeks! Nick picked up after the third ring and before he could end his greeting, Rachel cut him off.

'If you want me to work with you and your mysterious world ruling company, you need to start telling me the truth. Why have I got a six-week itinerary if I am only here for a few days?' she raged. 'I cannot work like this Nick.'

'Whoa whoa.' Nick interjected. 'Someone has done their research?' He laughed.

'Nick, I am being serious.'

'Have you read your emails?'

'What?' Rachel asked perplexed. 'What are you on about emails? Why would I read my emails?'

'Your work emails. I sent one to you explaining what would happen when you arrived there.'

Rachel shook her head even though Nick could not see her.

'Nick, stop changing the subject. There are clothes here, all in my size.' Her stomach turned over at the thought of someone touching the underwear they had bought for her.

'Yes, and they are for you. Arranged by Sandra. Brought over by Shannon who is the personal shopper for our company. You do not need to accept them, yet if you are going to stay and be part of us, you will have no time to buy other clothes. It is all explained in the email, read it!'

Calming down slightly, Rachel paused. 'You need to be straight with me from now on Nick. OK?'

'Agreed.'

'Well, I can tell you now, I can't stay for six weeks. Christmas is in two.'

'Says the girl that doesn't believe in Christmas.'

Ignoring him, Rachel carried on. 'And I cannot leave my house stood for six weeks, what if someone breaks in?'

'Rachel, I never dish out orders, yet I am about to. I command you to stop worrying. I would never put you in jeopardy. Your house has been put under surveillance and you get to spend Christmas with others. I will be in Cyprus over Christmas, visiting family. I want you to join us.'

'Visiting family?'

'Yes. Stay for a week, then make your mind up. I shall be with you in a couple of days and we can talk through any concerns you have.'

'OK.' Agreed Rachel.

'I have to go but read the email and ring me if you need anything. I will see you in two days.'

Putting the phone down, Rachel felt more comforted knowing that Nick would be here soon.

Deciding to take advantage of the heat, she took her binder and sat outside. The itinerary could wait.

Looking out towards the harbour, she relaxed. The view was stunning. The sound of crickets was the only noise in the quiet grounds of the villa. Making the decision to heed Nick's words, she would stay for at a week and hear him out. She had agreed to venture into this new world, therefore she needed to embrace it.

Feeling the heat on her shoulders, she physically relaxed and grabbed her work phone to read Nick's email. Scrolling down them, she noticed one from Caroline Bennett, the gun maker. Frowning slightly Rachel wondered why she would be contacting her through work. Everything between the committee needed to go through V.E.L.U.S.

The email seemed friendly enough, wanting to meet for a coffee whilst she was in Cyprus, offering to show her some sights, yet something about the email rang alarm bells. Her personal number was attached at the bottom, advising Rachel to contact her on that one as soon as she could.

Deliberating, Rachel checked the time. She had to get ready, Caroline could wait for now.

Looking at herself in the long stylish black and white maxi dress that was recommended on her itinerancy, she smiled. Her usual jeans or work attire did not expand to this type of clothing, yet she loved how classy it made her look. Pinning her hair up and adding another slick of lipstick, Rachel was surprised at the excitement that rose up in her.

Maybe she could get used to small surprises, she thought as she walked out of the villa to Yuri opening the rear car door for her.

Chapter 10
Joshua - Magda

'Come Jesus, you must be hungry.' Joseph said to Joshua as he led him to their house. 'Please feel welcome to our home and eat with us. We shall all help with the land tomorrow, but tonight you must rest after your travels.'
Joshua followed Joseph down the fields to the quaint farm house.
The house was a lot larger than he had perceived from the pod. Following Mary to the front of the house, Joshua soon found out why.
'We have a guest tonight.' Mary bellowed as she walked through the door. A stampede of feet was heard running through the house towards where Joshua was stood.
A chorus of adult and children's voices grew louder as the sound of the feet got closer to the entrance of the house.
'In this era, many families chose to live together.' V.E.L.U.S.'s robotic voice echoed in his head, making him question if V.E.L.U.S. knew what he was thinking.
'Please, come.' Mary invited Joshua into the kitchen, where a large table dominated the room. Counting twenty wooden chairs surrounding the table, Joshua realised Mary and Joseph had a large family.
The kitchen was sparse, yet functional, with high wooden tables featuring along each wall. A box near the kitchen door was stacked with wooden plates, bowls and cutlery, each with its own intricate design. A huge wooden bowl featured on the kitchen table showcasing its elaborate carvings to demonstrate it contained fruit.
Admiring Joseph's handiwork, movement in the corner of Joshua's eye caught his attention.
A young woman was standing at two huge stones in the corner of the kitchen. Intrigued by the machine, Joshua stared at the dark

corner. The young woman was moving the top stone slow and steady. Feeling she was being watched, the young woman paused and turned to look at Joshua. Thin material was wrapped around her face like a head scarf, leaving only her eyes visible. Joshua noticed her huge brown eyes open wide in surprise at his stark white protective suit, yet she nodded at him and he could see her smile through the thin fabric covering her head.

Returning to her vegetables she was chopping before Joshua's entrance, Mary resumed her position at the table and continued on with her chore. Chatting was still heard at the door way with the odd head popping around to take a look at the strange visitor.

'Please excuse our family, we do not have visitors often. Especially ones that appear from the sky.' Mary spoke to Joshua. 'Please come and sit.'

Joshua watched the young woman in the corner, feeding grains into the stones, grinding them into fine flour as he manoeuvred around the table and sat next to Mary.

'Magda, this is Jesus, a visitor to us this evening.' Mary shouted across to the woman in the corner. Mary lowered her voice and moved her head closer to Joshua. 'Magda over there is an angel sent from god. She comes and grinds our grains, and in payment, she takes some flour or bread to give to the less fortunate. She has dedicated her life to helping others, yet dislikes any attention she gains from her deeds. The poor of Capernaum and surrounding villages, would be lost without her.'

Joshua looked over at Magda, her hands constantly working as she fed the grain into the millstone, grinding it into flour and transferring into a bag on the floor efficiently.

Without thinking he stood up and walked across to Magda. Her hands red and cracked from the work of grinding the grain, he offered to help.

'No, you are a guest of the house.' She replied, looking at him and then Mary sitting at the kitchen table.

'If he is offering child, let him help, you work too hard.' Mary shook her head as she looked across to Magda and Joshua. 'I need to go and get some crops to finish this evening's meal.' As Joshua started to offer help she chuckled. 'I have sons to call upon. You stay with Magda. JAMES, PETER' She bellowed. 'Come and pick some crops for this evening's meal.'

Two men appeared at the door and shoed the children away. Looking at Joshua with disdain, one of them whispered into Mary's ear.

Shaking her head, Mary stood up. 'Magda will be fine. Our visitor has been sent to help us. Now come.' She instructed the two men who scowled at Joshua as they left the kitchen.

The two of them alone, he turned to face Magda, displaying his willingness to help. A curious look on her face as she stared intently towards him. 'Usually men do not help with milling the flour. You are different.' She spoke to him.

A piece of her dark wavy hair fell free from the scarf as she bowed her head down. Joshua's heart skipped a beat, he recognised that hair. Reaching across to her, he moved the head scarf away from her face and gasped. She was the image of Jess. Staring into her brown eyes, a lump formed in his throat as he thought about Jess and the others.

The longer he stared at her, the more it hurt remembering what he had left behind. Roughly wiping away the tears that had begun to form in his eyes, he noticed Magda moving closer to him, worry etched on her face. Realising she would ask questions, Joshua snapped out of his daze, this was not the time for reminiscing.

'Magda, please let me help. I feel uncomfortable watching you whilst I sit. I can grind, you can feed.'

Taking off her scarf, her long dark hair fell free.

'Here, wear this, it stops the dust from getting into your mouth.' She wrapped the scarf around his head and moved round him closer to the bag of grain.

Joshua could feel Magda staring at him as he worked the millstone. Turning to smile at her she looked away.

Grinding the grain was hard work, his muscles out of practice, began to stiffen up, yet his pride to impress this version of Jess made him push through.

Starting to sweat, he partially zipped down his suit to let some welcome cool air in.

'What is that?' Magda enquired, pointing at his zip.

'This?' Joshua moved the zip up and down. 'It is a zip.' He answered without thinking.

'It's fascinating.' Magda exclaimed. 'May I?' She gestured towards the zip.

Reprimanding himself to think before speaking, Richards's voice entered his head, reminding him to keep the technology safe to prevent capture and sentenced to death, yet, he could not refuse this beautiful woman.

Joshua nodded and let her examine the zip on the front of his protective suit. She moved it up and down, gasping in enchantment as it closed together and opened each time, she moved it. Over enthused, Magda pulled down too hard on the zip, yanking it down to his navel, exposing Joshua's chest. Gasping she tried to quickly close the zip back up, accidently brushing his skin in the process.

They both felt it.

Their eyes locked as the energy resonated through their bodies as her hand laid on his chest. Taking a step back, Magda blushed and looked away.

'Sorry.' She apologised, her eyes wide and innocent, looking at Joshua's chest and then down at the floor. Joshua touched her chin and pulled it up to look at him. 'Please do not apologise, I am hot from the grinding, you have helped me.'

Joshua removed his arms and let suit fall to his waist, revealing the top half of his athletic body.

Joshua saw Magda inhale at his physique. Placing her hand back on his chest, the electricity they both felt flowed through them. Intensifying, the longer they touched. Looking up and deep into his eyes, Magda moved closer to Joshua. Raising his hand, Joshua pushed her silky dark hair behind her ear and slowly stroked down to the nape of her neck. He pulled her gently towards him and stroked her jaw with his thumb. She looked up and pressed herself against him, her brown eyes intently staring into his, as if she knew what he was thinking. Her hand slowly made its way up Joshua's chest, caressing his athletic muscles, stopping on his smooth shoulder. Joshua placed his other hand in her hair and moved his head down closer to Magda's, their noses touching, he could feel her heart beating fast against his chest, her breathing heavily against his skin.

Mary's voice, berating James, warned them she was about to come into the kitchen. Jumping apart, Joshua turned back to milling the grain. His heart beating and face flushed, he glanced quickly at Magda. A little smile played on her lips as she fed the grain into the stones.

Mary sat back at the table and continued to chop the vegetables the two men had brought into the kitchen. Two women and a few children joined Mary at the kitchen table, chatting as they helped prepare the meal.

'Meet me after the evening meal. I need to talk to you.' Joshua whispered to Magda.

'I have to deliver the flour this evening.' She whispered back.

'Let me help you.'

Smiling shyly at Joshua, Magda nodded in agreement.

'Magda, you staying for the evening meal?' Mary asked across the noise of the now bustling kitchen.

'As long as you have enough.'

'There is always enough for you child.' Mary replied.

More people filtered into the kitchen area, helping Mary by taking the prepared vegetables to cook in the outdoor stove.

Finishing the last of the grinding, Joshua walked outside to catch some air. The suit was extremely warm for physical activity, yet he felt uneasy being half naked in front of all these people.

One of the men from earlier approached Joshua. Eyeing him curiously, he motioned Joshua to follow him. Once in doors, he led him through various passages until they arrived at a sparse bedroom. A wooden bed strewn with hay was pressed up against the wall whilst a small, exquisitely made wardrobe featured next to it. The man walked towards the wardrobe and opened it.

'Here.' The man took out a white dress robe and passed it to Joshua, still eyeing him apprehensively. 'My mother asked me to provide you with something more cooling. You cannot walk about half naked.'

'I appreciate this and will pay you back for your hospitality.' Joshua held his hand out to the man. 'I am Josh..., I mean, Jesus. And you are?'

'A man that does not know his own name will remain a stranger until proven otherwise. I am James. I will wait outside while you put that on.' James stalked out of the room.

Changing into the white robe, Joshua wondered why James was so hostile. Mary and Joseph were extremely welcoming, yet James seemed intent on making him feel awkward. Knowing he had to make friends not enemies, he decided he would inform James of his intention to rectify the damage he had caused. Joshua gathered his protective suit and walked out of the room. Seeing James, he lifted his suit in the air. 'I shall go and put this away and start repair on the land.' Joshua said to James.

'The evening meal will be ready, do not insult my Mother by missing it. You can repair the land after.' He grunted at a startled Joshua.

Following James back to the kitchen, he saw at least thirty men, women and children in the kitchen, most of them seated.

Scanning the crowd for Mary, he noticed Magda was beckoning him. She had saved him a seat next to her. Weaving between the people with his suit on his arm, he reached Magda and sat down grinning at her like a little school boy.

She reminded him so much of Jess, her looks, her caring nature, he felt a piece of home was with him. Yet she was not Jess and Joshua needed to come to terms with that.

Although, there was something about her that he trusted and needed.

Deep down, he knew she would be the key to complete his mission.

Chapter 11
Joshua - The Blue Pill

The evening meal had been surprisingly nice. Not knowing what to expect, the huge pot of fish stew had looked revolting. Mary dished it out in perfect circular wooden bowls and handed it out to each person. Small flat bread featured along the table on wooden plates and a collection of wooden spoons to be used as cutlery were scattered across the table. A smaller table and chairs had been brought in to accommodate the younger children and they chattered amusingly with each other. Dishing out the fish stew, Mary's face lit up with delight as compliments flowed with each bowl she delivered.

Looking around at the happy faces, smiling and conversing amongst themselves, Joshua thought back to his evening meals at home.

More often than not, he ate alone. His mother long deceased, his Father working all hours on the TT pod and Jess on call or at work in the hospital. He had yearned for company on an evening to be part of a big family, one that bickered and fought, yet always stuck together. He had seen this with Servians, family and friends uniting, helping each other out in times of need. Comforting each other through the worst times. Celebrating together the good times.

Being part of the Matriats at times was stifling, yes they were safe in the knowledge they would not get killed in the middle of the night, had ample food and shelter, yet showing affection or any type of emotion in public was frowned upon. Walking around like robots, only allowed to celebrate when Lamia had reclaimed another part of the Servians dwellings.

Scared to be caught displaying affection, it had seeped behind closed doors. Children were no longer cuddled, no one had friends, only work colleagues or acquaintances, birthdays and milestones were no longer celebrated. Lamia's one goal was to create a world of emotionless barbarians to undertake her brutal deeds, and unfortunately she had succeeded.

Without thinking, Joshua stood up in front of them all. A hush descending across the room as they all looked at the stranger from the sky, now dressed in a pristine white robe.
'I would like to take a minute before you eat to thank you all. Thank you for your kindness and hospitality. Especially to Mary and Joseph. When I arrived here, I was unsure what to expect, yet I could not have asked for more compassionate people. And to Magda.' He smiled down at her. 'Thank you for letting me help.' He cheekily winked. Her face growing flush at the thought of them earlier, she beamed back at him. Raising his wooden goblet full of wine he raised it to the room and towards Mary and Joseph who were now sat at the helm of the table. 'I drink to you. To arrive here in Capernaum, in a different dwelling, with different people, I may not still be alive. I owe you my life.' Seeing Mary's eyes fill with tears of happiness, he drank some of his wine.
In the corner of his eye he saw Magda raise her glass. 'Thank you for your daily kindness.' She smiled to the couple and drank some of her wine. Others followed, showering Mary and Joseph with their appreciation of all that they do.
As Joshua sat down, Mary stood up. 'I cannot express how happy you all make me, I am grateful to have each and everyone one of you in my life, even in bad times. I am blessed.' she said, beaming at Joshua. 'Now let's eat, before the food gets cold.'
Still beaming, she sat down next to her husband and kissed him.
A warm feeling wrapped around Joshua as he enjoyed being surrounded by happiness and love. He hoped he could be a part of this for a long time.
Following Magda's lead, he grabbed some of the flat bread from one of the wooden plates and tore off a piece. Dipping it into the steaming hot stew, he popped it into his mouth. The fresh flavours leapt about his palate.
'Wow.' He exclaimed through another mouthful. 'This is really good.'
Magda chuckled at him. 'Mary is a fantastic host. Making certain everyone has their fill, yet making sure there is enough left over for me to take to the less fortunate. She is an exceptional woman.'

Finishing off his bowl of stew, Mary offered Joshua more. Patting his stomach he motioned to her that he was full. The kitchen still full of indistinctive chatter and laughter, slowly hushed as the sound of dogs barking and horses neighing, indicated someone was outside.

Pushing his chair away from the table, James stood up. Giving a suspicious look to Joshua as if he had caused the unannounced visitor, he went to investigate.

'Good evening my family.' Boomed a voice a few moments later.

'John.' Cried out Mary who promptly stood up and rushed to embrace the man who had just entered.

Around the same age as Joshua, the man was dressed in a white robe with a leather belt around his waist. His beard and hair, extremely long and his thick chest hair could be seen through his clothing.

'I was in the mountains when I saw an object fly from the sky and into your lands. What has God graced you with my dear Mary?'

Mary grabbed John's hands and led him towards where Joshua sat. 'He brought this man John. God sent this man. Jesus, please meet John.'

Joshua stood up and backed away from Mary and John, his heart racing, his eyes wide, he began to panic. 'No, please, you have this all wrong. I can explain, I am not from God.' Looking at Mary and then at Magda, he pleaded with his eyes to help.

Magda stood up. 'Thank you for the evening meal Mary. Maybe tonight is not the night for answers. Tonight is for rest and talking tomorrow. Come Jesus. We must take this flour and bread to the poor.'

Mary nodded in agreement as she looked at Joshua.

'Yes, you are right, this evening is for resting, tomorrow is a new day for new enlightenments.' Beckoning John to come with her to the end of the table, she offered him some fish stew.

Politely declining John's eyes still rested on Joshua.

'Who is he?' Joshua whispered to Magda as he followed her to the bags of flour near the door.

'John is Mary's nephew. He lives in the mountains. He is harmless, yet odd. He eats only raw vegetation and honey and has given his life up to worship and spread the word of God to all. Do not fear him, he is a good man, although a bit different.' She whispered back

'Thank you.' Joshua said, for the intervention and the information on John. Joshua had little knowledge of religion, it had been abolished by Lamia's family years back and was only taught behind closed doors.

'You're welcome.' She whispered back. 'In return, I want you to show me more about your world. I want to see more zips.'

'My zip!' Joshua exclaimed and dashed back into the kitchen to see John holding up his protective suit.

'Jesus, what is this miracle?' John asked as he stroked the fabric of the suit.

Holding his breath, Joshua froze. He needed to get the suit back without raising suspicion. The less who knew about his technology, the better.

'It is Roman.' He replied to John. 'The Romans are trying a new armour and asked me to wear it and report back my findings.'

John threw the suit on the floor in disgust. 'Wars ravage this world, you should not be a part of it.' He spat at Joshua.

Grabbing the suit from the floor Joshua smiled at John. 'And that is why I am going to report back it is appalling.'

John roared with laughter and patted him on the back. 'I like you Jesus. Tomorrow we talk.'

Nodding to John as he walked out of the kitchen, he saw Magda loading the last bag of flour on to the cart and gesturing Joshua to get on. Throwing his suit over the flour, he jumped on the wooden trap and sat next to Magda.

The cart bumped across the rocks and dirt as they set off down the track towards the Sea of Galilee. Looking around the lush green fields and inhaling the fresh air, Joshua felt himself physically relax. He would leave the answers to their questions for another time and figure out a plan of action tomorrow, tonight would be for resting and learning about this new world.

He needed the help of others to make sure the world did not turn out like Lamia's, yet he needed people he trusted. If the TT pod and its contents fell into the wrong hands, Lamia's world would be created again, albeit sooner.

Joshua leant against the seat of the cart and gazed at Magda. The light of the setting sun, shone behind her head, creating a soft glow around her. Feeling his gaze, she turned and flashed a smile at him. Joshua's stomach flipped over.

He knew that Jess no longer existed, yet seeing this woman and the feelings he was gaining towards her in such a short period of time, made him feel guilty. He loved Jess, her selfless, caring nature was what drew him to her when they were just teenagers. Joshua closed his eyes and reminisced the times they spent together. Insignificant moments that made him yearn for her. Waking up to her arm draped across his stomach, stroking her soft skin as she still slept, softly kissing her forehead while the moonlight shone through the window, highlighting her flawless complexion. The way she fluttered her eyes open as she had looked up at him, love shining through them. Nudging her ear with his nose, as he whispered he loved her.

The cart abruptly stopped waking Joshua.

'Whoa, was I asleep?' He asked bleary eyed.

'Yes.' Magda smiled at him. Cocking her head to a side, she asked. 'Who's' Jess?'

Joshua swallowed, unsure of how to explain Jess, when a crowd of children came running up to the cart. 'Miss Magda, Miss Magda.' They shouted up at her in glee.

Joshua looked at the children, most were barely dressed. Two small boys, scarcely five years old, hung at the back of the crowd. A thin piece of cloth strung across both the boys waists. They had no shoes on their feet and dirty marks speckled all over their delicate skin. Bruises and cuts smattered across their thin little bodies. Yet their gaunt faced with tired eyes showed an untold story. Completely awake and rattled by the boy's appearance, Joshua grabbed some bread and made his way down to the boys. Kneeling down to their level, his stomach turned over. They looked like Servians that had escaped the Matriats.

'Here.' Joshua said as he offered them the bread. The boys looked at Joshua, then quickly put their heads down. Frowning, Joshua tried to offer them the bread again, yet they stood totally still, not moving a muscle.

'Who did this to you?' He whispered to the children.

'The Roman Soldiers.' They both whispered back, still looking down at their feet.

Magda joined the other side of Joshua and took the bread from him and passed it to the boys who hungrily ate it in front of them. 'Please leave them, they are scared of men. The Roman Soldiers use them as toys for entertainment. We have taught them to hide when they can. Most are homeless, yet no one wants to help, most of them do not have anyone to turn to.' Looking at him intently Magda's face was full of curiosity. Her eyes burning with questions. 'How do you not know this Jesus? Where have you come from? Why are you here?'

Joshua's mouthed opened, yet nothing came out. Saying out loud where he was from and why he was here, sounded ludicrous. Stuttering for words to placate Magda for now, he felt the electricity between them again, making him inhale sharply. Seeing her hand on his arm she looked deep into his eyes and smiled. 'I am sorry to bombard you, I can tell you are in a painful place, I will wait for you to tell me, when the time is right for you.'

Patting him as she removed her hand, Joshua realised he had been holding his breath. No one had the effect through touching him like Magda had.

Pushing those thoughts aside he looked at the two little boys as Magda gave them some more bread. The memories of the Servian children rattled through his brain. The torture of the poor had been going on far longer than Lamia and her families reign. Going back one hundred years would not have helped the innocent children that were slayed before them. Sitting down on the dirty ground he leant against one of the carts wheels, his mind in turmoil.

He needed to bring the divide of rich and poor closer together. He needed to ensure the future of humanity did not rest on using the less unfortunate as entertainment. He needed to create a world where they could live together, respectfully and equally. Like his Father would have wanted.

He needed a new plan. Looking at Magda, her hair glistening in the late sun, her laugh infecting all around her, her kindness known by many, he knew she would be the one, the one that could help him create a new world.

Riding in silence back to Mary and Joseph's, Joshua looked out on the horizon. The clear night's sky, making way for the moon to illuminate the path before them.

Taking a deep breath, Joshua was the first one to speak.

'Magda, I am not from here, but I think you already know that.'

Turning her head, she smiled at Joshua. 'Zips are not part of Capernaum.' She joked.

Smiling, knowing he had her trust, he continued. 'I am not from here, I am from a different country, and some would say a different world. I was supposed to travel to a place in my world, yet ended up here. After seeing those two boys and the pain that had been inflicted upon them, I think I came here, to this precise place for a reason. I need your help to carry out my mission as my Father intended.'

'Mission?' Magda questioned.

'My mission was to change the history of my world. One where children do not live in fear from soldiers, where people help one another, feed one another, live together as equals. I need to make this my mission, for this world.'

Magda looked at Joshua, 'But how?' She queried.

Sighing, Joshua put his head in his hands. 'Honestly, I do not know. I need help to create another way. I have no idea where to start. My Father sent me, his only son to complete this, yet I have already failed him.'

Stopping the cart, Magda put her hands on Joshua's. The electricity flowed through them, yet neither of them pulled away.

'The moment I saw you, I knew you were special, Jesus. I should be wary, yet something draws me to you. You have not failed your Father, just yet. We will complete his biddings together.'

A slow smile spread across Joshua's face. 'I cannot express my gratitude.' He squeezed her hand and looked into her eyes. They could both feel it, the way they made each other feel, he wanted to kiss her, yet withheld. She was not Jess, she made him feel safe and could accomplish anything, like Jess did, but he couldn't, not just yet, it didn't feel right.

Magda moved her hands away to start the cart back up. Relieved, Joshua exhaled and turned to face the road ahead. He needed to keep his head focused on his plan.

'If you are in this with me, I need to show you how I came here. Carry on past the house and I will direct you.'

Magda carried on past the house and Joshua guided her to the TT pod.

As they rounded the corner, moonlight glinted off the TT pod. Magda gasped at the huge, white capsule that stood before her.

Climbing off the cart, Magda cautiously approached the pod. Looking at Joshua, to confirm it was safe, she wandered around, stroking the smooth metal surface.

'This is the TT pod' Joshua explained to Magda. 'This is what I arrived in.'

'And these?' she pointed at the damage from the landing.

'They are just dents, the TT pod bounced a few times when we landed.'

'We?' Magda enquired. 'There is more than one of you?'

Joshua laughed, thinking of V.E.L.U.S. 'No there is only one of me, I shall show you soon what I mean by 'we'.'

At the rear of the TT pod, Magda followed the indentation in the ground from where it had slid to a stop. 'Does it ever end?' She laughed, pausing to trying to see where the TT pod initially hit the Earth. 'You have created quite a mess. Lucky it was Mary and Joseph's land. Anyone else's, it could have been a very different story. We will arrange for the land to be ploughed tomorrow.'

Joshua shook his head. 'It's fine Magda. I can …'

Magda cut him off. 'Jesus, I know people that can help. You do not know anyone here!' She exclaimed. 'You helped me, let me help you.'

She looked up and stared at Joshua with determination. Not able to tear himself away from those hypnotic eyes, so dark, so much like Jess', he felt himself melting under her gaze. The emotions grew inside him as he stood, gawking like a teenager. Using all his strength, he wrenched his eyes away from hers, he needed to keep his head straight, and he needed to formulate a plan first.

Joshua took Magda's hand and started to lead her back to the TT pod. 'Magda, I do not need help as I have something that can do it for me, yet before I show you, I need to explain a few things.'

Reaching the TT pod, he walked along to the lettering. 'Here.' He pointed at the J.E.S.U.S. and spelt out the letters. 'J is for Joshua and E is for East, the SUS is my Fathers Company, SUS Industries.'

Magda just looked at him blankly. 'So, your name is not Jesus?' She asked, confusion spreading across her face.

'No, my name is Joshua. When I first landed, Mary asked me what the symbols were. I spelt them out and did not correct her when she thought my name was Jesus. There is a reason which I will explain.'

Joshua located the makeshift stairs Joseph had made him. 'The inside is on a slight angle from landing, please be careful. V.E.L.U.S. open the door'

Magda's eyes showed her astonishment as the TT pod's door partially opened and laid on the makeshift mud stairs.

'Watch your step.' Joshua told Magda as he guided her inside.

Magda's eyes were wide with amazement as she entered the brightly lit pod. 'Where is the sun coming from?' She enquired.

Yet, before Joshua could answer, V.E.L.U.S.'s voice boomed round the pod.

'Good Evening Mr East. I see you have a visitor.' Magda looked around the TT pod, her eyes frantically searching for the source of the female robotic voice.

'This is Magda, V.E.L.U.S. and she has come to assist with the mission. Please make her feel welcome, I will try to explain who you are.'

'Of course Mr East. Do you require any drinks or meals whilst I commence reconstruction of the land?'

Seeing the scared look on her face, Joshua touched Magda's cheek. 'Do not be afraid. The voice you hear is my on-board companion, V.E.L.U.S., it is a lot to get used to, but you will understand. Please sit.' Joshua motioned towards the chair in the middle of the TT pod. 'Would you like a drink? Water? Wine?'

Magda sat on the chair, looking around the TT pod in amazement. 'Can I have a wine please?' She asked meekly.

'V.E.L.U.S., we require two wines please and display a 360 view whilst the land is reconstructed.' Joshua stated.

A white tray emerged from underneath the console with a large bottle of water, two glasses and a blue pill. Retrieving the tray, Joshua sat next to Magda.

'V.E.L.U.S. helps me with things. She is not human, nor a living thing, yet from where I come from she is a part of life as we know it.'

Unscrewing the top of the bottle of water, Joshua dropped the blue pill inside. Securing the lid back on, he shook the bottle as the water inside turned red. Pouring the red liquid into the glasses, he passed one to Magda and continued. 'She will be able to reconstruct this land quickly. Please look over here.'

The monitors had sprung into life and gave a 360 view around the pod. 'We can watch from inside while V.E.L.U.S. completes her reconstruction.' Joshua pointed towards the monitors as Magda held her glass open mouthed.

She watched through the monitor's, mesmerised as a metal arm protruded from the pod and stuck into the ground. The land began to shake before their eyes, yet the TT pod stayed still.

The piles of dirt and vegetation, shook and moved to its original place, before the TT pod had landed. Magda's eyes grew wide as she saw the huge indentation reformed to its original appearance. The TT pod started to move slightly as the mud underneath it went back to its rightful place.

'Hold on to your wine.' Joshua instructed Magda as the TT pod slowly moved to an upright position. The floor no longer sloping, Joshua stood up and stretched.

'Reconstruction of land complete.' V.E.L.U.S. confirmed once the metal arm was safely back into the TT pod.

Magda moved towards the monitors and looked at the surroundings in more detail. The once indented land, now back to its original fields. Trees and bushes that had been destroyed by the TT pod, now back in place, swaying in the night breeze.

Speechless, Magda turned to Joshua. Her mouth open, her eyes still wide with surprise. 'How....' She stammered. 'I have never seen anything like this.' Sitting back down on the chair in the middle of the TT pod, Magda's skin turned pale.

Asking if she needed anything else, Magda shook her head. 'I know I asked for more zips, but ...' She trailed off.

'I know, yet, there is more to come.' Joshua smiled at her whilst taking a sip of wine.

Following Joshua's lead, Magda took a tentative sip from the glass she held.

The look of delight as the rich, flavoursome wine danced on her palate made Joshua beam.

'How?' she said holding the glass up before her. 'I saw the clear water. I saw you put a blue pebble in. I saw it turn red. This is not wine, yet it tastes like wine.' She exclaimed.

'From my world, we have many different things. I can take simple water and turn it into many different drinks. It was not a pebble, but... .' Joshua tried to think of something that Mary would understand.

'In this period, many would use herbs to heal people.' V.E.L.U.S.'s voiced echoed around the TT pod, making Magda jump and look around nervously.

'Yes, V.E.L.U.S.' Joshua agreed, noticing Magda's worried look. 'You will get used to her.' He soothed. 'She means you no harm, yet I can understand she will seem a little scary at the moment.' Taking a sip of his wine, Joshua continued. 'The pebble is like a herb from my world. It is made very small so we can carry lots of them. We have many different ones. We use them for drinks, for food, to help people that are ill.

'You can heal people with this wine?' Magda looked at her glass in amazement.

'Not with the wine.' Joshua laughed, we have a different pebble for that.

'Ahh' Magda said, taking a bigger sip of her wine, yet still not grasping the concept.

The wine relaxing her, Magda implored Joshua to tell her more from his world.

'It will take a while.' He answered.

'We have all night.' Magda replied raising her glass to him.

'Well, I think we should maybe start with this.' Joshua retrieved his protective suit that he had placed folded near the chair. He went to the inside pocket and took out two handwritten letters and sat down next to Magda.

Passing them to her, he swallowed the lump in his throat as tears started to form in his eyes at the sight of his Fathers handwriting. He cleared his throat and composed himself. 'I shall translate.' He whispered.

Chapter 12
Rachel - Nick's Revelation

Sitting at the dining table in the villa, Rachel could not believe it had been a week since she first landed here.

On one hand, it had passed in a blur of meetings and discovery's, each one more surprising than the last, enlightening yet chilling, that she had been part of this profound company for many years with not an indication of its enormity.

Although on the other hand, it felt like she had not been home for months. The December wintery weather of England seemed a distant memory in comparison to the hot climate of Cyprus.

'You've caught the sun.' Nick pointed out as he sat with Rachel at the table.

Wearing an off the shoulder dusty pink top, teamed with white denim jeans, Rachel had never worn so much colour in the past week. Her usual go to items, black or dark blue, practically in oversized, had never made their way out of her case. Yet she was loving this new look. Shannon the personal shopper for the company was extremely gifted, each item fitted perfectly and complimented her stature and skin tone.

With a mouth full of moussaka, she nodded her head in agreement to Nick. Her nightly invitations to the complex's pool, along with sitting on the villas terrace on an evening had given her a glow.

'I hope you are remembering to wear sunscreen, the sun can catch you out here.' Nick carried on.

Smiling at him, her mouth still full of moussaka Nick laughed at her.

Swallowing the last of her food, she put her cutlery down. 'Weird really, being a responsible adult, I wear sunscreen daily.' She teased him. 'Yet there is something burning that I need to talk to you about.'

'Ha ha, very funny, go ahead. It's about my family isn't it?' He replied.

'Well yes, there was few questions I wanted to talk to you about. The most burning question was obviously about your family, but the other one is about the Caroline Bennett. Can you tell me more about her?'

Nick frowned at her. 'Why?'

Rachel grabbed her phone and showed Nick. The last week she had sporadically been receiving emails and messages from Caroline. Not wanting to appear rude, Rachel had replied to one of the messages, instructing she had free time after Christmas. Her phone had immediately rang with Caroline on the other line. Slightly cold at the beginning of the phone call, Caroline had sleazed her way through the call. Taunting Rachel on how she was Nicks prodigy, then backtracking, uttering she wanted to learn from Rachel and the way she overcame her previous life. Explaining to Rachel the discussion that happened about her within the committee and how she was to be used. Caroline asked if they could meet up for dinner on the Marina one evening, enabling them to discuss how Rachel could work for her once the committee had chewed her up and spat her out.

Shocked and confused, Rachel said she would check her commitments and get back to her. The phone call had shaken her up, so many different temperaments through one five-minute call, yet Caroline's last words had run through her head all day. Her past often prevented her from trusting people whole heartedly, yet she had done with Nick. Wondering if Caroline was playing her, or Nick actually was just using her, she had decided to come clean with Nick and gauge his reaction. Rachel was unaware if it was the Cypriot atmosphere or the discovery's of the last week that had cooled her hot headed temperament, yet she was proud of herself for waiting until her and Nick were alone.

Nick gravely looked over the emails and messages, and listened silently with a stony face as Rachel retold the conversation with Caroline. Rachel saw the fire in his eyes as she found the courage to ask him if any of it was true.

After a tense few minutes, Nick finally spoke. 'You did the right thing telling me this.' His voice broke slightly, surprising Rachel. She had never seen Nick like this.

'After all these years working together, I hope you know my nature and realise I would never have been able to keep up the pretence. This has shocked me. We need to be careful Rachel. Bide our time. Caroline is a powerful woman brought into the committee, not just because she inherited the place from her Father, but also because of her contacts. She slowed the production of ammo and paid a lot of her own money to seek out underground dealers. She knows some, but not all of what we do. I would suggest to not meet with her, yet if you must, let me know and I will ensure Yuri takes you. If you feel threatened or uncomfortable, press your panic button and Yuri will interrupt your meeting with some emergency.'

Rachel's hand went up to the gold necklace that hung around her neck. The encased pearl pendant housed a small panic button Nick had given her on his arrival to Cyprus. 'Just in case.' He had winked, trying to put her at ease.

Nick ran his hands through his light brown hair, the tension showing in his face. 'Rachel, I feel I need to be honest with you. You were among a number of people that I looked at for this position. Wild cards one.' Nick held his hands up at Rachel as she pulled a disgusted face at him. 'Please just hear me out.'

Fiddling with his cutlery, Rachel had never seen Nick so nervous. He spoke about his wife, how he fell in love with a woman here, bringing her into the cult of S.U.S. Industries. It was not what he wanted, yet he had an obligation to carry on his ancestors undertaking. A wonderful woman she had accepted Stefan for who he was and what he needed to do, yet refused to leave Cyprus. He split his time between his wife, son and his responsibilities in England. Watching his son grow up, teaching him the knowledge as he was taught by his Father, he knew his son was not made for the committee. His son had shown resilience and had made his standing known that when the time came for him to fulfil his position, he would refuse it. Therefore he went searching for a replacement. People from different backgrounds, gifted, rich, average and abused. Rachel had flinched, knowing Nick was talking about her. After a year, he had whittled it down to five children, Rachel being one of them. He had watched Rachel as she struggled through life, yet always fighting on.

Angry tears pooled in Rachel's eyes. 'Let me get this right. Whilst I tried to survive my childhood, surrounded by strangers shooting up in front of me, watching my own mother bouncing away on a man for money, scavenging food from the neighbour's bins, sold to the highest bidder to violate, you just stood from afar and watched it all happen?' She whispered.

'No, it wasn't like that.' Nick pleaded. 'I can promise you, I ensured food was in the neighbour's bins for you to eat, and if I was not around, I made sure someone put it there for you. When I discovered when you had been sold ...' He trailed off; his voice caught in his throat as he remembered when he got the call Rachel's mother had sold her to a local paedophile for a bag of smack. The gut wrenching feelings were still there, the feeling of helplessness being in Cyprus whilst he waited for the word they had tracked her down. 'We rescued you.' He said in a small whisper.

'You rescued me?' She screeched. 'You think putting food in bins is rescuing me? You think taking me from a paedophile to put me straight back into a crack house is rescuing me? I can't listen to this anymore.'

Rachel stood up and walked outside towards the wrought iron fencing at the end of the terrace. Her hands on the rail, she bent over the railings looking at the drop below. Her cries uncontrollable as the memories from the past rose up.

Nick could have saved her, yet she was just an experiment to him. All trust she had in the company, in Nick, was gone in a split second.

Sobbing she saw movement next to her. 'Please let me continue.' She heard him say. 'After all these years, I think of you like a daughter, I want to explain why I am protective, why I think all this is a mistake and why I do not want you to meet Caroline.'

Outraged, Rachel laughed out loud. 'You think of me as a daughter yet you stood by as I got raped for money. Would you put your own flesh and blood in that position? Thought not. I need you to leave.'

A shameful look on his face, Nick placed a hand on her shoulder. Flinching at his touch, she moved away. 'I will come back tomorrow.' He said, turning around to leave.

Bending over the railings she screamed into the steep decline. Her pain echoed around the complex, bouncing off the walls as she screamed a second time before crumpling against the railings. Hugging her knees to her chest, she wiped the tears away from her eyes. She was Rachel Nichols, she had fought all her life and she would fight again. Not thinking about the consequences, Rachel marched into the Villa and grabbed her phone.

Punching out at text, her finger hovered over the send button as her mind whirled over what had just happened.

Determined she pressed send, she would meet Caroline, where and whenever she wanted.

Chapter 13
Joshua - The Beginning of John's Persuasion

Thudding on the TT pod, awoke Joshua.
Blearily, he opened his eyes. His head was pounding and his limbs felt heavy and stiff. Realising he was laying on the floor, he put his hand to his head. Regretting the wine he had consumed last night, his stomach flipped over as the events of yesterday ran through his mind. Too much had happened in the last twenty-four hours for him to have been granted this hangover.
'What is that?' He heard a female voice say.
Sitting up from the floor, he saw Magda, half asleep on the chair, a blanket covering her.
The banging on the TT pod was getting louder.
'V.E.L.U.S. switch on 360 view and get me a water and a hangover cure please.' Requested Joshua.
The monitors lit up with the surrounding area, as a tray revealed itself from under the console. Grabbing the water and pills he offered them to Magda.
Shaking her head, he unscrewed the water and gulped it down with the pills. 'Do you feel alright after last night?' He enquired.
'I am fine.' She answered surprising Joshua. Shaking his head at her resilience to his potent wine, he looked at the monitors and saw a man walking around the TT pod. His head ringing with every bang on the TT pods metal shell.
'Joshua, that's John.' Magda said rubbing her eyes. Her long dark hair swung in front of her as she sat up. 'Joshua, let him in. Of all the people I know, he would be beneficial to our cause.'
Joshua grinned at Magda. 'You called me Joshua.'

Smiling shyly back at him, she replied. 'From now on, everyone we meet will know you as Jesus, at least I can keep a little bit of who you really are alive, by calling you your true name.'

Joshua and Magda had sat in the TT pod until late. Reading out loud the hand written letters from his Father and Darias, Joshua had started the story from the end and worked his way back. Explaining about everyone, including Jess.
Magda had listened quietly to it all, had wiped his tears when he had shown her the goodbye messages and the photographs of his Father. Asking questions only when he had stopped talking and had almost collapsed with excitement when shown the 3D projections of the Earth. Waving her hand through the blue light, her glee was contagious as she laughed and clapped in enjoyment at the sight. It had been a welcome distraction from the emotions running through him whilst relaying his past.
Magda had insisted she be shown the last moments of Rylitte. He did not want her to see the mounds of dead that filled the street, yet she had insisted it would help her understand his world. V.E.L.U.S. had brought up CCTV of the day he left, showcasing the Streets of Rylitte. Seeing so many men, women and children dead in the streets, he turned away not wanting to relive it a second time.
A tear ran down Magda's beautiful face as the monitors displayed scenes gathered from a Matriats body cam whilst in a Servian Village raid.
'How can people act like this?' She whispered, distraught at what she was seeing.
Putting his arm around her for comfort, she softly wept into his shoulder. He regretted agreeing to show her the scenes of Rylitte and the Servian villages and whispered sorry into her ear.
Soothing him she said it was her that needed to see this. Seeing those poor children, defenceless against the army of the Matriats slayed for nothing other than entertainment destroyed her, yet her pain was nothing compared to theirs. It had cemented her belief in Stephens's vision of how the world should be and how it could be, with Joshua's gifts from his world. Magda gave her word she would do anything required to help Joshua complete his mission to direct the human race onto a different path.

'V.E.L.U.S. audio on.'

John's voice could now be heard in the TT pod.

'Jesus, I have seen the new lands, I have seen your miracle, please speak to me. I want to spread the word of your coming.'

Magda nodded at Joshua, confirming he needed to speak to John. 'He is well connected, he will know how to get the word out. He can be trusted so long as you tell him the truth.'

Not fully confident, Joshua trusted Magda's judgement and asked V.E.L.U.S. to open the door. Making his way towards the door as it opened, he saw John stood there opened mouth.

'Good Morning John. Please, come in.'

'Mary of Magdalena, what brings you to be inside this miracle with the one from the sky? Have you been chosen?' John addressed Magda.

Raising his eyebrow, Joshua looked at Magda. 'Am I not the only one with a different identity?'

Magda laughed. 'Ah no, my story is not as interesting as yours. There are many Mary's. I originally come from Magdalena, thus use Magda so people know who they are talking to.'

'Interesting.' Joshua grinned at Magda.

Joshua held out his hand to help John inside the TT pod. Motioning him to sit next to Magda, the door of the TT pod slowly shut, enclosing them inside.

John started to speak but Joshua held his hand up to stop him.

'I know you have many questions John, but please hear me out first. I have not been sent by God to you, yet I have been sent here for a reason. I need your help to complete my mission given to me by my Father. I will be carrying it out, as his only son, in his honour.'

Feeling more confident as Magda smiled at him, encouraging him to continue, he retold the events leading up to his arrival. John watched as the monitors displayed the horrific crimes from the future.

John had sat their quietly, not a murmur over the few hours as Joshua had taken to recall his story.

Showing him the handwritten letters, John examined the foreign writing.

'You do not need to know what these say, yet if you wish I can translate.'

John looked up at Joshua, wide eyed.

'You say you are not from God, yet see your mission. See what you want to do. This is God's vision.' He said tapping the letters.
'I must go. I know what I can do. Wait for me here.'
John stood and the TT pods door opened.
'I will not be long.' He said looking back at Joshua and Magda's worried faces as he walked down the steps. 'Stay here.'

Needing some fresh air, Joshua followed him and lent against the metal sphere. Sighing, he looked up at the sky. The clouds floated carelessly across the sun as Joshua pondered if he had made the right decision confiding in John.
'It was the right thing to do.' Magda said, causing Joshua to jump.
'I feel too many people know about me and the TT pod.' Joshua advised, recalling Richards's words to hide the TT pod. 'I do not want to be captured before I have set a plan in place. People will be scared of my technology and destroy it when it can help so many.'
Stroking his face, she turned his head to face her. 'Do not worry Joshua. I know this must be frightening for you, not knowing who you can trust, yet you need to believe in yourself, like I believe in you.'
Sighing he looked back up at the sky.
'You must be hungry. I shall venture to Mary's and return with food, while you wait for John to come back. It will be a good distraction while we wait.' Magda proceeded to walk away.
Not wanting her to leave, Joshua grabbed her arm. 'I have food in the TT pod, I shall bring it out. You can have a morning meal from my world. We can eat it out here whilst we wait for John.' He said with a glint in his eye.

After feasting on pancakes and bacon, Magda and Joshua relaxed outside of the TT pod, enjoying the soft breeze as Joshua retold stories of his world.
V.E.L.U.S.'s voice echoed out of the TT pod.
'Approaching, one male one female.'
Shielding his eyes from the sun, Joshua surveyed the field and saw two people approaching. Squinting at the distance, he could see one of them manically waving as they both hurried towards the TT pod.
'John has returned with Mary.' Magda informed Joshua whilst waving back at them, smiling.

Feeling his stomach turn over, Joshua deliberated to himself why John would bring Mary with him. She had already seen the TT pod, yet Joshua was not ready to explain to another person what brought him here.

Mary rushed up and embraced him, kissing each cheek. 'I have been so worried Jesus, you did not return last night. I did not sleep. I wondered if you had been taken away from us. Or James had scared you away.' Mary rambled. 'John told me you were alive and well. I cried and thanked him.'

Joshua could feel the protective love radiate from Mary, though she hardly knew him. It was a nice feeling, knowing he had people that treated him as family after such a short period of time.

'I have returned. And I bring Mary.' John announced to Joshua as if he had not noticed their arrival. 'You will be wondering why I bring this kind, good woman with me. Huh?'

Joshua nodded, not knowing whether to laugh or be afraid. 'Mary tells me your Mother was also called Mary? To help you disperse your mission, you will need someone to look after you. Mary will look after you like a Mother. She will provide you with clothing, food and a place to sleep and give you comfort when you need it. Joseph will teach you carpentry, then you can sell your items to blend in with others. In return, you will help Mary with your miracles. Such as wine, and harvest time. I will scour for helpers to bring peace on this world. Ones that will deliver the message, yet loyal to you.'

Smiling at the anticipation on Mary's face, Joshua agreed.

Squealing in delight, Mary hugged Joshua. 'You can call me Mother or Mary, either is good, but now you are my son Jesus. She squeezed him tighter.

'There is one more thing Jesus.' John addressed Joshua. 'Before you spread your word, we need the people to know of you and accept you. You need to be baptised and show the many who you are. We shall have a celebration for all to join. Many will flock to the celebration. I will baptise you Jesus, and that is what you will be known as, hence forth.'

Joshua refused. 'I have not been sent by God John, I will not be baptised when I know nothing about him.'

Mary and John gasped. 'But you must.' Mary pleaded.

Joshua shook his head. 'There must be another way. I cannot lie to the people I am supposed to protect. I cannot spread the word of a God I do not know about.'

A silence descended across the four of them before John grinned at Joshua and put his arm around him.

'Come let me teach you.' He said as he led Joshua towards the house.

Chapter 14
Rachel - The Pretence

Opening the front door, Rachel checked the road leading to her villa was still deserted.
Unlocking the silver car door, she got in and started the engine. Thanking her lucky stars, it was automatic, she reversed out and followed the satnav on her phone towards the Marina to meet Caroline. Driving down the hill, Rachel felt apprehensive. She had only sent the message late yesterday evening, and now here she was travelling to meet her for dinner at 8PM.
Parking up and walking towards the restaurant, Rachel looked longingly at the tourist families milling around on the Marina. They all seemed carefree and happy, and Rachel envied them. Her past always simmered below the surface, threatening to overspill if jolted, she wished she could have just one carefree happy day without the memories of her past marring the perfect moment.
A tall burly man blocked her path and grunted at her, interrupting her thoughts.
'Sorry.' Rachel apologised, assuming she had not seen him whilst caught up in thought.
As she tried to manoeuvre around the muscular male, he grabbed her arm firmly. 'Miss Nichols?' he enquired, in a clearer voice.
Rachel nodded at him in confusion.
'Miss Bennett is waiting for you, please follow me.' The man instructed.
Rachel complied and followed the man to a nearby restaurant. His short crew cut hair, large muscular stature and steely stare, alarmed Rachel slightly.
'Rachel, you made it.' Rachel heard Caroline's voice before she saw her.

Turning around, she watched Caroline stand up from the table and eagerly walk towards her. Wrapping her arms around Rachel, Caroline embraced her like an old friend and motioned to sit at the sea front table.

'Thank you for meeting me Rachel. I know you have a busy schedule, yet I wanted to see you in person. It is an honour to dine tonight with THE Rachel Nichols, our newest member of the committee.' Caroline put her hands up in the air.

Rachel blushed as she placed her bag onto the floor, wondering why Caroline was acting like she was a celebrity.

The large man sat next to Caroline; his steely stare still fixed on Rachel as her eyes opened wide in apprehension. She was unaware that Caroline would be accompanied by anyone else. She should have brought Yuri with her.

Seeing her distress, Caroline laughed. 'Please ignore Craig.' She said as she pointed towards him. 'He is a man of few words, yet amongst a small number of people I whole heartedly trust. He is a fantastic bodyguard, but a better friend. I would be lost without him.' Caroline looked at him adoringly with a slight smile on her face. Looking back at Rachel's awkward face, Caroline laughed again. 'Please do not get the wrong impression, Craig is a married man with children, he is dedicated to his position with me as much as he is dedicated to his family. You wouldn't think this scary man would be such a big softy underneath.'

A slight smile flitted quickly across Craigs face.

Nodding in acknowledgement at Caroline's statement, Rachel smiled awkwardly.

'I have taken the liberty in ordering drinks and food already; they should be along shortly. Again, please do not take any notice of Craig, he will not let me go anywhere without him.' Caroline leant forward and whispered to Rachel. 'I have had a few death threats in the past due to my line of work and Craig takes his position at Brodells seriously.'

Rachels' eyes opened wide in surprise again. 'You've had death threats?' She whispered.

Caroline's face turned grave. 'Yes.' She nodded seriously. 'Unfortunately, in my line of work, it is more common than you think. Mostly from the do-gooders that no longer want weapons in the world. They think as I am the last in line of Brodells, if they get rid of me, the Brodell empire will cease to exist, therefore no more weapons. What they do not understand is there is a board of directors and the company will continue to operate, with or without me alive.'

'Are you not scared? You seem so calm about it all?' Rachel asked.

'I have learnt to not be consumed with negative thoughts Rachel. We all have little boxes in our minds that we try and keep our darkest fears inside. I ensure the lid of mine is always shut.' Caroline replied. 'Craig here thinks I should be more diligent, yet he has been by my side for nearly twenty years now and has got me out of some tricky situations. I know I will always be safe when I have Craig with me.'

Rachel smiled at Caroline in gratitude. Finally, she had met someone just like her. Caroline had fears which she kept hidden, yet she had the ability to keep everything within the box.

The evening past quickly, the food had been delightful, and she had relaxed within Craig's presence, yet there had been no mention of the original reason Caroline had asked for them to meet.

'Caroline, tonight has been lovely, getting to know you and Craig, yet I thought you had originally asked me to meet with you to discuss what was going to happen with the committee?' Rachel asked.

Caroline put her fingers to her lips. Leaning across the table, Caroline whispered into Rachel's ear. 'Not here, too many people could be listening. Are you free tomorrow?'

Rachel nodded.

'I will send instructions regarding tomorrow. This is too serious to discuss openly.'

Leaning back onto her chair, Caroline clicked her fingers and Craig stood up.

'I will escort you to your car.' Craig said gruffly to Rachel as Caroline stared icily at her.

'I...I'm sorry if I offended you.' Rachel stammered as she rose from her seat. 'I just thought there was a reason for this evening.'

'We shall discuss it tomorrow.' Caroline thinly smiled whilst waving her hand, signalling the conversation and evening had ended.

Craig accompanied Rachel to her car in silence and watched her until she had drove out of sight. Letting his daunting demeanour slip slightly, Craig leant against the wall of a shop and let out a big sigh. Closing his eyes, he thought of his wife and children at home. Only a few more years of being Caroline dogsbody and he could give up the security business for good and complete his dream of opening a bakery with his wife. He knew Caroline would make it difficult for him to leave, he knew too much of her what happened behind closed doors, yet he hoped the loyalty he had shown through the years would soften the blow.

The next evening, Rachel found herself checking to see if the road leading to her villa was deserted again before she started the silver car.
A note had been slid under the villa of her door, only five minutes earlier with the address to meet Caroline and orders to burn the note immediately.
The air was still warm for 7pm, yet Rachel had chills as she drove towards the destination. This evening seemed different then last nights. The burning of the note and Caroline's icy stare as she left. Rachel felt lost and thought about the events of the last few days.
Nick had tried to contact her, yet she had been non-responsive. Plastering on a smile daily, she had continued adhering to the itinerary and learning about the company. She had learnt a lot, some of it unbelievable, yet the conversation with Nick had always been in the back of her mind whilst she took notes and asked questions. She had been mature enough to be pleasant to Nick when anyone else was present, yet if they had been left alone, she had been less forgiving. How could she work with someone that was able to watch a child suffer and just walk away, leaving them until the time was right? How could someone stand by and watch a distressed young girl wallow in poverty and abuse, and then call her his daughter? Rachel could not understand it, nor did she have the stomach to listen to his excuses. The conversation between them had opened the box that she had stored those dark memories inside. The old memories of her childhood that had been hidden, were now raw and at the forefront of her mind.
Rachel's only reprieve from her own thoughts was when she was with Yuri. It felt strange driving on her own without him.
The journey seemed longer without his chatter. She enjoyed his ability to talk about anything. He was the only person that didn't push her for information of why she was in Cyprus, the only person that didn't test her and she appreciated that.

They had grown close over the few weeks he had been her driver, though not close enough for her to confide in him the altercation with Nick.

Yuri was mischievous, charming and made her feel like a normal person. She could relax when she was with him, she could be herself, she could just be, Rachel. She wasn't an addition to the committee, or the abused child, she was Rachel, happy carefree Rachel.

The night of Nick's revelation, Yuri had saved her. His caring nature and offer of Christmas day with his family had raised her spirits. Without him realising, he had given her the strength to stay in Cyprus for now.

Dark thoughts had entered her head that evening. Thoughts of returning to Trinity Estate. To join her kind. To go down the road she was born to go down. Selling her body would not be an issue, the gift of having a child had been taken away from her by the paedophile she was sold to. Damaging her little body so severely, the only option was to operate, rendering her childless for life.

Rachel very rarely drank, yet that night, in her emotional state, she had grabbed a bottle of wine from the fridge. Downing half in one go, she felt the liquid swirl in her stomach. The warm glow from the alcohol spread through her body, numbing the pain that had reared its ugly head.

Still holding the bottle, Rachel walked towards the patio doors, leading to the terrace. Her plan was to finish the bottle outside, watching the sun go down on her miserable life, yet a knock on the front door had stopped her in her tracks. Yuri was standing there when she opened it. Seeing her tear stained face, he asked if she were OK and would inform the office if she could not attend her meeting tonight.

Confused and slightly light headed by the wine, Rachel informed Yuri she had a night off. Thrusting his paperwork towards her, it clearly showed in black and white his instructions were to pick her up at 8.30pm and drop her off at the Marina. Inviting Yuri in, Rachel grabbed her itinerary and showed Yuri he was not required this evening.

'Maybe its fate this has got mixed up.' He said throwing his papers in the air. 'It looks like you need a friend tonight.'

'Not tonight Yuri, thanks, I just need to be alone.' She replied, exhaustion setting in from the crying.

'I don't want to leave you like this.' Yuri said, worried. 'Just wait there, I have an idea.' He said rushing out of the door.

'Yuri, no, please do not get anyone. Not while I'm like this.' She shouted after him, yet he was already out of ear shot.

Sitting on the black leather couch, her head started to spin from the half bottle of wine she had just downed. Clutching her head to stop it from spinning, the effects of the wine and the night's events caught up with her and tears spilled down her face. Catching a glimpse of her reflection in the switched off TV, made her feel even worse. Her neatly pinned up hair had come down in places, mascara streaked down her face and her eyes were all red and puffy.

Not having the strength or the choice, Rachel sat staring at the open door, feeling sorry for herself, as silent tears ran down her face.

Yuri returned with a small black box in his hands.

'What you need is a distraction.' He said smiling that cheeky grin of his. 'But first, go wash your face, get some comfy pyjamas on and I'll make you a coffee.

Too tired to argue, and slightly relieved someone was taking control, Rachel did as she was told and returned to a coffee outside on the terrace with Yuri sitting there shuffling a deck of cards.

'Let's play.' He said with that mischievous smile.

Dealing out the cards, he had asked if she knew how to play black jack. Rachel nodded. Ignoring Rachel's mournful aura, Yuri sorted his cards and talked about the squid he had eaten that day.

Perplexed by Yuri's random conversation, Rachel started to engage with him and her night improved dramatically, passing in chatter and laughter.

Although Rachel smiled and laughed, the anger and disappointment in what Nick had done, still simmered below the surface. He was the only person she had grown close to trusting, proving to her, she could depend on no one.

Turning into a poorly lit street. Rachel parked up the car. A waste land spread out before her with run-down cattle sheds to her left. Thinking this could not be the place, she cursed herself for following the rules and setting light to the paper as instructed. Just as she was about to grab her phone, car lights moved alongside her. Looking up, Rachel watched Caroline as she got out of her car and motioned her to wind her window down.

'They may have tracked your car and your phone. If you are committed to discussing the committee like you said, leave the car and your belongings here and come with me.'

Rachel sat there like a rabbit in headlights, she had not been expecting this, yet she was curious about what Caroline had to say.

The crunch of gravel alerted Rachel another car was approaching. Tentatively, Rachel looked around eyes still wide open in panic.

'Do not worry, that is Craig.' Caroline explained. 'I know Craig joined us last night, however, this meeting will just be me and you Rachel, no one else. I understand if the trust between us is not there yet, however we need to be quick. If they track your car and see it is parked here, they will come looking.'

Caroline was right, Rachel did not trust her just yet, leaving her bag and car would be reckless.

Feeling Caroline's cold blue eyes staring at her as she grew impatient, Rachel heard Craig's car door open as he wandered across to Caroline. Rachel heard them whispering as she closed her eyes, her heart hammering, knowing she needed to think clearly and not with anger. Nick had warned her Caroline was dangerous, and to only meet with Yuri, yet Caroline did not seem dangerous last night. She was pleasant and showed Rachel that we all have a little box of fearful memories in our minds. The altercation between her and Nick jumped into her thoughts. If she had to pick one to trust right now, it would be Caroline over Nick. Making her decision, Rachel climbed out of the car.

'Leave your keys in the ignition. They fob will have a tracker too.' Caroline said.

Putting the keys back into the ignition as Caroline advised, Rachel shut the car door, leaving her belongings.

Caroline pulled out her phone and rang a number. The interior of Rachel's car lit up as if she was receiving a call.

'Sorry, just had to check.' Caroline said as she put her phone away.

Driving off into the darkness, Rachel felt apprehensive. Caroline was being extra cautious, and she wondered why. Her demeanour was different from last night. Whereas Caroline was warm and welcoming, this evening she was cold and silent.

Looking out of the window, watching the landscape speed past, she slipped her hand into her denim jacket pocket to feel if it was still there.

The car gathered speed as it hit the motorway, heading towards the airport.

A smile of relief quickly passed Rachel's lips as she wrapped her hand around her personal mobile phone.

Chapter 15
Joshua - The Baptism

Carving a design in the base for his statuette, Joshua was amazed at the natural ability he had for woodwork alongside the enjoyment he gleaned from it. Watching Joseph and the time it took him to create his pieces had given Joshua an idea. Adapting tools, he had in the TT pod, had worked perfectly. They saved both him and Joseph time in their carpentry, along with a more precise incision.

Whilst the tools helped him greatly with his carpentry, the real skill came in his gift to form art. He had captured the essence of Magda in his carvings and attached the model to the intricately designed base. Presenting it to her in the TT pod she had been delighted and recommended setting up his own shop near the Sea of Galilee. Tourists would marvel at his carving abilities, thus spreading a good name when he eventually started to put his mission into action.

Within a couple of weeks, Joshua had set up his shop and it had been a roaring success.

At the same time, Mary's nephew John had set up a ministry to spread the word of God.

The close proximity and Johns relentless badgering about him being baptised began to grate on Joshua.

After another successful day at his shop and another pestering from John, Joshua sat moaning to Magda.

'Seriously Magda, I cannot go on with John pestering me like this. It's driving custom away with his constant nagging.'

'Why don't you move your shop somewhere else and not tell John?' Magda had suggested.

'He'd only track me down.' Joshua laughed.

'That's John.' Magda chuckled along with him. 'Once he has a notion, he does not stop until it's completed.'

Sighing, Joshua recited to Magda the long conversation he had with John that day.

Trying a different angle, John had spoken at length to Joshua about him being the spokesman for the people. The people being the ones that were not able to speak for themselves, creating a following that bunched them together, like a flock of birds, making them stronger so they were not so much as a target to the King or Romans.

Joshua refused, he was not leader, nor would he want to repeat what happened in his world. A rebellion and look what happened there.

Again, John took a different approach. Being more sympathetic, John declared he understood of Joshua's frustrations and explained it was not a rebellion he would be leading, but a strength in numbers, a strength in people. Making the Romans and Kings of this world realise, the poor are not toys; they are people and gifted people at that. Rewarding the poor would create loyalty and peace. The people as a whole, want safety and harmony, not to be angry and vengeful. He explained Joshua needed to utilise his gifts he brought with him, use them to spread the word.

Thinking about the medication and how he could distribute it, Joshua began to waver. The people of these times would not have access to the technology, knowledge or remedies he had with him. Instead of impressing the Romans or people with power with his gifts, Joshua could use it on the sick. The rich and powerful would only use his gifts for punishment, yet the poor could benefit from better homes and medical treatment, although John told them this would be a delicate operation. Joshua could not go around shouting he had the cure for diseases, he need to complete these subtly. Word needed to spread by mouth, only the truly sick and needy would benefit.

Joshua had asked for time to think and John had agreed to come and see him the next morning.

'What are you going to do?' Magda had asked as they both made their way out of the TT pod to gaze at the stars.

'I'm still not sure. I do not want to be a fraud. Getting baptised is saying I believe in God, yet I do not know much about God to believe. Am I making sense?' Joshua said as he laid down on the grass and looked up at the stars.

'Where do you think the stars came from Joshua?' Magda asked as she laid down next to him.

'In my world, everything was scientific. You did not believe in something you didn't have hard evidence for. No one can prove God was real to me, only retell stories from long ago.'

Turning her head to look him, Magda spoke softly. 'But you are not in your world anymore.'

Joshua sighed 'I know Magda, I need to stop thinking about the past and onto the future.'

Jess flashed across his mind as he spoke those words to Magda. Wondering if this was a sign from Jess to pursue Magda, he shook his head. All this talk about God was sending him crazy, Jess wouldn't come and give him a sign.

As he lay there, he felt Magda's fingers entwine with his. 'God is not just about believing, it is about helping out others, saving each other and giving people hope life will get better. You have a good heart Joshua, you do what you feel is right.'

Turning to lay on his side he looked at Magda. Stroking her silky soft dark hair he knew deep down, this new world was not making him think straight.

'I'll decide tomorrow about the baptism.' He said to Magda. Then taking her by surprise, he kissed her.

Gasping she asked if he was sure.

'It is the only thing I am sure about right now.' He said as he continued to kiss her.

Joshua was in an extremely good mood the next day, whistling as he stood at his stall, a smile permanently on his face as he recollected the previous night. Yet, as he spotted John walking towards him, his mood dipped slightly.

'I am making a decision this afternoon John.' He shouted across to him, hoping he would leave and come back in the afternoon.

Instead of leaving, John shouted two fishermen across to join him at Joshua's shop.

Seeing John smirk at him as he watched the two men walk towards them, Joshua eyed him suspiciously.

'What are you up to John?' Joshua questioned.

'If you do not wish to spread your name by baptism and the word of God, I will have to spread it this way, through the truth.' He said through gritted teeth.

'You're blackmailing me?' Joshua asked stunned 'But you are a man of God? You preach against this!' He stuttered as the two fishermen approached his shop.

'Good Afternoon, Andrew and Peter, have you met Mary's son, Jesus before.' John asked as he pointed at Joshua.

The two men indicated they had not.

Joshua looked at John in shock. A man that professes he lives by Gods word was bribing him! Grabbing a couple of intricately designed bowls he had, Joshua offered them to the fisherman. The two men looked at the wooden bowls, and whilst distracted, Joshua hissed at John. 'Don't do this!'

Ignoring him, John picked up one of Joshua's carvings.

'Behold this statuette. It is good yes?' John smiled at the two men. 'What if I were to tell you Jesus had made this with tools he brought with him on his travels?'

The two men shrugged, many people travelled to the Sea of Galilee.

'But what if I told you, this man, Jesus fell from the sky with his tools?' John said, turning to Joshua and smiling, a glint in his eye.

The two men gasped. 'What do you mean?' Peter asked.

'This man, Jesus, was sent to us by God. He fell from the sky and was taken in by Mary and Joseph. He has miracles with him. He can heal the sick, he can create masses of food from tiny pebbles and he can make the sun glow in the dark.'

The two men scoffed at John.

'I will show you were he fell from the sky.' John carried on, ignoring the men's laughter. 'Meet me this evening, at night fall, on the road that leads to Mary and Josephs, and I will show you.' John smirked at the two men.

'Do not listen to this crazy man. He is not feeling well.' Joshua laughed and rolled his eyes at the men 'I will ensure he gets the rest he so obviously needs.' Grabbing Johns arm, Joshua started to lead him away, yet John struggled. Holding onto John's arm firmly, Joshua agreed to the baptism. 'I will do what you say, I will be baptised, but do not EVER, pull this stunt again.' He hissed into John's ear.

Breaking free of Joshua, John turned back to the two men.

'I got your attention did I not?' John spoke to the two men whilst Joshua's face grew in anger. 'You found it entertaining? Well Great news! You two are invited to the baptism of Jesus, son of Mary and Stephen at the River Jordan the day after tomorrow. It will be a great day.' John smiled at Peter and Andrew.

The two men walked off bewildered and confused, yet happy with the gifts Jesus had given them. Agreeing John was a source of entertainment, they decided to attend the baptism in two days' time.

Irritated, Joshua shut his shop early and left for Mary and Joseph's house, followed by John.

The last couple of months had been a whirlwind of activity, and although Joshua had enjoyed it and the freedom that came with it, he knew it would change, yet it would change on his terms, not Johns.

'I cannot believe you just did that, to strangers.' He seethed at John.

'But they are not strangers to me.' John arrogantly replied.

Turning to face him, John could see the fury in Joshua's eyes, which amused him. 'We do not know if we can trust them.' Joshua seethed at John. 'You have told them where the TT pod is, they could tell anyone. If the TT pod falls into the wrong hands... do you realise the damage that could do?'

John laughed at him, angering Joshua even further. 'Peter and Andrew are good men. If they were not, I would know, and I would not chance your miracles to be taken. Yours is not the only baptism I will be completing, I have others to do. There will be a crowd of people, good people. Bring your miracles. Now come, we must inform Mary, she will be extremely happy!'

John danced off up the rugged road, leaving Joshua alone with his anger. He had known John would be trouble, yet had given him the benefit with him being a relation of Mary's. He should have known Johns flighty nature would be a cause for concern, yet he would have never thought he would be so devious. Surrendering the TT pod to total strangers just to get his own way of baptising him.

Joshua continued down the dusty track, his mind going over the incident that just happened. The anger leaving him the more he walked, was replaced by the memories he had made over the last few months.

He had enjoyed spending time with Joseph, his calming nature and patient abilities made him a great teacher for Joshua as he learnt the carpentry techniques.

The meal times were his favourite, as he admired Mary's ability to serve delightful and delicious food, day after day, and enjoyed the chatter and laughter that joined every meal.

He spent most evenings with Magda in the TT pod, documenting what they had done so far or showing her something new from his world. The electricity between them was still there, pulling them together. Trying to stay platonic for the sake of the mission, yet failing most nights.

Maybe John was right, maybe it was time for him to move on to the next phase of his mission.

As he neared the house, Joshua heard his name being called out. Mary was waiting outside for him, hopping up and down excitedly.

'John told me.' She said as she embraced him on each cheek. 'You my son have made me very happy. We shall have a celebration tonight in your honour.'

Seeing the celebrations Mary and her family had quickly put together in his honour, he felt his heart swell with love and pride. Looking around the table at the cheering and excited chatter, he felt part of something special. Joshua knew with his family by his side, he would be able to take the next step in his mission, even if he didn't agree with it.

On the day of the baptism, Joshua travelled down to the River Jordan with Magda before the sun had risen.

As the cart bumped along the road they chatted and watched the sunrise together.

He had spoken to her in confidence about John holding him to ransom over the baptism in front of Peter and Andrew. Listening with a grim look on her face she had patted him on the arm. Now that he had agreed to be baptised, Magda assured John would not pull the same trick again.

Arriving at the River Jordan, Joshua saw his family, friends and others he had met throughout his time at Capernaum. His friends Philip and Nathaniel greeted him as he approached.

'Big day eh?' Philip said to Joshua as they laughed and joked.

Joshua had never had male companionship before. It was all new to him. Initially standing at the side of gatherings Magda had taken him to, she slowly coaxed him into friendly chatter with people his own age. Finding more out about them at each meeting, he was fascinated by how they knew each other. Their extended families were complex, each seemingly related to another, interwoven by their huge families, yet friends by choice. All different in their own way through employment, family standards or high ranking standings, yet seeing them altogether, happily talking amongst themselves, their statuses vanished, levelling them all out to equals.

Joshua's new brothers approached him, James, Jude and Simon. Celebrating, they carried him, throwing him up and down, laughing as they walked him to the edge of the water. Joshua had never felt so happy, this is what the world should be like, everyone coming together to celebrate.

Laughing with James, he was pleased they were now close. A few weeks after he initially landed, James had invited Joshua for a walk, explaining as they sauntered along the fields near their house, he was especially protective of his Mother. He worried about her, often her kind nature was taken advantage of, seeing Joshua was not part of the less fortunate she usually helped, he wanted to ensure Mary was safe in Joshua's presence.

In that moment, Joshua knew James would be an ally. Seeing his loyalty towards his family, he knew he would able to trust him with his life.

Leading him to the TT pod, Joshua briefly explained why he was there. Not going into as much detail as he had with Magda and John, James had accepted it all immediately.

'Say no more Jesus.' James had said to Joshua. 'I understand why my Mother needed to protect you. I will be here by your side. I will be at your service.'

Smiling at the memory and quick loyalty of his now brothers, he laughed as they put him down on the shore.

Watching others being baptised in the River Jordan Joshua's heart practically stopped beating. John fully submerged the man he was baptising. Keeping his head under the water for at least five seconds, pulling him up to repeat this process four more times.

Smiling John walked towards him.

'Ahh, Jesus. It is now your turn.'

'John, I need to speak to you.' Joshua whispered

'Do not tell me you are having doubts again. Will I have to shout?' John cried out putting his hands in the air.

A few heads had already turned towards them both. Grabbing his hands and forcing them down, Joshua muttered to him. 'No, I am not having doubts but I need to speak to you before the baptism.'

Motioning John to follow him to somewhere more discreet, Joshua whispered. 'John you cannot hold me under the water. Bad things will happen if you do.'

John scoffed. 'Jesus, you come all this way to tell me how to baptise someone? You do not tell me how I baptise. I run my own Ministry. I am the word of God. You are to be baptised how I say, or not at all.'

Walking away from Joshua, he turned around and shouted at him. 'I refuse to baptise you.'

The crowd on the shore line grew quiet at John's outburst.

Walking up to John, the distress clearly in his eyes, he whispered to him. 'Please you need to understand, I cannot be submerged under water, and if I am, you will see what happens. Bless me with water, splash it in my face, but I beg you, do not immerse me under the water.'

Joshua could hear the murmurs flowing through the crowd as John still refused and walked away.

Grabbing his arm, he pleaded with John. 'You are right, I need to be baptised, to spread my word, to lead the poverty stricken people of Capernaum and the surrounding villages into a better world. This is your Ministry, you are the word of God, you have the power in you, and you can create a new way of baptism that will be done for centuries after you have gone. Practice this new baptism on me today, I beg you.'

John nodded his head in agreement 'Just this once Jesus because it is you.'

Walking towards the River Jordan, John instructed Joshua to be extremely still while he submerged him up to his neck when he was in the water. Giving the illusion he was fully submerged, John would stand in front of him and splash his face with water, blessing him.

As they neared the shore line, Joshua could hear the cheers of his friends and family. Smiling at the love he felt radiate from them, he followed John into the River Jordan. His robes floated around him as the water slowly swirled around his waist.

Turning around towards the shore he could make out his family. Mary stood there, delight on her face as she waved at him. His friends Thomas and Judas, arriving just in time to see the baptism go ahead.

John addressed the crowd and a hush descended. Requesting God cleaned Jesus of his impurities and sin, John put an arm around Joshua's waist. He slowly lowered him down into the water as his other hand rested on top of his head.

'I surrender you Jesus, to God, to remove your uncleanliness, to purify you from this day on.' John screamed as he used his full force to push Joshua under the water.

Joshua's eyes shot wide open in the murky water as he struggled to get back to the surface, yet John's firm grip held him steady. Joshua could feel the water slowly penetrating inside his ears.

'Mr East, you cannot fully submerge the ear piece.' He heard V.E.L.U.S.'S voice ring in his head. 'It is only splash proof.'

'I know.' He wanted to scream, yet John was holding him firm.

John's arms still firmly wrapped around Joshua's waist, he brought him to the surface. Spluttering, gasping for breath, he tried to shout to John, telling him to stop, he could not be submerged.

Yet John continued to shout 'TAKE AWAY HIS SINS. MAKE HIM PURE AGAIN.'

Joshua's long hair, now sopping with water, stuck to his face, leaving him unable to see. Joshua's arms flayed around him as he tried to grab hold of John, pleading with him to stop. Yet John ignored his protests and submerged him once more, causing Joshua's open mouth to fill with water. Choking on the water, Joshua's body jolted, trying to repel the liquid invading his lungs, yet John held him firm under the water.

'Esta, coeaj, ahf.' V.E.L.U.S.'S voice rang through his head. Her words making no sense, Joshua could feel his ear growing hot.

John brought him to the surface again. A high pitched noise screeched from his ear. Yet John continued on. His force no match against Joshua's failing body.

John finished his baptism and pulled Joshua's weakened body up. The pain reverberating through his ear and throat, rendered Joshua speechless. Joshua heard a crackle, followed by the feeling of hot needles shooting through his head, the ear piece was short circuiting.

A cloud of smoke dispensed from Joshua's ear and floated up into the sky. The crowd that had gathered stood silent, watching in awe as the smoke exited Joshua's limp body and into the sky. Watching the cloud float higher, forming it's self into a bird like shape, murmurs began to filter through the crowd.

No longer able to hear, Joshua laid limp in Johns arms. Barely able to open his eyes through the pain, he looked towards the shore line. He could just make out Mary and Magda, screaming at John, motioning at him, telling him to bring Jesus to them.

Joshua's throat started to close up. The struggles and choking under the water had dislodged the V.A.I. in his throat.

His throat started to spasm involuntary, making his fully body jolt, as the V.A.I. tried to reattach itself. His throat growing hot, Joshua closed his eyes. Feeling the vibrations, he knew the V.A.I. was speaking on its own accord, yet his mouth remained closed.

John carried Joshua's lifeless body towards the embankment.

Feeling a pop in his ear, Joshua could slightly hear again, yet the pain continued.

Without warning, V.E.L.U.S.'s booming voice came out of Joshua's throat, causing John to drop Joshua into the River.

With no fight left, Joshua let himself sink to the bottom. V.E.L.U.S's booming voice still penetrating out of his throat. Knowing this was the end, Joshua opened his eyes, looking up towards the swaying surface of the water and sent a silent apology to his Father. He had failed him.

His eyes slowly shut, letting the darkness engulf him as the last few air bubbles floated from his mouth to the surface.

Chapter 16
Rachel - The Meeting

Pulling up outside a double metal entry gate, Caroline waited until they were fully open before driving though. Parking in a garage adjacent to the vast grounds they had entered, Rachel watched as Craig stopped his car next to them.
Rachel mirrored Caroline's movements, removing herself from the vehicle.
Craig led the way as they walked outside the garage and round through to the back, the gravel crunching under their feet as they moved.
Walking through a wrought iron arch, Rachel admired the garden she had just entered. Trees and bushes swayed in the night breeze as a sprinkler sprayed the lush green grass. Craig still walked ahead, a flashlight in his hand, illuminating the way as they walked along the grass and not the stone pathway. Not a sound could be heard barring the rustling of leaves through the wind.
As they neared the end of the garden, Rachel spotted a small, stone statue of a cherub hidden between two trees. Immaculately carved, with a bow and arrow at its back, Craig stopped as they reached the small clearing and turned off his light. Placing a finger over his ear piece, Craig nodded at Caroline, before she placed her hand over the cherub's smooth, chubby arm. The statue glowed blue as the bushes behind it parted slowly, exposing a red metallic door.
Slowly and silently, the door opened revealing a dark metal corridor behind it. Motioning Rachel to follow her, whilst Craig stood stationary at the entrance, Caroline and Rachel walked down the passageway. Their shoes twanged on the metal interior, echoing loudly as they continued to walk down the sloping corridor. Small LED lights dotted around the interior, lighting

only on approach, giving just a few feet of visibility in the seemingly never-ending passageway.

'Not much further.' Caroline's voiced ricocheted around the metal interior. The corridor was getting hotter and stuffier the further they walked down. Veering to the left slightly, the corridor opened into another series of tunnels. Taking the right one, Rachel noticed red metallic doors, similar to the entrance one along the passage. Stopping at the third door down, Caroline removed her phone from her pocket. Holding it up to the door, a thin blue light shone over Caroline's eye. A clicking noise signalled the door was now open and Caroline walked through.

Rachel followed her into a lavishly furnished board room. Comfortable couches featured on one side, with a highly polished six seater oak table on the other. A projector screen adorned the wall closest to the table with a drinks cabinet, coffee maker and fridge to the left. Feeling the cool air on her skin, Rachel could see the air conditioner high on the wall, giving the room a welcome breeze from the stuffy corridor.

'Please sit.' Caroline beckoned to the pale cream couch. 'Cold drink?' she questioned.

Rachel shook her head as she made her way across the red and gold carpet. 'No thank you. I am fine.'

'We may be here for a while; I am having a gin. Are you sure you do not want one?' Caroline questioned.

'I will have a water, maybe something stronger later.' She laughed nervously.

'As you wish.' Caroline said as she poured gin over a tumbler half full of ice. Passing Rachel a bottle of water, she set her crystal tumbler down on the coffee table between them and sat adjacent to her.

'I hate to get straight into business, yet I suspect your car will have already been discovered, therefore we do not have as much time as I would've hoped.'

Taking a sip of water, Rachel held her hand up to pause Caroline. 'Before we start, what is this place?' She said with more confidence than she felt.

Caroline smirked. 'This place is my bunker. It is where I complete a lot of my meetings. Along the corridor are rooms full of merchandise to show potential buyers.'

'Merchandise, you mean weapons?' Rachel interjected.

'Merchandise, guns, whatever you want to call it, it is still a product that I am selling. Do you feel special Rachel?'

The question caught Rachel off guard. 'Should I be?' She asked.

'You should. You are the first of the committee I have ever brought down here, this location is extremely on a need to know basis. The committee are far too involved in everyone else's business, their higher than mighty charade fools no one, thus my Mother secretly built this, and I carried it on, expanding beneath Cyprus. This is not the only bunker I have. I have others scattered across the world. Yet that conversation is for another time.'

Bewildered, Rachel nodded, signalling Caroline had her undivided attention.

'I know your skills Rachel, you learn fast, negotiate better and win people over with that innocent face, yet startle most with your sharp tongue. Strong minded, yet open enough to accept anything. The type of woman I like to have in my circle.' She smirked at Rachel.

Leaning back on the chair, Caroline's blue eyes shone out. Her dark poker straight hair shone under the florescent lights. 'So, Rachel, tell me what you know so far about the company.'

Although she was still angry with Nick, his grave face, full of concern replayed in her mind when she had shown him Caroline's message. She gave her the chills. Caroline's pale face smiling, yet it not quite reaching her cold, steely blue eyes.

'Where do I start?' Rachel laughed. 'One minute I was a buyer for steel, the next I was part of a global committee that ran the world! I am still unsure as to what my role will entail.'

Caroline's eyes narrowed as she leant forward towards Rachel. 'The problem with S.U.S. Industries and the committee, is they treat us all like children. Spoon feeding us slowly, gauging our every reaction to each revelation they feel us worthy to know. We all get it.' Caroline threw her hands in the air. 'That Joshua East was our founding Father. That his mission was to rid the world of poverty and evil, yet S.U.S. Industries are hypocrites. Globally ruling the world, stating free speech for all, yet raging war against the ones that do not comply. Have you learnt about Joshua East's world yet?' She spat.

Rachel nodded.

'The alternative future, ruled by Matriats, yet what is happening at the moment? We are ruled by a descendant of a Matriat, a clever one. The current Matriat ruler, boasts of peace and love, yet underneath, is a cruel and calculated man. One that doesn't care about the people, just stands by and watches until he needs something from them.' Caroline paused, watching Rachel's reaction and Rachel did not disappoint her. Shuddering involuntary as the memory of Nick telling her he watched as she was abused came to the forefront of her mind. Smiling, Caroline picked her gin up and swirled it around the tumbler.

'Do you want to know why you was brought in Rachel?' Caroline's blue eyes gleaned as she leant even further towards her. Swallowing, Rachel nodded.

'I am sorry to have to tell you this.' Caroline sarcastically said, leaning back whilst putting her hand over her heart. 'But you were brought in as an experiment.' Caroline caught a glimpse of anger ignite in Rachel's eyes. Staring at her intently, knowing Rachel was on the verge, she continued. 'The committee has never had a normal person, no offence, on it before. We had others we could have brought in, yet the committee agreed we needed to go in a new direction. Stefan, well you know him as Nick, presented you. You were a walking advert. Neglected, abused, raped, starved, you had it all.' Caroline laughed. 'Bringing someone like you into the committee would apparently give us an insight into the scummy estates that litter our world. What made the dregs of this world tick? How we could stop them from draining the economy? And most importantly, how we could get rid of them? Mostly their weaknesses are drugs, yet they are clever. The vermin of society would run scared after a few hundred deaths, seeking a new way to get high. They chose to be this way, they choose to sell themselves for the next hit and normally the apple doesn't fall far from the tree.'

Caroline paused as she looked at Rachel, seeing her sitting there seething, yet saying nothing.

'Yet, look at you! You are one of a kind!' Caroline added, not wanting to push Rachel too far, just yet.

'Our almighty leader is not what he perceives to be. He is a fraud, as were his ancestors. Once he no longer has use for you, he will spit you out and leave you where he got you from. Have you seriously never questioned how you got an apprenticeship? Given opportunities far more than other employees have been given? Stefan was grooming you Rachel, grooming you for his experiment, just like your Mothers pimp,'

'Enough!' Shouted Rachel. Caroline had gone too far. 'What exactly do you want from me?' She questioned her.

Amused, Caroline stood up and walked towards the drinks cabinet to top up her drink. Speaking more softly, she knew she had Rachel exactly where she wanted her, it was time for her charm offensive. 'I want you to be my ally, Rachel. I want you to tell me everything they teach you, and when I hear the time has come for Nick to get rid of you, I want you to join me, at Brodells.' Caroline answered smiling as she took a sip of gin.

'What use could I be to you at Brodells? All I have ever known is S.U.S. Industries.' Rachel questioned.

'You see, Rachel. You can give me something no one else can. Inside information that I am not privy to. You will join me in taking down the hypercritical company S.U.S. Industries is, and always has been. Together, we will give the world back to the people.' Pausing she looked at Rachel, trying to gauge her reaction, yet Rachel's face remained blank. 'Think about it and get back to me tomorrow. I am seeing a couple of potential clients in the day, the evening I will be free.'

Rachel's head jerked up in surprise.

'I do not celebrate Christmas either. Surprising? Why would I celebrate a fraud?' Caroline smiled. 'I have heard you are going to see where it all began in two days. Is that true?'

Rachel nodded, still not uttering a word.

'If we are going to work together to overturn the East's ruling us all, I need us to meet again, before you go to Israel. Just message me a Yes or No tomorrow and I will arrange the rest.'

'Why do we need to meet before I go?'

'Because young Rachel.' Caroline said as she walked back towards her, drink in hand. 'I have never been to the landing site, nor seen the TT pod that still originates there, and you can help me find it.'

'I'm not sure about this.' Rachel said, suddenly finding her voice. 'There is obviously a reason why you haven't been taken to see it.'

Sitting down next to her this time, Rachel saw excitement flicker in Caroline's eyes as she spoke. 'The TT pod has technology, far more advanced than what we have now, that only the elite of S.U.S. Industries have access to. To overcome S.U.S. Industries, I need to understand the technology.'

'Why am I allowed to go?' Rachel queried, whilst she frowned at her.

Caroline obnoxiously laughed. 'Like I said Rachel, you are an experiment. You will not understand the complexity, the magnitude of the TT pod and its technology. Think of it like this. The TT pod has been standing there for over two thousand years, yet it still has power to function. Imagine if we could get hold of that technology and pass it out to the people? Everyone in this world could have electricity for free, no more gigantic wind turbines cluttering up our countryside, no more solar panels sitting on the roofs of buildings, no more burning of fuel to power generators. The power would be given to the people, energy companies would cease to exist, the people of this world would have one less bill to pay, children would no longer sit in freezing cold dark houses as their parent's frittered away money on themselves. It would be the start of a new world Rachel, and you would be part of it. You would save children, children just like you were, from freezing to death in the cold of winter.'

'I need to think about it.'

'Good girl.' Caroline smirked as she finished off her drink. 'Before we leave, I need to show you something.'

Motioning Rachel to follow her out of the board room and down a series of metal tunnels, she led her to a door with a large X on it. Opening it up with her phone and eye scanner, she leant in and switched the light on and asked Rachel to look in.

Horrified, Rachel recoiled from the room. Caroline pushed her back in and told her to take note. The stench was the first thing she noticed, death and rotting meat. Taking in her surroundings, Rachel noticed the walls, damp and murky were sprayed with blood. A group of rats scattered from a human limb they had been feasting on, as Caroline pushed her further into the room. Rachel put the sleeve of her denim jacket over her nose, as she tried to stop her stomach heaving from the repulsive sights and smell. Different stages of decayed skin hung from rusty iron hooks around the room, whilst human excrement mingled with rotting food scattered the floor. A wooden chair displaying red leather restraints, featured in the middle of the room with indistinguishable body parts dotted around it. Rachel stood there, hand over her mouth, frozen.

A groan from the corner of the room, made Rachel turn her head slowly. Not able to distinguish if it was male or female, Rachel could see the person's bones jutting out of their paper thin skin. Only a few wisps of hair remained on their head as they struggled to turn around and look at Rachel.

'Please, help me.' Rachel heard it whisper.

Taking a step towards the tortured individual, she felt Caroline's bony hand on her shoulder, stopping her proceed any further. 'Do not help it.' She snarled. 'This is what happens when I am betrayed.'

Hearing the skin and bone cry in the corner, Rachel turned to Caroline. 'Is this what you do? Torture people for betraying you? How can you stand there and not want to help? No matter what this person has done, no one should suffer like this!' She stood firm, her eyes steadily looking into Caroline's steely blue ones. 'This person has not done anything to me, I will help them.'

'As you wish. I will have it arranged for them to be delivered to your villa.' Caroline sadistically smiled as she cocked her head to one side. 'Because I know where you live.'

Not knowing if Caroline was threatening her, Rachel still stood firm. 'I shall expect delivery latest tomorrow then.' She answered crisply as she walked out of the room. 'I feel it is time I left, I have a lot to think about.' She said as Caroline shut and locked the door.

'I agree, you do.' Caroline smirked as she led Rachel out of the tunnels.

Getting into her silver car as Caroline sped away, Rachel let out a sigh of relief and sagged back into the driver's seat. That whole meeting including the drive back had been exceptionally tense.

Pulling her personal phone out of her pocket, she pressed stop on audio. Playing it back Caroline's voice rang out clear as day. She would tell Yuri it worked, when she visited him for Christmas dinner tomorrow.

Chapter 17
Joshua - Forty Days

Opening his eyes, Joshua groaned. The bright lights of the TT pod blinded him. Feeling slightly dazed he looked down. The IV's running into his arm slowly coming into focus.
'What?' He whispered questioning himself. Turning his head quickly to the right and then the left, he looked for signs this was not Déjà vu. Feeling a familiar wave of sickness come over him, he closed his eyes and groaned.
'Joshua?' He heard a female voice say.
'Magda?' He replied in hoarse whisper, slowly opening his eyes that were adjusting to the bright lights in the TT pod.
'Thank goodness, Joshua.' Magda cried, her face coming in to view as she moved closer.
Kneeling beside the bed in the TT pod, all the emotions Magda had been carrying spilled out as she sobbed on his shoulder.
'Hey.' Joshua soothed. Moving his arm, Joshua tried to comfort her, yet the IV's stopped him. 'Hey, don't cry, what's happened? Are you OK?' He asked.
'I thought we had lost you.' Magda cried. 'I just... I thought...' She stammered.
'Magda, what's happened?'
'I need to tell Mary, I promised I would let her know as soon as you woke. She has been here day and night. Oh Joshua we have been so worried.' She kissed his forehead.
'Slow down Magda.' Joshua tried to chuckle at her excitement, yet the soreness inside his throat made him cough.
'Relax Joshua, you need to rest.'

'Magda what is happening?' Joshua asked once his coughing had stopped. 'Why am I here in the TT pod? Why do I have IV's in my arm, you need to explain what's happened.'

'Here, take these.' Magda instructed as she popped some pills into his mouth. Giving him some water, Joshua swallowed them, amazed Magda knew what to give him.

'Magda, please tell me what happened.' He pleaded

'Maybe I can be of assistance.' V.E.L.U.S's voice boomed out.

'Yes, V.E.L.U.S., please explain to Joshua what happened and I will fetch Mary.' A weary Magda said, walking towards the entrance of the pod, then coming back, kissing Joshua's forehead again and eventually leaving.

'Mr East. What do you remember?'

Screwing his eyes shut, Joshua went through his last memories. 'The last thing I remember is John convincing me to be baptised.'

'Do you remember travelling to the River Jordan?' V.E.L.U.S. asked.

'No.'

V.E.L.U.S retold Joshua the events that happened at his baptism.

'I asked him not to submerge me, yet he still did?' Joshua asked in disbelief, whilst shaking his head.

'Yes.' V.E.L.U.S. answered. 'As you know, submerging the V.A.I. can have grave consequences. Which is why it is only used in extreme circumstances. The V.A.I. short-circuited not only in your ear, but also in your throat, causing major internal burns. The quick thinking of Magda is what saved you. Wrapping you in a blanket she laid you on the back of the cart, the side with the ear piece facing down. The jolting of the cart as she sped towards the TT pod, managed to dislodge trapped water in the ear piece and trickle out onto the blanket, drying it out quicker. The movement also moved the wires inside the ear piece into safe mode, thus stopping any power going through it. Magda brought you straight here and asked for my assistance. I have managed to reinsert the V.A.I. on your vocal cords and in your ear, yet your throat may still be sore from the burns. You had a 23% chance of survival Mr East. You have been extremely lucky.'

Shaking his head in amazement, Joshua laid there taking it all in. 'How long have I been recovering?'

'Forty days.' V.E.L.U.S. replied. 'The chair has been massaging your muscles, therefore you should still be at full capacity. I am 99% sure you will make a full recovery.'

'Forty days?' Joshua exclaimed. 'What… how?'

'Magda and Mary have been alternating watch. You have had visitors, yet I will leave that to Magda or Mary to explain.'

Visitors? Joshua thought, hoping it was not John. The thought of being anywhere near that devious man made his blood boil.

'Where is he? Where is my son?' Mary's voice chimed into the TT pod, making him smile.

Crying, she touched his face tenderly. 'Oh my boy, I have been so worried.' She said smiling down on him, tears in her eyes. Joshua looked at Mary's face. Deep worry lines etched her normal happy face and dark bags hung under her eyes.

'Oh Mother, please do not cry.' He said, trying to soothe her.

Mary let out a loud cry, 'Oh my son, you called me Mother. The first time you called me Mother. I am so happy. I thought you were going to die. We have all been so worried.'

Joshua, did not reply. He did not have the heart to tell Mary, it was a slip of the tongue. He wanted his real Mother, the one that was there day and night for him until she died. Nursing him through illnesses instead of passing him to appointed staff, she was always there when he needed her. And right now, he needed her more than anything. Not wanting to cry in front of Mary and Magda, he asked V.E.L.U.S. to sit the bed up so he could talk easier.

With the bed now into a chair, Joshua grabbed the bottle of water and took a huge drink to soothe his throat.

'So, what have I missed?' He asked Mary and Magda, their faces suspiciously telling him he had.

'We have never seen anyone survive without food for 40 days Jesus. You are a miracle.' Mary said quietly. 'We thought you were going to die. We had close family and friends visit you to say their last goodbyes.'

'What?' Joshua exclaimed! 'In the pod? No, no, you should NEVER bring anyone to the TT pod. V.E.L.U.S. needs to be protected. In the wrong hands …' He ranted, yet Magda cut him off.

'We spoke to V.E.L.U.S. about this and she had a solution. V.E.L.U.S. would you like to show Joshua?' Magda asked.

The TT pod disappeared and a sandy desert could be seen for miles around. Sitting up straighter, Joshua looked in awe as he could see the sun setting in the distance over the dunes. He laughed as he saw the chair he was once sat on was now a mound of sand, supporting him.

'V.E.L.U.S. I had no idea you could do this.' He exclaimed.

'You never asked Mr East.'

Magda and Mary laughed.

'Anyone who wanted to visit was brought here, yet brought by cart and covered with a thick blanket so they could not see the TT pod. My poor horse spent hours walking around this field as we made the illusion we were taking them to the desert. There is one more thing we need to tell you.' Magda looked at the floor.

'Go on.'

'Seeing you laid there, Peter and Matthew asked many questions. We was unsure what to say and the words just came out.' Magda said, still looking at the floor.

'What came out?' Joshua asked, his voice still horse.

'We told them you were in a trance, asking God for guidance and would not eat until you had an answer. I thought it would be better than telling them the truth. Although now everyone is asking when you come back from your fast, will you be opening a ministry?'

'Why would I open a ministry?'

'Because many already want to follow you. They witnessed the malfunction of the V.A.I., they are describing the cloud of smoke as a dove and V.E.L.U.S.'s voice as the voice of God.' Answered Magda.

'Are you being serious?' Joshua chuckled. 'What did V.E.L.U.S. say?'

'V.E.L.U.S.'S voice boomed out, I knew it was V.E.L.U.S. yet the words she was speaking was not of Aramaic. I didn't know what they were. Yet people are saying God spoke to you once you had been baptised. They say you are the messiah.'

'Please, no.' Joshua whispered startled.

'I have spent nearly forty days here, and I have spoken to V.E.L.U.S. a lot, we both agree, this is a good thing. The people of Capernaum and the surrounding villages, have grown up surrounded by preachers, we can use this to help spread your mission.'

Joshua looked across at the desert still featuring inside the pod. The sun had now set and stars twinkled in the sky. V.E.L.U.S. had calculated this would be the best option to complete his mission, therefore he decided he would be a fool not to follow her advice.

'Yes, let's do this.' He said grinning at Magda and Mary.

Mary squealed excited. 'My son the Messiah, I knew you was special as soon as you came to us.' She told him. 'Now Magda, release him from the IV's and let's go and get you some proper food.

The TT pod switched back to its white padded interior as Mary removed Joshua's IV's. 'You must have lived in a wondrous world.' Mary whispered to Joshua as she finished.

'We had some wondrous things Magda, yes, yet I prefer it here.' He smiled at her.

Helping him down the stairs and into the cart, they travelled the short distance to Mary's house just in time for the evening meal.

Shouting and laughter could be heard coming from inside the kitchen. As Mary, Magda and Joshua walked in, a hush descended over the people seated at the table.

Joshua did not know where to look as thirty pairs of eyes stared at him.

James stood up from the table, surprise across his face. Walking towards him, he grabbed Joshua's shoulders and looked him in the eyes. 'Is it really you?' He asked in bewilderment.

'It is me.' Joshua smiled.

Cheering, James turned around to the rest of the people sat at the table. 'It is him, it is really him. My brother has returned. We must celebrate!'

Every person sat at the table, got up and surrounded Joshua. Each one individually hugging him, crying tears of happiness and giving thanks to God he had come back to them.

The kitchen alive with laugher and chatter again, Joshua sat at the table with Mary on one side and Magda on the other. Looking across at James sitting opposite, he watched as he silently picked up his wooden goblet of wine, smiled and raised it to Joshua. Smiling back at him, Joshua grabbed his wine and raised it back.

Happy and content in this little bubble of Mary's kitchen, he knew tomorrow would be an entirely different day.

Chapter 18
Rachel - Yuri's Father

Waiting for the kettle to boil for her morning tea in the kitchen, Rachel looked at her phone. Tempted to turn it off aeroplane mode to see if she had any messages, she resisted. The audio from last night would load straight to the cloud service she had, and anyone with authority could access it.

She had received a message from Caroline last night, saying the package would be delivered at 10pm this evening. Tossing and turning, Rachel's sleep had been peppered with images of the poor innocent person, starving and tortured. Its paper thin skin showing every vein and bone in its frail body. Still unsure if she would take the tortured soul to hospital or nurse it to health at the villa, Rachel wondered if Caroline would stick to her word.

The doorbell rang distracting her from her thoughts.

Tying her silk dressing gown around her, Rachel padded to the front door of the villa.

Tentatively opening the door, Rachel saw Yuri with a huge smile on his face, his arms filled with presents and a set of reindeer antlers on his head.

'Merry Christmas.' He cried.

Laughing, Rachel opened the door wider. 'You know I do not celebrate Christmas Yuri.'

'I know, but it is only fair I buy you presents like I do everyone else. Giving is better than receiving.' He replied, trying to waggle his finger at her under the mound of presents.

Yuri walked into the villa and placed the five presents on to the dining table, one large, one medium and three small ones. 'Do not open them until I get back.' He said smiling as he went back to his car. Rachel looked at the presents, exquisitely wrapped with white and silver paper, white ribbon and a gift tag made to look like a snowflake.

Never having celebrated Christmas, it felt strange seeing these presents on the table for her. Rachel's childhood Christmas' had consisted of her mother treating herself to an extra-long high, and since she had been on her own since she left Trinity Estate, it was easy not to celebrate it.

Yuri returned with a hamper in his hands. Shutting the front door with his foot, he made his way into the kitchen.

'Yuri what are you doing here? What's in the basket?' Rachel asked trying to peek in the hamper.

Waving her away, his normal happy face turned serious. 'Rachel, this is your first Christmas of many.' Holding his hand up to shush her protests, he continued. 'I am not asking you to celebrate Christmas, I am asking you to have a good time with me, and later my family. Christmas is not about Jesus' birthday or a religious holiday, it is about spending time with your loved ones, and I know you love me.' His face broke into his usual cheeky grin. 'It's about letting go of all your troubles for one day and to celebrate the life you are living.'

Turning back to the hamper, Yuri started unpacking sausages, bacon, tomatoes and beans.

'Yuri about letting go of your troubles...' She said as she watched him pull more and more food out of the basket. 'I met with Caroline last night.'

Yuri paused, a tin of tomatoes still in his hand as he slowly turned around to face Rachel. 'You did WHAT?' He exclaimed.

Yuri surprised her. He never questioned her, nor raised his voice. Ignoring his out of character request, Rachel continued. 'I cannot tell you Yuri, nor will I tell you. I am not putting you in danger, that's if it was dangerous.' She added seeing the angry concern on Yuri's face.

In a total change of personality, Yuri put down the tomatoes, walked slowly but confidently towards Rachel and sat opposite her at the dining room table. 'Rachel, you will not leave this table until you tell me what happened.' He said firmly. Watching her stance change from friendly to defensive, he softened his voice. 'Rachel, I hope you listened to my suggestions from the other night when we discussed it, yet I am unhappy you went without telling me.'

'I thought it was better this way. I do not want to drag you into all this.'

'Yet, I am already involved Rachel.' He said sliding his hands across the dining table to cover hers.

'How?' She asked.

'As your driver and your friend, it makes me involved. You need to tell someone Rach, you can't keep everything bottled up. It will send you crazy.'

Rachel sighed and Yuri sat silent as Rachel retold the full night's events, finally playing him the audio recording.

Running his hands through his shiny black hair, he looked gravely at Rachel. 'What are you going to do?'

'I'm going to say yes.' Yuri sharply inhaled and shook his head at her response. 'But.' She continued 'I have not made the decision if I am going to get the committee involved or stick with Caroline. I need time to think and I was hoping you had some infinite wisdom you could bestow upon me.' She smiled at him.

'Rachel, this is no laughing matter, Caroline is extremely dangerous. Who wants to save the world, yet leaves tortured souls to rot to death in that room? Why does SHE have the power to destroy anyone that crosses her? Do not say yes right now. You need to think. I know you are not on the best terms, yet I think you need to tell Nick.'

Frowning, Rachel looked at him. 'How do know about me and Nick?'

'I was waiting outside in case you needed to go anywhere and I heard.' He said, his eyes not able to meet Rachel's.

'Why didn't you mention it?'

'None of my business Rach. If you wanted me to know, you would tell me when you were ready.' Seeing her alarmed face, he patted her arm from across the table. 'I have not told anyone what happened. Chauffeur code.' He said as he saluted making Rachel grin at him. 'What you need is a traditional English breakfast to help make your mind up.' He said as he got up from the table and moved to the open plan kitchen.

'Need any help?' Rachel volunteered.

'No, go get ready and your breakfast shall await you, when you come back.'

Rachel walked towards her en suite bathroom. Getting under the hot shower while she heard Yuri singing as he cooked, made her smile. In the last few weeks her world had dramatically changed.

Nights in on her own had been replaced with evening meals on the harbour, or added reading about the upcoming visits she had. The mundane tedious life she led, now a rollercoaster of emotions. Not knowing which she preferred she was glad she had Yuri.

Wrapping a towel around her, she chuckled as she heard Yuri trying to reach a high note in his singing.

Dressing in a simple yet elegant, knee length, Christmassy red wrap dress, paired with sparkly, strappy heals, Rachel walked into the open plan living room, just as Yuri was placing the breakfast down on the dining table.

'Wow weee.' Yuri commented as she shimmered in.

Twirling around at Yuri's compliment, Rachel giggled.

'Make sure you don't get any breakfast down you.' He laughed as they both sat down.

Chattering to each other, Rachel relaxed. She would heed Yuri's advice and leave problems for today. Well, until this evening when she had to give Caroline an answer.

After they finished breakfast, Rachel complimented Yuri on his cooking skills as he passed her the presents from the other side of the dining table.

After trying to refuse to open them until she bought Yuri something, he rebuffed her protests by explaining the wrapping paper cost more than the actual presents inside and to not get her hopes up.

Opening the presents, she laughed her way through the gimmicky items. Ones that they had joked about whilst riding in the car. A warm fuzzy feeling came over her as she realised, he had remembered their conversation. She smiled to herself and wondered if this is what it felt like to be part of a family.

Opening the last present, Rachel gasped. A diamond bracelet shone inside the case she had just opened. Pushing it towards Yuri she had told him to take it back, it was far too much.

Sliding it back across the dining table, Yuri explained. 'I noticed you were not wearing your necklace Nick had bought you. It can be a scary world out there, and after what you told me, you need it. This is not just a diamond bracelet, it is an SOS.' Turning the bracelet over he showed Rachel the last diamond before the clasp had a small red dot inside. Push this gem if you ever feel in danger. I get notified immediately with your location.'

'Yuri this is lovely, yet I can't accept this. Come on, diamonds?' She exclaimed.

Yuri laughed. 'You think a chauffeur like me can afford diamonds Rach, they are imitation. You worry too much.'

Relieved, Rachel examined the bracelet more carefully. 'They look so real.' She gasped as Yuri helped her put it on.

Rachel sat at the table, admiring the sparkly bracelet as Yuri started to clean up. 'Leave that.' Rachel said. 'You cooked, I will clean.'

Taking the plates from Yuri she stacked the dishwasher.

'Shall I drive to yours later? I wasn't expecting you to come here.' Rachel asked Yuri.

Refilling his orange juice from the carton, Yuri shook his head. 'No Rachel. As it is your first Christmas, I will be spending the full day with you.'

Rachel objected, Christmas was a family day and Yuri needed to be with his. Surprising herself with the warm glow she felt when Yuri said she was now family as they had been spending so much time together, she took her drink out on the terrace before she got emotional. She was unsure if it was something in the Cypriot air, or the events that had happened to cause all these emotions she was feeling. Usually she prided herself on being a strong independent woman, yet recently, she had grown to rely on Yuri. Looking across the horizon at the marina from the terrace, she sighed in contentment, she would never tire of this view.

The day passed with her and Yuri playing cards, laughing and walking around the marina. He had only been in her life for a short time, yet she could not picture life without him. Pledging to stay in touch when she eventually returned to England, Yuri advised it was time to go to his parents' house.

Getting in the back of the car felt weird now, Yuri felt like a younger brother. As he opened the back door, Rachel bypassed it and headed straight for the passenger seat of the vehicle.

Yuri looked pleased at her choice and jumped in. Instead of switching on the aircon, Yuri put the windows down and blasted out Christmas tunes. Shouting the lyrics out of the window as they sped down the road, Rachel could not remember the last time she felt as happy and as carefree as she did right then. Yuri smiled at her, before joining in the out of tune singing. Relaxing into her new cheery persona, Rachel wondered once more, if this was what a normal family felt like.

Turning off after 20 minutes, panic started to rise in Rachel's chest. This was the way to Caroline's villa.

'Yuri, where do your parents live.'

'Not much further now.' He said in-between singing.

'Yuri, where are you taking me?' Rachel sat upright in her seat, her heart beating wildly, as they continued to travel the exact way Caroline took her. 'Yuri I don't like this, where are you taking me?'

Yuri looked at her in surprise. 'Rachel, you look like you have seen a ghost. What is it?'

Twiddling with the bracelet Yuri had given her, she turned and looked at him. 'This is exactly the same way Caroline took me. Is there something you want to tell me?' She said with more confidence than she felt.

Yuri's face softened. 'There are many villas in private grounds in this area. Purposely built near the golf course.'

Rachel's apprehension simmered slightly. Yuri was not taking her to Caroline's, yet how did Yuri's family afford to live in a gated villa. He was a chauffeur. Sure he had the confidence of a rich person, yet he was extremely down to earth, nothing like the stuck up rich kids she had encountered previously.

Pulling up outside some gold gates, Yuri pressed the intercom.

'Hello?' Crackled a stern male voice through the speaker.

'Yuri here with Rachel.' He cheerfully answered.

The golden gates opened smoothly as Yuri drove through.

The gravel crunched under the cars tyres as it made its way down the drive. As they approached the house, the drive opened into a huge circle with a round, grey, fountain in the middle. Driving around the fountain, Yuri parked the car outside of the entrance to the villa.

Rachel tentatively got out as she took in the vast mansion. The stone stairs leading up to the grand front door were adorned with carvings on each step. Two columns either side of the steps held up a stone canopy that displayed another set of exquisite carvings around the sides. A traditional wreath hung on the huge oak door with flashing Christmas lights surrounding the window panels either side of the entrance. Stained glass featured above the door, exhibiting a family all wearing robes. Shutters covered the many windows either side of the mansion as ivy grew up the walls, giving it a more English cottage look than a Cypriot villa.

Yuri opened the door and announced their arrival. A cocker spaniel ran up to Yuri yapping excitedly followed by a lady in her forties who was an older female version of Yuri. Wearing a

Christmas apron and reindeer ears, she hurriedly walked towards Rachel greeting her into their home. Her smile and nature made Rachel relax instantly, glad that she had accepted Yuri's invite for the festive dinner with his family.

As Yuri's mum led them into the kitchen area, Rachel whispered to Yuri. 'Why did you not tell me your family are rich?'

Looking at Rachel he raised one eyebrow. 'Would you have accepted me as a chauffeur and a friend if you knew?' He replied.

Giving Yuri's mother the bottle of wine she swiped from the fridge, she felt awkward and inadequate. It may have been better to not have brought anything she thought to herself as his Mother studied the bottle.

'My favourite, how did you know?' She exclaimed as Rachel breathed a sigh of relief. Wondering if Yuri's mother was lovely, or the wine was a favourite of hers, Rachel sat on the kitchen bar stool that Yuri's Mother had offered. After declining Rachel's offer of help with the food preparation, Yuri's Mother passed a glass of buck's fizz to them both.

Turning her back to Rachel and Yuri, she attended to a bubbling pan on the stove. 'Yuri, go get your Father now our company has arrived.' She instructed as Yuri saluted her. 'I have eyes in the back of my head young man, I know what you are doing.' Rachel laughed as Yuri scarpered to get his Father.

'I am so happy you are here Rachel. I have heard so much about you.' Yuri's Mother chattered as she continued cooking.

'Thank you. I am sorry but I do not know Yuri's surname, thank you Mrs …' Rachel trailed off waiting for Yuri's Mother to complete the sentence.

After a pause, Yuri's mother replied. 'Call me Maria. You are part of this family, we are not formal.'

'You have a beautiful house Maria. Thank you for inviting me here to spend Christmas with your family.'

'You're very welcome.' Came a male voice from behind her.

Turning around, her face dropped.

'I think you may already know my Dad.' Yuri said as he stood there awkwardly.

Rachel froze, as Nick walked towards her.

Chapter 19
Joshua - James' Wedding

'Joshua! Joshua!' He heard Mary shout.
'Yes Mother.' He replied turning round and smiling as she ran towards him at the TT pod.
'James is to be married!'
'James? My brother James? To who?' Joshua asked.
'To a delightful lady called Damaris.' Mary whooped.
'Damaris? Since when?' Joshua asked thrilled.
'Joseph and I have been finishing the agreements with the family. They are to be married in two weeks in Cana.'
'Wait, what? I have never heard of a Damaris. James never spoke of a lady in his life. In two weeks? Do I need to speak to him?'
Mary laughed at Joshua's serious reaction. 'No, we have been waiting one year. The family is a good family. One that will love James like their own. He is at the house. Come and see him.'
Joshua followed Mary to the home and congratulated his brother James.
'Sorry I have not been about to help much, but I've heard your mission is going well?' James said to him.
'It is thanks James. I know what John did to me was evil, and I won't ever speak to him again, yet he did make sense. Talking to people about God, it breaks the ice as everyone here knows who God is!'
James laughed and shook his head. 'I still cannot believe in your world there was no religion. It's all everyone talks about here!'
'So, do I get to meet the lucky lady before I see you marry her?'

'Of course! She is over there.' James pointed to a petite woman in her early twenties. With her long dark hair and olive skin, he could see why James had been attracted to her.

'How did you get a woman like that to marry you?' Joshua joked with James.

'I do not know Jesus.' James laughed. 'Maybe that is why the wedding is in two weeks, so she cannot change her mind!'

They both laughed as James led Joshua to Damaris and introduced them.

A gorgeous sunny day dawned on the day of the wedding. Magda and Joshua were meeting the rest of the family in Cana after visiting the needy in Capernaum.

'The poor do not need feeding just because we have a wedding to attend.' Magda had scolded Joshua.

Not being able to contain himself, Joshua grabbed Magda and kissed her hard.

Pulling away from him, she laughed. 'What was that for?' She asked.

'For just being you.' He smiled, his heart bursting with pride at the woman she was.

They had grown extremely close over the last few weeks, spending every moment with each other, Magda had helped him with his new ministry. It was all new to him, religion, God, getting members, yet Magda had taken it all in her stride. She had taken control and pushed him forward. Joshua knew if Magda had not taken control, he would have still been in the planning stage of how to complete his mission. However, Magda's ability to spread the word yet ensuring their privacy had not only increased his following, it had made their relationship blossom.

After feeding the less fortunate they made their way to Cana.

As Magda and Joshua approached the wedding, they could hear the music and joyful laughter from inside the venue. A choir was singing, and they managed to slip in unnoticed, just in time for the wedding feast.

After much food of fish, fresh vegetables and a huge selection of fruit, the bride's family signalled the celebrations were about to start.

Excited and enthralled, Joshua watched as the bride, dressed in white, sat under a highly decorated canopy. Her eight bridesmaids smiled with happiness as they arranged themselves around her.

Joshua had never attended a wedding before. As religion and celebrations had been prohibited by Lamia, weddings were null and void. Joshua watched in awe at the festivities as Magda lent over and explained each part of the wedding as it occurred.

Damaris beamed as songs and blessings were sung to her and gifts presented. Joshua watched as James strode through the throng of well-wishers wearing a blue robe and purple cloak. The beam on his face was all that was needed to show the happiness and love he felt for his new wife, Damaris.

Joshua sat at his table mesmerised as Mary sat next to him on his right and Magda on his left. As he observed James and Damaris exchange words of love, promises and compliments, Joshua put his arm around Magda. James held his hand out to Damaris who accepted and stood up to be next to her new husband. As they kissed the full congregation cheered. People arose from their tables and made their way to the happy couple.

'Come.' Whispered Magda. 'We will get blessed.'

Explaining to Joshua all couples were to be blessed under the canopy, Joshua grinned at her. 'Shall we get married; shall we do this?' He asked as gestured to the happy newlyweds.

Tears in her eyes, Magda replied. 'Yes, I would love to be your wife Joshua.'

The rest of the day had been as joyous as the first part, the merriment had gone long into the night.

Magda had arranged for someone else to feed the less fortunate the next day so they found themselves sleeping in the cart in preparation for the third day of celebrations. Covering them over with a blanket Magda snuggled up to Joshua.

'We will not tell anyone of our intent to marry just yet, we do not want to take away the focus from James and Damaris and spoil their celebration.' She yawned.

'Anything you say.' Joshua kissed the tip of Magda's nose, his heart brimming full of love for this selfless woman.

The next day they awoke to another glorious day, servants were setting the outdoor tables up and Magda went to find Mary to use her facilities to get ready.

Spotting his friends Thomas, Judas and Bartholomew, Joshua jumped off the cart and approached them.

'Good Morning Jesus.' Thomas greeted him. 'I am hearing great things about your ministry and your abilities to heal the sick. I'm getting asked if you are single from every female I come in contact with.'

'Don't worry.' Interjected Judas. 'He does not come into contact with many females!' They all laughed and chatted amongst themselves, animatedly catching up as they made their way back to the venue.

Magda joined the group as they approach the wedding and the music started up again.

'Can't beat a good wedding, eh?' Bartholomew shouted as he led a pretty young woman to dance.

Joshua smiled at Magda and whispered. 'It will be us next.'

Giggling she went to sit at the table with Mary and Joseph.

A few hours passed and the celebrations were in full swing. Joshua had been introduced to so many people from both sides of the family, his head was spinning.

Rolling his eyes as another well-dressed person approached their table, he fully anticipated an introduction, yet Mary stood up and followed the gentleman to the edge of the celebration. Joshua could see the worry flash across her face as she nodded and proceeded to beckon him across to her.

Telling Magda to stay and enjoy herself, he wandered across to where Mary was anxiously standing.

As soon as he neared her, she burst out crying. 'Oh Jesus. I have failed as a mother, I have failed your brother James.'

'Why what's happened?' Joshua grabbed her shoulders and bent down slightly to look into her eyes. 'Mother, tell me what has happened.' He exclaimed, worried.

Looking at the people enjoying the celebration, she placed her face close to his ear and whispered. 'We have run out of wine.'

'What?' he asked her confused. 'Does it matter if we have run out of wine, we can just ask people to go get some more!' He replied, trying to soothe her.

'No Jesus, you mustn't. This family is a good family, a priest family. It was agreed I would provide the wine for the wedding. If I do not fulfil my agreement the wedding will be stopped. James will lose the precious Damaris and our reputation will be in tatters.' She said wiping her tears with the scarf from her head.

'Mother do not worry, I will fix this.' Spotting six large stone jars behind Mary, he turned her around and pointed to the jars. 'Get someone to fill those with water and wait for my return.' He ordered as he walked away.

Walking to the cart, Magda caught up with him. 'Is your Mother crying?' she asked.

'Yes.' He replied. 'They have run out of wine.'

Magda gasp. 'Oh no, your poor Mother, she must be extremely upset. What are doing?'

'Who was it that told me to always bring pebbles?' He said to her as he rummaged through the cart for the correct pills.

'The wine pebbles.' Magda clapped with excitement. 'Thank goodness for your marvellous science!'

Joshua, flashed her a smile as he stuffed the little plastic bag firmly into his belt. Joshua walked towards the six stone jars, now full of water and popped three pills in each. Watching as the blue pills fizzed and turned the water red, he turned to Mary. 'Mother, you now have wine.'

Her mouth opened wide with astonishment. Managing to stammer a thank you, Joshua just smiled, nodded, and returned back to his table. He was glad he had the ability to repay back some of the kindness Mary had shown him, yet still puzzled that this wedding could have been stopped over such a small mistake.

Managing to gather herself back together, Mary instructed one of the servants to take a glass to the steward to taste. Praying what Joshua had done, worked, she watched as the steward put the wine to his lips.

Tasting the wine, surprise crossed the steward's face. Worry still etched across her face, Mary watched as he made his way to the happy couple and apologised for serving the best wine last. Relieved, Mary walked back towards her family.

As Joshua sat, arm round Magda, continuing to watch the dancing that was now occurring, he was approached by Thomas, Judas and Bartholomew. Excited, they took it in turns to explain they had watched him turn the water into wine and asked if he could show them again. Looking at Magda, she had slowly shook her head, signally to not get caught up in it, it was not time. Joshua knew this wedding was neither the time nor place to explain his mission. Too much alcohol had been consumed.

Deciding to laugh it off and play dumb, Joshua knew he would not be able to keep his miracles secret for much longer.

Chapter 20
Rachel - Christmas at Yuri's

'What the hell!' Rachel exclaimed when she finally regained control over her frozen body.
Looking at Yuri then Nick and back again, she could not comprehend how the two of them were related.
'Yuri favours his Mother.' Nick explained seeing the confused look on Rachel's face.
'I didn't mean that! I meant this situation. How could you not tell me? Either of you?' She stammered.
Maria excused herself from the kitchen as the three of them just looked at each other.
'You!' Rachel pointed at Yuri. 'I thought you were my friend. I thought I could trust you!'
'You can trust me Rachel. You would never have spoken to me if you knew who my Fathers was.' Yuri said sheepishly.
'Too right I wouldn't.' Rachel said indignantly. 'I bet you have told him everything.' She said throwing her hands up in the air. 'This is why I do not put my trust in anyone. They ALWAYS betray you.' She said, her eyes growing dark with anger. 'Is that why you invited me here? Because you have told him all about Caroline!' She seethed, now pointing her finger at Nick.
'What about Caroline?' Nicks face became grave.
'Don't pretend Nick. I know Yuri will have told you. This was a mistake.' Rachel said getting up from her stool and snatching her purse off the breakfast bar.
Grabbing her arm, Nick stopped her going any further. 'What about Caroline?' He repeated with more authority in his voice this time.

Shaking his hand off, she looked at him with fire in her eyes. 'You know exactly what about Caroline. He would have told you.' She spat pointing her finger at Yuri.

'Honestly, Rachel, I have not said a word. Anything between me and you stays between me and you.' Yuri pleaded at Rachel. 'Do not tar me with the same brush like everyone else does. Just because I am Stefan Easts son, does not mean I am Stefan East!'

Rachel pulled a face at Yuri, yet he moved closer to her and continued. 'I did not tell you about any of this, because I liked you. If I told you who I was, you would have acted differently around me, just like everyone else that knows does. It gets lonesome. I hate being bowed at, fawned over. I did not choose to be born into this family, yet I choose to be my own individual and live my own life. I have refused to take over my Fathers role like all our predecessors have.'

As Yuri paused to breath, Nick interjected. 'Yes, Yuri. We understand you have chosen your path not to be involved in the dealings of S.U.S. Industries. Now I need to know, what about Caroline?'

Rachel shook her head. 'I can't ... I'm...' Rachel stammered. 'I don't know who to trust anymore or what to do.' The last few days caught up with Rachel and she put her head in her hands. She had never felt as lonely as she did right now. Tears formed in her eyes. The thoughts of returning to Trinity Estate flitted across her mind again. It was her only path, the path she didn't choose, yet would always end up on. Like Caroline said, the apple doesn't fall far from the tree.

Marias voice rang out, disturbing Rachel from her thoughts. 'You two get out of my kitchen, I will not have anyone upset in my house on Christmas day.'

Her voice growing softer as the two men exited, she comforted Rachel. 'Today is about family and joyfulness, not tears and inquisitions.' She had said to Rachel while wiping her tears away.

'I don't have a family, nor anything to feel joyful about.' Rachel said miserably.

'We shall soon see about that. Grab an apron, you're helping me.'

'What?' Rachel's head shot up in surprise as she watched Maria walk across to the stove.

'Put that apron on.' She said pointing to an apron hung next to an array of knives. 'You can listen to me whilst we finish this together.'

The next 45 minutes lifted Rachel, yet she had no idea how Maria did it. Instructing her in between her chatter about her life, Rachel was lulled into a safety net. Speaking about her childhood and her family, Rachel normally got envious, yet Maria had to leave most of it behind for the man she loved. Her childhood sounded idyllic and Rachel enjoyed listening to her stories of chasing the farm animals or shimming up trees for lemons. 'Not that I could do that now.' She laughed as they put the finishing touches to the plates.

'Dinner is ready.' She bellowed as the two sat down at the table and waited for Nick and Yuri to return.

As Yuri went to open his mouth to speak to Rachel, Maria put her hand up. 'There will be no more talk from you two tonight. I will have no tears on Christmas Day.'

Throwing a grateful smile towards Maria, Rachel felt her gently pat her hand to say she understood.

Chattering on still about her background, the table was soon full of laughter. Crackers were pulled, pudding was served and then cheese and crackers. Maria's mobile rang and she answered, chattering away in Greek. It was a family member wishing her a Merry Christmas. Greek being one of the languages Rachel knew, she was glad that Maria was exactly who Nick said she was. A Cypriot woman that fell in love with Stefan East, who was pretty much the current ruler of the world.

'You speak excellent English Maria, you have the accent down to a fine art.'

'Why thank you Rachel. Years of dealing with English tourists and of course Stefan.' She looked at him lovingly. Leaning over to Rachel she whispered into her ear. 'He is a good man, though he is only human, humans make mistakes, especially when they have the weight of the world on their shoulders.'

Rachel smiled, her anger at Nick softening slightly.

Although her mood changed dramatically as her mobile tinged with a message. Knowing who it would be from, she read it, her stomach turning over.

'Who is it?' Yuri asked concerned.

Not speaking, Rachel's heart started beating widely as she read the message from Caroline, demanding an answer.

'Is it who I think it is from?' Yuri asked.

Nodding her head, Rachel's heart started to beat faster. The time had flown by, it was now 9pm and she needed to get back in time for her delivery, yet had still not made a decision.

Standing up she spoke to Maria. 'You have been a fantastic host. Thank you so much for your delicious food and your time with me today. It has been a very special first Christmas for me, yet I need to return to my villa.'

Before Maria could protest, Yuri stood up. 'I need to take her Mama, it has been a long tiring day.' Kissing his Mother, he said bye to Nick and motioned Rachel to follow him.

As Rachel neared the door she stopped. Her hand on the door frame of the kitchen, she thought about her personal mobile phone in her bag. Marias' words about Nick being a good man echoed in her mind. Turning around, she addressed Nick. 'You asked about Caroline? I have about 20 minutes before I need to leave. I have a package coming for me at 10pm that I need to be there for. I hope this is not a mistake.'

Standing up abruptly Nick stumbled towards Rachel.

'This way.' He hurried towards his office.

Locking the door behind them as Yuri stood guard outside, Rachel gave a brief overview of what happened with Caroline. Keeping an eye on the time, Rachel could only play a small amount of the audio recording.

Pressing stop as Nick was listening, Rachel informed him she needed to leave. Refusing to leave her personal phone, he nodded his head in agreement, gesturing, he understood why.

'I will call you on Yuri's phone as you are travelling back. Caroline will have access to your work phone.'

As Yuri drove, Rachel played the rest of the audio recording over Yuri's mobile. Once it had finished Nick stayed silent.

'Hello?' Rachel said into the speaker.

'Yes, I am still here. Is there any way you can stall her before giving an answer?' Nick asked.

'No. You saw the message. I have a feeling, if she delivers the package tonight, she will want an answer, or I'll be swopped with the package.' Rachel replied.

'What is your gut feeling Rachel?' Nick said, the worry evident in his voice.

'To agree and go from there.' Rachel sighed

'Caroline is extremely dangerous. I don't want you on your own.' Nick informed her.

'It'll be too suspicious if anyone else is around.' She responded.

'I think you should say no Rachel. Let Yuri stay at your villa tonight and we'll arrange security for tomorrow.' Nick instructed.

'I am saying yes. This sounds laughable, yet I think Caroline wants world domination.' Rachel chuckled in amusement at how bizarre the words sounded out loud.

'Caroline was always a risk to bring into the committee.' Nick's voice rang out from the phone. 'Her Father before her was a fantastic man, yet his wife turned out to be cold and callous, much like her daughter has turned out to be. Sandra and I agreed to only take Caroline places of low risk and I am glad we did. The power source for the TT pod cannot be moved. We have not figured out the technology for it yet. If removed from the TT pod, it will be extremely unstable, we cannot risk another explosion.'

'Another explosion?' Rachel exclaimed.

'Yes, another explosion.' Nick confirmed. 'We tried to remove the power source to a secure location to find out the basis of the energy it still has in 1981, yet when we tried to remove, an explosion occurred. It was a strange occurrence. Energy ran through the ground and blew up in Southern Lebanon sparking a war. We cannot confirm, yet we have a suspicion Caroline was behind the search for the TT pod. Knowing we were trying to remove it, she sent her own soldiers to search and kill everyone in their path that stopped them. Field Marshal Sanderson used his contacts in Israel to declare Operation Peace in Galilee, thus helping keep the TT pod safe.'

Rachel exhaled loudly. 'Has she tried to get anyone from the committee before to help her?'

'Not that we know of, yet we have had a couple of members resign and then disappear, which is unheard of. If someone is alive, we can find them.' Nick's voice was tinged with sadness.

Rachel thought of the torture chamber and knew that is where the other members would have ended up.

'I am due to go to Galilee tomorrow.' She said. 'Caroline wants an answer tonight. If I say yes, she wants to meet me before. My gut feeling is telling me to say yes and use it against her to keep the TT pod safe.'

'If it were anyone else, I would agree with you, yet I feel it is too dangerous for you Rachel.' Nick said, trying to persuade Rachel from agreeing to help her.

'I'll go with her.' Yuri interjected.

'Are you sure Yuri? You never wanted to get mixed up in this fully.' Nick's voice came over the phone.

'You know my training Dad, she will be safe with me.' Yuri glanced at Rachel and smiled.

'Thank you for the offer Yuri.' Rachel looked at his athletic stature, wondering how he would be able to protect her. 'But wouldn't Caroline get spooked if Stefan Easts son turned up with me?'

'No one knows I am married or have a son Rachel. It has been extremely hard, yet I wanted to keep them safe, away from all this. Only a select few people know and they are the people that I trust with my life. I hope now you know this, you realise how much you mean to me, to us as a family.' Nick replied.

Yuri looked at Rachel and smiled. 'You are like a big sister to me.' He said to her. 'Or an Aunt.' He said chuckling.

'Hey.' She said hitting him playfully. 'I am definitely not old enough to be your aunt!'

'You two, this is serious business.' Nicks voice came across the phone. 'I agree with Yuri, he has been trained by Special Forces. Do not let looks deceive you Rachel. Yuri has trained since the age of ten, has fought in tough situations, it is why I asked him to be your driver.'

Rachel stared at Yuri, his soft curly hair, his cheeky face, and innocent aura. She could not imagine him being a trained solider with the ability to protect her.

'If you are intent on going ahead with this, I shall postpone your trip to Israel for one day. It will give us more time to get prepared.' Nick continued. 'Yuri, stay with Rachel tonight, yet stay hidden. And Rach?'

'Yes Nick?' Rachel answered.

'Be careful, we do not know what Caroline is capable of.'

Rachel gulped as Nick put the phone down.

Yuri pulled up outside of her villa at 9.50PM. As Rachel got out Yuri whispered to her to use her bracelet if she needed help. He would be inside the villa in seven minutes.

Walking towards her front door, she opened it and switched the lights on.

Texting Caroline a simple yes. She sat on the leather couch opposite the front door and waited in silence.

Not a sound could be heard inside the villa. Time seemed to slow as Rachel watched her phone click to 10PM.

The doorbell rang. Though she had been expecting it, the noise still startled her and her heart started beating widely. Rachel's shoes echoed around the room as she walked across the smooth tiles towards the front door. Opening it slightly, she peered outside.

'Good Evening Rachel.' Caroline smirked. 'I thought I would deliver your package personally.'

Chapter 21
Joshua - The Temple

Word soon got round about Joshua's water wine trick. His family tried to protect him as best they could from those that suddenly wanted 'help' from Joshua, yet some still managed to get through. Joshua didn't mind the ones that truly needed help and he was their last resort, however he had no time for those that wanted to make a profit from his good deeds.
Joshua was amazed at how quickly all this had happened. Magda's way was great, slow and steady, building up his ministry with trustworthy people that would spread his word and be rewarded if they showed compassion to others without wanting gain. It was simple, it worked, and he had control over it.
Yet now this. Joshua could not walk anywhere in Capernaum, or even Galilee without being harassed. He needed a break.
Another night holed up in the TT pod, he held a meeting with Magda, Mary and James asking their help on what he should do next.
'You are always welcome to come and stay with me and Damaris in Cana. Travel at night and no one will see you leave. We will keep you safe there, until all this dies down.' James had offered.
'Thank you James, however I cannot stay with newlyweds just yet. I shall let you have time on your own first.' He winked at him, as James grinned back.
'I've heard Jerusalem is nice at this time of year.' Magda said. 'Why don't we go there for a few days? Clear your head without the pressure of thinking someone will find you?' She suggested.
'You mean like a holiday?' Joshua contemplated.
'A holiday?' Magda asked.
'A holiday is when you spend time away from your home, relaxing or trying something new.'

'Ahh, yes, like a holiday then. You need time to think and also some respite.' Leaning across to Joshua, Magda whispered into his ear 'You still have not fully healed after the baptism. You need to take it slow to recover, yet you have not stopped since you awoke here after forty days!'

'Yes, yes. Let's go to Jerusalem.' Joshua said over enthusiastically, trying to hide from James what Magda whispered.

'I have family in Jerusalem.' Mary suggested. 'You can stay with them, say you are Aaron, Joseph's son.'

Nodding in agreement, Magda and Joshua made the arrangements to leave that evening.

Leaving just after their evening meal, the sun was already beginning to set. The evening looked cloudy, with a little promise of visibility from the moon and stars. Grabbing a torch and the tablet from the TT pod, Joshua programmed in their destination and checked for the quickest route. Sighing to Magda, he showed her the fastest way to Jerusalem. According to V.E.L.U.S.'s calculations, it was going to take them a just over ten hours of travelling to get there.

Magda laughed at him. 'Of course it will take a long time, we do not have TT pods like you! It will be fun, I will make it fun.' She said to him.

They arrived in Jerusalem early hours of the morning. Locating Mary's relatives place, they moved the cart further out of the city to rest for a few hours before the relatives awoke.

The bright sunshine and laughter from children around their cart alerted them they had slept longer than anticipated.

Stretching up and yawning, Joshua flipped a couple of copper coins towards the children. 'Go treat yourself.' He shouted to them after they thanked him and argued over what they would buy.

'Why did you do that?' Magda asked, still exhausted from their journey.

'Doing something nice is the best way to start the day!' He smiled at her.

Jumping out of the cart, Joshua walked around stretching his legs. 'Don't be too long, those children will be back with others wanting more coins!' She shouted after him as she prepared the horse and cart for departure.

Walking through the market, Joshua was amazed at how crowded the area was. More like a city than Capernaum, he watched the people with amusement as he strode along.

Stopping to buy some bread, he noticed shouting coming out of a temple. A man stood against one of the pillars at the entrance, preaching about the sins of the world. A ruckus could be heard whilst men carried crate after crate inside, packed with animals. Craning his neck, Joshua tried to see where the shouting was coming from, yet his curiosity was interrupted by the woman at the bread stall.

'Sorry, what was you saying?' Joshua asked the old woman.

'I was talking about the temple, I feel sorry for the poor.' She said to Joshua shaking her head. 'They save up every coin they can get, to spend it in that temple, praying for better times to come. If only they used the coins they gathered to feed their children, there would be a lot less deaths in this city.'

'Seriously?' Joshua said confused. 'What is the temple used for? I am not from round here.'

The old woman's laughter at Joshua's obvious statement, turned into a hacking cough. 'I can tell because of your accent and your shiny teeth. Where are you from?'

'My family moved to Galilee some years ago, yet I have never ventured up here. What is the temple used for?' He asked repeating the question as he pointed at the temple.

'Crooks and thieves. It was a nice temple once, yet the crooks took over. Stealing animals from nearby farms at nightfall, to bring here and sell at a high price to offer to God. Turns my stomach how much they charge. Luring the poor in by telling them they only have to roll some dice to win money. Shocking behaviour.' She said, shaking her head. 'I have seen many a person walk into that temple with lots of money and walk out again with no shoes on his feet or clothes on his back. Lost it all on that stupid dice game, but will they listen? Never.'

Joshua thanked the woman for her time and paid for the bread.

Making his way back to Magda, the old woman's words rang in his ears. His face still grave as he contemplated the issue at the temple, he jumped on the cart. Noticing his sombre mood, Magda asked him what had happened. As she made her way through the streets of Jerusalem towards Mary's relative's house, Joshua relayed his conversation with the old woman.

'Bad things happen Joshua, the people that go in there are adults, not children. They have a choice and if they choose to throw their money away, then it is their own fault.' Magda explained.

'Those crooks are giving the poor false hope! They need to be stopped!' Joshua replied.

'Joshua, No! We have come away for a few days to let all the excitement at home calm down. You need space to think, not take on another problem.'

'I know, but…'

'No buts, listen to me.' Magda ordered. 'We are going to have a few days, just me and you. No arguments you need to rest!'

Sitting in silence for the rest of the way to Mary's relatives, Joshua's mind was in overdrive. The theft of the animals were frustrating, especially the thieving part, yet the gambling really struck a nerve. Less fortunate families going into a temple that should bring them peace and hope, yet they leave poorer and hungrier than before. Crooks scheming off desperate people needing to feed their families, for what? A bigger house? A better horse? Joshua wondered how they could sleep at night. He would think and discuss the issue with Magda when he got back to Capernaum. He knew this is one issue he would need to solve, yet not on this trip, Magda would not allow it. He would return when he was back to full strength and give the people back their temple.

Pulling up outside the house, Mary's sister rushed out. The same kind face as her sister, she embraced Joshua and Magda.

'Good Morning.' Joshua said. 'I am Aaron, Joseph's son and this is Magda, visiting Jerusalem for a few days.

'Yes, yes, come in. Mary sent word you were coming. I am Delilah.' Gesturing them to follow her inside, Magda and Joshua, looked at each in surprise, both thinking the same thing. How did Mary get a message to Delilah faster than they arrived?

Delilah chattered away as she led them through to the back of the house, shouting at people on the way.

She took them through the back door and into a courtyard surrounded by nearby houses, creating a square stone suntrap. The air was still, with no breeze, blocked by the structures around them, yet trees with branches full of fruit, overhung the courtyard, giving welcome shade from the hot sun.

A table had been set up with chairs surrounding as if waiting for their arrival.

'You must be hungry after your travels?' Delilah said as she offered seats to both of them. 'Wait here.'

A few minutes later, Delilah reappeared, followed by members of her household bringing dish after dish of food. Looking at each other, Magda and Joshua laughed. Delilah was definitely Mary's sister.

'Please help yourself.' She instructed as more people filtered into the courtyard.

Wishing he had not eaten the bread he had bought this morning, Joshua filled his plate high and sat next to Delilah.

Her plump hand patted his knee as she leant over to whisper in his ear. 'I saw you at the wedding, helping Mary with the wine. Your secret is safe with me.' She winked before standing up and addressing the courtyard full of people.

'My nephew Aaron and the beautiful Magda will be staying here for a few days, please make them feel welcome.'

Joshua smiled at Delilah, grateful for her discretion.

The morning passed in joyful chatter. It was getting easier now for Joshua to socialise with new people without Magda by his side. He was more confident, and Magda did not have to fill in the awkward silences to keep the conversation flowing.

Delilah's two sons Elijah and Jacob invited Joshua for a walk through the city centre to show him the sights.

Delighted, Joshua accepted leaving Magda in Delilah and her daughter's capable hands.

Elijah and Jacob were great company. Constantly chattering and playfully insulting each other, Joshua warmed to them immediately.

As they neared the temple Joshua had seen earlier that morning, Elijah stopped.

'Won't be long.' He cheerily waved, leaving Joshua and Jacob outside.

Jacob sighed as Joshua looked at him puzzled. 'Please do not tell my Mother, she would die from shame if she knew what Elijah was doing.'

'Why? What is he doing?' Joshua asked.

'He owes Farrow money.' Jacob explained. 'Yet I have no idea where he got it from.'

'Farrow? Money for what?'

'The dice man. Elijah wanted some extra money to impress a girl he knows. He had seen a man win a lot of money when he was in there sacrificing a goat for Mother a few weeks prior. Elijah played one game and now he is hooked. He goes there most days, sometimes he wins, yet most of the time he loses, he is always in debt to Farrow.' Jacob explained sadly.

'How did this happen? Isn't it supposed to be a holy place?' Joshua scratched his head as he looked at the people going in and out of the place of worship.

'The temple was a holy place. A place where you could pray or sacrifice an animal to show your allegiance to God. Many people that went there, did not have access to animals, nor had the crates to bring them to the house of God. A crook took advantage of this situation, bringing animals to sell outside of the temple. More crooks joined him and they gradually moved inside. Demanding those that did not have an animal to sacrifice, was not worthy to be in the temple. Telling them God would think they had lost faith and damn them to poverty and sickness. Not wanting God to think they had turned their back on him, many sold everything they had to buy an animal from the crooks. One day, a young man could not afford an animal and asked if he could roll two dice, if it landed on the same, they would give him an animal for free. The crook gave the animal to the young man in exchange for his dice, thus starting the gambling ring that now takes place inside the temple.'

Curious, Joshua walked inside the temple looking for Elijah. Spotting him sat at a table with a fat dirty looking man, coins piled high next to him, Joshua instantly knew it was Farrow. Walking closer towards them, Joshua's eyes opened in shock. Farrow was holding a ruby red ring in the air, with one eye closed and his tongue poking out the side of his mouth as he examined the fine piece of jewellery.

Joshua knew that ring, it was Magda's. The piece of jewellery had once been his Mothers and Joshua had given it to Magda. He knew that ring inside out and not one other person of this time would have a ring like that. Furious, Joshua stormed across to the table where Farrow and Elijah were sitting.

'Where did you get that ring?' He roared at Elijah.

'I...I...' Elijah stammered.

'It's not his ring.' Farrow sneered at Joshua. 'It's mine now. He just lost it on a game.' He laughed.

Anger surged through Joshua as he looked around at the poor passing money over to the snivelling fat crooks that scattered across the room. Women with children at their feet, crying, asking for more time to pay back their debts.

Grabbing a piece of leather that dangled from the animal cages, Joshua walked behind Farrow. The dirty fat man, still laughed in amusement, not paying attention to what Joshua was doing. Wrapping the length of leather around each of his fists, Joshua pulled it taught before he wrapped it around the crook's neck. Spluttering Farrow started choking and struggled, yet Joshua kept a firm grip, pulling the leather tighter and tighter around Farrows chubby throat.

Elijah looked up fearfully, and slowly edged away as Joshua glared at him in anger. As Farrow struggled and tried to remove the leather from around his neck, he kicked his legs out involuntarily, causing the table he and Elijah had been sat at, to topple over. The coins that were on the table scattered across the dirty stone floor of the temple.

The noise from the coins falling to the ground, alerted the other crooks around the room. Seeing their fellow thief slowly starting to lose consciousness, they moved towards Joshua, forming a circle around him. Letting the now unconscious Farrow slide to the floor, Joshua's eyes alit with the anger still pulsating through him.

Picking up Magda's ruby ring that had fallen from Farrow's hand, he secured it in his secret pocket inside his leather belt and pulled out a small metallic pencil. Flicking it open, the pencil extended into a razor sharp flexible piece of steel.

Moving it like a whip, Joshua flicked the metal to the nearest crook and skilfully wrapped the end of the whip around his ankle. Flicking his wrist once again, the metal whip retracted in itself, bringing the crook towards Joshua.

Fear could be seen in the crooks eyes as Joshua placed his foot on the man's throat, daring him to move.

The man, turned his head slightly, looking to the table he was just sat at.

'Money?' Joshua roared. 'Is that all you care about? Money?' Joshua, flicked the metal whip again and pulled the table towards him, scattering any money that laid on it.

'Is this what you want? Is this worth it?' He screamed at him. The man's ankle bled out onto the dirty floor of the temple as he cried out in pain and fear.

The man tried to cover himself up, yet the stench of urine filled Joshua's nostrils, as wetness spread across his clothes.

Too angry to care the crook had wet himself out of fear, Joshua, rampaged around the temple. Upturning tables and screaming as the people inside ran out crying.

Joshua turned to Elijah and the crook with the injured ankle.

'If I ever come here, and see any of this again, I will kill you and your family.' He threatened and then stormed out.

Jacob, was waiting anxiously outside as Joshua exited the temple.

'Are you alright? Where is Elijah? What happened?'

'Your brother is a thief.' Pulling Magda's ruby ring out of his belt, he held it up so Jacob could see. 'This is my Magda's ring, there is no other one like it in the world. Elijah had it, was using it to gamble with, that is where he got his money from! Thieving from his own family! I will not have ANYONE take my Magda's possessions and get away with it.'

Jacob stood there open mouthed as Joshua stalked off.

Arriving back at Delilah's on his own, he shouted for Magda.

Looking at his face she asked him what was wrong.

Giving her the ruby red ring, her eyes opened in surprise.

'We need to leave, now!' He said.

Chapter 22
Rachel - The Package

Grabbing Rachel's wrist through the door, Caroline examined her bracelet.
'What a lovely bracelet Rachel. I do not seem to remember you wearing that last night.' She sneered, letting go of Rachel's wrist and walking into the villa, her black stilettos clicking over the tiled floor.
'This old thing?' Rachel laughed while she nervously fiddled with the bracelet. 'I've had…'
Caroline spun round and held her hand up to silence Rachel. 'You may want to open your patio doors. I am not sure the package will fit through that.' Caroline said pointing at the larger than normal front door.
Still twiddling with the bracelet, Rachel walked as confidently as she could to the patio doors leading on to the balcony. Opening them wide, she turned and faced Caroline. 'If the package is not as agreed, the deals off.'
Laughing Caroline walked closer to Rachel. 'This is what I like about you Rachel. The fire you have inside you.'
Holding her hands in the air, Caroline squawked, 'The deals off. The deals off.' Imitating Rachel. Laughing at her own impression, her face suddenly grew stern. Clicking her fingers to the burly man stood guard outside the door, Rachel noticed it was Craig, Caroline's right hand man. He turned to look at Caroline as she raised her chin up at him, giving a silent signal. Craig nodded back and pointed to someone out of Rachel's eye line.
Adrenaline pumped through Rachel's body, nervous at the crazy woman in her villa and what she would do next. Not holding out much hope that Yuri would be able to make it into the villa

unseen, Rachel decided to keep Caroline talking, unsure how this night was going to pan out.

'I have seen people wander about this street. What if someone spots you bringing in the package, all skin and bones?' Rachel questioned her.

Caroline walked towards her, stopping close. In her six inch heels, Caroline towered above Rachel and looked down, straight into her eyes. A slow condescending smile, spreading across her face. 'Oh Rachel. You must think so little of me. I have been in this world far longer than you, and have been taught more than you will ever know.' She stroked her face. 'The place is surrounded by my people, there are no residents in eye line of this villa. Yet how would we disguise skin and bone?' she said sarcastically, putting her finger to the side of her mouth. 'Oh look, you shall find out now.'

A noise at the patio doors caused Rachel to look. Two large men, dressed in black, held a hefty square wooden shipping crate between them. Carrying the wooden box through the patio doors, they sat it on the floor in front of Rachel. Hearing the groans from inside, Rachel knew Caroline had made good on her promise.

'Not there you simpletons.' Caroline shouted as the men had started to head out of the front door. 'Put it out the way, in one of the bedrooms.'

Rolling their eyes, the two men picked the crate back up. Moving around them, Rachel opened the spare bedroom door with the most room and directed them in there.

Whispering thank you to the men, they looked at her puzzled before leaving the villa in silence.

Walking out of the bedroom, Rachel found Caroline rifling through her fridge.

'No Cristal? Dom Perignon? Even Moet would do! Rachel, this is a night for celebration. Two independent women coming together, chasing after the same goal.' She said, animated.

Slamming the fridge shut, Rachel flinched. Catching a glimpse of Caroline's smug smile as she walked towards the front door frightened Rachel. Her mood switches were unpredictable. Fiddling with her bracelet, Rachel watched as Caroline whispered into Craig's ear. Craig nodded in acknowledgement at Caroline, and Rachel could just make out him signalling to someone out of her view.

'The Cristal will be with us shortly. Now sit.' Caroline instructed, pointing for Rachel to sit at the dining table. 'Before you open your present you asked for, we need to have a little chat about tomorrow.' She said, sitting opposite Rachel.

Rachel jumped as the Caroline's right hand man, Craig came into view, and placed a small black box on the table.

Nervously laughing, Rachel looked at Caroline. 'I was too busy concentrating on what you were about to say, I did not hear him.' She stuttered, trying to stay confident, yet underneath her heart was beating wildly.

'You are funny Rachel. You will get used to my stealthy security, since they will be with you everywhere you go now.' Her conceited smile directed straight at Rachel, informing her this was non-negotiable.

Gulping Rachel's mind went into overdrive. How would she be able to speak to Nick and Yuri if she had surveillance following her?

'Now about tomorrow, I have …' Caroline continued.

'I'm not going.' Rachel cut her off.

'What do you mean you are not going?' Caroline said. Rage alighting in her eyes.

'Nick emailed me, they have postponed until the day after.'

'This is not good.' Caroline stood up. 'Did he say why?'

'No. Told me to take tomorrow off and recommence the schedule a day later than originally planned.'

'I have not been informed of this. Have the other members of the committee?' Caroline said pacing up and down. 'Craig.' She screamed as the security guard came running. 'What do you know of Rachel's schedule changing?'

N…Nothing.' Craig stammered.

Turning her steely blue eyes on to Rachel she slowly walked towards her. 'You wouldn't lie to me would you Rachel?' She asked, a cold chill running through her voice.

Feeling her face flush under Caroline's scrutinising stare, Rachel shook her head.

Caroline crouched down to Rachel's level as she still sat at the table. Grabbing her face in between her bony fingers, she forced Rachel to look at her. 'Because bad things happen to those that lie to me.' She snarled.

Rachel could feel Caroline's hot breath on her face as she quietly seethed, waiting for Rachel to answer. 'Honestly Caroline, I am not lying. Why would I? We're in this together.' She tried smiling as Caroline's bony fingers still crushed her cheeks together. 'I can show you the email if you want.' Rachel offered, trying to buy time.

Throwing her face to the side, Caroline instructed her to go and get the email. Running into her bedroom, she fumbled for her laptop.

'What's taking you so long?' She heard Caroline half singing half shouting as she grabbed her laptop. Not entirely sure what her plan of action was, Rachel sat on the edge of the bed and placed the laptop on her knee. There was no email from Nick. Cursing herself for saying something so stupid, Rachel switched the laptop on and waited for it to boot up.

The wardrobe opened a fraction. Jumping in fright, the laptop slid from her grasp and crashed to the floor.

'Shhh' said Yuri, his head now poking out. 'I've made my Father aware, Caroline will get an email any second.' He whispered as they heard the clicking of Caroline's shoes heading towards the bedroom.

Standing up as Caroline entered, Rachel went to pick the laptop up.

'I hope you are not trying to destroy any evidence of what you and Nick are up to?' Caroline demanded.

Reassured that Yuri was with her and adrenalin running through her body, Caroline's attitude angered her.

Looking straight into her cold eyes, Rachel threw the laptop on the bed 'Take it, look through it yourself. YOU find the email.' Watching Caroline's eyes open wide with surprise as she watched the laptop land on the bed, Rachel continued. 'Caroline, if you want us to work together, you need to adjust your social skills. Don't ever grab my face again.' She said as she stalked out of the room, leaving a surprised Caroline picking the laptop up from the bed.

Rachel could hear Caroline laughing at her outburst as she walked back into the living room. Running her fingers through her hair in exasperation, she wondered how she had managed to get herself into this situation, Caroline was a maniac.

Standing in the middle of the living room at a loss of what to do, the security guard, Craig, hurriedly pushed passed her, heading towards Caroline. Seriously, she thought to herself, what could be happening now?

Hearing the click of Caroline's shoes along the floor, Rachel braced herself for what was about to come.

Caroline rounded the corner with a smile on her face. 'Sorry about all that Rachel. I sometimes have a tendency to let my emotions run away with me.'

No kidding Rachel thought, as she watched Caroline sit back at the dining table, cradling Rachel's laptop. Placing the laptop on the table, she motioned for Rachel to sit opposite her.

'I have just received an email confirming your adjustment to the schedule.' She said picking an imaginary bit of fluff from her cream top. 'However, I do wonder what Stefan is up to. Have you spoken to him recently?'

Rachel shook her head.

'Good, good. I will need a list of people you have been in contact with over the last forty-eight hours. We cannot take any chances now can we?' Caroline waggled her finger in Rachel's direction.

Nodding in acknowledgement and agreement, Rachel let Caroline continue.

'Now on to the reason I am here. I had hoped this would all be fresh in your mind for tomorrow, yet I am sure with your memory you will remember everything I tell you.'

Opening the black box in front of her, Caroline revealed a diamond broach. 'Merry Christmas' She trilled with ohhs and ahhs as she placed the box closer to a perplexed Rachel.

'This broach is your new best friend.' Taking it out of the box, Caroline explained Rachel needed to wear it when she visited the TT pod. 'No scanner can detect it. To the average eye, it is just a broach, to the trained eye, it is an exquisite diamond broach, to us, it is surveillance. It will track your location as well as sending live feed directly to me.'

Craig placed a single piece of blank A4 paper between them.

Puzzled, Rachel looked at Caroline. Smiling she pulled out her mobile phone. 'You have heard of UV light before?' Caroline asked.

Rachel nodded thinking of the crime scene shows she used to watch when at home.

'Welcome to CB light.' She exclaimed as a pale pink light shone out of her phone. 'That's Caroline Brodell light to me and you.' She whispered to Rachel winking.

Smiling at her absurd mood swings, Rachel watched as Caroline shone her phone over the blank piece of paper. As the light hit the paper, words revealed themselves as Rachel looked on in amazement.

Tapping the paper, Caroline continued. 'On my magical paper, you will see a series of questions. These. Must. Be. Asked.' She said tapping her finger along with each syllable.

Stealthy Craig revealed himself again, placing a mobile phone on the table next to Caroline.

'This.' She said holding up the mobile phone. 'Has been programmed with the light. Use the time you have tomorrow to memorise these questions and burn the paper afterwards.' Cocking her head to one side, she looked at Rachel. 'I am trusting you on this. Do not fail me.' Abruptly standing up, Caroline clicked her fingers as Craig followed her.

'Enjoy your present.' She shouted as they left.

Staying sat at the table, Rachel slowly closed the box of the broach. Hearing something behind her, she whipped her head around. Breathing a sigh of relief when she saw it was Yuri, she put her finger over her mouth, signalling to stay quiet. Looking outside to ensure all the vehicles had left, she carried the black box containing the broach to her bedroom and placed it into the bedside draw. Slowly shutting the draw she tiptoed out and shut the door to the bedroom.

Sighing as she leant against the door, she waited a few moments, composing herself before finding Yuri.

Seeing him stood near the counter top, she walked towards him.

'Did you hear everything?' She whispered.

'Yes.' He replied gravely. 'I also brought some supplies, which I think we may need.'

Looking at him puzzled, he picked up a backpack placed next to him. Opening it, he showed the contents to Rachel. 'Where did you get all this?' She asked.

'No time to explain, yet I always have these resources in my car. Shall we?' He replied.

Rachel took a deep breath and nodded.

They both slowly made their way towards the bedroom that contained the package.

Opening the door, they could hear the weak groans inside.

Walking up to the wooden box that lay next to the bed, Rachel called out to the person inside.

'Do not be scared. I am the woman you asked for help. You may hear some banging as we open the box.'

Pulling out a crow bar from the back pack, Yuri used it to lever open the top. Tentatively lifting up the lid with one arm, Rachel quickly looked away. The stench of the rotting person inside the box flooded the room. Knowing it was a risk to open a window, Rachel kept the box open slightly whilst she leant over and grabbed a towel from the bed, quickly wrapping it around her head. Looking inside, the sight of the skin and bone naked, cold and shivering against the side of the box, brought tears to her eyes. Rachel could only just make out the person weakly repeating please, over and over again.

Furious that Caroline could do this to another human being, Rachel wrenched the top of the wooden container off. The creature inside started screaming, lifting its weary hands, trying to block the light streaming inside the box. 'Yuri, switch off the light.' Rachel shouted as she tried to shield the box.

Yuri immediately reached for the light switch and the room plunged into darkness. Rachel walked to the blinds and slowly opened them, letting the moon and street lights softly illuminate the room. The frail person's screaming turned into a quiet sob as it slowly moved back into the foetal position.

Indicating to Rachel the person was too frail to get out of the box, Yuri used the crow bar again to remove the side of the vast wooden container.

Speaking softly as he entered and scooped the weary person into his arms, Yuri gently told them he was there to help. Laying the skin and bones on the bed, Yuri sighed.

'How can anyone do this?' Rachel whispered as they both noted the full extent of the visible inflicted wounds.

Fully naked and laid on the bed, they finally realised the poor tortured soul was a woman.

Yuri took out a first aid kit and bags full of fluid from the back pack and started to assemble them. Fetching the tall coat rack from near the front door, he used it as a stand for the IV's.

Rachel sat on the bed, talking softly to the woman whilst she covered her with a tin foil blanket and then a sheet. Wiping her arms down ready for Yuri, Rachel noticed track marks running up and down her arms. She had grown up around drugs users to not know what they were.

Whispering to Yuri her findings he nodded, advising he would not use any opiates in the pain relief.

Unsure if it was the woman's own doing or something Caroline had subjected her to, Rachel sat down next to her, stroking the wisps of hair as she spoke softly, telling her that no more harm would come to her.

The woman was trying to talk, yet Rachel could not make out what she was saying. Her dry cracked lips moving over her brown teeth as barely a whisper came out. Her gaunt face, pleading with Rachel to come nearer and listen to what she had to say. Rachel moved closer and leant over the woman. Putting her ear near the woman's mouth, Rachel felt her rancid hot breath, blowing on her cheek.

'I knew you would come back Chantelle.'

Sitting upright in alarm, Rachel yelled out. 'No, No, No.'

'What's matter?' Yuri asked alarmed.

Standing up, Rachel grabbed the woman and roughly turned her on to her stomach. Locating the now faded round scar on the woman's back, Rachel gasped.

'No, no this cannot be happening.' Rachel walked backwards away from the woman.

'Rachel, what are you doing?' Yuri shouted as he moved the woman on to her back and made her comfortable again.

Rachel felt the wall of the room stop her from walking backwards any further, all the time staring at the woman that laid before her.

Yuri, had started to insert the IV's as Rachel slid down the wall. Sobbing into her knees, she heard Yuri take off his surgical gloves and bend down near her.

'Who is it?' Yuri whispered as he put his arm around her.

'It is my Mother.' Rachel whispered back.

Chapter 23
Joshua - The Many Healings and Catching of Fish

Deciding against going straight back to Mary and Josephs house, Magda and Joshua had a couple of weeks touring around.
Stopping off in wonderful villages and towns, they had been taken in like family by most people. Gate crashing weddings and celebrations, people embraced them like old friends.
Throwing caution to the wind, Magda and Joshua decided to get married and had a secret, simple ceremony in Nazareth.
Accompanied by only a married couple they had met the night before, Magda had married Joshua in a borrowed wedding gown, with Joshua wearing his protective suit he brought everywhere with him.
The married couple, Gabe and Naamah, were excellent company. After their wedding vows, Magda and Joshua changed into their normal dress and headed into the city centre with Gabe and Naamah.
Intending on celebrating like a wedding party should, Joshua ensured he had plenty of wine pebbles with him.
All four of them walked about Nazareth in high spirits. Joshua, picked up Magda and spun her around. She was now his wife, his beautiful dark haired wife. Kissing her hard, he swayed.
'I think I may have drunk a little bit too much wine.' He slurred.
'Mr Joshua, you can, as it is your wedding day.' Magda hiccupped back.
Gabe and Naamah, loving the free alcohol, were as drunk as Magda and Joshua.
'Its good stuff.' Gabe complimented. 'Anytime, you are here, you come straight to me. Best friends for life me and you.' He said as

he slowly slide down a wall. With one eye closed and holding a cup of wine, he pointed at Joshua. 'You are the best.'

Pulling him up whilst laughing, Joshua supported him as they carried on walking down the street.

Seeing a crowd of people around a man shouting, Joshua asked Gabe what they were doing.

'That's the synagogue Josh.' Gabe replied putting his arm around him. 'It is were Jewish people listen to the bible. I like it. The man reading has a very soothing voice.'

'Do you think I have a soothing voice?' Joshua said, narrowing his eyes to try and focus on Gabe.

'You have the most soothing voice I have ever heard!' Gabe said. 'Naamah, Magda.' He shouted. 'Come here.' The two giggling girls ahead of them stopped. Turning around, Magda looked at the man preaching to the crowd.

Running to Joshua she grabbed his shoulders. 'Joshua, they are talking about you, listen?'

All four of them listened to the preacher's voice. '…To proclaim good news to the poor. He has sent me to bind up the broken hearted, to proclaim freedom from the captives and release from darkness the prisoner's...'

Looking at Magda with wide eyes, he nodded his head. 'Yes, he is talking about me. I help the poor, I free the little bitty children that the soldiers capture. Should I go up there?'

Gabe whispered in his ear. 'You should do it. You have the soothing voice. Go sooth them Josh.'

'I'm going to do it, I am going to let them know I have come to save them all.' He shouted at the top of his voice whilst punching the air.

Naamah giggled as she watched Joshua pushed his way through the crowd to the preacher.

Climbing up the steps to the podium, Joshua noisily stumbled a couple of times before he reached the platform. The preacher stopped reading the scripture that lay in front of him and looked at Joshua, dishevelled and smelling strongly of alcohol. 'Please, step down. I am addressing my followers. This is not the time to approach me.' He looked down at Joshua in disgust.

Smiling with his eyes half shut, Joshua slowly edged his way in between the wooden pedestal that held the Book of Isaiah and the preacher. Successfully shuffling in-between, he turned around quickly to address the crowd. Holding on to the pedestal to stop him swaying, he began.

'I come in peace.' He shouted as a murmur went through the crowd. 'I am here to be of service to you! If you need to be healed, I can heal. If you need food, I can give it to you, if you have a broken heart, I can fix it.' He said winking at the women at the front. 'I am the person that can grant all your little wishes.'

Hearing Gabe shouting encouraging words in the background, Joshua continued. 'I have been told, I am the messiah, I AM THE ONE. The one that will make this world a better place, the one that can point you all in the right direction, yet you must heed my advice...' Hiccupping, Joshua paused. Placing his hand over his mouth, he felt sick. His head was spinning.

'You're not the messiah, I know you! You are Joseph of Capernaum's son. You sold me a bowl!' A man from the crowd shouted.

Eyes closed, swaying, Joshua smiled lopsidedly. 'But what a good bowl that was.' He said pointing and winking at the man.

'Enough!' The preacher sternly said. 'You have made quite a fool of yourself. Return to your friends and leave.'

'I haven't finished.' Joshua whined at the man. Holding onto the pedestal still, Joshua felt the preacher moving him out of the way. No longer in control of his body, Joshua fell backwards, still holding on to the pedestal, brought it down on top of him, the scripture included.

The crowd gasped and fell silent as the preacher picked up the scripture and tried to move the pedestal off Joshua.

Laid there, the world spinning, vomit flew from Joshua's mouth, all over the preacher's feet. Groaning, Joshua looked at the sick and up at the preacher. Trying to say sorry and explain why he was so drunk, the preacher looked down on him with horror and disgust. Putting his head in his hands, Joshua vowed never to drink as much again, even whilst celebrating.

The crowd now angry, grumbled as they waited for the preacher to instruct them. 'Seize him! Seize him!' The preacher cried as he tried to shake the vomit off his feet. 'Make him pay for his sins.'

Joshua felt himself be picked up and carried, yet the movement made him feel ill again. Throwing up over the people that were carrying him, Joshua felt himself fall to the ground as the crowd dropped him in revulsion. The alcohol running through his veins had helped the numb the pain from the fall, yet Joshua knew he would be suffering tomorrow. The last bought of sickness had made Joshua feel slightly better. His head had stopped spinning, and he was thinking a little more clearly. Deciding to stand up and face the people he got on his hand and knees, yet was kicked back down by a tall, muscular angry man covered in vomit.

'You will die for this.' He grimaced.

Picking him up over his strong shoulders, the crowd surrounding them cheered as Joshua was carried to a cliff edge.

'Are you being serious?' Joshua said out loud 'I didn't think you actually meant you would kill me.' He tried to say to the man as he stood at the cliff edge.

'I always do what I say.' The man replied pushing Joshua up in the air. The man outstretched his arms and pushed Joshua up towards the sky, as he waited for the signal to throw the imbecile, he was holding off the side of the cliff.

Sobering up quickly as he stared at his imminent death, Joshua needed to think and quick.

'If you throw me, you will die also.' He shouted at the man.

The man scoffed and wavered under Joshua's weight. 'You are not the messiah. God will not strike me down.'

'You are right, he will not strike you down, yet if you throw me, I will hold on to your arm and pull you down with me.' Joshua said as he clasped his hand around the man's wrist.

Still dangling above the man's head, Joshua waited for him to speak.

'What if I put you down and kick you off?' The man said.

'That would work.' Joshua answered truthfully.

As the man lowered Joshua down to a standing position, he took his chance. Kicking out at the man so he stumbled backwards, Joshua burst out running along the cliff edge. Parts of the land crumbled away as he ran, bumping its way down to the rocks below. Not stopping to look, Joshua sped on as the crowd followed. Two men ran after him, speeding their way along the edge of the cliff, yet misjudged their footings and fell to the depths below. Again Joshua carried on running, ignoring the shouts behind him.

As he ran, Magda came into view on the cart, worry etched across her beautiful face.

'Start the horse moving, I will jump on.' Joshua screamed as he neared her.

The cart slowly started to move as Joshua launched himself on the back. Pulling himself to the front, the horse lurched forward and ran faster than Joshua had ever seen her run before.
Making their way out of Nazareth, Joshua looked behind him and could see they were not being followed. Blowing out a sigh of relief, he laid his head back and his heavy breathing eased.
Grabbing Magda's hand, he told her she could now slow down.
Seeing a dense wood, Magda guided the horse into it and stopped the cart.
'I really should not be in charge of this horse and cart whilst drunk.' She said smiling at Joshua. 'Yet that was a close one.'
'Stroking her dark silky hair, he looked into her brown eyes. 'Please never let us drink like that again.'
'I promise.' She said kissing his nose.

Laughing as they reminisced the last two weeks on the way back to Mary and Joseph's, Joshua admitted he felt responsible for the two men chasing him and falling to their deaths.
'Why?' Magda asked. 'I understand you were a nuisance and you did vomit over them poor people, yet I find being sentenced to death for vomiting is a bit harsh. The men did not need to follow you, yet they chose to which led to their deaths. I know you do not believe in God Joshua, but I do feel he was looking out for you today. I am not sure anyone else would have been able to talk around that giant man holding you up like you did, nor would anyone be able to run on a cliff edge and not fall like I saw you do. You was not responsible and I do not want to hear another word about it!'
Nodding his head in agreement, Joshua stroked Magda's silky hair. 'Cannot believe we will be back at Marys soon. Do you think Delilah would have sent word about our departure?'
'I think she may have, yet I feel she would have been too ashamed to tell her why.'
Agreeing with Magda, they stayed in companionable silence for the rest of the journey home.
Seeing Mary dashing out of the house as they arrived, always made Joshua smile.
'How have you been Mother?' He asked embracing her as she often did him.
'Good, yet I hear you have been getting into mischief.' She said waggling her finger at him. 'Mother's find out everything. Being

sick on a preachers feet. It is a good job you are the messiah or I would have put you over my knee.' She laughed, clearly not believing a word of what she had been told.

'Come, eat and tell me all about your travels. I suspect you will be busy catching up with your ministry tomorrow.'

Joshua nodded, smiling at Mary as they walked towards the kitchen, into the love and laughter he had grown accustomed to.

A few weeks passed, and Joshua had been busy with his ministry, whilst building a house near the TT pod in his spare time for him and Magda some privacy.

Meeting a tradesman to order more wood for his new home, Joshua saw Peter and Andrew looking rather glum at the side of the Sea of Galilee. After placing his order, Joshua walked up to them both and asked if everything was alright.

'We are fisherman Jesus. Not much chance of us earning a living if there are no fish in the sea and my wife's mother is sick. We need to pay for a healer to see her. I am not sure what my wife would do if her mother died. Then to make matters worse, we have money due to the tax collectors.'

Peter sighed and looked at the floor.

'Listen, I am addressing my followers tomorrow afternoon. Giving a speech on be kind to others and stuff. Can I address them from your boat? It'll stop them from getting too close.'

'Yeah, sure.' Andrew shrugged his shoulders. 'Not like there are any fish for us to catch to take the boat out anyway.'

'I may have something that will help with that. Leave it with me and we'll try it after the sermon. Make sure you keep this to yourself though.' Joshua put his finger to his nose and winked at the two men.

Looking a lot happier, Peter and Andrew agreed.

Whistling as he walked back to the cart, Joshua saw his friend Matthew, a tax collector. What are the chances, Joshua thought to himself. 'Matthew.' He shouted across to him. As Matthew looked across, Joshua waved him over. He liked Matthew, rich and a lot more educated than the rest of the people he knew, but with a heart of gold. He enjoyed his company and could talk to him about outlandish subjects without being laughed at.

'Hello Jesus, great to see you.' Matthew embraced him. 'Congratulations on the wedding. You are one lucky man landing

Mary of Magdalena. She is a true Queen of Galilee to the people here.'

'Is it really that long since I last saw you?' Joshua said stunned. 'We need to meet up more. We'll get something arranged when my house is finished, come round for a meal one night.'

'Yes, that would be lovely. Keep me updated.' Said Matthew.

'Sorry you weren't invited to the wedding, it was just me and Magda. Mary and Joseph were not happy when I told them, neither were Magda's parents. Anyway, the reason I called you over was about Peter and Andrew over there.'

'Ahh, yes, the sons of Jonah.' Matthew nodded.

'They're having a bit of a hard time at the moment, they are not catching any fish to sell, Peters mother-in-law is sick, and their taxes are due. I would help them out, but, between you and me, Magda is expecting a little one, hence the house build.'

Matthew gasped. 'Congratulations again.' He whispered. 'Your secret is safe with me. You know I am huge believer in your work and what you do Jesus. I would love to contribute to your ministry.'

'Contribute how?' Joshua asked.

'Instead of working in your shop, selling your items, I would pay you a wage to spread your word full time.'

'Are you being serious? You would pay me to make the world a better place?'

'Yes I would. I believe in you Jesus. You and Mary of Magdalena are what keeps Capernaum and the surrounding areas alive.'

'I don't know what to say.' Joshua said.

'Do not say anything, accept my offer and I will speak to the sons of Jonah and give them a week's grace.'

'You sir, are a Godsend.' Said Joshua,

Matthew laughed as he walked away shouting. 'No Jesus, you are the God send!'

Returning to Mary's that afternoon, Joshua couldn't stop thinking about Peter's mother-in-law. What if Mary was ill and no-one helped her? Walking to the TT pod he grabbed some pills and his first aid kit. Telling Magda where he was going he explained it was his duty to help as he had the items to heal.

Kissing him as he left, she added. 'This why I married you.'

Peter was surprised when Joshua arrived at his house. Explaining he should be able to help, Peter led him through to where his mother-in-law was laid.

The sheen of sweat glistened off her as she mumbled incoherently. Kneeling by her side, Joshua placed his hand on her forehead, feeling the heat from the fever before his hand touched her skin. Seeing her grey sweaty skin, he knew he needed to act quickly, the pills he had brought would not work fast enough. Pulling out a small syringe from his medication kit, Joshua swiftly injected the contents straight into her veins before anyone could see.

Patting the injection mark with his hand until it faded, Joshua arose, telling Peter and his wife she would be fine in a few minutes.

Packing everything he used back in his bag, he looked around to see her skin turning back to a healthy pink colour.

'Mother?' Peter's wife called out as her mother sat up.

Running his fingers through his hair, Peter looked at Joshua and then his mother-in-law as he watched her stand up.

'Would anyone like some tea?' She asked, as if she had not been near death moments before.

'How?' Peter asked bewildered. 'She... I... My wife...I just cannot believe my eyes!'

'She will be fine now, if she gets ill again, just come and get me. Although I am pretty sure she will be fully recovered.' Instructed Joshua.

'I can't thank you enough.' Peter said, amazement featuring across his face. 'Please, let me buy you a drink at Tobias' Inn. I wish I could offer you more.'

'No need to thank me. I only ask you pass the kindness on in the future, make sure you help anyone in need.' Joshua replied smiling. It felt good being able to help people.

'Of course, but please, let me buy you a drink. I think I need one after what I have just seen.' He smiled at him.

Joshua laughed and nodded his head.

Walking into Tobias' Inn, Joshua marvelled at how busy it was. Wooden tables and chairs were full of men and women, drinking and laughing. The noise of the happiness made Joshua smile as he approached a bar made of stones and wood.

Nodding to acknowledge Peter, the bar man came straight to him.

'How's the mother-in- law Peter?' He asked. 'Samson came in and told me you were all having a rough time of it.'

'Tobias, I need you to pour an extra-large drink of anything this man wants.' He shouted as he slapped Joshua on the back. 'The healer wouldn't come and see the mother-in-law without payment, Jesus here turns up and heals her, just like that.' Peter clicked his fingers. 'She was grey, the way you look just before you die, sweating and mumbling about her dead husband. I honestly thought she was a gonner. Don't ask me how he did it, he is a miracle worker.'

Tobias looked at Joshua. 'Is this true?' He whispered just loud enough so Joshua could hear him over the noisy crowd.

Joshua nodded as Peter answered for him. 'Of course it is true. This man is a saviour and all he asked in payment is for me to help anyone in need.'

Passing him a stone tumbler, Tobias filled it up with wine and leant over. 'I heard you can also turn water into the finest wine anyone has ever tasted.'

'Oh I don't know about that.' Joshua replied nervously as he sipped his drink.

'Can I ask you something?'

Joshua nodded.

'My wife burnt her hands on a fire when cooking our evening meal a couple of weeks back. No healer can help. I will pay anything to stop my wife's pain. Would you look?'

'Of course, when would like to me to come and see her?' Joshua asked.

'I will go get her now.' Replied Tobias. Joshua watched as Tobias rushed out from behind the bar and climbed the stairs at the back of the inn, two at a time. Unlocking one of the doors at the top, he hurried in.

Peter leant over to Joshua as they waited for Tobias to return. 'Her hands are bad Jesus. Tobias blames himself. He fell asleep while he was supposed to be watching the children. The children went searching for their mother and found her outside cooking on an open fire. She had her back turned to them. They decided to sneak up on her and give her a big cuddle, however, when they did it pushed her forward and her two hands went straight into the fire. The screams could be heard from miles around.'

Joshua watched as Tobias helped a woman down the inn steps. She slowly moved down the stairs, pain etched across her face, her hands wrapped in sheets, sodden with a mixture of blood and pus.

Shouting at the customers on the table nearest to the stairs, Tobias moved to sit his wife down, as the full inn fell into silence.

Joshua walked towards Tobias' wife and sat opposite her. Gesturing to give him her hands, she slowly lifted her arms and placed the saturated sheets on the table. Her brow furrowed as she closed her eyes to breathe through the pain.

Joshua, moved around to sit next to Tobias' wife and whispered into her ear. 'I am going to give you something for the pain and then look at your wounds.

Nodding at him, tears running down her weary face, he reached into his bag and pulled out a syringe already full of numbing agent. Injecting both arms, he whispered into her ear again. 'Do not be afraid, your hands will feel numb but just for tonight.'

Turning she smiled at him and whispered back. 'The pain, it has disappeared, thank you.'

Looking at her tired face, he talked to her whilst he undid the home made bandages.

The burns were bad, yet nothing he could not sort. Pulling out a cream and some artificial skin, Joshua got to work fixing the woman's hands.

Tobias stood guard at the table, ordering anyone that came near to gawp at his wife was barred from his inn.

Finishing, Joshua instructed Tobias and his wife to keep the new bandages dry for three days, then to remove and the hands should be back to normal. Any problems to get Peter to fetch him.

Tobias' wife stood up, tears streaming down her face. 'I can never thank you enough, I am free from pain. Please, tell me, what coins we need to give you.'

Joshua smiled at her. 'The happiness I see on your face right now is the only payment I need.'

Packing up, Peter came up to him. 'Jesus, there is someone else asking if you can help them.'

Sitting back down, Jesus asked Tobias if he could use this table to help another person in need.

Patting him on the back, Tobias told Joshua he could stay there all month if he wanted and signalled to his staff to bring Joshua a drink.

Word spread and many turned up to ask Joshua for help. Not able to turn anyone away, he stayed at Tobias' Inn most of the night, healing the ones he could and asking others to come back to the Inn tomorrow morning, if he needed different medication.

Worn out he headed home to Magda. Falling on his bed, he was thoroughly exhausted, yet he fell asleep with a smile on his face, knowing he had made the world just that little bit better.

After he saw the people he could not help the night before, Joshua returned to the Sea of Galilee. Checking the pocket inside his belt, he could feel the smooth metallic disc he had promised to bring. Walking towards Peter and Andrews's boat, Joshua could see a crowd had already formed. Moving his way through the crowd, a scarf covering his face as to keep him incognito, he heard Peter's voice ring out.
'Jesus will be delivering a speech from THIS boat today.' He bellowed. 'Make sure you come quick as places near the front are filling up fast.'
Joshua chuckled as he climbed onto the boat and walked towards Andrew. 'What's all this about?' He asked him, pointing towards Peter.
'There was only a few people about, Peter said he was going to drum up some new members for you. He's been shouting for the last 20 minutes. People are getting excited!' Andrew replied laughing.
Patting him on his back, Joshua crossed the boat, pulled off his scarf and put his arm around Peter. 'You've done a great job. I have never seen so many people here.' He whispered into his ear.
'The least I can do after what I saw you do last night.' Peter replied smiling.
Joshua's speech went well, addressing the crowd, he told a story from his world. Changing the names of Matriat's and Servian's to Romans and Galileans, he spoke about a Servian child, dirty, starving and tortured by the Matriat soldiers. The child laid by the side of the road, near death, bleeding. He asked the crowd 'Would you stop and save the child?'
The crowd murmured no, there was no point, the child was almost dead. He told the crowd, his Father picked the child up and brought him home. He nursed the child back to health, and kept him hidden. All the while knowing if he was caught by the Matriats, they would both be sentenced to death. That child grew strong. His Father began to teach him, to read and write and the child took it all in, the child grew stronger more intelligent. That child ended up a doctor.

'That now grown up child told me, he saved others, just like he was saved. A small act of compassion, turned into not saving not just one human, but many. Help humanity, spread the kindness.' Joshua ended with cheers from the crowd.

Coins and flowers were thrown at him as the crowd chanted 'Jesus, Jesus, Jesus.'

Thanking, smiling and waving he told the crowd he must go, yet to come back tomorrow and he will speak once more.

The crowd started to climb into other boats, trying to get to Joshua, shouting what acts of kindness they had already done.

'Peter, we need to leave.' Joshua said, looking at the crowd growing restless. 'Remember, spread the kindness.' He shouted at the crowd, hoping to calm them down slightly.

Joshua pulled a horrified face at Andrew, while he laughed at him. 'How do you do it Jesus, you seem to send everyone crazy.' He chuckled as he helped Peter steer the boat out into the sea.

As they sailed through the waters, Joshua looked back. There were still a few boats that were following them. Directing Peter into different waters to where they normally fished, he looked back. The boats that followed, had now stopped barring one. Satisfied, they were safe he told Peter to anchor the boat.

Kneeling down on the deck, he gestured to Peter and Andrew to do the same. Forming a circle, Joshua pulled the out the small metallic gadget and placed it in the middle of them.

'What I am about to show you, you must not tell anyone or I will never help you again.' He declared.

The two men nodded.

'This.' Joshua said as he showed them the gadget. 'Is from another place.' Peter and Andrew's eyes grew wide as they looked at the metallic disc.

'Is it a pebble?' Andrew whispered.

'Yes, it is a kind of pebble.' Joshua replied. 'This pebble, fish love. When I drop this into the water, the fish will swim as fast as they can to come and find this shiny pebble.' He tried to explain.

The men nodded in awe at Joshua.

Checking to see how far away the other boat was, Joshua knew they had time to fish before the boat reached them.

'Tell me when you are ready with your nets and I will drop it into the water.'

The two men scrambled and proceeded to get their nets ready and throw them into the sea.

Joshua silently thanked Richard for his careful preparation. He had literally thought of everything. Scoffing at him when he had presented him with the fish magnet, Richard had said it made him sleep better knowing Joshua would be ready for any eventuality.

The fish magnet worked on a releasing a chemical smell to attract the fish, acting like tasty food. Once the fish go to eat it, it shocks the fish with a burst of electricity, killing it immediately. The fish magnet was activated by water, thus came with a thin wire to pull out when enough fish had been caught. Joshua wrapped the thin wire around his wrist.

'Ready.' Shouted Peter as he threw the nets into the sea.

Throwing the magnet after them, Joshua counted to ten and then asked them to pull up the nets.

Struggling to pull them up, Joshua quickly retracted the magnet and ran to help. Heaving the weighty nets, Joshua smiled to himself, knowing the magnet had done its duty.

The net inched up little by little and as it rose, the shiny scales of the fish glinted in the late afternoon sun.

As Andrew spotted how full the nets were, tears sprang into his eyes. Heaving the net onto the boat, the ropes groaned under the weight of the fish. Not able to hold the net any longer, Andrew and Peter let go of the rope as fish spilled out over the deck. The huge quantity of fish that swirled onto the deck, knocked the men over and they laughed as they were swept to the other side of the boat. Still laughing in astonishment, Joshua pointed out that they still had a full net on the other side.

Noticing the other boat sail nearer, Peter shouted out to it. Turning around excitedly to Andrew and Joshua, he informed them it was his brothers James and John.

Waving them over to collect the other net. Peter fell to Joshua's feet.

'I can never thank you enough for what you have done. Anything you ever want, come straight to me. I will do anything you ask.'

Pulling him up, Joshua hugged him. 'It is just nice to see you happy.' He smiled.

Chapter 24
Rachel - The Mother

Picking her up, Yuri softly carried Rachel into the living room of the villa and laid her on the leather couch. Grabbing the covers off her bed, he covered her over. Placing a pillow gently under her head, he was at loss of what to do. He couldn't bare seeing Rachel sobbing like this, yet he knew no words would bring her comfort.
Grabbing a box of tissues, he passed them to Rachel. Checking over his shoulder as he walked into the kitchen, he was glad it was an open plan area. Making them both a sweet tea he placed Rachel's next to her, still unsure what to say. Yuri knew about Rachel's childhood, what that woman did to her.
'You can leave if you want.' Rachel said, her sobbing subsiding.
'I need some time on my own.'
'I am not leaving you like this, and with …' He trailed off.
'You can say it. Your Mother.' She spat.
Yuri sat at the dining table in silence and sipped his tea. He thought he had been trained for anything, yet this proved he had not.
Rachel broke the silence and spoke first. 'Sorry for snapping Yuri.' She said quietly as his phone started to ring. Looking at the caller ID, Yuri frowned and then put it away.
'Answer it. It might be important.' Rachel said.
'It was my Father. I am not sure if you want him to know about this. About what was in the package.'
'I'm not sure about anything anymore Yuri. All I know is I wish I had left her there, in Caroline's torture chamber.'
Walking across to Rachel laid on the couch, he knelt down to face her. 'It's not what you're going to want to hear right now Rach, but you've got to snap out of this pity party you're having right now.'

Rachel sat up in surprise, distracted her from crying. 'But ...I'm not, I'm...' Rachel stuttered.

'You are. Look at you. You was abused, neglected by that woman in the next room, we know this.' Yuri paused as Rachel's face grew angry.

'This is exactly what Caroline wanted, she knew exactly what she was doing. She knows you too well Rach. She wants you knocked down, pliable, someone she can mould into what she wants. That woman in there is not your Mother, she has never been a Mother, she is reminder of what you got through to make it this far. Do not let the past damage your future.'

Seeing the realisation on Rachel's face Yuri knew his tough love was working. 'Let's use this against Caroline. We can speak to that woman, ask her how she got here and what she knows.' He said, his voice growing softer.

'I know. It was just a bit of a shock, seeing her after all these years, and seeing her like that.'

'It's bound to be Rach, don't let it define you.'

'I thought she was dead. I got told she was dead.' Rachel said, the tears threatening to start again.

Yuri turned round and looked at her puzzled. 'Who told you she was dead?' He asked.

'About six months ago, police showed up on my doorstep and told me they had found a body. It was too decomposed for anyone to ID visually. They asked my permission for someone to come and take blood tests for DNA. I agreed and was told it was a match.'

Yuri sighed, stood up and walked to the patio doors. 'Did you tell anyone about this?' He asked as he looked at the evening sky.

'No-one, I leave my past in the past where it belongs.'

'Your mothers DNA would have been on file already due to her drug abuse. I do not think they were real police.'

'Are you saying it was Caroline?' Rachel asked suddenly feeling foolish. She should have asked for ID or demanded to see the body, yet at the time, she was in disbelief. She had not spoken or been in contact with anyone from Trinity Estate, including her mother, since she was sixteen.

'Maybe.' Yuri gravely replied.

'Does she know about my past? Does the full committee have access to my information?'

Yuri nodded at Rachel and returned to looking outside. A shadow caught his eye. Moving slightly to the side so the curtain concealed him, Yuri pulled out some glasses from his inside pocket. Tapping the side of the glasses, his sight zoomed in to where he saw the shadow. A man, dressed all in black was pacing up and down, holding a gun.

'Rach. Do not make a sound. I am going to turn the light off.' He whispered as he slowly moved back to the light switch.

'Why?' She whispered back.

'I think the house is being guarded. Wait here.' Yuri silently moved towards the bedrooms, walking down the corridor he slipped out of the window.

Rachel pushed the bed covers off her. Her heart hammering out of her chest she stood up, too nervous to stay sat down.

Hearing a groan come from the bedroom, Rachel scowled towards the door. Her sadness had left, replaced by a burning anger and loathing of what was contained in that room.

Pacing up and down, she tried to distract herself, yet the moans and groans coming from that wretched woman were exasperating.

Walking towards the patio doors, Rachel looked outside at the evening sky. Yuri was nowhere to be seen. The moon, situated on the other side of the villa and lack of street lamps gave no assistance to the landscape at this time of night. The desolate wild grassy hill was covered in darkness, with only the road, miles away at the bottom, shedding any light in the area. Hearing the soft rustle of the breeze through the window, gave Rachel chills. Anything could be out there.

The groans got louder.

'SHUT UP!' Rachel screamed at the door, the hatred building inside her.

The whimpering continued. Walking to the bedroom, Rachel hammered on the door. 'I SAID, SHUT UP!' She screamed once again as the moaning continued.

Not being able to abstain any longer, Rachel wrenched the door open.

The skin and bones that laid on the bed, disgusted her now. Once where there was pity, was replaced with a seething hatred of what this repulsive human had put her through.

The woman's eyes focused on Rachel. 'Chantelle.' She whispered.

'What do you want? Why are you here?' Rachel spat at her.

'I need to talk to you, to whisper in your ear. I am in so much pain.' The woman cried.

Rachel took a step forward. 'I can hear you from here.'

'Please come closer.'

Rachel inched closer and bent over the bed. The stench from the woman's breath made Rachel heave inwardly. Turning her head away from the rancid smell, she let the woman whisper into her ear.

'Caroline said you had it here. Can I have it please?'

'Had what here?' Rachel said.

'She said you would be pleased to see me. That you have missed me. She said you had a present for me.'

Standing up and looking at the grotesque woman in of front her, Rachel's patience was running out. 'I have no idea what you are talking about Lynn. Spit it out.'

The woman laughed. 'Still call your old mum Lynn.' She said, the laugh turning into a hacking cough. Motioning her to come close again, Lynn whispered into her ear. 'Caroline said it was hidden in the fridge. You had brought it just for me, wrapped it up like chocolate.' The gammy woman's wrinkly mouth, moved into a smile, showing her decaying blackened teeth.

Storming out of the bedroom, Rachel headed to the kitchen. Opening the fridge door, she rifled through it until she spotted a metal box. The words *Chocolate for Chantelle*, embossed on the top. Before she opened it, Rachel knew what was inside.

She had carried a tin like this around for years. Given to her by a neighbour when she was six, it was originally full of chocolate. She remembered the feeling she had when she opened it, full to the brim of small, colourful, individually wrapped parcels. Excitedly as she unwrapped the first one, she had almost cried with happiness as the sweet flavour alighted her taste buds as she popped it into her mouth.

Sat in her safe place, in the cupboard under the stairs, the door had opened and Rachel had been yanked out by Lynn. Her smokers laugh still rang through Rachel's ears as she ridiculed her daughter in front of the others shooting up in the house. 'Chantelle's box, Chantelle's box.' She sang. 'I know many who would like Chantelle's box.' She laughed as she grabbed the tin whilst Rachel cowered. Empting the contents onto the floor, Lynn grabbed money from a dirty mattress and put it in the tin.

'Go.' She screamed as Rachel ran out the door and to her mother's dealer. Swopping the money for a hit, tears ran down her face as she walked back knowing the chocolate would be long gone, given out to her mother's 'friends'.

The tin provided some happiness for Rachel. Once she heard it rattle with money, she knew she would be left alone for a couple of hours while the others got high. She had some reprieve to go and find food, or sleep without being beaten or abused, yet the sight of it still turned her stomach. She was transported back to the house, back to her childhood, back to the life she wanted to forget. This tin seemed smaller, yet the writing looked the same, but faded. Stroking the lettering on the top, tears sprang into her eyes again. Roughly wiping them away after promising she would not cry over her past anymore, she opened the box.

A lighter, spoon, needle, syringe and heroin lay in the box. Dropping it on the floor, Rachel bent over and retched into the kitchen sink. Caroline had brought drugs into her villa. She knew exactly what she was doing. Yuri's voice echoed in her mind. Only moments earlier had he said Caroline was playing her.

Anger pulsed through her veins as she stood up. Wiping the sick from her mouth she marched into the bedroom where Lynn still lay with a smile on her face. Breathing heavily, Rachel's chest moved up and down as the resentment and rage flowed through her. She wouldn't crumble like Caroline wanted!

'Did you get it?' Lynn whispered. 'Chantelle's box? I still had it, after all these years. Surprise!'

Looking at Lynn laying there, her eyes shining, waiting for gratitude for bringing that shit into her life again, caused all the hurt, betrayal and anger inside Rachel to unleash.

Grabbing the pillow from under Lynn's head she put it over her face. Her weakened body no match against the strength coming from Rachel.

'I should have done this a long time ago, bitch.' Rachel spat as the struggling started to subside.

Holding the pillow down with all her strength, tears running down her face from the emotions surging through her body, Rachel noticed the wetness spreading across the sheets covering the frail body. Seeing Lynn soil herself, disgusted Rachel and made her grasp onto the pillow more tightly. Her knuckles turning white the longer she clung onto it.

Rachel felt her body suddenly lurch backwards, away from Lynn. Still clinging on to the pillow, Rachel watched as the old woman gasped for breath. Fighting to get back to her, to finish the job, yet strong arms held her back as she heard a soothing voice whisper into her ear.

'She's not worth it.' Nick murmured as he clung on to Rachel.

Chapter 25
Joshua - Confirming the Twelve

Turing the fish over on the outdoor fire, Joshua felt contented. His ministry was going great, spreading the word far and wide. He was helping the poor, the sick and the needy and their house was complete.
He looked over to where Magda was sat with the other women, cradling their week-old baby girl, Prisca.
'Heard you was up all-night Josh, and not in the good way.' Judas laughed, slapping Joshua's on the back.
'Tell me about it, Prisca can be loud when she wants to be!' Joshua replied, laughing, whilst trying to bat Judas' hand away from stealing the fish.
'You'll give us a bad name.' James joined them, passing Joshua a goblet of wine. 'You took the baby out didn't you? To give Magda some rest?'
'Prisca, the gorgeous baby she is, has not slept properly since she was born. Poor Magda has not had a wink of sleep. I couldn't just stand by and watch while Magda cried with the baby.'
'I know but going hiking up the mountains was a bit much!' Judas said. 'That's what women are made for, to look after the children.'
Joshua shot Judas a warning look. 'Too far Judas. Magda does more for the ministry than you will ever know.'
'You thought about that?' Asked James.
'About what?' Judas probed, grabbing some more of the fish.
'Word has spread, and I mean really spread about what I have been doing and the stories I tell. I have been invited to attend many cities to deliver speeches, yet now we have Prisca, Magda will not be by my side. It's just not feasible to continue completing it on my own.'

'You won't have had time to think about that with the new baby and walking through the mountains in the dark.' Judas laughed. 'Gluten for punishment you.' He said, swigging the last of his wine. 'You got anymore?' He asked Joshua holding up his wooden goblet.

Ignoring Judas, Joshua carried on talking to James. 'Walking up the mountains with Prisca helped me more than it did her. It gave me a lot of time to think. I have some really great friends that have been a fantastic support with everything.' Joshua raised his eyebrows to James, indicating Judas did not know about the TT pod.

James smiled and nodded, signalling to Joshua to carry on.

'Matthew is supporting the ministry, yet we are receiving a lot of donations as well. I reckon I would be able to pay my most supportive friends to carry on my work. I can teach them the way I deliver my speeches, give them stories and they can travel on my behalf, well that is if they want to do it. I'm going to ask everyone individually tonight.'

'I'll do it.' Judas interjected. 'You want me, I am your man!'

'I'll speak to you in more detail tonight, Judas. Here, have this wine.' Joshua said rolling his eyes at Judas, and passing him the goblet of wine James had brought him.

Seeing Matthew arrive, Joshua waved him over. 'Matthew, so glad you could make it. You are looking really well.'

'Thank you Jesus. I am delighted to have been asked to celebrate the birth of your daughter, yet I also have some bad news.' Joshua passed the cooking of the fish to James, as Matthew pulled Joshua to one side. 'Have you heard about John? John the Baptist?' Matthew asked.

'I heard he got imprisoned for shouting his mouth off about King Herod's marriage a while back, yet I thought they had let him go.' Joshua answered.

'That is true, yet they captured him again. King Herod threw a party for his birthday. A lot of wine was consumed, it all got a bit messy and he ended up getting far too close to his step daughter! Apparently, she stood on a table, danced, and started taking her clothes off one piece at a time, all the while staring straight at King Herod. The guests, including her own Mother, Heriodia was cheering her on! Anyway, after her dance that ended up with her naked and sat on King Herod's knee.' Matthew looked at Joshua's eyes wide open. 'I know, her own step father!' He acknowledged as Joshua let him continue, mouth agape with this news. 'King Herod asked what kind of payment she would be looking for if they were to slip away somewhere more private, if you know what I mean.' Matthew said wiggling his eye brows up and down. 'Without hesitation, his step daughter asked for Johns head on a platter! How sick can you get? Dancing naked for your step-father and asking for John the Baptist's head on a platter in return, you just couldn't make it up. Apparently Heriodia had planned it with her daughter as she was still seething about John telling everyone their marriage was a sham. Let's face it, it is a bit weird that she was married to his brother before him!' Matthew exclaimed.

Joshua, sat on the grass while he took in what Matthew had just told him. 'After what he did to me… well, I never spoke to him again. Neither did Mary, yet I wouldn't have wished beheading on him. I wouldn't wish that on anyone.' Joshua looked up at Matthew. 'Does Mary know?'

'I'm not sure.' Matthew said as he sat down next to Joshua. 'I've just heard now before I came here, from one of Herod's Guards. He said that Herod did exactly what his step-daughter wanted him to and put Johns head on a platter, even garnished it with tomatoes and lettuce.'

'Sick bastards.' Joshua said shaking his head. 'Just because he is the king, he can't go round beheading people because he wants a bit of his step daughter.'

'Do you want me to speak with Mary?' Matthew offered.

'No its fine, I'll speak to her in a minute. I just can't believe it.'

'I know me either.' Matthew said shaking his head. 'Anyway, how's Fatherhood?' He asked, trying to get them onto a happier subject.

'Prisca is beautiful, takes after her mother. Although I am not sure where she gets the loud mouth from!' They both laughed.

Interrupting them Judas held up his empty goblet of wine. 'Is that seriously what you wanted to talk to Jesus about in private, his baby? I cannot listen to this baby talk anymore. Where is the wine?' Judas asked.

Joshua pointed him in the direction of the big vase of wine with a collection of people around it. James followed him laughing and shaking his head.

'While I have you alone, there was another reason why I asked you here tonight.' Joshua said to Matthew and explained he wanted him to be part of his ministry. He thanked him for being a generous benefactor, yet knew he could provide more if he concentrated on the ministry instead of just donating money.

A tear came into Matthews's eye. 'Are you sure you trust me? Am I good enough to help you?' He said in astonishment.

'Matthew you have a heart of gold, I have shown and told you about the TT pod and all the pebbles I brought with me, yet you have not mentioned a word of it to anyone. You have shown your worth on more than one occasion, I would be honoured if you stood by my side on this.'

'It is my honour Jesus.' Matthew said, bowing his head slightly to Joshua. 'Have you asked anyone else?'

'Not yet, but when I do, I will tell them to come and see you.'

Seeing Mary near the vase of wine, Joshua stood up. 'Sorry Matthew, I need to go and see Mary before anyone else tells her. I am unsure of how she will react.'

'Understandable Jesus. You go. I will be waiting for you when you need me.' Matthew replied with a big smile on his face.

Joshua ran up to the people stood around the huge vase of wine and asked Mary to come into the house with him.

Sitting her down, he explained what Matthew had told him about John. Putting her hands to her mouth, Mary sat there in shock.

'Did we do this?' She finally whispered. 'Did we force him to another city because we cut him out of our family?'

'John did this to himself. He should know he is not above the law and certainly not able to criticise King Herod in public. Do not blame yourself.'

Patting his hand she nodded. 'I need leave, to go and see Johns Mother.'

'Understandable.' Joshua replied.

Leaving Mary to gather her things and get Joseph, Joshua walked outside to attend to the others that were turning up to celebrate the birth of Prisca.

The warmth of the afternoon heat was perfect for this occasion. He looked across at James who had returned to cook more fish on the outdoor stove. He saw Damaris handing out bread next to him.

Many people had turned up to celebrate and Joshua had ensured he had plenty of wine ready for the celebrations, yet before everyone had a bit too much to drink, he needed to speak to the ones he was closest to.

The night had drawn to a happy end. Magda put the sleeping Prisca down in her basket and turned around to her husband. Wrapping her arms around him she asked who had accepted the job offer.

'Twelve. Which I am extremely happy about, considering I only asked fifteen.' He replied.

'Who accepted?' Magda asked.

'James and John, the sons of Zebedee. Thomas, Bartholomew, Philip and Judas.'

Magda rolled her eyes at Judas' name.

'I know you think he is a waste of space and he does crave attention, yet he is a great distraction at times. When the pressure gets to us, Judas is the one that always brings us back up again. He is reliable, dependable and has always been loyal to all of us.' Pulling Magda closer, he kissed her head. 'I know you find him annoying, but underneath all the bravado, he has a heart of gold.'

'On your head be it.' Magda said, pushing away from Joshua and clearing up the goblets. 'I do not trust Judas, he is loud, brash and I know he has taken items from Mary's house before, do you really think he would keep the TT pod to himself?' She asked.

'He saw me use the pebbles at James' wedding and did not tell anyone.'

'That you know of.' Interrupted Magda.

'I am sure Magda dearest, if Judas would have told someone, they would have come and begged for my pebbles themselves.' He said grabbing her and swinging her around until she squealed.

'Joshua, stop, you'll wake Prisca.'

Laughing Joshua put her down.

'Did you ask Matthew?' Magda said.

'He was the first one I asked, and he leapt at the chance.' Joshua smiled

'I like Matthew.' Magda agreed.

'Me too. Jude, James ...' Joshua continued.

'Your brother James?' Magda enquired.

'No, Matthews's brother. I asked my brother James but he didn't want to commit just yet. He invited us to stay with him if things get out of hand here, however, James mentioned they are wanting a little one like Prisca.'

'Aww how lovely. Their child would be beautiful.' Magda cooed.

'It would, although I did ask my brother Simon the Zealot and he said yes. And Andrew and Peter. Did you know Peter's name is actually Simon?' Joshua said laughing as Magda shook her head. 'Apparently when they were younger, my brother Simon and Peter, were always getting mixed up with having the same name and looking very similar so his Mother decided to change his name and started calling him Peter and it has stuck ever since!'

Joshua let go of Magda and sat down next to the basket that Prisca lay in. Staring at her long dark eyelashes and smooth skin as she slept, Joshua had never felt as happy as he did right then.

Magda placed her hand on his shoulder. 'She is so precious isn't she?' She whispered.

Nodding in agreement as he still looked at Prisca, he was determined to change the world one bit at a time so Prisca, and the generations ahead of her, will no longer have to live in fear.

Chapter 26
Rachel - The Landing Site

Placing the broach on the lapel of her suit, Yuri stood back. 'Are you sure you are OK to do this?' He asked.//
Nodding she grabbed her folder and bag. 'It is the only way.'//
Getting ready to go to the landing site and see the TT pod, Rachel felt strangely calm and determined. The last twenty-four hours had proved, she could get through anything.

After Nick had pulled her off Lynn, her anger turned into hurt. Sobbing into his shoulder he had manoeuvred her out of the bedroom and onto the black leather couch. Softly stroking her hair as she cried, he let her sob her heart out on his shoulder before addressing the issue.//
Exhausted and cried out, she looked up at Nick. His heart contracted at her tear stained face and sadness in her eyes, wishing he could take the pain away.//
'Sorry Nick.' She said as she pulled away from his shoulder and grabbed a tissue to wipe her eyes.//
'What for?' He asked.//
'For this.' Rachel said indicating the tears.//
'Never apologise for crying, it is the bodies way of coping with emotions.' Nick informed her.//
Rachel scoffed. 'You never cry.'//
'Ask Yuri, I cry often. It is done in private. And it is a scientific fact, crying out your emotions is the best way to keep a level head.' Standing up and stretching, Nick looked at Rachel and smiled. 'It has not been the best first Christmas.' He joked, causing Rachel to laugh a little. She supposed she did feel a little better.

Yuri came through to them both and advised he had a colleague arriving tomorrow morning. She was going to sneak in through housekeeping and look after Lynn. Any information she extracted, she would pass to Nick directly. Rachel would not have anything else to do with Lynn if she did not want to. Standing up, Rachel headed to the fridge to get a bottle of water and noticed the drug paraphernalia and her childhood tin box had been removed. Offering Nick and Yuri one, they both shook their heads.

Listening as Yuri informed Nick, he had spotted eight men patrolling the area surrounding the villa, Rachel presumed they would be feeding back all her movements' to Caroline.

Yuri advised Nick he was going to stay the evening and Nick agreed, telling them both he would call tomorrow with a plan of action before they left for Israel the following day.

Checking all windows were locked and shut, Yuri had taken to sleeping on the floor next to Rachel, a gun on his chest.

After a fitful night's sleep, Rachel and Yuri went through the plan with Nick via a secured telephone line.

Rachel was to go to the landing site as planned, wearing the broach. Nick would have someone infiltrating the location Rachel was at, sending Caroline the wrong signal and hopefully blocking the visual.

At all times, Rachel would have protection, she may not see them, yet they would be there, Special Forces, people Nick trusted with his life. Yuri would be her driver as usual to prevent any suspicions.

Taking a long breath in, Rachel looked out of the patio doors, it was going to be a long day. The excitement of going to see the landing site, marred with the thought of Caroline watching her every move was making Rachel anxious.

'See you outside in 30 minutes.' He winked at her.

Giving him a little wave, she waited until he was clear out of site before removing the cover off the broach.

Her phone rang. Looking at the caller ID, she saw it was Caroline.

'Morning Caroline.' Rachel said confidently.

'Good Morning Rachel, you never thanked me for your present.' Caroline mocked.

'What present?' Rachel asked.

'The package.' Caroline replied, slightly annoyed.

'Oh, yes, thank you. The woman is doing well.'

'The woman?' Caroline probed.

'I think she said her name was Linda or something but she is so weak, I am just letting her get well before I talk to her.' Rachel said cheerfully whilst gritting her teeth. Closing her eyes, she regained control. She needed to make Caroline believe, she had no idea who was in the package.

'Hmm' Caroline said, clearly annoyed. 'Well I wanted to invite you for dinner tomorrow evening after your little excursion.'

'I'll still be in Israel Caroline.'

'So will I. I'll send you the details. Wear something nice. We will be entertaining.' She replied before promptly ending the phone call.

Rachel frowned at the phone as she moved it away from her head. Why would Caroline need her to entertain anyone?

Checking her watch, she had ten minutes before Yuri came in the car. She was glad he had arranged a colleague to look after Lynn, not because she wanted her to get well, but because it stopped her from going in there and finishing off the job.

Landing in Haifa, after flying in the company's own light aircraft, Rachel was whisked through security with Yuri. A car was waiting for them outside. Unsure if the broach was sending her location and a visual, Yuri and Rachel kept conversation light.

'Be just over an hour before we get there Miss Nichols, would you like any music on.' Yuri asked.

Smiling at his professionalism, Rachel replied. 'No thank you Yuri. I have work to do.'

Travelling in silence, Rachel went through the details she had been given. The place it all began.

Scrolling through the information on the tablet, she still had doubts that their founding Father of S.U.S. Industries was Jesus. It sounded ludicrous. Nick and Sandra had been adamant she needed to go and see the landing sight. 'Seeing is believing.' Sandra's voice echoed through her head, though she is not sure what more information the TT pod could give her. She had spent hours reading through the S.U.S. Industries version of the New Testament and was positive she knew all there was to know about Joshua and V.E.L.U.S.

Reading through, she envied Joshua. Landing in unknown territory, he was taken in by his adoptive mother Mary, found a wife and entrusted the secrecy of the TT pod and the powers he brought with him in his twelve best friends. It all sounded so simple. Nothing like her life.

Yuri's voice interrupted her thoughts. 'Miss Nichols, we will be arriving at the guesthouse shortly. I will accompany you to your room when you arrive with your luggage.'

'Thank you Yuri.'

Rachel had a swift look at her itinerary. Andreas will be meeting her in the dining area of the place she was staying at 12.30pm for lunch, she had around an hour to herself.

Getting out of the car, Rachel looked around at the guest house. Set near the Sea of Galilee, the place was stunning. Made from grey stones, edged with beige, the guest house overlooked the water with the mountains behind. Rachel walked around the building marvelling at its uniqueness. Whilst fully modern, the building still kept an historic edge with its huge arched windows. Wandering back towards Yuri, Rachel passed the patio area. High raised stone planters featured in the mosaic styled, vast courtyard. Wooden tables and chairs dotted about, keeping conversations private, but still in view of the striking building.

Yuri led her to a room, opening it with a key he already had and passed it to her.

Walking inside, Rachel looked around. The room was sparse but had everything she needed. Two single beds, a wardrobe, desk and attached bathroom. Tea, coffee and a kettle sat on the desk. Pulling her luggage into the room, Yuri nodded at her and left.

Taking off her suit jacket, Rachel hung it up in the wardrobe, picked up her phone and walked out of the room. Yuri was leant against the wall to her right.

'You ok?' He whispered.

Nodding her head, she looked at Yuri. 'I'm a little nervous about what Caroline is seeing, yet I am looking forward to seeing where it all began.'

A huge grin spread across Yuri's face. 'You will love it.'

'Before I meet Andreas, I'm going to sit outside and just have a few minutes to myself. It's been a crazy few days.' She smiled.

Yuri laughed. 'I'm glad you are OK though. There are very few people that would be able to act normal after what you have been through. You're made of strong stuff Rach.' He said putting his hands on her shoulders. 'I'm proud of you.' He added seriously. 'And I am only a button away.' Nodding at her bracelet.

Rachel's phone rang. Caroline flashed up on the caller ID. 'At least we know she is watching.' She said to Yuri as she went back into the room. 'Caroline Hi. I have just arrived and got into my room.'

'Yes you have and where is your broach?'

'On my jacket, ohhh.' Rachel hoped she sounded convincing. 'I did not want to crease it before my lunch with Andreas.'

'Get it on.' Caroline hissed. 'Do not push me if I think you cannot be trusted.'

The phone went dead.

Rachel got the jacket out of the wardrobe, not sure what else Caroline could do. She had no friends or family that she could threaten her with.

Putting the jacket on, Rachel's phone alerted her to a message.

Watching the video she had just been sent, Rachel's hand went to her mouth. Two children looking around five and six years old, dirty and thin huddled together in the corner of a damp and dark room, the camera the only source of light. The look of desperation in their eyes as they tried to block the light with their tiny arms. A whip could be seen on the edge of the video, held by Caroline's bony hand. Smacking the whip on the dirty stone ground, the children huddled together even closer, crying in fear.

Caroline's voice echoed out on the video. 'Last chance Rachel. Anymore mistakes and these are taken to the room your mother was in. You know it was your mother inside the package. Remember I am always watching!' She hissed before the video stopped.

Closing her eyes, Rachel breathed through the nausea that was now rippling across her body. Caroline seemed to know everything about Rachel, her weak spots, even what she was thinking, yet how did she know about her mother.

Her phone rang. 'The deals off Caroline.' Rachel answered, not letting Caroline speak. 'You won't use the TT pods energy to help the world, you'll be using it for yourself.' Grabbing the broach and tossing it to the other side of the room, Rachel heard Caroline laugh.

'Has the penny finally dropped? I thought you were smarter than this Rachel, I thought you would have already known why I wanted it. I thought someone as bright and intelligent as you would have done her research on my company and the sectors we are currently going in, yet you have been distracted just lately haven't you?' Caroline mocked.

'I don't have to listen to this. It is about time I alerted Nick to your plans.' Rachel said as she was about to end the call.

'I'm telling Nick.' Caroline mocked her in a high pitched voice. 'I wouldn't do that if I were you.' She trilled, her voice growing excited.

Rachel knew she should just end the call, yet something made her stay on the line.

'Do you recognise those two little angels in the video I sent?'

'Why should I?' Rachel said trying to sound disinterested.

'Well I am shocked Rachel, how do you not know your own brother and sister.' Caroline gleefully enlightened her.

'What?' Rachel whispered. 'I do not have any siblings.'

'Well maybe not full siblings, but born from the same mother, you and those little children are definitely related. They are so good, always do what I tell them.' Caroline cackled.

Rachel's blood ran cold as she sat on the edge of the bed. 'I don't believe you.' She whispered into the phone.

'Ask your mother. Anyway Rachel you should be thanking me. I saved them from the same life you had at that age. They have the rats to play with and eat.'

Caroline was too happy to be lying.

Anger blew up inside Rachel. 'You bitch! Where are they?' She spat.

'That's more like it!' Caroline sneered. 'I may deliver them when you return from Israel, dependant on how good of a job you do. No more mistakes Rachel, remember I see everything.' The phone went dead.

Going back to the messages, the video had disappeared. Standing up, Rachel paced up and down the floor. The revelation going over and over in her mind, picturing them two little frail children, scared and on their own.

She needed to get a message to Nick, to stop him from scrambling the location, she couldn't risk her own flesh and blood going to that torture room.

Grabbing her stuff, she left her room and went to the terraced area. Sitting at the table, a waiter came across and asked if she wanted anything.

Plastering a smile on her face she asked for a gin and tonic. Just the one to take the edge off these emotions. Putting her head in her hands she felt ashamed. She sounded just like her mother. The drugs where always to take the edge off, and it was always Rachel's fault. She had grown up hearing the story of how Lynn had got into drugs countless times.

Lynn had been introduced to her Father on a night out through friends. A military man, he had only been in Stanis briefly attending a meeting before he needed to leave. A few days was all they needed before Lynn fell head over heels in love with him. Being an only child to elderly parents that had recently died leaving her nothing, Lynn rented a room from a work colleague. When Rachel's Father had asked Lynn to move in, she jumped at the chance. He had a house in Stanis and after moving in, their relationship grew from strength to strength, having an idyllic couple of years together.

Lynn knew he was in the army and what he worked on was top secret. Proposing to her the night before he was called away, Lynn delightedly accepted. They would wed as soon as he got back, albeit his deployment would be at least a few months.

A month later, Lynn discovered she was pregnant. Thrilled, she counted down the days until he returned to give him the good news.

One week before he was due back, thudding in the middle of the night awoke Lynn. Scared, she crept out of bed and onto the landing. Trying to see through the darkness, a bright light shone into her eyes. 'Who are you? What are you doing here?' Demanded a male voice.

Using her arms to shield the light, she felt a strong hand from behind her, grasp her arms and wrench them behind her back. A gruff male voice told her to keep still as he tie wrapped her wrists together.

'I am only going to ask you once more.' The male growled as she felt the cold metal of the gun against her head.

'I live here with my fiancé; we are due to get married in 4 weeks.' Lynn tried to explain.

'What do you know?' The intruder demanded.

'I don't know what you mean.' Tears streamed down her cheeks as she tried to shield her eyes from the glaring light.

'She doesn't know anything. Get rid of her.' The man ordered.

Lynn felt herself being hoisted up and over someone's shoulder and carried down the stairs. Bundled into a car outside, still in just her nightgown with her arms tied behind her back, she saw the man that had carried her dressed all in black whisper, to the driver. As she stared ahead, the driver looked in the rear view mirror, and smiled at her. His head was also covered with a black balaclava, and in the dark of the night, all Lynn could see was the two gold teeth glinting at her.

Starting the car, the driver reversed slightly, looking at Lynn's tear stained face, he grinned again. 'You're in for a treat tonight.' He said in his husky voice.

Driving through the deserted streets of Stanis, Lynn looked at the stars twinkling in the sky. Silently praying her and her unborn baby would be OK, hoping her parents were up there, looking down, ensuring her and her child's safety.

The car stopped and the driver dragged Lynn out, hands still tied behind her back. Taking her into a boarded up house, Lynn wrinkled her nose as the smell of vomit, filth and burning filled her nostrils. Holding on to the tie wraps, the driver kept Lynn close to him as he took out some money and a small plastic bag and threw it at a scrawny woman laid out on a mattress.

'You know the drill. Her first.' The driver instructed.

The woman checked the money and scrambled to her paraphernalia. Emptying the contents of the small plastic bag onto a metal spoon, she licked her lips, revealing her brown rotting teeth.

Seeing what she was doing, Lynn started to struggle. 'No, I'm not doing it, I can't do it. I'm pregnant.' She cried out.

'You won't be for much longer.' The man hissed in her ear as he punched her in the stomach. 'Now stop moving.'

As the scrawny woman held up the spoon to her face, watching as the acid and heroin bubbled away, Lynn noticed a man, wearing only tracksuit bottoms, crawling along the floor. Turning onto his back, he started laughing manically. 'Where'd you get it from T? You owe me.' He said mesmerised by the flickering light beneath the spoon.

'No, her first Carl.' The man looked at Lynn, not noticing the driver stood behind her.

'Who is she T? Fuck that, you know I'm first.' Carl said as he stood up, fire in his eyes. No one would stop him getting a hit first.

Lynn felt before she saw the driver pull out a gun.

The world slowed as the shot echoed around the room. Carl's eyes wide open in surprise as he watched the bullet fly through the air towards him. Hitting him in the forehead, he fell backwards, dead.
T was still sat on the floor, shaking, holding the syringe in the spoonful of ready Heroin.
'Get on with it or you're next.' The driver growled at T.
T shakily stood up and walked over to Lynn. Surprisingly strong for such a gaunt person, her steely fingers gripped onto Lynn.
'I can't do it with her hands behind her back.'
Taking a knife out, the driver cut the tie wraps and pushed her down so she was sat on the floor.
T grabbed her arm once more whilst the driver held onto her firmly, to stop Lynn from struggling.
The effects where instant, as she drifted off to a place she had never been before, she looked at the driver straight in his eyes.
'My fiancé will kill you for this.' Her voice now slow and slurring, Lynn found her own voice unrecognisable.
'Your fiancé is dead.' He laughed as her eyes fluttered shut.
That had been the start of Lynn's drugs abuse. When Rachel was born, Lynn cried. She was the image of her Father. Her dark brown hair and big brown eyes. Rachel was a constant reminder of what she had lost and what she had been through. Seeing her every day, intensified her need for another fix to dull the pain.
Therefore, it was always Rachel's fault.

Rachel's phone rang, distracting her from the thoughts of her mother.
'Good choice of drink.' Caroline's voice rang out, confirming to Rachel that the broach had audio as well as visual.
'What do you want Caroline.'
'I want to remind you Rachel, that I am watching everything. No more than the one gin, we know how you can spout your mouth off when you've had one too many.'
The phone clicked off, signalling Caroline had ended the call.
Exasperated, Rachel turned on the tablet but was unable to concentrate on the information before her. Grabbing the piece of blank paper from her bag, Rachel used the CB light from the phone Caroline had given her to memorise the questions. She could not slip up now.

It was Yuri that brought her drink over and not the waiter. Swiftly hiding the paper, she looked at Yuri and smiled, motioning towards the broach with her head.

'Your order Miss Nichols. Mind if I join you?' Yuri said making no reference to the broach.

Surprised, Rachel shook her head and gestured to Yuri to sit with her. Trying to mouth, the broach has audio, Yuri looked away from her while he talked.

'I am sorry to inform you, Andreas has been taken ill and will not be able to lunch with you today. I can arrange something to be delivered to your room or you can dine with me.' Yuri smiled at her.

'Yuri, thank you for the offer, yet I have lots to catch up on, I will forgo lunch today.' She replied smiling back him.

Nodding, Yuri stood up but she could see the confusion in his eyes.

Sipping the gin and tonic, she needed to keep focused until Caroline had got what she wanted. If not, her childhood would be a walk in the park compared to her newfound siblings.

Reading an extract from Joshua's log, Rachel looked up as a shadow loomed over her table. Yuri was stood there. 'Sorry Yuri, I am still not interested in lunch.'

'No Miss Nichols. Due to Andrea's lunch cancelling, I have been asked to take you to your next meeting earlier than planned. Please if you would like to follow me to the car and we can go.'

'Now?' Rachel asked surprised.

'Yes.'

'Who authorised this?' Rachel asked.

'The order was delivered by Mr S East.' Yuri replied showing her an email on his blackberry.

Nodding, Rachel got up. She began to feel uneasy, one wrong move and that's it for her brother and sister.

The drive was only seven minutes and although Yuri did not say it, they both knew it was to the entry of the landing site in Capernaum. The car beeped as it passed through an archway into the grounds of a mansion.

Seeing the worried look on her face, Yuri reassured her it was just a scan of the car, a security measure to make sure there were no weapons present.

Following the drive way to the left, they continued on for a couple of minutes until they reached a double fronted stone bricked house. Opening the car door for her, Yuri advised he would be waiting here, until she was ready to go back to the guest house.

Nodding at Yuri in acknowledgement, Rachel grabbed her laptop, tablet and folder and got out of the car. The crunching of gravel made her look up to see Nick waiting to greet her.

'Rachel! Great to see you. I heard Andreas has been taken ill. So unfortunately you have me as your tour guide today.'

Trying not to show how surprised she was, Rachel smiled awkwardly, praying Caroline would know this was out of her hands.

Taking her devices and binder from her, Nick walked through the entrance of the house.

Once inside, Rachel realised the house was actually offices. Tall glass walls featured either side of her, with a plain brick wall two metres from the door, creating a small entrance. Looking through the glass, Rachel could see the bottom floor was mainly open plan and showed a team of people working away at their desks. Blue projections hovered above two of the desks with three people around them, moving the parts of the blue projections around. Two guards stood at the brick wall, one protecting the only entrance into the offices and one at a conveyor belt that disappeared through into the next room.

Placing her items onto the conveyor belt, Nick pointed through the glass to the three stood together at the blue projections. 'This is our team of scientists, they are constantly working to improve anything S.U.S. Industries uses. Currently they are working on vehicles and how we can power them with just water. It can work, yet the sheer amount of water is uses is not viable at the moment. It is a great work in progress though.' He said proudly.

Watching her possessions on the conveyor belt disappear through the wall, Nick carried on talking. 'Just your usual scanner, like an airport one, however the scanner you are about to go through is different to any other. The room will be dark when you first go in, just follow the instructions and wait for me on the other side. Don't worry, it is to check for any transmitters, which we both know you don't have.' He said as he laughed and patted her on the arm.

Gulping, she hoped Nick being overzealous did not rouse Caroline's suspicions.

Walking tentatively into the body scanner the room was black.

'Please raise your arms above your head.' Rachel recognised the robotic voice from the office. It was V.E.L.U.S.'s.

Florescent horizontal strip lights blinkered on, casting a pale orange light in the small rectangular room. Swiftly looking behind her, Rachel could see the lights were protected by a sheet of glass in front, and behind her.

'Please close your eyes while detection is initiated.' V.E.L.U.S.'s voice rang out.

Rachel caught a glimpse of red as she closed her eyes. The bright red light shone through her eyelids as she tightly squeezed them shut. The air around her, began to grow warm as Rachel could feel the heat from the lights on her skin. The room was silent, barring the buzzing from the strip lights behind the glass. Feeling the room increase in temperature, beads of sweat began to form on Rachel's brow. Moving her hand slightly to wipe her forehead, V.E.L.U.S.'s voice rang out. 'Please keep extremely still while detection is completing.'

Inhaling deeply to try and distract herself from the red glare that still shone through her eyelids, the heat started to penetrate through her clothing onto every part of her body. Her clothes started to stick to her as the room grew hotter and her skin felt like it was on fire. Feeling the beads of sweat run down her face, Rachel wasn't sure how much longer she could keep still in this intense temperature. Her clothes now drenched in sweat stuck to her as the heat increased even more. Her heart thumping rapidly, she could hear the whooshing beats in her ears as the brightness inside the room, painfully radiated through her closed eye lids. The temperature inside the room was now too high and her head started to spin. Feeling herself wobble, Rachel was on the verge of passing out. Focusing all her energy on not fainting, she felt the bile rise up in her throat.

Collapsing to the floor, the room suddenly plunged into darkness and a cool air blasted onto Rachel.

'Detection complete.' V.E.L.U.S.'s voice rang out.

Panting, Rachel saw the door at the other side open letting light into the room.

Slowly getting up, she stumbled towards the door and into Nick's arms.

'You did amazing Rach.' He said smiling at her as he supported her towards a chair. 'The transmitter has been destroyed.'

'No, it can't be.' Rachel looked up at him with terror in her eyes. 'She'll kill them.' She whispered.
'Kill who?'
Nick placed Rachel into the chair. Still panting from the intense heat, Rachel gave Nick a quick overview of the video she was sent and Caroline's threat.
Outwardly, Nick was calm and collected, yet Rachel could see the fury in his eyes.
'There is water and a change of clothes in there.' Nick said pointing her towards a ladies changing room. 'Leave it with me, I will deal with it. Do you need help to get to the changing rooms?' Nick asked as he stood up. Rachel shook her head.
'We can recover deleted videos Rach, get a shower and sit and drink the water. You took a battering in there from the heat.' He said before he went to retrieve Rachel's phone.
Standing under the shower of the ladies changing room, Rachel let the cool water run over her skin as she tried to convince herself Nick would find her brother and sister.
Hearing the door open she switched the shower off.
'Rachel, you OK?' She heard Yuri's voice.
'Yeah. I'll be out in a minute.' She shouted, wrapping a towel around her.
'We've recovered the video and are working on tracking the location it was filmed. I thought you'd want to know.'
Rachel quickly opened the shower door. 'Did you see it?' She said looking at Yuri.
Looking down he nodded. 'I just can't... I have no words Rach. I feel this is all our fault.' He shrugged his shoulders.
'How can it be your fault?'
'We, well my Father brought you into this, and look what's happened. Look at everything you have been put through.'
'Yuri' Rachel paused and looked at him with a smile on her face. 'Right now, I have never felt like I have, but in a good way. I have a younger brother and sister. I have family. Something I have never had before, yet always wanted. I would go through all this again, if it meant I had something to live for, instead of just existing. Will you let me know as soon as you have tracked them?'
Yuri nodded and left to let Rachel finish getting ready. Drying her hair in the mirror, she smiled at herself. She had a brother and

sister and she knew they would soon be with her safe. She would make sure of that.

Walking out of the changing room feeling refreshed, Nick shouted across to her. 'Rach, we have tracked the children. They are two hours from where you were staying in the Turkish part of Cyprus. Field Marshal Sanderson is infiltrating and personally overseeing a Special Forces team to get them before Caroline finds out. We believe they will be in the underground tunnels you described.'

'You sure they will be safe? Caroline will know the broach has been destroyed. She may move them if she gets suspicious.'

'We have field surveillance watching her. Two people have been shot, we have it on good authority it was because of the failure of the broach.'

Bile rose in Rachel's throat. 'I got two people killed?'

Walking across to her, he put an arm around her. 'No Rachel, you did not get two people killed. The people working for her know what they are doing. They got themselves killed. I have Field Marshal Sanderson on the radio to give me any updates while we are here. We can reschedule the tour for another day.' Nick passed Rachel her phone. 'You have two missed calls from Caroline. What do you want to do?'

Taking a deep breath, Rachel looked at the phone. 'I'll have to call her back.'

Before she could change her mind, Rachel pressed redial and Caroline answered straight away. 'Why did you not answer?' She screamed.

'I had to make sure I was not in ear shot of anyone, they've been giving me a tour around the offices. I didn't want any questions asked why you were calling.'

A moments silence passed before Caroline replied. 'Yes, you were right not to arise any suspicion, but next time you make your excuses and you answer. You got that?'

'Yes.' Rachel agreed.

'There's been a problem with the broach.' Caroline informed her.

Rachel gasped, hoping it gave the desired effect of surprise. 'What kind of problem, I've not touched it.'

'Yes, I know. It malfunctioned when you went into the body scanner, which I had been assured was FOOL PROOF.' Caroline screamed again. 'It is extremely frustrating when you cannot rely on your staff. Yet, I can rely on you can't I Rachel? And we both know why!'

'You tracked me to where the landing site is, though didn't you?' Rachel asked.

'Yes, we have that, but I need to see the TT pod. I need you to video call me discreetly when you are there. Do you still have the questions? Ask Nick when you are at the TT pod. Got it?'

Before Rachel had chance to say yes, Caroline had put the phone down.

Rachel looked across at Nick. 'Did you hear?' She asked.

Nick nodded. 'Looks like we are going to have to take that tour. Are you comfortable with that?'

Rachel nodded and followed Nick to the back of the house. 'It's not far.' He instructed.

Following him outside, Nick rounded the corner and walked towards a barn attached to the house. Motioning Rachel to put her finger on the scanner, the doors opened, and she walked through. The door slammed shut behind her as a blue light, scanned up and down her body. The next set of doors opened. Walking slowly, she gazed at awe at the vast metal capsule in front of her. She understood now what Nick and Sandra meant. Seeing is believing. The TT pod was bigger than she expected, yet it felt magical being in its presence.

'You can touch it.' Nick said as he came up behind her.

Placing her hand on the cold smooth metal, she jumped as a door opened and stairs formed from the TT pod.

'Welcome back Magda.' V.E.L.U.S.'s voice boomed out. 'It has been a long time.'

Chapter 27
Joshua - The Letter

Joshua and Magda had been extremely busy. With the help of V.E.L.U.S., they had organised the requests from other cities and sent word of who would be going, and when.
One by one, the new employees of Joshua's ministry had been initiated. Joshua spoke to them individually, telling them about his life in Rylitte, how he had become to be there and finally had shown them the TT pod.
Introducing them to V.E.L.U.S. had been eventful. Judas had jumped out of his skin, screaming demon until he saw Magda and Joshua laughing at him.
'You could have warned me!' He said grumpily.
'I did.' Joshua laughed. 'You chose to fiddle with the buttons instead.'
Finally, he read the letters, leaving his Fathers until last. No matter how many times he read it, the lump in his throat formed, and his voice broke with emotion.

My Dearest Son Joshua,
If you are reading this, two things will have happened. First the war has broken out and Lamia has ordered for the deployment of the NESRE.
Secondly, I am no longer with you, and it is time you learned the truth.
My Mother and Father, your Grandparents, had always been advocates for the Servians, using their status and wealth to protect them as much as they could, without repercussions. Servians are humans just like us, just born into a different life.

My parent's position in society involved socialising with the elite of Rylitte and using this to their advantage. My parents tried to eradicate the mistreatment of Servians when they could.

When I was twelve, my parents and I were invited to dine at Lamia's parents, Lamashtu and Seth. A full-blown dinner party with at least fifty guests seated around a huge table in the ballroom of Rylitte Hall.

Waited upon by Servians, I ensured my manners where present and thanked each server that presented me with exquisite food, or topped up my favourite drink of the time, Paxipunch. One of the servers whispered into my ear. Asking me not to speak to them, if the guards saw the interaction, they would get beaten for daring to engage with us.

Horrified, I told my mother. Stroking my head, she whispered back into my ear. 'That is why we fight against this darling. Yet we must keep our fighting secret, and discreet.'

I had seen what occurred to the ones that defied the Rylitte's. Every Saturday, public killings were held, to show the world what happened if you spoke against the Leader. Broadcast live on every TV channel, Lamashtu ensured the publicised front row was filled with only the most famous and respected people of that time. Although, Lamashtu was the star of the show, announcing each victim by name, location and crime they had committed, to show the world not one person was safe from her.

My mother knew if they were uncovered, even I would be involved in the public killings.

After dinner had finished, Lamia sought me out. Her bony fingers touching my shoulder made my skin crawl. She whispered in my ear, I was one of the chosen few, it would be announced that very evening, I needed to be prepared.

My eyes furiously searched the crowd, as I looked for my parents. Seeing my mother talking to Lamashtu, her shocked face found mine. The colour had all but drained from it, Lamashtu had told her.

Nodding politely at Lamashtu, my mother walked towards me, we had an hour to prepare. Entering a private room, my mother held me, tears in her eyes. 'I will do everything I can, to stop this.' She whispered. 'Yet we must play along for now.'

Looking at her I shook my head, I wanted to do this, I could change everything that was happening. If Lamia was to choose me as her husband, I could change her, show her how people were more loyal through love, not fear.

My Father walked into the private room, bringing with him a small black box. 'You must give this to Lamia. She will be impressed, yet it will impress her mother more, and Lamashtu is who you need to win over.'

Opening the black box, I could see a blue sapphire ring. Slowly lowering the lid of the box, I looked at my father and nodded in appreciation, I knew what it was.

The time came for me to present my gift to Lamia.

I met with four other well-known boys my age outside of the ball room.

Led into the golden gilded room, all eyes were on us as we walked single file towards Lamia, Lamashtu and Seth, who were sat on cast iron chairs covered in gold and purple fabric. They had changed into more elaborate outfits since the evening's banquet.

Lamashtu addressed the crowd as they stood watching, her silver dress sparkled under the ball room lighting, accentuating her harsh pale white face against the black of her hair. Lamashtu looked pure evil.

I was fourth in line. I waited whilst the three others gave their presents and the meaning behind them.

I walked up to Lamia. Much to my surprise, my voice was clear and confident as it echoed around the room.

Lamia's eyes lit up as she opened the box and I explained the emerald ring was not just a ring. Placing it on her finger I asked her to point it at the block of stone the Servian worker had just brought in, and to squeeze her hand together. The laser shot from the ring towards the huge rock, causing it to explode. Cries and delight came from the crowd as I watched Lamashtu smile. I explained it would keep her safe until I was her husband, there to protect her.

The smile from Lamashtu vanished. 'A woman of Lamia's standing does not need protection from a lowly man.' She hissed. 'Men like you should know your place. This is a woman's world, and women will continue to run it forever!'

I lowered my head; I had blown it. Searching the crowd for my parents, my eyes landed on them. The encouraging smile they wore, were all I needed to know. I had not failed them.

It was the fifth and final boys turn. He opened a large wooden box that was next to him and brought out a beautiful girl, my age. He retold the story of how the Matriats greatest warrior Avali had been defeated by pure chance at a disrespectful little Servian's hand.

I quickly looked back at my Mother. Gone was the encouraging smile, replaced with worry, her face had paled. The weak smile she flashed me confirmed it, the disrespectful little Servian he was talking about, was Caelan.

Presenting the girl to Lamia, he introduced her as Aniela, the only living relative of Avali's slayer. He had hunted her down personally to prove the respect he had for the Leader, and what they stood for. His head turned to me as he spoke of how he knew his place and would be loyal, truthful and fulfil any demands required of him.

Bowing after he spoke the crowd clapped and cheered.

Lamashtu arose and thanked the boy for his gift, she would be the highlight of this week's Saturday show.

The girl turned her head and looked at me. As our eyes locked, I felt like she was staring into my soul. I needed to rescue this girl from the clutches of the Rylitte's, yet I only had one day.

The fifth boy, Azazel, was chosen to be betrothed to Lamia when she came of age. I no longer cared about the betrothal, all I cared about was Aniela.

I knew she would be kept in the prison cells underneath the kitchen. Lamia used to take me down there when we were younger, to torment the poor people locked up.

I waited a few hours until all at the party where completely inebriated and falling amongst each other.

Slipping out of the ballroom I made my way to the kitchen, yet the servants where still cleaning. I edged around in the shadows, hiding behind the huge serving trolleys they had used to feed us all. I eventually managed to get to the entrance of the holding cells and slipped down the stairs before anyone could see me.

Leaning against the wall at the bottom to catch my breath and let my eyes get used to the darkness of the prison, I heard footsteps coming towards me. Darting across the corridor I opened the door that I knew housed the cleaning equipment for the kitchen. In my haste, I ran headfirst into a tall stocky man and froze, this was it, I could save myself, but I would not be able to save Aneila.

The man bent down, recognising me. My Father had saved him from death at the hands of another Matriat and he had never forgotten. I told him Aneila's fate. I will never forget his smile.

His smile told me I was doing the right thing, his smile told me I gave him and the Servian's hope of a better world.
On his words he told me to run and free her.
I ran when the shelves of equipment came tumbling down, forcing the guards to run towards the clatter.
Grabbing the card, the guards had left on the desk I ran to Aneila's cell. Holding the card to the door, it unlocked. As I entered Aneila, stood up and smiled. I did not have to say anything, she trusted me implicitly, she knew I had come to save her. The card still in my hand, I looked at the end of the corridor. The guards had lost interest in the clatter and were beginning to turn around. Without thinking, I began to open the other cells, letting the prisoner's free, some were innocent, some were meant to be there. A larger than life Servian stomped out of one of the cells I had opened. Battle crying, he thumped his chest ready for a fight. He looked at Aneila and I, to our hands holding, the scared look on our faces. He knelt down to us both in the midst of the chaos. He grunted he wanted the card, immediately I passed it to him. 'I will see you out of the grounds, then you are on your own.' He growled. The easiest trade I have ever made.
He stayed true to his word and led us out of Rylitte Halls grounds. I then knew Aneila was safe. Staying hidden was easy in the darkness the evening brought. Staying near trees and bushes, I soon made it home, hoping my Mother and Father had noticed me missing and left before the prisoners were set free.
They were not there. Calling upon the only other person I trusted, I took Aneila to Caelans' room.
That night was the only time I had seen Caelan show emotion. He swept Aneila up and hugged her, burying his head in her shoulder, silently sobbing at the last member of his family.
With my Fathers permission, Caelan had tried to track his family down, yet he had only found one remaining. Azazel was not lying, he had indeed brought the last family member of Avali's slayer, to Lamia.
Caelan called my Mother and Father and let them know I was home safe. They returned not long after, chastising me for the worry I had caused when they could not find me in all the chaos.
They sat and told us the carnage that was happening at Rylitte Hall. Lamashtu was furious and vowed to slowly kill those who had ruined her daughters pairing ceremony.

The next day, Caelan and my Father formed a new identity for Aneila, knowing she would not be safe back with the Servian's.

They coached and taught her the Matriat way, along with formal education. Aneila was extremely intelligent and took everything in her stride. After six months Aneila was ready to be introduced as Liz's niece from another country. It was a risk, Lamashtu was still looking for her, yet she underwent surgery to change her eye colour and transformed her hair style. She had grown in the six months, not just in shape and size, but in confidence. She seemed such a different individual to the one I rescued months previous.

The introduction to school and the Matriat world was a success. In the same classes, I stayed close to ensure her safety, yet I did not need to. She blossomed, the confidence we had given her shined through and people flocked to her. She was made for the Matriat and Servian world.

Years passed and we formed an unbreakable friendship that turned into love.

Your Mother Mary was Aneila.

You son, are part Matriat and part Servian. Showing love knows no boundaries. It hurts to think this does matter in our world, which is why we could not tell you of your Servian heritage until now. I could never imagine loving anyone as much as I loved your Mother.

We still lived in fear each year that passed, wondering if someone had broken our secret. When Lamashtu died, we thought that would be the end of it, yet Lamia pledged to continue her mother's unfinished work, upping the raids on the villages, sending troops to burn down their houses while their children slept, wanting someone to give up Aneila.

Your Mother cried every night on how many people had been slaughtered at her expense, wanting to give herself up, yet I knew this insanity would continue even if Aniela had been caught. Lamia loved ruling with fear too much. Azazel behind her at every announcement, his smug smile taunting, knowing no one could touch him.

I made sure we built a network of people, trying our best to give protection to the Servians and recruiting more Matriats to stop this madness.

We made good progress, now the baton has now passed to you son, you need to continue this fight to reunite the world. Make it stronger as one.

I know you will make me proud, as you did your Mother.

Your Loving Father x

Each one of Joshua's friends sat in silence as he read the letter, tears streaming down his face as he finished. Every time he read it, he wished he had been there for his mother. To hold her while she cried, to promise her he would do anything in his power to protect her and his heritage. He wished he had done more while he was back in Rylitte, yet now he had to continue his mission to change the world. To show people love, kindness and support is what really matters. Being there creates loyalty, creates peace, creates a carefree happy world.

Each one pledged their loyalty to Joshua, to go forward and spread the word as Joshua did, so the next generation of their families will live in a world of safety and not in fear, regardless of their heritage.
Sending them out to their visits, Joshua walked the short way to his house.
Kissing the top of Prisca's head, he still had tears in his eyes.
He wished his Mother and Father could see their beautiful granddaughter, and he hoped her children, and her children's children will live in the world her grandfather had imagined for them.

Chapter 28
Rachel - Rachel's Father

'I can't believe it.' Nick whispered. 'I thought… but…' He picked Rachel up and spun her around. 'Do you know what this means?' He asked, his face animated with excitement.

Nick put Rachel down. 'Nick what's happening, why did V.E.L.U.S. call me Magda?' Rachel asked, puzzlement on her face as she watched the two people in lab coats cheering and hugging each other.

'This is the original V.E.L.U.S.' Nick explained. 'The V.E.L.U.S. we use, is not on the same programme as this one. We duplicated her programming and kept them separate in case there were secrets hidden within this one that did not copy across, and we were correct. She is the safety net of the power source and information locked in there. We have managed to get so much, yet a lot of it is hidden until an authorised person is here to do so. Rachel, you are the authorised person. YOU ARE MAGDA!'

Rachel looked at Nick, puzzlement still on her face. 'Nick, I am still confused. I have no idea what you are talking about.'

Telling the two scientists to go take a break, Nick led Rachel to the computers they had been at and sat her down.

Holding her hands, he looked her straight in the eye.

'Rachel, do you know who your Father was?'

Exasperated, Rachel sighed. 'What has this got to do with anything?'

'Please, just answer my question, do you know who your Father was?'

Rachel rolled her eyes. 'A sperm donor that created the life I lived as a child.'

'No, No Rachel, he wasn't.' Nick said, the excitement on his face. 'Your Father was part of us. He sat on the committee just like you are doing. He was a good man.'

'Nick, please do not say you knew my Father, and you left me with that piece of shit of a Mother.'

Looking into his eyes, she could see him inwardly pleading with her to listen to him. 'I did know your Father, yet we never knew you existed. We tracked down the team that murdered your father a couple of weeks after he went missing. Under interrogation, one of them gave us your Mother's name. He described how she was engaged to your Father and how they had taken care of her. He didn't know the location, only knew the driver had returned without her, confirming she was dead. Not one of them gave up the dump site address. Every single body that was found, we investigated, yet none were your Mother, she had vanished. The driver was fond of dismembering his victims, we wrongly assumed this was your Mothers fate. We were alerted your Mother was still alive when her name flagged up after she was arrested for shop lifting, along with you name as a dependant. Looking at the dates, we knew you could potentially be Major General Marbery's daughter. As soon as I saw the photographs captured by Special Forces, I knew you were his. I just needed to prove it, yet it was hard getting close to you. I went to Trinity Estate and left food and water out for you. I waited until you ate and drank, then took the empty water bottle to have your DNA verified. You say you were not born for this, yet you were.'

Rachel sat there and listened; doubt written all over her face. 'You said I was one of many, an experiment, your wild card remember?' She questioned him.

'You were, we had others. Not your Fathers.' He added seeing the disgust register on Rachel's face. 'Yet ones that were born part of this, without them knowing. We needed a replacement, one that had the blood of the original committee running through their veins, yet had not been corrupted by others, or that turned their knowledge and heritage into a cult.'

'You mean James Smith?' Rachel said referring to Nick's cousin who had taken his heritage to heart and formed a cult. Claiming to be the Messiah reincarnated, James recruited his followers, just like Joshua did, feeding them bits of information about the alternate future and how enriched their lives would be once they followed him into the new world. However, the more followers he gained, the more his eccentricity developed, which inevitably ended terribly. Rachel could see the similarities between Joshua East and James when she reviewed the photographs included in an article she was required to read. Part of her knowledge involved showing the good and the bad of the S.U.S Industries timeline, and she had wondered how James became to think he was the incarnation of Joshua East.

'Yes, exactly like James Smith.' Nick replied. Still holding her hands, he squeezed them slightly harder. 'You, Rachel, are a direct descendant from Magda's twin sister, Martha.'

Rachel frowned. 'There is no mention of a Magda having a twin sister anywhere, I hope you are not bullshitting me Nick.'

'You heard V.E.L.U.S. when you entered. You are the image of Magda and Martha. Identical twins share the same genetic makeup. These genes are passed down continually through generations until it is matched up again. Your genetic makeup is that of Magda and Martha's, your DNA maybe be slightly different, yet it will be that marginal, you will pass V.E.L.U.S.'s security checks.'

'Why has Martha barely been mentioned in the New Testament and never in S.U.S. Compendium?' Rachel replied.

'Magda and her twin Martha were private. They ensured their survival and bloodline through discretion. Joshua brought the technology and idea of the new world; they were the ones that delivered Jesus to the people. As you know there is not much reported on Magda and even less on Martha and that is how they wanted to keep it, yet unfortunately there is always a leak. Your Father was murdered to keep Martha's bloodline under control.'

'By whom?' Rachel asked.

'Caroline.' Nick replied. 'She wanted to be the only one left to keep the bloodline pure.'

'I am related to Caroline?' Rachel replied astounded 'And she killed my real Father?'

'Yes.' Nick had the decency to hang his head in shame.

'You knew this, and you still let me meet her?'

'Yes, I knew you were related but no, I never knew Caroline was behind it until yesterday evening. After your meeting with her, I had everyone that is security cleared digging into what she was involved in. I knew something was not quite right, yet never suspected how involved she was or how long this has been going on for.'

'Are you kidding me?' Rachel shouted. You never suspected Caroline, an arms dealer?'

'Her family has been in the committee for generations Rachel, you cannot dismiss someone just because you have a hunch. You need solid evidence.'

'Are you, or are you not the MD of this business, whatever it is?' Rachel said throwing her hands in the air. 'You have the power to follow your hunches.'

'I did Rachel, I have had her looked into time and time again. Caroline is extremely clever; she covered her tracks. The information on the audio you played gave me details of a meeting we knew was going ahead but with an underground organisation called NIGHT WAVE for the supply of weapons.'

'Isn't NIGHT WAVE responsible for the terrorist attacks that happened around the world 3 years ago?' Rachel asked.

'Yes, the NIGHT WAVE is a worldwide terrorist organisation, who we have never been able to pinpoint. Constantly off the grid, we had managed to infiltrate an encrypted message between them and a buyer. Your audio about the meeting matches with the information we were given. Caroline is the one heading NIGHT WAVE. We had the head of a terrorist organisation on the committee for all these years. I knew there was something, but I would never have expected this.' Nick shook his head. 'She had access to everything. We knew we had a leak as NIGHT WAVE were always one step ahead, but Caroline? Therefore, she needed you Rachel. Why she is so intent on messing with your mind, bringing up your past, so you do not stray from her and you give her what she wants, the power to the TT pod.'

'So, Caroline wants the power source. Why doesn't she come and get it herself?' Rachel asked trying to make sense out of everything that was being said.

'We had a break-in about six months ago. Until now we had no idea who it was. Nothing was touched, no prints were found, and the security wiped. Only someone with access and coding skills can wipe the security. I have a feeling it was Caroline, and this is when she realised, she could not access the power source. She needs you to infiltrate the TT pod. She knows now that genetics need to match, not just have part DNA.'

'But can't you open it?' Rachel asked still confused.

'No, bloodline is only one part, you need to have the correct genetic makeup. I knew you was the one Rachel; I knew as soon as I saw you.'

Rachel stood up, trying to take it all in. 'But why wait until now? Why not bring me here years ago?'

'I needed to bring you in without causing suspicion. I knew my timeline would work. Progressing you through the languages, the negotiating, coaching, communicating to a higher level of personnel, preparing you, yet I did not prepare you well enough.' Looking up at her, she could see the true regret in his eyes. 'I am so sorry I put you through all this, I didn't realise all of this would happen.'

Rachel paced up and down. She needed to think.

'What would you do with the power source if I authorised removal?' Rachel finally asked. 'If Caroline cannot access it here, surely this is the safest place.'

'Caroline can get to you Rachel, look what she has unearthed already, look what she has put you through over only three days, imagine if she had longer. We can move it and not tell you the location, you would be useless to her then.'

Nick paused while Rachel absorbed the information.

'What if I told V.E.L.U.S. I was not Magda?'

'V.E.L.U.S. will always recognise you as an authorised person regardless of what you tell her. Look, you don't have to make a decision now, come examine the TT pod.' Nick saw Rachel stall. 'You have to speak the command to release the power source. It cannot be removed without your approval.' He said smiling at her, the excitement returning to his face.

Rachel agreed to be led into the TT pod, it would be a welcome distraction after what had happened so far today.

Climbing the steps, V.E.L.U.S. welcomed Magda once more. Looking around in awe, Rachel was amazed at how homely it felt. The leather white chair and plush carpeting still looked brand new, not over two thousand years old. It had been well preserved.

Nick explained that everything in the TT pod had been coated in a substance to prevent wear and tear, something that had not been invented in our time. Going into further detail than anything she had read so far, Nick described what they had discovered from Joshua's future. For their time, they had been a lot more advanced in technology. Everything was preserved or recycled. Everything was reused. Whilst the world he came from was a cold, joyless one, with milestones and events not celebrated; slaughter and cruelness was rewarded, they had ways in which this future could learn from. Reusable energy such as the TT pod's electricity source, there was no landfills as nothing was ever destroyed or thrown away, it was recycled. Furniture production was stopped and instead altered or sold if you wanted a change. Shops no longer existed, everything was delivered. Food produce came in huge trays that slotted into cupboards or refrigerators, the empty trays returned when the shopping came. The food was grown in controlled environments with accelerant technology, taking one day to produce a tree full of apples. Diseases were still apparent, yet they had the technology to cure.

Rachel's mind buzzed with this alternative future.

Nick showed Rachel how to replay footage of Rylitte and the future they would never see on the TT pods monitors. Watching them in amazement, she turned to Nick.

What would happen if Caroline got the power source from the TT pod?

'I think you know Rachel, Caroline has turned out to be this futures Lamia.'

Thinking of her brother and sister and the life she could potentially lead with them, she turned to Nick hoping she had made the right decision.

Nodding at him she took a deep breath. 'OK, I'll do it, I'll authorise the removal of the power source.'

Chapter 29
Joshua - Molecular Regeneration and Electro Magnetics

The arranged speeches had been a success. After some training, Joshua gave the twelve people he now employed medication. Telling them to go wherever the road took them and to find those that required aid and to give them the help they needed. Asking only in return for a bed at night and food for their troubles, yet to never to accept money.

A couple of weeks passed, and all twelve staff had sent word all was going well.
Playing with baby Prisca, Joshua heard a knock at the door.
Picking her up, Joshua answered and saw one of King Herod's guards standing there. Four other guards were in the background, standing watch.
'Jesus of Joseph, in the town of Capernaum. You are requested to join me and travel to our Ruler King Herod's residence and dine with him tomorrow evening.'
Magda joined him at the door. Passing Prisca to her, he motioned for her to take her indoors.
'You want me to drop everything and come with you now?' Joshua exclaimed.
'Yes, that is the request of King Herod.' The guard informed Joshua.
'No. I am not leaving now. I will send word when I am able to attend.' He replied.
The guard spluttered at Joshua's refusal. 'But you must. It is on King Herod's orders.'
'I said no. I will come when I am ready. Tell King Herod, I heard of him beheading John, I am unsure of what motives he has

towards me. Once I feel confident I am not at risk of being murdered, I will attend.'

The guards face turned red at Joshua's obstinacy. 'You are ordered to come with me.' The guard demanded.

Hearing a commotion behind him, Joshua looked over the guard's shoulder. It was Matthew racing up the hill on a horse.

Jumping off as he neared, he ran towards Joshua.

'Jesus, we did as you asked, we healed as you taught us, and we told them your stories. All twelve of us have been followed back. They want to meet you, they want to meet the man that gives the power of healing. There are hundreds of them.' Matthew said breathless and hurried.

Joshua turned around to the guard. 'I suggest you leave before you are mobbed by crowds wanting to see me.'

The guard nodded at his men as they mounted their horses. 'We will return and that time, we will not leave without you.' He shouted at Joshua as they began to ride off.

Watching the men leave, Matthew turned to Joshua. 'I am sorry, I did not want to lead the people to your door, yet I needed to tell you.'

'No, it is fine. Thank you, Matthew, you have done the right thing.' Joshua patted Matthew on the shoulder and went back inside the house. Seeing Magda stood there rocking Prisca, concerned etched across her face, he knew she would understand.

'We need to leave, and quickly.' Joshua said.

Magda nodded. They had talked about this. He wanted to keep her and Prisca safe, away from all it all. They knew the introduction of the others spreading the word would gather traction and grow into something big, yet they had not anticipated it being so quick and being brought to their front door.

Running to the TT pod, Joshua grabbed some food packs and pebbles. Stuffing them into a bag he placed them on to the cart as Magda brought out baby Prisca. Checking the horse was properly attached, he jumped in the back of the cart with Prisca

'Where do you want me to head?' Magda asked.

'I don't know. I can't think of where you two will be safe.'

'We'll go to my sisters in Bethsaida. We should be safe there.' Magda replied as she clicked for the horse to go.

Matthew ran to the cart. 'I'll try and create a diversion.

As the cart started to move, Joshua shouted thanks to Matthew. 'Meet us in Bethsaida with the others, and make sure no one sees the TT pod.'

Matthew nodded and waved, as the horse started to gather speed.

Hurtling through the countryside, Joshua caught a glimpse of the hordes of people through the trees. Holding Prisca tight, he tapped Magda on the shoulder. 'Have you seen this?'

'Yes.' She shouted over the noise of the horse and cart making its way down the dirt tracks towards Bethsaida. 'I think they know where we are heading. It won't be long before they find us. We need to make sure the TT pod is safe. I shall drop you at Bethsaida, take Prisca to my sisters and go back to the house.'

'No. You are not going alone.' Insisted Joshua.

'I'll stop at Marys and ask one of your brothers to join me. I promise I will be safe, we need to know the crowds have been drawn away from the TT pod.' Magda advised.

Although he was not happy, Joshua agreed, if he went back, they would follow him. This would be the best option.

'Promise me you will get Aaron or Jedidiah, or both. Do not go on your own, promise me.'

Magda promised Joshua and dropped him near the Sea of Galilee in Bethsaida and left towards her sisters. It was not long before Matthew joined him.

Full of apologies, Joshua reassured Matthew there was nothing he could have done as he watched hundreds of people appear behind him. The other members of his ministry soon caught up, bringing hundreds more with them.

Strapping his bag firmly to him, he watched as his twelve friends formed a circle around him. Linking their arms they moved slowly around Joshua, trying to protect him from the crowds flocking in their direction.

'What should we do Jesus?' Judas shouted as he looked behind him. 'There must be at least five thousand people here, all wanting to see you.'

'Peter, Andrew. Come in the middle with me and hoist me up above the crowd.' Joshua directed them.

Carefully unlinking arms so no one could get through, Peter and Andrew joined Joshua in the middle as the circle got smaller.

More people were ramming into the circle, trying to crawl under the men's legs and climbing over their heads, just to touch the almighty healer.

Peter and Andrew crouched down near each other, shoulder to shoulder as Joshua sat in the middle of them both, carefully lowering himself on their shoulders. Holding one leg each, they wobbled as they stood up.
Their faces red with Joshua's weight they patted his leg, signalling they were steady for him to address the crowds.
As Joshua rose up out of the circle, a hush descended across the masses. He looked at the faces, many men, some women. He could see the sick had been left on the outskirts of the crowd as their family members had tried to clamber to speak to him, Joshua. Dismayed at what he saw, he knew he had created this carnage. He had made them fight amongst each other for survival.
'Good Afternoon my good people. I understand you have come to see me, come to ask for my help, my guidance. I will only help those that wait patiently. I will not help those that demand it, or fight to see me first. Anyone that has caused harm to a member of my ministry will be turned away. Return to your friends or family you have brought with you, sit in large groups along the sand and wait, with patience, until I see you.'
Signalling to a relieved Peter and Andrew to put him down, he gestured to the others to come closer.
'I want them in groups of fifty. Go round to all the groups. Tell them to talk amongst each other, find out an interesting piece of information from someone they do not know in the group. I will be asking a select few from each group to tell me that fact. Tell them to be prepared, I do not have a lot of time for people to waste it today.
The twelve members went and did as instructed and the people all sat in huge groups. The once chaotic angry crowd was now a peaceful serene of happiness and laughter.
Matthew was the first one back to Joshua. 'You make it look so easy. I have never seen a crowd disburse and change so quickly. You really are a miracle worker Jesus.' He said in wonderment.
'You need to have faith in yourself Matthew. Confidence in your own ability, commands respect from others, you will learn and you and your families, will carry this on for generations after we are gone.' Joshua said smiling at him as he walked to the first group of people.
'How are we all?' He addressed the eager faces. 'I hear you have travelled far to come and see me.' He smiled as his attention was

drawn to a frail teenager. Joshua walked around the group and knelt down. 'And what is your name?' He asked the teenage boy.
'Samson.' The boy replied.
'You do not look well, how can I help?' Joshua asked.
The boy looked at his Mother and she nodded, giving him reassurance he was allowed to speak.
'My mouth hurts, I cannot sleep, I cannot eat. I am so tired and hungry. Sometimes, I there is a horrible taste in my mouth and liquid comes from nowhere.' The teenager mumbled.
Joshua instructed him to open his mouth so he could see inside. An angry abscess was on the teenager's tooth. Asking him to lay down, Joshua injected him with a numbing agent, drained the abscess and then coated the infected area with medication.
'I have taken the naughty pain away, it should be fine from now on.' Joshua told the teenage boy. 'Your mouth may feel slightly strange for a few hours and you may talk a little differently, yet this will pass. Try and eat some food now while I am here, so I can check everything is working fine.'
The teenager now smiling, looked eagerly at his Mother, yet she shook her head. Looking at Joshua, she meekly spoke. 'I am sorry sir, messiah, Jesus, sir, we do not have any food. We have walked for three days to come to you as Thomas was unable to heal my son. We are hungry, but please we are so grateful. Thank you.'
Bowing her head down shamefully as she did not have any food, she put a protective arm around her son.
Joshua stood up frowning and addressed the rest of the group before him. 'Does anyone here have any food?'
The mumbled replies where the same of that as the teenage boy.
Shouting at Nathaniel, he asked him to go and ask the rest of the groups. Reporting back, Nathaniel brought with him a young boy carrying five loaves of bread and two fish in a brown wicker basket.
'This all we could find Jesus, this young boy offered it.' Nathaniel informed Joshua.
Thanking the young boy, Joshua took the basket from him and patted him on the head. 'You will do great things for this country and this world. Keep being generous and kind, and good things will follow.' The boy smiled in acknowledgment and ran off.
Kneeling over the basket, Joshua took out a small silver packet from his bag.

'This.' He said shaking the packet at Matthew. 'Should only ever be used in extreme circumstances.' Shaking the dust like contents over the bread and fish, Joshua watched as it was absorbed into the food. 'Watch carefully.' Joshua instructed as he gently broke off a crumb from the bread. Matthew watched in amazement as it expanded to the size of his hand.

'Molecular regeneration. Works on the same principles as if you cut a worm in two, it can grow back its tail. Show the others and pass the food out. One piece of bread and one smaller piece of fish. It expands further when in your stomach. Tell anyone if they are finished and are still hungry, they can come and ask for more, yet I do not think they will. And as always, keep it between us.' Joshua tapped his nose as Matthew looked at him in amazement.

'Of course.' He stuttered, raptured once again by Joshua's abilities. 'You never cease to shock me Jesus.'

Joshua laughed as Matthew headed off to pass out the food.

The day ended on a high note, the people were happy, fed and delighted with the miracles Joshua had performed. Asking them all to treat others with the same kindness he had treated them, he smiled as he had managed to help them all.

Seeing the dark clouds form, many left the beach in search of shelter. Bringing the last of the bread and fish back, Joshua saw there was still a loaf and a half of bread and one fish left.

'Keep it for now and we can pass it out to others if we need to over the next few days.' Joshua instructed Matthew.

Matthew nodded in acknowledgment and pointed to a boat anchored in the sea. 'James and Johns Father turned up not long ago in his boat, their sister has had a baby. We're sailing across the water to see them and help them celebrate the birth, are you coming Jesus?'

'I'll catch you up. I need to go and see if Magda returned to Martha's safe.' Joshua advised.

'No problems, give Prisca a kiss from me!' Matthew said before turning to join the others.

As Joshua walked to Martha's, it started to rain. Running to the house, he managed to get under shelter before the thunder and lightning started.

Magda was there with baby Prisca in her arms. 'Your Father thinks I am incompetent to do anything doesn't he Prisca?' She said mocking Joshua as she laid Prisca on a blanket in the room.

'I cannot help it if I worry about my wife.' He replied, kissing her and then Prisca. 'Zebedee is a grandfather.' He told her. 'His daughter gave birth today. All the members of the ministry are going across on Zebedee's boat to see her and celebrate.'

'Why are you not with them?' Magda asked in between blowing raspberry's on Prisca's stomach.

Watching his daughter laugh, he knelt down to join them. 'Why would I want to be anywhere else, other than here with you two?' He said as he pulled his wife in for a kiss.

'The TT pod was safe and sound. V.E.L.U.S. advised to bring the tablet with me so she can alert me if anything happens. As I logged today's events, V.E.L.U.S. advised me to give you this.' Magda walked towards the table at the other end of the room and retrieved a large leather bag from underneath it. Bringing it across to Joshua, she pulled out two clear boots and a clear hat.

Joshua exclaimed in delight. 'My snowshoes and hat! Where did V.E.L.U.S. find these? I never knew they were packed!'

'Snowshoes?' Magda questioned. 'V.E.L.U.S. said you would know what they were. I knew there were some kind of shoe, but…'

'I wore them for the snow.' Joshua interrupted. 'Snow is like powdered water. I'll show you what it looks like on the TT pod monitors when we go back home. I wonder why V.E.L.U.S. thought I would need them?' Joshua said turning the snowshoes over, examining them.

'She said it was for the storm that was coming. V.E.L.U.S. predicated the thunderstorm would be extremely violent this evening. She said you would need them if you were to travel back tonight. I have spoken to Martha, and she has set us up a bed to sleep here. I do not think we should risk going out.' Showing Joshua the tablet, he looked at the weather V.E.L.U.S. had anticipated. If she were right, it would be one terrible storm.

'What do the shoes do?' Magda asked examining one.

'They wrap around my feet, watch.' Slipping one on, the clear plastic material moulded onto Joshua's feet to look like he was not wearing anything. Just a thin outline could be seen if you inspected it closely.

'Josh, that is magical.' Magda said, examining where the boot was on his foot.

'Now watch this.' Joshua said as he opened the front door of the house. The rain was now lashing down outside, and the roads where covered in running water. Putting his one booted foot in the rainwater, the bottom part inflated. Tiny little fins all around the boot came out, stabilising his foot. 'I do not get wet and I can stay upright, even on water. We never got as much water as this in Rylitte as we had drainage systems.'

'Drainage systems?' Magda asked.

'They are round pipes that water runs into and takes to other parts of the country so roads do not flood like this.' He said.

'Why did you need these shoes if you never had rain like this?' Magda asked, whilst waving her hand to get Joshua to come back inside.

'We had snow Magda, the most amazing weather of all. When snow falls, it covers everything in white powder. The white powder builds up and up. Normal shoes or boots would not be able to walk in it, but these.' He said holding the one snowshoe not on his foot. 'These help you to stop slipping. They stabilised you so you stay on top of the snow, and most importantly, they kept you extremely warm. Snow is very cold.'

Magda frowned. 'Not sure I like the sound of snow.' She said. 'What does this do?' she asked holding up the clear hat.

'This moulds around my face, helping me see through a snowstorm. It stops the snow, or rain getting into my eyes, keeping me dry and warm. If my snowshoes fail and I did fall over, my snow hat inflates, and uses the little inbuilt propellers to get me to safety.'

'You've lost me.' Magda laughed. 'Show me when we are back home and in the TT pod.' Yawning she looked outside at the torrential rain. 'I'm tired, it's been a long day. Do you mind if I go to bed?'

'Course not, leave Prisca with me, we'll follow you soon.' He said, kissing the now sleeping baby on her head.

Magda smiled as Martha came in, heavily pregnant. 'Won't be long now and Prisca will have a little cousin to play with.'

Joshua gasped. Magda and Martha looked up at him. 'Zebedee, the members, they are out on the water in this storm.' Joshua said as thunder and lightning crackled through the sky.

Magda's eyes grew wide in shock. 'Martha, Zebedee's daughter had her baby today, all the members of the ministry have gone across the water to celebrate.'

'I need to go, I need to make sure they are safe.' Joshua said putting the other boot on and watching as it moulded to his foot.

'No Joshua, you can't, it's too dangerous. The storm might hit you, then what will we do? We cannot lose you.' Magda pleaded.

'Magda, wearing these, I will be fine and protected. Do not worry.' Grabbing the tablet, Joshua activated V.E.L.U.S. in his earpiece. 'V.E.L.U.S. where is the storm right now?' He asked.

'It is directly above the Sea of Galilee, winds current sixty-seven mph.' V.E.L.U.S.'s voiced echoed in Joshua's head.

'Can a small boat survive in this weather?' Joshua panicked.

'Thirty-four percent chance of survival with the waves approximately 11.7 metres tall.' V.E.L.U.S. answered.

'Is there anything we can do to stop the storm?' Joshua asked as Magda and Martha sat in silence, staring at him wide eyed.

'You need to drop a tracking rod near the storm. It will attract the lightening and I can suck the power from the storm and disperse it safely.' V.E.L.U.S. advised.

'Do we have a tracking rod?' Joshua demanded.

'At the TT pod, yet you can make one from items in your cart.'

Joshua put his hat on as Magda and Martha watched in amazement as the clear plastic moulded to his face then disappeared. Running to the cart, he grabbed the pieces V.E.L.U.S. told him to get. Relieved he had used one of his diminishable blankets as a cover for the back of the cart, all the items he required were dry. Back inside Martha's V.E.L.U.S. instructed him how to assemble the rod. Quickly following V.E.L.U.S.'s instruction, the tracking rod was assembled swiftly.

Standing up with the rod in his hand, he quickly kissed Magda and Prisca goodbye and waved at Martha.

'Be careful.' Magda shouted after him.

Running towards the Sea of Galilee he could see the high waves crashing up and down with the storm directly above it.

V.E.L.U.S. guided him to switch the tracking rod on. The electro magnetics in it would keep the water level around him, so he did not have to climb the waves.

Turning it on Joshua cautiously edged towards the water. Sticking the long metal rod in the sea, the waters around it immediately calmed, leaving a level surface for Joshua to walk on.

Stepping on the water tentatively, he found he still had the balance to walk in the shoes as they inflated. Walking slowly, then a little quicker, he soon started to run across the waters. Asking V.E.L.U.S. for predications where the boat was, his heart dropped when V.E.L.U.S. announced she was unable to locate. Advising

Joshua to keep looking she would track the positions he had already been and try and direct him to different areas. Joshua's run slowed into a little jog as he searched the waters for Zebedee's boat. Continuing to look across the sea, he spotted a little fleck on top of a wave. Changing direction, he sped towards the speck, hoping his eyes had not deceived him.

As he neared, he could clearly see the boat. The people aboard looked terrified. Continually heaving buckets full of water from inside the boat to try and prevent it from sinking, yet wave after wave came, bashing against the side of the little vessel, spraying water back in. Still making his way towards the boat, V.E.L.U.S. told him to drop the tracking rod five metres from approach.

Joshua shouted over the high winds and rain. 'It's metal V.E.L.U.S. The rod will sink.'

The calm robot voice echoed inside Joshua's head. 'Mr East, the tracking rod is designed to stay upright, but float from halfway. Drop it vertically down and it will instantly come back to the surface, settling half in the water and half out of the water.'

Joshua did as instructed when he was five metres from the boat and continued walking.

Peter saw him, wind and rain lashing on to his face as his mouth hung open watching Joshua walk towards him, calm waters shrouding him.

Alerting the others, some stood with wooden buckets in their hands, gawping, as the rain continued to fill the boat. Not able to tear their eyes away, they stared as Joshua walked on water towards the vessel.

Reaching the boat, he waved at them.

'How…what?' Peter stammered. 'I cannot believe my eyes.'

'I have shoes on from the TT pod.' Joshua laughed. 'They make me float.'

'But the water is so calm around you.' Judas exclaimed.

'The storm will be gone soon, do not worry.' Joshua tried to reassure them.

Lightning struck the tracking rod. The people on the boat, covered their eyes at the bright light behind Joshua.

Opening his eyes slightly, Peter saw Joshua, stood there in his white robes, the wind and rain howling around them, yet near Joshua all was calm. The bright light shone out behind him, creating a glow around his white robes which gently moved from the calm lapping waters surrounding him. Peter had never seen nor experienced anything as striking as this moment. Gasping, he put his head down away from the light, smiling to himself, knowing this man would be the saviour of the world.

The wind and rain abruptly stopped. The men looked around in surprise at the dramatic change in the weather and at Joshua still stood on the sea.

'Aren't you going to invite me on the boat?' Joshua said laughing at their surprised faces.

'Jesus, how are you standing on the water?' Peter asked.

Walking to the edge of the boat, he told peter to climb down. Taking off his clear plastic hat, he laid it on the surface of the water.

'Stand on this.' Joshua instructed. 'It will wrap around your feet and hold you above the water. Don't move too quickly when you stand on it or you will lose your balance and fall. Shuffle towards me, slowly.'

Peter gingerly put his feet on the plastic hat and watched as it curled around and disappeared. Shuffling gradually towards Joshua, a smile of joy slowly spread across his face.

'I'm doing it Jesus, I'm doing it. I'm walking on the sea.' He excitedly shouted moving towards Joshua faster.

'No Peter, it is only a hat. Not too fast.' He shouted as Peter fell into the water. Grabbing him and releasing the hat from his feet, Joshua pulled his head up above the sea.

Bending over, he whispered into Peter's ear. 'Remember always have faith in what I say.' He said as Peter spluttered out of the water. Telling him to hold onto his legs, Joshua pulled him along the water towards the boat.

Climbing aboard the vessel with Peter, Joshua removed his boots and hat and securely folded them into his leather belt.

Standing up, he looked at the now clear night sky. V.E.L.U.S. did well on her advice.

Turning to the sopping wet men that were still looking at him in shock, he smiled at them. 'Come on, move this boat, we have Zebedee's Grandchild to celebrate.' He said looking at them all in amusement.

Chapter 30
Rachel - The Power Source

Relief washed across Nicks face. 'Thank you Rachel. You do not know what this means, not to just S.U.S. Industries, but now for the worlds survival.'
Smiling in acknowledgement, Rachel continued to look around the inside of the TT pod. The inside was not as large as she anticipated. 'Why is it so small on the inside?' Rachel questioned.
'The TT pod was designed for all eventualities, therefore a lot of storage was essential. Medication, ration packs, all different types of electronics and lots more. We found an inventory stored on V.E.L.U.S. years ago, which showed us everything that had travelled back in time with Joshua.' Nick explained as he pushed a few buttons on the console. 'Quite a few electronics were still left on the TT pod unused, and unfortunately we have no idea what they would have been required for!'
'Have you not asked V.E.L.U.S.' Rachel asked.
'Yes, yet we are still none the wiser. Let me show you.'
Guiding Rachel out of the TT pod and around the back, Nick double tapped on a small indentation. A section of metal retracted slightly, and then moved in on itself, revealing a chamber inside the TT pod. The opening was small, and Rachel crouched to look inside, whilst Nick instructed V.E.L.U.S. to turn the lights on. Pulling herself in to the now bright, white storage compartment, Rachel realised it was bigger than the main part of the TT pod. Metallic blue apparatus hung on the surrounding brilliant white curved walls inside the storage area. Clear empty boxes were stacked against the walls.
'These.' Nick said pointing at them. 'Where full of ration packs, medication and other items from the alternative universe. They

were all long gone by the time our technology would have been able to extract the data of what they were made of.'

Nodding to acknowledge she was listening to Nick, Rachel stood closer to the gadgets that littered the wall. 'How are they attached?' She asked Nick.

'Honestly, we do not know. We have asked V.E.L.U.S. yet have not been able to decipher the coding and components on the information she has given us. It is fantastic technology though. Watch what happens.' Nick placed his hand in front of a cube of metal that was attached to the wall. Holding his hand a couple of centimetres away, the cube wobbled then shot towards his hand. Catching it, he turned and grinned. 'The shake from the cube is a warning it is about to remove itself.' Holding the cube back up to the place it came from, it wobbled again. Nick opened his hand and released the metal cube. Shooting back into its original place, Nick turned around to Rachel, still entertained. 'I never get bored of showing people that.' He laughed. 'No matter what piece of equipment you take, it will only wobble and return to its original place. V.E.L.U.S. downloaded the software onto our network, yet the coding is too specialised for our systems. We have had two engineers working on the encryption for the last thirty years. We are not as advanced as our alternate future.'

Rachel walked around the storage compartment. 'If the energy source is removed, would the TT pod stop functioning? Would all these apparatuses fall from the walls?'

'We know there is a small back up power source in case of failure of the main one, yet we do not know if this is working. It has never been used and we have never been able access it.' Nick replied.

Thinking and nodding, Rachel paced around the storage compartment. 'As I will be removing it, I will need a day accessing the files and all details about it. I need to ensure, mine and everyone's safety. Especially with what happened the last time you attempted to remove it.'

'Agreed.' Nick replied. 'We wouldn't be prepared for removal for at least a week. Preparations for its transportation have not been put in place. We wanted to ensure you could unlock the power source along with agreeing to do so before we made preparations.' Nick smiled at her.

Feeling reassured, Rachel continued to look at the gadgets adorning the curved walls of the storage compartment. There were so many, all different shapes and sizes. It was crazy to imagine these being over two thousand years old. There was not a speck of dust, nor dirt on any of them.

Nicks radio crackled, disturbing Rachel from her thoughts. Putting in an earpiece, he told the caller to go ahead.

Heart pumping, Rachel knew it would be Field Marshal Sanderson giving an update. Nick climbed out of the storage compartment, muffling his replies. Darting after him, Rachel pulled herself out of the small exit and followed Nick as he paced outside of the TT pod. Clicking the radio off, Nick breathed in heavily.

'What's happened?' Rachel asked panicked. 'Nick look at me, and tell me what is going on? Have they managed to pick them up?'

'I…I'm sorry Rachel.' Nick stammered. 'The children were not there when Special Forces arrived. They continued the search on Field Marshal Sanderson's orders, yet they lost contact. We are unsure of the situation, if they have been captured, killed or their radios were scrambled. Field Marshal Sanderson will report to me as soon as they have re-established communication.'

Grabbing her phone from her pocket, Rachel's face was red with fury. 'I'm ringing Caroline.' She said as she unlocked her phone.

Snatching it from her hand, Nick held the phone at arm's length. 'No. Do not speak to Caroline. She will know you sent them. The children will be kept alive until she has the power source. You need to ask her for proof they are still alive prior to sending the video of the TT pod.' Nick ordered. 'Once received we can track their new location. Do not let her know you are behind the raid.'

Rachel's chest heaved up and down as she breathed heavily, furious with Caroline. Nick was right, she needed proof her siblings were still alive. 'We need to get his video done and quick.' She said.

Nick silenced V.E.L.U.S.'s volume to ensure she did not welcome Magda when they walked in.

'Ready?' Nick said as they stood outside the building. Rachel nodded as she set the phone to record and placed it in her breast jacket pocket.

Going through the motions, Nick played his part extremely well, excitedly taking her into the building and showing her around the TT pod. Rachel tried to act as surprised as she could, yet there was still fury simmering underneath. Stopping her phone recording, she breathed a sigh of relief as Nick flopped into a nearby chair.

'Easy bit over, now to call Caroline.' Rachel said.

'Wait.' Nick put his hand up to stop her. Looking at the notification he had just got from his mobile, his face paled. 'She blew up the tunnels.' He said.

Rachel walked towards Nick and sat in the seat next to him. 'What?'

'Erm, Caroline.' Nick said, fumbling with his words as he replied to the message he had just received. 'She blew up the tunnels with the Special Forces team in it. Causing a chain reaction from two other rooms full of explosives. The Turkish are reporting it as a terrorist attack. As soon as they find the bodies of the Special Forces, they will retaliate on us. They have the weaponry. This could start a war.' Nick ran his hands through his hair. 'Caroline planned this.'

'How could she have planned Special Forces being in the tunnels?' Rachel asked obstinately.

'I'm not sure, yet I am certain she planned for this to happen. She knows, Rachel. She knows we sent them. She used your family ties as an advantage, she knew you would tell me, and I would arrange some kind of rescue mission. She planned this to distract me from you, and the TT pod. I need to call an emergency meeting.'

Rachel followed Nick into the main building and up into the glass panelled meeting room in silence. Yuri was already sat at the table with a grave look on his face.

'I've sent all office personnel home. Security have stayed and army presence are on their way.' Yuri informed them.

'Good. How long?' Nick asked as he sat at the mahogany table.

'Immediate response will be here in fifteen minutes, the rest may take over an hour. I have commenced lockdown procedure, the TT is being lowered as we speak. Sandra and Field Marshall Sanderson are ready when you.' Yuri looked at Rachel's pale face. 'I am sure Caroline will not have harmed your brother and sister. She needs you, and you need them.' He said. 'I will continue the search when we are in full lockdown.'

Rachel flashed him a weak smile, not daring to ask what lockdown is as she sat adjacent to Yuri.

'Is everything ready for the presentation?' Nick asked.

Yuri nodded. 'All ready when you are.'

Reaching forward, Nick placed his palm on the middle of the table. The glass panels frosted over and then plunged the room into darkness.

Gasping as V.E.L.U.S.'s voice boomed out in the room, Rachel listened as she announced the meeting members. The individual blue lights projected, slowly revealing Sandra Callaghan, Field Marshal Sanderson, Marshal of the Royal Air Force Voysden, England's Prime Minister Edward Thompson, and HRH the Queen of England. Gulping, Rachel straightened her sitting position as the Queens outline began to form within the darkened room.

Addressing all the members individually, Nick quickly reviewed why they were there. Listened intently, Rachel grimaced as he informed them, the Special Forces team had died within the tunnel walls on a rescue mission. Her stomach turned over as Edward Thompson relayed the Intel they had on the explosion in Cyprus, confirming the Turkish military had found the Special Forces team in the debris and were calling it an attack on the Turkish Government. The President had been informed yet had not reached out to him asking for validation. They were preparing for retaliation. She looked at the blue projection of the Queen, her face grave at the news. Silent, yet nodding in acknowledgement at all information imparted.

Field Marshal Sanderson advised all defence plans had been put into action. The Marshal of the Royal Air Force Voysden confirmed they were in communication with all Forces personnel and defence plans are on track.

A 3D projection appeared, mid-air above the table, casting light into the darkened room. The blue presentation was outlining the plans for the next forty-eight hours. A silent tear ran down Rachel's face, roughly wiping it away before anyone saw. This was no time for pity she thought to herself. She caused this chain of events. People had already died because of her, and now many more will if Turkey launch an attack. If Caroline had a hand in this attack, she knew they would be well equipped.

Staring at the contingency plan, Rachel could not concentrate. She needed to remove the power source and give it to Caroline, maybe then she would stop this. Feeling a hand on her shoulder, Rachel had not noticed Yuri move to the seat next to her. Leaning over, he whispered into her ear. 'None of this is your fault. It is Caroline's. She wanted this to happen and she made it happen.'

Yuri patted her shoulder and removed his hand as he lent back. She turned around slightly and flashed him a weak smile, Rachel knew he meant well, yet this did not stop her feeling she had caused it.

The presentation over, the blue projections switched off. The glass surrounding the office, turned from blackness to frosted, letting light back into the room.

'Yuri, can you take Rachel to the bunker, make sure she is settled and return here.' Nick instructed.

'What will you be doing while I am in the bunker?' Rachel asked.

'Speaking to our contacts, seeing if we can get intelligence on the imminent threat.' Nick replied whilst typing on his laptop.

'I can do that, you know the languages I'm fluent in, give me a list, I can call people.' Rachel pleaded. 'Please, I need to help. I was the cause of this.'

Nick looked up sharply. 'Rachel what the hell are you on about? You were not the cause of this. Caroline was the cause of this. We need you Rachel. You are the key to the power source, to information stored in the TT pod. You are the only person in this world that can do it and we need you. We need to keep you alive, not just for that, yet also for future plans. We need to protect you, not put you in harm's way. I will explain when this is all over but trust me when I say, you are the most important person in all of this. Now go.' He shouted, as Yuri guided her out of the meeting room.

Following him down the stairs, Yuri took her to a thick metal door. Using his thumb print, it unlocked and led them into a small concrete corridor. Jogging down the corridor and then two flights of stairs, Rachel wondered where he was taking her. Trotting along another concrete corridor, they arrived at what looked like a large safe door. Turning the dial this way and that until it clicked, Yuri wrenched open the door, spun the dial and closed it again. Hurrying down a metal corridor this time, he looked at Rachel's surprised face. 'I know many would think the safe door dial is old and outdated, yet sometimes the old ways are the most secure. You can't computer hack into it to release the door, you need to drill for hours!' He said smiling.

Coming up to another metal door, Rachel was now panting. Not sure if it was due to the situation or how unfit she was, she asked Yuri how much longer.

'This and another door and we are there.' He answered opening the metal door with a key card. Going through into the next corridor, Rachel knew they were near. The walls were all brilliant white, and softly lit. A frosted glass door straight in front of them. 'We have to go in individually.' Yuri instructed. 'V.E.L.U.S. only lets authorised personnel in.'

Walking up to the frosted glass door, Yuri instructed Rachel to place her hand just above the handle.

Pressing her palm firmly on the glass, blue light glowed underneath it and expanded across the door. The door opened as V.E.L.U.S. welcomed Rachel. Walking through into what looked like a fully furnished living room, Rachel waited for Yuri.

Joining her, Yuri guided her around the underground shelter. As she was shown the kitchen and bathroom, Rachel thought it was more like a house than a bunker with all the amenities. Yuri took her to the last door, opening it to reveal an identical room to the barn above ground, complete with TT pod.

Seeing the surprise on her face, Yuri explained. 'Whenever there is a breach or threat, the TT pod gets lowered into the bunker to keep it safe.'

'You mean the power source?' Rachel questioned.

'Not just the power source, but all the other information it holds. Even the tools, the original V.E.L.U.S. along with the metal it is made from. It could be dangerous in the wrong hands.' Yuri replied.

Walking back into the living room area, Yuri explained he had to leave but his mother would be joining her shortly.

'If you want to look at the TT pod in more detail, just ask V.E.L.U.S. if you have any questions. Keep this on you at all times.' Yuri passed her what looked like a pager.

Frowning, as she looked at the small black device, the screen on it lit up.

'Hook it anywhere you want. If you need anyone, speak their name into this. We'll speak to you through it as well, if you hear a voice, it will be one of us trying to get through to you.'

'Thanks Yuri.' Rachel smiled.

'You're welcome Rach, I'll be coming back here, I just have to help my Dad with a few things first.'

Rachel nodded, feeling slightly awkward she had been brought down, she started fiddling with the shiny black gadget, 'Yuri, I know it is not the best time to ask and I most probably already know the answer, but would you ask your Dad if I should send the video to Caroline? In all this commotion, I wasn't sure what he wanted me to do.'

'Yeah, course. I'll let you know through the comycon.'

'Comycon?' Rachel queried. 'Oh, the comycon.' Rachel said holding up the imitation pager.

'It is the only secure way to communicate with each other at the moment, we have no idea what Caroline has hacked into.' Yuri explained as Rachel hooked it onto the belt attached to her trousers. 'It also works on a unique signal, therefore if all satellites are down, we can still communicate through the Comycon.'

She smiled awkwardly and watched as Yuri left through the frosted glass door.

Pacing around, Rachel was at a loss what to do. There was not much she could do to rectify the position she had put herself, Nick, Yuri and the TT pod in, yet she felt she needed to do something productive. Grabbing a bottle of water from the fridge, Rachel made her way to the room that now housed the TT pod.

'Welcome Magda.' V.E.L.U.S. boomed. 'Is there anything I could assist you with today?'

'V.E.L.U.S. can you show me some footage from Rylitte.' She asked.

Sitting down on the chair, V.E.L.U.S. displayed different times and areas of Rylitte. Absorbed in looking at the alternate future, she jumped when she heard Yuri's voice sound out.

'V.E.L.U.S. pause.' She instructed before picking up the Comycon. 'Hi Yuri, I am here.' She said into the black gadget.

'Dad said to send the video with a message saying he had gone into a meeting and you were having a tour with one on the lab techs. Make her think everything is happening as usual, yet my Father has been called away urgently.'

'Yes, I'll send it now.' She said into the comycon before hooking it back onto her belt. Firing off the video of her entering the barn with the TT pod with a message, Rachel sat back and sighed at her phone. There was an anxious feeling in her stomach, she felt so lost and so alone right now. Hoping her brother and sister were not harmed in the blast, all she could do was wait until Nick or Yuri contacted her.

Asking V.E.L.U.S. to recommence the footage, Rachel tried her best to concentrate on learning more about the alternate future, yet it was bugging her Caroline had not replied. Something was clearly wrong, Caroline always replied. Asking V.E.L.U.S. to pause again, Rachel got up. Yuri's Mother, Maria should have been here by now, nearly an hour since Rachel first entered the

bunker. Walking through into the living room, Yuri burst through the door. 'Rachel you need to come with me now.' He demanded.
'What?...Why?' Rachel asked shocked.
'No time to explain, follow me quickly.' Yuri panted.
Yuri ran ahead of her, guiding them through the many doors they had passed on the way there.
Taking her back to the frosted glass board room, her eyes wide in surprise as Nick stood there watching a monitor.
'I'm assuming Caroline never contacted you back?' Nick said, not taking his eyes off the monitor displaying the area outside of the offices.
Walking towards the monitor, Rachel sharply breathed inwardly.
'No, she can't be.' She said freezing at what was displayed.
Quickly turning around, Rachel darted for the door. Yuri grabbed her around her waist. 'Wait.' He abruptly said.
'Rachel, there is no easy way to say this.' Nick gravely said. 'Caroline has demanded the power source in exchange for your brother and sister. She said it is non-negotiable and if she does not get an answer in the next 6 minutes, one of them will die.'
A tear ran down Rachel's face as she continued to watch Caroline with the two scrawny, young children, dressed in rags in front of her. Her bony hand on the shoulder of the little girl, holding her still whilst she sobbed. In Caroline's other hand, a gun pressed against the back of the little girl's head.
'I have to do it.' Rachel whispered. 'She can't kill them. They are only children.'
'I'm sorry.' Nick said. 'We cannot put the power source into Caroline's hands. Millions of people will die. You need to think about this Rachel. Do you choose millions of people and freedom or those two children?'
'Those two children?' Rachel shouted. 'Those two children are the only family I have got, and the only reason those two children are here is because of me! I had no one when I was younger, I will not let it happen to MY siblings.' She screamed at Nick as she squirmed away from Yuri.
'Rachel. I am ordering you NOT to remove the power source. You do not realise what she can do with it!'
Ignoring Nick, Rachel wrenched the frosted glass door open and ran towards the entrance of the building.
Running down the stairs and out into the open, Rachel stopped as she saw Caroline's smug smile. Three black cars were parked on

angles, doors open, blocking the road to prevent any car driving in or out. A black van parked at the back, had its rear doors open as if waiting to be loaded with a package. Knowing what package the van was waiting for, Rachel quickly counted ten people all dressed in black behind the cars, pointing guns towards the entrance of the door. Shock registered as she spotted soldiers, faced down, scattered along the gravelled drive. Their army immediate response had been assassinated. Breathing heavily, Rachel's eyes narrowed at Caroline. She knew Rachel would do anything for her newfound brother and sister.

'I knew you would come Rachel.' Caroline sweetly smiled. 'I think I already know your answer.'

'You know I would do anything for them two.' Rachel said to Caroline through tears. 'Yet even if I do get the power source, you have revealed yourself to who you truly are. It will only be a matter of time before someone catches up to you and all this will have been for nothing. You will be locked up or dead.'

'Oh, Rachel of little faith. You really do think I am simple, don't you?' Caroline sniggered. 'My cover was broken as soon as you blurted your mouth off to Yuri. I warned you I was always watching.' She tutted as she waved her gun towards Yuri that was now beside Rachel. Placing it back on the little girl's head, Caroline continued. 'Yet I still needed that power source, so I played your game and bided my time until I got the distraction I needed, and you did not disappointment me Rachel. You played well and truly into my hands. That video you sent me was hilarious, great acting by the way Nick.' Caroline smirked as she slowly inched closer to Rachel, the gun still pressed against the little girl's head. 'With the threat of World War Three about to start, no one will have time to search for little old me.' Cocking her head to one side, she smiled. 'So, Rachel, you have about thirty seconds to fetch me the power source or someone you love is going to go bye bye.'

'You know I cannot get the power source within thirty seconds. If you shoot my sister, the deal is off.' Rachel shouted as Caroline cocked the gun, ready to shoot.

'Twenty seconds Rachel, tick tock.'

'I can't... it's impossible. You will not get the power source if you kill my sister.' Rachel screamed.

'Zero.' Caroline said.

Rachel flinched at the bang as the echo from the shot bounced around the car park.

Rachel stood there frozen, the ringing in her ears muffled the noises that surrounded her. Touching the wet sticky liquid on her face with her trembling hand, she tried to make sense of what had just happened. Her mind seemed to have stopped working as she tried to comprehend the last few seconds. Everything seemed to move in slow motion as she looked at Caroline's smiling face and the people running to the cars behind her.

Rachel looked at the floor and heard an almighty scream. It was her scream; the noise was coming from her mouth as she realised what had happened.

'No, no, no, no.' Rachel repeated as she fell to the floor, scrambling to the dead body that lay in front of her.

Chapter 31
Joshua – Homesick

Joshua and his trusted circle of friends had a great night celebrating Zebedee's first grandchild. They had partied until the early hours of the morning and after seeing the delightful baby, Joshua had pangs to get back to his own family.

Dishing out hangover pebbles, Joshua informed them all he was making his way home and they were welcome to join him if they wanted. All twelve decided to walk back with Joshua.

Laughing and telling stories of their most recent travels as they walked, Joshua listened as Thomas retold his account of when he was questioned by one of Herod's guards.

'…And then he asked me if I thought Jesus was John the Baptist reincarnated.' Thomas said as the whole group roared with laughter. In between laughing, Thomas continued. 'So, I explained that Jesus and John the Baptist were alive at the same time. He then asked if Jesus was Elijah.' The group stopped walking, and most fell to the floor in laughter.

Joshua approached Thomas. 'Who's Elijah?' He asked.

'Elijah was John the Baptists Uncle, died before John was born, yet you would have known they were related. Apparently, Elijah and John the Baptist had the same outspoken, peculiar personalities and looked relatively similar too.' Thomas replied.

'What did they say about me?' Joshua asked.

'They didn't say anything, was just asking questions who you are and what you are doing. I think King Herod is wary of your intentions.'

'What did you tell them?' Joshua questioned.

The group fell silent with the serious tone in Joshua's voice. 'I...I just told them you were wanting to help the needy and sick to make the world a better place.' Thomas stammered.

'And you?' Joshua pointed at Philip. 'Has anything like this been asked of you?'

Philip nodded. 'Yes, Jesus. I have been asked a few times from different guards and members of the royal household. I said the same as Thomas.' Philip replied as he looked at the ground.

Going round the group, Joshua was told similar stories. Lastly, he asked Peter.

'Peter, what has been asked of you?' Joshua questioned.

'The same as the others, yet I replied with something different.' He replied proudly puffing his chest out. 'I told them you were the Messiah and you had come to change the world.'

'No, no, no.' Joshua replied remembering the time he was nearly thrown off the cliff by the angry crowd. 'Please do not tell them I am the Messiah. This will anger people, especially King Herod. If he beheaded John the Baptist for just saying his marriage is a sham, he will surely see me dead for saying I am the son of God. Please, keep this, and my story to yourself.'

The group murmured and nodded at Joshua as they set off walking again. Joshua hung back from the group, needing to think about what actions he was required to take next. If questions were being asked, it wouldn't be too much longer until King Herod's guards came for him again.

Peter dropped back from the rest of the group and started to walk with Joshua.

'Sorry Jesus.' Peter apologised. 'Everything you have done for me, for my family and the people in these areas, I wanted you to have the recognition for it. You have done so much, people need to bow at your feet.'

Joshua laughed. 'Thank you, Peter, yet I do not need anyone to bow at my feet. The feeling I get from helping people, is all I need. My family are healthy and happy, and I have great friends. I do not need recognition or payment, I enjoy it. However, I am concerned about King Herod's intentions towards me. Last time it was pure luck I managed to get away from the guards, next time, I am not sure I will be as lucky, especially with the interest more and more people are taking in me. I have a feeling when I am found, King Herod will keep me, and kill me.'

Peter gasped. 'No Jesus, he cannot, he will not, I will not allow him to do this.'

Joshua smiled at Peter's loyalty. 'Thank you, yet I do not want you to risk your life for mine.' He said patting him on the back. 'If this does happen, I need you to make sure Magda and Prisca are protected and well cared for as well as continuing to spread the word. Promise me.'

'I promise you Jesus.' Peter replied.

Stood in a trance, biting his fingernails, Joshua looked out across the fields at the end of his garden. The soft breeze blowing his hair as he thought about what he had discovered over the last few days.

'Josh, are you listening?' Magda waved her hand in front of Joshua's face.

'Sorry Mag's did you call?' Joshua replied suddenly becoming aware Magda was next to him.

'Are you alright?' Magda asked. 'You've not been yourself the last few days. You're worrying me'

'Come here.' Joshua said, wrapping his arms around Magda. 'I'm sorry if I have worried you, it's just there are a few things on my mind lately.'

'No kidding.' She laughed. 'Remember you can always talk to me.' She said planting a kiss on his cheek.

Squeezing her a little harder, they gazed across the fields together. Joshua sat Magda down on the grass and explained the information his friends had told him on the walk back from Zebedee's.

'That's nothing to worry about.' Magda soothed 'It is just people being inquisitive.'

Joshua shook his head and explained how Matthew had been carrying out his own investigation, collecting gossip from his old tax collector friends about King Herod's interest in him.

'Herod intends to have me arrested Mag's.' He told her. 'From then on I am not sure what he is going to do, yet I have a feeling, I won't be around for much longer.'

Looking at her striking face glowing from the orange sunset, he did not think he had ever seen her look more beautiful. He watched a single tear run down her cheek before she quickly brushed it away.

'We will hide you in the TT pod. I will get people to guard it, no one will discover you. We will say you left for Jerusalem or

Bethlehem and have not returned.' Magda said to herself as she stood up and walked around Joshua. 'Yes, we will arrange for you to go into hiding. With your friends and family, we will ensure you are protected.'

Grabbing both of her hands to stop her from pacing up and down, Joshua made her look at him. 'I am not putting you and Prisca at risk. And we definitely do not want Herod getting his hands on the TT pod. Imagine what he would do with it.' Joshua said.

'I will consult with V.E.L.U.S. and secure our most precious data and items on board there. Herod will not know how to open it. I will ensure it is protected, with you inside.' Magda informed, a determined look on her face.

'I agree, speak with V.E.L.U.S. and secure everything we need to keep secret, yet I will not be hiding in it. I am not bringing the guards to our front door Mag's, I won't put you and Prisca at risk. The twelve trusted friends we have will keep you safe, I will make sure of that. Out of everyone I know in this world, you are the most precious one to me and the one I rely on the most. If the time comes and I am captured, you need to promise me you will carry on the work we have started. Not for me, but for Prisca, and her children.'

Magda quietly started to sob into Joshua's shoulder. 'I know it is hard Magda. I don't want to leave you or Prisca, yet if me leaving keeps you both safe, I know I have done one thing right.'

'I am not sure if I can live without you Joshua.' Magda said quietly in-between sobs.

'I know Mags. If there was a way I could be with you two forever, you know I would be there, yet, I cannot put you in harm's way. Let us not think about it just now. Worrying is wasted energy, lets enjoy our time.' Joshua kissed the top of her head.

Silence elapsed between them as they watched the sun set on the horizon.

Clearing her throat, Joshua looked across at Magda. 'There is something I had come out here to tell you.' She said anxiously.

Cupping her head in his hand and stroking her cheek with his thumb, he gave her an encouraging smile. 'You look nervous Mags. You know you can tell me anything.' Joshua whispered.

'I thought it would be good news, yet now, after this I am not so sure.'

'What is it Magda.' Joshua asked.

'I'm pregnant.' She replied.

Holding her close, a tear slid down Joshua's face. There was no choice for him now, he needed to move Magda and Prisca to somewhere secure, somewhere she would be safe.

They held each other in silence until the sky turned black and the stars twinkled in the sky.

Returning into the house, Magda went and checked on Prisca, rubbing her stomach as she walked.

Guilt racked through Joshua, she shouldn't be stressed at a time like this he thought to himself. Grabbing his protective suit, Joshua checked to see if the small, black, portable jexton was still secured inside the pocket. Feeling it was still there, he told Magda he was going for a walk. Seeing the sad look in her eyes, he smiled weakly at her. Kissing her forehead, he cupped her face. 'I am so happy about you carrying my child, this should be a celebration.' He said looking into her sad brown eyes. 'I cannot celebrate until I know you, Prisca and this little one is safe.' Bending down, Joshua kissed the small bump he had not noticed was there. 'I will be back, and I will be back with a plan.' He said, holding her tighter than usual. Kissing him back, she made him promise to come back safe.

As he left the house, Joshua saw Peter, John and James walking towards him. Stuffing his protective suit into the bag he was holding, he waited for them.

Explaining he was heading out for a walk up the mountain, James advised they would accompany him as it was imperative they spoke to him immediately. Agreeing, the three men followed Joshua as he made his way to up the mountain.

'We have news Jesus.' Peter instructed. 'And it is not good.' He said sadly. 'Matthew asked us to come and take you to a protected area. King Herod is apprehensive at the amount of people that are willing to follow you. His guards have been asking the people if they would prefer you or him as King. Majority of the people have advised they would prefer you to be King. He is paranoid and angry the people do not respect him as much as they do you. It is only a matter of time before the guards come looking and ... we know what follows. I am sorry Jesus.'

Joshua nodded and continued walking. 'I had a feeling this was going to happen.' He replied, his voice steadier than he felt. 'I need some time, to get away from the crowds and think clearly. Not for me, but to make sure Magda and Prisca are safe. If I am sent to trial and killed, I need you to keep them safe.'

Peter, John and James nodded in acknowledgement and followed him up the mountain in silence. Reaching the top, they all sat and looked at the view. Joshua passed out bottled water to them as they chatted and watched the sunrise.

Wrestling with his conscience slightly, Joshua watched all three of them grow sleepy from the pills he had laced their water with. He appreciated their protective nature, yet he needed some time on his own, to be with his former loved ones. Facing death, he had never felt more alone than he did right now. Mary would not be around forever to look after Magda and though he had brothers, sisters and friends, he longed for the people he had known his entire life.

Checking they were fully asleep, Joshua turned around from them and retrieved the jexton from his inside pocket. Slipping the protective suit over his shoulders, he looked at the small black oval jexton he was holding. Switching it on, he placed it on a rock a metre in front of him. A blue projected screen shone out from it, displaying a menu. The names of his former friends and family were listed. Selecting his own Mother first, he watched as she spoke about how she loved her son and husband and could not imagine life without them.

Tears ran down Joshua's face as he whispered quietly. 'I really need you right now Mum. I miss you so much.' Wrapping the protective suit further around him, he pictured her making it, the time and effort she had painstakingly put into this suit, yet she would never know how precious it was.

The video ended and reverted to the main menu. A pang of guilt flashed through him as he looked at Jess' name. He could not watch hers, it would be too painful. He had promise he would never forget her, yet here he was, married with a second child on the way.

Shaking his head to disperse the guilt swirling around inside him, he decided to select Liz's next, he knew hers would be interactive.

'What's happened for you to be contacting me on here?' Her joyful voice echoed through the mountains.

Laughing through his tears, Joshua chatted with the blue projection of Liz, understanding that her answers where limited due to it being pre-recorded, yet her quirky remarks made it feel like he had never been away.

He moved on to Richard next, then Sarah the housekeeper and his only acquaintance Michael, that he had known since his school days.

Hearing a noise behind him, Joshua looked around to see Peter stirring. He knew he did not have much time left before they awoke, and he wanted to keep his previous future life separate from his current one.

Selecting his Father and Caelan at the same time, they both projected out to him. Interacting with each other as well as Joshua, he told them about Magda and Prisca and that they had another one on the way.

'Your Mother would be so proud of you, just as I am.' Stephen's projection smiled down on Joshua.

Caelan joined in the on the conversation, telling Joshua how he thought of him like a son as much as he thought of Stephen like a brother. 'Whatever you do in this new life, it will always be the right decision. You have a good heart, like your Mother and Father. Whatever you have done and how ever far you have got, I know it will be a success, even if you cannot not see it yet. You were a warrior and hero in the Servian world, just as you will be in this world.' Caelan said proudly, as tears pricked in Joshua's' eyes.

Knowing their answers would be limited, Joshua asked their advice on his impending capture and potential death.

Stephen was the one to answer this. 'I have been honoured to call you my son, watching you grow into the man you have become has been a pleasure. The hard part is to tell you when to admit defeat and when to keep fighting. Only you will know this, yet just remember, me, your Mother, Caelan and Liz will always be there, inside you. We will be with you ever step of the way, even when you are staring death in the face, we are there, right here.' Stephen touched his forehead. 'And here always.' He said touching his heart.

A noise behind Joshua distracted him from his tears. Looking behind him, he could see Peter trying to sit up. Joshua quickly fumbled for the jexton to turn it off. Picking it up from the rock, Joshua turned it over casting the mountain in a hazy fog with the blue projection as Stephen continued to talk. 'You son are the chosen one and you need to listen....' Joshua managed to turn it off as Peter started to exclaim.

Stashing the jexton firmly into the inside of his protective suit, he took it off his shoulders and put it back into the bag he brought with him.

Offering Peter, John and James some food he had brought with him, they hungrily ate what was offered, yet Joshua was not in the mood for food. He had decided. If he were to be sought out and arrested by King Herod, he wouldn't fight, he would show the people of this world that violence was not the answer. Anger would only increase the divide between everyone. Instead they would need to unite and show love was more powerful than hate, even when faced with death. He would not inflict pain onto others that were following orders, he would co-operate and die with dignity. Hopefully they would see the error in their ways and show compassion to those around him after his death.

He knew he needed to tell Magda, unsure of how much time he had left. He needed to speak to Matthew and ask him to find out when the instructions for his arrest and capture would be ordered. It could be months, or it could be tomorrow. Standing up and stretching, Joshua began the descent down the mountain with the others. Most of the journey was passed in silence and small mutterings between the three. Joshua ignored them, he needed to speak to Magda and let her know of his decision.

Arriving at the bottom of the mountain, Joshua, Peter, James and John were greeted by a large crowd that had formed. Turning to James, he asked who had told the crowd he would be there. Anxious that the orders for his arrest had already been issued, he slowly walked down the last part. A man was shouting from afar at him, yet Joshua could not make out what he was saying. Afraid to go any further in case he was arrested before he had chance to speak to Magda, Joshua turned to John and asked if he knew what he was saying.

'He is asking for your help Jesus, saying his son is foaming from the mouth and is possessed by a demon.' John replied.

Relieved it was not an order for his arrest, Joshua hurried towards the man.

'Teacher, please help me. My only child, my son has been possessed by a spirit, he suddenly screams, his eyes role into the back of his head and his body shakes as he foams at the mouth. I have tried all people at the ministry, yet no one can remove the demon from my son. It hardly leaves him.' The man shouted at Joshua.

Sighing heavily, Joshua looked at Philip who stood next to the man. It would have been him that told the crowd he was up the mountain. Joshua would need to leave Magda. He would not be able to give Magda and Prisca the concealment they required. The crowds and Herod would see to that.

Walking to Philip grinning at him, Joshua's face was like thunder. 'I have told you already what you need to do with a child with these symptoms, you are unbelievable bringing these people here.' He shouted as Philips face dropped.

I...I'm sorry Jesus.' Philip stuttered as Joshua held his hand up to silence him and ordered the man to bring him his son.

Joshua knew the child had epilepsy before he was brought to him. Grabbing Philips bag of medication, he took out a needle and a vial of medicine. Withdrawing the liquid from the vial into the syringe, Joshua watched as the man carried his son towards him. The man was only a few metres away from Joshua, when the child started fitting and foaming at the mouth. Rushing across to the child as the father laid him on the floor, Joshua knelt down beside the boy. Holding his head still, Joshua quickly injected the medication into the child. The boy immediately stopped fitting and began to quietly moan in confusion. Checking all his vital signs, Joshua passed the boy back to his Father.

'He should be fine now. Any problems, please find Philip who will be happy to assist you.' He grimaced at Philip.

The crowd were overjoyed watching Joshua heal the boy so quickly, yet Joshua was still angry. He needed to get to Magda and make sure she was safe.

Chapter 32
Rachel - Caroline, What Have You Done?

'Caroline, what have you done?' Nick gasped. His eyes wide open in shock as he ran his hands through his hair. As he stared at Caroline, the world seemed to slow. People were screaming around him, two cars were reversing and screeching off down the gravelled drive, yet it all sounded muffled. Slowly looking at what lay before him, the tears welled up in his eyes.

Kneeling on the floor next to Rachel, he felt nothing as the sharp gravel ripped through his trousers and dug into his knees.

Nick looked at the commotion happening around him, his brain was foggy. He couldn't register what had just happened. It looked real, it sounded real, but he refused to believe it was real. He could feel his heart pounding, the blood thumping in his ears. He wanted to talk to Rachel, but a lump formed in his throat and nothing came out. He felt someone tugging at his shoulders, shouting at him to move but he couldn't, he had frozen. He could not remove his eyes away from the hole that now featured in his son's head. As he watched the blood trickle from the wound, the world stopped spinning.

'Yuri, son, come on. We need to get you to hospital.' Nick softly spoke to him. 'Come on Yuri. You need to get up.' Tears ran down his cheeks as Yuri laid there motionless. 'Yuri, come on. We need to go. We have lots to do.' Yuri's eyes were closed as if he were sleeping. The blood seeping from the wound in his head, pooled underneath him as Nick's voice got louder. Grabbing his shoulders, Nick started to shake him. 'Get up now Yuri.' He shouted as no reaction came from Yuri's body. 'I said get up!' Nick yelled.

Tears ran down Rachel's face as she watched Nick trying to wake Yuri up from an everlasting sleep. Her trousers were seeped in his blood. Removing her hands away from Yuri as Nick shook him more, she held them up in front of her face. Looking at the blood that covered her hands, Rachel wailed. It didn't look real; it couldn't be real.

'Yuri, please, get up.' Nick was pleading now. 'Please son.' He wept. Bending his head over to Yuri's chest, Nick howled.

Rachel could only look on as Nick broke down before her, sobbing into Yuri's chest, grasping onto his once white shirt in anguish.

'Yuri, son, please. I'm sorry, please get up. I…I need you. Please Yuri, don't leave me.'

The crunch of gravel, alerted Rachel someone was approaching. Hearing Caroline's laughter above her head, she looked up.

'So then Rachel, you off to get the power source you promised. You can lead the way if you wish.' She smiled.

'I warned you the deal was off if you killed someone.' Rachel shouted at Caroline.

'Actually Rachel.' Caroline smugly replied. 'You said the deal was off if I killed your sister. I didn't kill the little darling, so you best go get me the power source before I get angry.' Crouching down to Rachel, her face only millimetres away, Caroline's face switched from smug to pure evil. 'Don't make me angry Rachel. I make a better friend than enemy.' She snarled.

Rachel could see Nicks enraged face in the corner of her eye. It all happened so quickly; Rachel only could register a blur of clothing before she realised Caroline was now laid on the floor next to Yuri.

Caroline and Nick grappled along the floor. Straddling her, Nick wrenched the gun from her hands and threw it on the gravel.

Pulling his fist back, Caroline laughed at him. 'Stefan East, holier than thou, direct descendant from Jesus himself, would never hit a woman. You wouldn't be able to live with yourself if you did.' She giggled.

Nicks clenched fist stayed raised above his head. His face a mixture of emotions, displaying the war raging in his head.

'I knew you wouldn't be able to do it.' Caroline sneered at him.

'No but I can.' Rachel said as she punched Caroline in her face.

The anger that simmered below the surface inside Rachel spilled out as she delivered blow after blow. The games Caroline had played, monitoring her every step even prior to Rachel joining the committee, bringing her mother back into her life. Then Yuri, poor innocent Yuri. He had not even wanted to be part of this life yet killed because of her. Rachel felt every choice she had made, had been the wrong one. She had caused too many deaths and Yuri's was the last straw.

The tears of rage and sadness blurred her vision as she started to punch into thin air. Rachel felt strong arms wrap around her midriff and pull her away from Caroline.

Squirming as much as she could to get back to finish what she started, the arms stayed strong across her waist and pulled her further away. Roughly wiping her eyes with the sleeve of her denim jacket, she felt the wetness of the cuff across her face. Looking at it in puzzlement, she saw the cuff was darkened in blood, Yuri's blood. Her heart constricted as the image of Yuri being shot reverberated through her mind. The strong arm around her waist held her tight once more as she tried to get back to Caroline again. Screaming at Nick to finish off the job, Caroline's bloodied face turned towards her, her teeth stained with blood as she smiled at Rachel's reaction and then at Yuri.

The more Rachel wrestled to get away, the further away she was taken. Her eyes flitted to Yuri, not moving. His sharp suit and white crisp shirt he always wore, now bloodied and dirty. His angelic face and soft curly hair now marred by the bullet wound in his forehead. Reaching her arms out to Yuri, she felt her head being held as two people were murmuring behind her. A hand placed on the side of her forehead, forcing her head against her right shoulder, straining out her neck. Feeling a sharp prick, followed by warm fluid running around her body, she knew she had been injected. Fighting with all her strength to get away from whoever had their tight grip on her, was useless. Feeling her eyes drooping, she screamed and threatened Caroline. Rachel started to slur her words as her view of Caroline's demonic smile and Nick still holding her down became blurry.

Fighting to keep her eyes open, she could feel her body not responding and growing heavy. She took one last look at the blurred shape of Yuri on the floor before everything went black.

Rachel fluttered her eyes open. Hearing beeping, she looked to the left. Seeing the machine monitoring her heart and blood pressure, it only took a second of confusion before the image of Yuri laid on the floor swam into her mind. A wave of nausea came across her and tears sprung into her eyes as she relived the moment. The memory replayed in slow motion repeatedly. The bullet exiting from the gun Caroline held and into Yuri's head. A sob escaped her as she remembered the delight in Caroline's face as she watched her and Nick's reactions.

Knowing she needed to see Nick, to catch up on what happened, she tried to sit up, yet felt a shooting pain across her stomach. Crying out in pain and surprise, Rachel started to move the blanket that covered her to examine her abdomen.

'Rachel, you need to rest, please lay back down.' A female voice said.

Stopping what she was doing, Rachel looked to the right and saw Maria sat in a hospital chair. The blue blanket draped around her fell, as she sat up and rubbed her tired eyes. Observing Maria's dishevelled appearance, Rachel knew she had been by her bedside for a while.

'Maria.' Rachel said surprised. 'I am so sorry for your loss.' She said sorrowfully. Looking down with guilt, Rachel wrung her hands together as tears escaped down her cheeks. 'It is all my fault, I should have never got involved with Caroline and now…' Rachel's voiced choked up, she couldn't express the words.

Maria stood up and made her way to the bed. Putting her arms around Rachel, she cradled Rachel's head to her chest. 'Shush, sweetheart. This is not your fault. None of this is your fault. You need to rest.' She spoke softly, stroking Rachel's hair as she fought back the tears. 'The two children are safe, they are here in this hospital.'

''My brother and sister?' Rachel whispered back. 'Can I see them?'

'They are in the children's ward. You will be able to see them, yet only when you are well enough, for now it can wait, they are safe.'

Tears ran down Rachel's face. 'I am so sorry, I didn't have a choice, I…I needed to save them and then …' Rachel trailed off.

Holding Rachel's head in her hands, Maria looked deep into her eyes and softly whispered. 'Only Caroline had a choice in all this. We would have all reacted the same. You were not responsible for Yuri's death. What I need you to do is take this time to recover. We all need you back to full health. You are the only person that will be able to bring Caroline to justice for what she did to my son.' Gently letting go of her head, Maria put her arms around her and hugged her gently. 'The surgery went well. They managed to stop the internal bleeding and stitch you up. It was touch and go for a while, yet the doctors have confirmed you will make a full recovery. For a moment, we were unsure if we had lost you too. Stefan was beside himself. That is why you need to give yourself time to heal, you will only prolong the recovery process.'

Rachel jolted her head up in surprise. 'What do you mean surgery? Internal bleeding?' Rachel asked, her tear stained face looking intently at Maria.

'Do you not remember?' Maria extracted herself from Rachel.

Shaking her head, Rachel watched as Maria pulled the pale pink leather chair to the bed and sat down. 'The last thing I remember is being pulled off Caroline, being held as I fought to get back to her.' Rachel said as Maria grasped her hand.

'I arrived just as the security guards were pulling you away from Caroline.' Maria explained. 'Stefan was still preventing her to get up. Her face was a mess, bloodied and broken, yet she was laughing as you struggled with the security to continue the beating you were giving her. Pietro, the security guard, injected you with a sedative, to calm you down, yet you collapsed. Stefan ran to you, screaming at Pietro, asking him what he had done. Checking you over, what they originally thought was a mixture of blood from Yuri and Caroline, was actually your own. The army arrived as I reached you and Yuri. I knew there was nothing I could do for Yuri, so I came to you. You were only just breathing with a weak pulse. The pool of blood underneath you were growing larger, it had to be coming from somewhere. I pulled up your shirt and saw the gaping wound in your side. Putting pressure on it to try and stem the bleeding, Stefan called for the army medic. He was able to stabilise you before we transported you to the hospital. You have been unconscious for two days.'

Confusion swept across Rachel's face as she pulled up her hospital nightgown to look, her abdomen was covered in bandages. 'How? When?' Rachel asked.

'We weren't sure until we reviewed the CCTV. It showed Caroline wheedling a flick knife out of her side pocket as she talked Stefan out of hitting her. As she went to stab him in the side, you unexpectedly came flying in. Caroline plunged the knife into you, instead of Stefan. You saved my husband Rachel, I can never thank you enough.'

'But I never felt anything?' Rachel said in astonishment. 'I would have felt something if I had been stabbed by Caroline.'

'So much happened in such a short space of time Rachel. Your body maybe did not register the pain as you were so focused on Caroline, or what had just happened to Yuri. We have the CCTV, yet I do not advise watching it just yet, it is not pleasant viewing.'

Rachel laid her head back in astonishment. She knew adrenaline was rushing around her body at the time yet did not feel a thing. Rachel stared at the bright white ceiling, only just registering what Maria had said earlier.

'Maria?' She questioned. 'What did you mean when you said I am the only person that can bring Caroline to justice? Where is she?'

'We don't know.' Maria looked down at the floor in sadness. 'She escaped. When you collapsed, Stefan released her and ran towards you and chaos erupted. Her people started shooting at us all, distracting us whilst they removed her and placed her into the only vehicle that was left near the house. Their visit to the TT pod and house was not a spur of the moment decision. Caroline had known she could not move the power source and needed you to retrieve it. All of her meetings with you, had been to lull you into a false sense of security. Caroline had planned for every situation, including being surrounded. As the vehicle sped off, it headed towards the grassy area bordering the house. The ground shook and the noise was deafening as they had detonated bombs to bring down the wall on the East side of the perimeter, just wide enough to fit her car through. The army did their best to stop her, yet her car was bullet proof.'

'Is the power source safe?' Rachel asked, wide eyed at all she had missed.

'Yes, it is.' Came a deep voice from the door of the hospital room. Rachel felt relief wash over her as she watched Nick come in and greet his wife. 'I was notified you were awake.' He smiled as he kissed Rachel on her cheek. 'We were so worried about you.'

'Nick, I'm so sorry about …' Again, Rachel trailed off, she couldn't say the words.

Nick nodded. He looked like he had aged since she had last seen him. Frown marks cemented in his brow, made more obvious by the paleness of his face. The bags under his tired eyes, emphasised by the flecks of grey now in his floppy blonde hair. 'Yuri's life will be celebrated, and we will morn in time, yet the safety of the human race is currently in our hands and this is our priority. When you have recovered from your wounds, I will update you with all that has been happening, but for now you must rest, we need you strong and back to the old Rachel.' Nick advised.

Rachel shook her head. 'Apparently, I have slept for 48 hours, I am recovered, albeit a little sore, yet that would not heed my ability to listen. You can update me now.'

'Not just yet. I need you fully functional.'

'You have kept a lot hidden from me Nick. I had only just begun to trust you from your last revelation, don't make the same mistake again.' Rachel firmly ordered.

'I agree.' Maria said placing her hand on Nick's arm. 'Stefan, you need to tell her.'

Nick looked at Maria and nodded.

Maria stood up and offered her seat to Nick before leaning over to Rachel. Kissing her cheek, she whispered into her ear. 'Listen to Stefan, do not judge and work together, you both want the same goal, make sure you reach it at the same speed. I have given him the same lecture.' Returning Rachel's smile, Maria made her excuses and shut the hospital door behind her, leaving them both alone.

'I'll get some water and food brought to us, you must be hungry and thirsty.' Nick said as he tapped on his mobile phone.

Rachel nodded, her mouth was incredibly dry and all of a sudden, she felt ravenous.

Nick tapped away on his phone before he put it back into his jacket pocket. 'How are you feeling?' Nick asked. 'About everything?'

Rachel couldn't look at him, she knew he meant about Yuri.

'I can't really talk about it just yet.' Rachel answered, her voice breaking.

Relief washed through Rachel as the door opened interrupting them. She was not ready to talk about Yuri. A nurse brought a trolley in containing bottled water, two teas and some biscuits.

'Lovey to see you awake dear, you have surprised us all with your recovery so far.' The nurse smiled at Rachel. Putting the tea, water and biscuits on the tray across the bed, she advised their order of food would be along in thirty minutes. Closing the door behind her, Nick cleared his throat as Rachel grabbed a bottle of water.

'I'm not going to lie, the last few days have been hard.' Nick said grabbing his cup of tea whilst not meeting Rachel's gaze. Sitting back down, Nick stared into the drink on his lap. 'The guilt of

Yuri is eating away at me, little by little. My boy, my son, my only child was taken away from me, yet I need to push all that aside until we stop Caroline. This is so much deeper and ingrained into everyday life, more than we could have ever imagined. I have been working day and night since Yuri was killed and you were stabbed, following every single thread entwined in Caroline's life. Every single update is on a shared drive that I have had installed onto a laptop for your use. I had intended on giving it to you when you had recovered, yet I will get it brought here so you can read it. What she is involved with, what she has done, is sickening. Yet none compare to her endgame. The reason she wants the power source.

She has designed a weapon of mass destruction. One that would wipe out half of the population. The other half would have no choice but to bow down and be at her disposal.

Her ultimate goal is to rule the world. She wants people to turn against each other, to clamber over their friends and family members to prove their loyalty and allegiance to her and her alone. She wants to be the centre of each and everyone's life. Everything we have built up over the years, the creation of Christmas, celebration of birthdays, encouraging everything we could to teach people to stick together, looking out for one another. Even producing a book that society could live by since Joshua began this path of equality and peace within the world. Over two thousand years of dedication and work, will all be for nothing if she gets her hands on the power source.'

'Do you think she got the idea from Lamia?' Rachel asked.

'I cannot answer that, all I can say is she is on an equal path as Lamia and her daughter Sophia. There is one other thing that I have not told you, which I should have done from the start.' Rachel's eyes narrowed as she waited for Nick to continue. 'There will be a file on the laptop labelled 5th April. Read it. This is the real reason we need you to move the power source.'

'Can you not just tell me why?' Rachel asked.

'There is only three people in the world that know why we need to move it. Once you have read it that makes four. Even Maria does not know. The laptop will only let you access it when there is no one else in the room. It will scan around to ensure authenticity and privacy. I cannot take the risk us being overheard whilst we talk.'

The hospital door opened, making Rachel jump. The nurse from earlier chattered away as she wheeled in the food Nick had ordered.

Smiling and raising his eyebrows at his point being proved, he stood up.

'I'll leave you to eat.' Nick said as he walked towards the door. 'Andreas will visit you in an hour and drop off anything you may need.' Smiling a sad watery smile at her, Nick left as the nurse placed the hot steaming plate of food on her tray. She was famished earlier, yet now her appetite seemed to have disappeared.

'Do you need me to feed you?' The nurse asked.

Unaware why, the nurse's comment made her chuckle inwardly as she shook her head and placed some of the mashed potato into her mouth. Satisfied, she was eating, the nurse left. Rachel placed her fork back down on the plate. The food was delicious yet, she was too anxious to eat. She needed to know what was on the file labelled 5th April.

Chapter 33
Joshua - The Additional 72

Having had the knowledge of his impending arrest verified, Joshua and Magda put their plan into action. To ensure the world changed significantly enough to prevent the war between the Matriats and the Servians, they needed to spread the word faster than they were doing already. Recruiting a team of people, Joshua held a gathering near the Sea of Galilee. Announcing to them all what they were required to do, Joshua advised he would be arming them with medication and wisdom on how to help the sick and most vulnerable in society.

'If your heart is not in it, leave now.' He instructed the crowd from Peter's boat. 'This job is not easy, it does not pay well, yet it will fill your heart with happiness.' Some of the crowd petered away.

Turning to Peter, he instructed him to count how many volunteers they had left and form them into equal groups. Joshua climbed down from the boat as Peter returned breathless, advising he had counted seventy-two and had separated them into nine groups of eight people. Nodding in approval, Joshua moved to the first group.

'Matthew will tell you which villages and towns you will be travelling to. You will travel in twos. Once you get to your location, knock on the first house you see, advise them you come in peace and ask if they need assistance. If they accept you, take anything that is offered, eat and drink what they give you but provide no payment in return, barring helping the sick. Use their facilities and sleep if it is presented. If they turn you away, note down the house and explain you will inform the rest of the village of their actions and forbid any help to be forthcoming. It is a hard lesson for them to learn, yet they need to be gracious to strangers, we need to unite this world as one. Got it?' The group of eight nodded their heads. 'If a town or village rejects you move on to the next. Make sure you send message to me of which towns and houses refuse as I will pay them a visit myself. When they treat you with disrespect, they also treat me with disrespect. My word is my bond. DO NOT TELL A SOUL OF THIS TO ANYONE WHEN YOU WALK THE ROAD TO YOUR DESTINATIONS. UNDERSTOOD?'

The people nodded wide eyed at Joshua. 'If you tell anyone what you are doing and who you are working for, they will crowd you and no doubt try and steal what you have. Do not put yourself into this position.' The crowd relaxed slightly, understanding Joshua's words. 'Any questions?'

A strapping young man stepped forward. 'Not so much a question, yet a request.'

'Go on.' Joshua acknowledged.

'I know we are leaving tomorrow, yet I need to bury my Father who passed away yesterday. Let me bury my Father first and I can join on afterwards.' The young man requested.

'No.' Joshua shook his head and paced closer to the man. 'Let the dead bury their own dead. Your Father is dead, he will not know if you are at his burial or not. You leave tomorrow or do not leave at all.'

Leaving the group and walking towards the next, Simon caught up with him. 'Jesus that was a bit harsh, he only wanted to say goodbye to his father.'

Stopping in his tracks, Joshua turned around to face him. 'You of all people know I do not have time for this. They go tomorrow or they do not go at all, time is precious.' He informed Simon.

Continuing to the next group, he explained the same. This time a man in his twenties stepped forward. 'I will do anything you ask, yet please let me go home to say goodbye to my family. They will worry about where I have gone.'

'No.' Again Joshua shook his head and walked closer to the man. 'No one who has emotional ties to a family at home is fit to complete this mission and service for the good of the world. You leave tomorrow or you do not leave at all.'

Walking away to the next group, Joshua looked at Simon, yet this time he remained silent.

Giving them all their instructions to leave the next morning, Joshua returned home to Magda exhausted.

'I had to be strict with them today. Some had families they wanted to go home to first, yet they cannot complete this mission if they are not whole heartedly in it. It was hard to say no, yet at least we know if they stayed, they will be loyal and spread the word like we need them to before I am arrested.'

'Shush. Enough talk of that. This is out last night together, and I want to make it special.' Magda said whilst wrapping her arms around him. 'I will ensure your work is continued if you are arrested. I will tell Prisca and this little one...' She said looking down at her expanding stomach. '...about you every day. I will make sure the world knows about you and what you have done to try and save us all from ourselves.'

'If the worst happens Mags, all I care about is you and the children are safe and well. I want you to find someone that will look after you when I am gone, someone that knows you and appreciates everything about you the way I do.' Joshua said squeezing her that little bit tighter.

Tears in her eyes, Magda whispered in his ear. 'I will never find anyone that will compare to you and how I feel about you. We were meant to be together, even if we were born two thousand years apart.'

Joshua chuckled as he pulled away from Magda and kissed her stomach. 'I hate that I won't be here to see this one.'

'Any thoughts on names?' She asked.

'No, just make sure that both Prisca and this one are called after me. Prisca East, sounds good doesn't it?'

Magda smiled at him as she watched him make his way to a sleeping Prisca. 'They will know exactly who their Father is. V.E.L.U.S. has lots of recordings of you. The TT pod will be where they play.'

'I'm glad.' Joshua said checking his bags, ensuring he had everything ready for the morning.

Sitting down with Magda curled up next to him, Joshua stayed awake for the full night, not wanting to miss his last precious moments with Magda, Prisca and his unborn child.

A week later, Joshua was wondering how Magda was getting on when the people sent out to spread the word, began to return. Their smiling faces were all confirmation Joshua needed to know it had gone well. Hearing the chatter and laughter spread amongst them as they swopped tales, confirmed to Joshua he had done the right thing. Although this did not ease the loneliness he felt being separated from Magda. She had moved to Bethsaida to be with her sister, and he had stayed with Peter in Capernaum, yet he knew his location was still too close to his family, for them to be safe.

'Matthew, I need to draw the crowds away from here, where do you think I should go? It is not fair on the residents of this village to be swamped with many people.'

'Jerusalem is a city, the many people that would follow you would not be as noticeable in Jerusalem.'

'Jerusalem it is, I will set off on foot tomorrow and do as my appointed have done. I will ask for nothing in payment for my services barring a place to sleep and food to eat on my journey there.'

'I will tell the others where you are heading and move these people from Capernaum.' Said Matthew.

Joshua looked at Matthew, one of a few people he could trust. 'Please could you keep an eye on Magda, if the day comes, and she gives birth before my arrest, would you please come and tell me directly?'

'Of course, Jesus.' Matthew replied. 'I will ensure Magda, and your children are safe.'

Joshua's travel to Jerusalem was eventful, healing the sick and helping the needy was what he enjoyed, yet it was the questions he was asked, or the arguments that he had to settle that riled him. He gave speeches on how to settle arguments to the crowds of people that flocked to him daily. He was invited to Pharisee's to dine yet grew tired of their pompous ways. He understood that religious leaders needed to be respect, yet how could he respect a religion that used donations from the poor to fund their lavish lifestyles. Instead of thanking them for their meal, he thanked the servants that made it and served him. He informed the Pharisees that they would never be as important as a servant unless they learned how to serve others. Instructed them they would be nothing without their status and money and they needed to learn how to be kind and help others instead of using someone's weaknesses against them. Angered by the way Joshua spoke to them, he was kicked out of their houses. Pharisees and their high-powered friends told Joshua he was never welcome to grace their houses again and his name would be mud to everyone they spoke to.

Joshua was not in least bit bothered, he hated dining with the rich and pretentious. Materialistic in nature was not the type of person he needed in his mission. He needed the crowds, the ones that could influence their future generations, the ones that saw the good in people and knew that others mattered, not the ones that only cared about what riches they had. They only seemed to be interested if someone of their stature had fallen on hard times and for all the wrong reasons. It was entertainment for them, they relished in one of their own falling from grace. It would not be them that would help the fallen get back up again, only gossip about how far they had fallen. Joshua needed the ones good of heart and had not been corrupted by materialistic evil narcissists.

Arriving to Jerusalem tired and hungry, Joshua sought out Mary's sister.
Opening the door, she greeted him. 'I thought you would never come back after what that scoundrel of a son of mine did!' She said ushering him into the house. 'He has changed though, the thieves from the temple moved away and it was restored to the way it should be. Elijah was the one that helped renovate it to a peaceful place, and now many can go and pray.'
Smiling through his tiredness, he welcomed Delilah's gratitude. Asking if she had a place he could sleep; she ushered him into an empty room.
'Rest young one, come and find me when you wake and I will gather food, I hear we have a lot to catch up on.'
Laying down on a bed made from straw, Joshua soon shut his eyes and fell into a deep sleep. The tension from arguments with the rich and the ignorance of the poor had taken their toll on him over the last few days. Yet as he relaxed within the safety of Delilah's house, the worries left him as he fell into a deep sleep.
Awaking some hours later, Joshua felt well rested and able to face the world again, even with the impending doom of his death weighing heavily on his shoulders.
Seeking out Delilah, she told him to go and wait in the back while she fetched him a meal.
Walking out into the calm of the courtyard, Joshua relished the peace and quiet while he could. It had been such a long time since he had been on his own without crowds following him. He needed this.

Hearing Delilah's footsteps, he stood up to help her with the copious amount of food she had brought out.

'Sit please.' She instructed, as Joshua smiled at her gratefully. 'You eat and then tell me what is bothering you and why you are here. Do you need me to send word to Mary?'

Joshua shook his head. 'No, Mary knows where I have headed, I needed to get away from Capernaum and far away from Bethsaida.'

Knowing his words would be safe, he retold Delilah all that had happened since he had seen her last, including the hearsay arrest that was coming.

'What should I do?' Joshua asked her. 'Stay hidden, moving from place to place in disguise? Or hold my head up high and let what happens, happens?'

'That is only a decision you can make my child.' Delilah replied. 'Yet I feel you already know the path you are going to take. It is the reason you are here. I hear your name daily whilst walking through the centre of Jerusalem and I am proud to call you my nephew. Herod is scared of the following you have gathered through compassion for others. He has never lived in a world where kindness gathers loyalty, only loyalty through fear and violence. You have enriched many lives, think about how many more lives you can enrich if you continue your journey, you saved my son from himself. I do not want to think of the man he would have become if you had not intervened. Do take to heart what others think of you, only take to heart the good you have done for the people.'

'Thank you, Delilah.' Joshua said as he finished his meal. 'I do not want appreciation for what I do, yet sometimes I need to hear what I am doing is right. I think I may take a walk to the temple and see what changes have been made.'

Giving him a big hug, Delilah nodded at him. 'Yes, you need to be shown the good you have done for the people of Jerusalem. Remind yourself, and relish in the happy faces you will see.'

Standing up, Joshua thanked Delilah for the meal and left for the temple.

He felt a lot lighter as he walked through the crowded streets of Jerusalem. Talking to Delilah had helped him realise he had made the right choice.

Approaching the temple, he saw the happiness on people's faces as they left the building. Walking inside he could see why. Gone were the thieves and crooks, replaced by chairs, flowers and an overflowing alter of food. Left not for god, but for the hungry and poor. A man stood at the rear of the church, doling out the food to ones that required it.

'Elijah.' Joshua cried as he realised it was him.

Elijah came running towards him. 'Jesus. I cannot thank you enough for what you did. I was on the road to destruction, you woke me up, showed me the error of my ways, and now I repay the debt in your honour. Telling everyone that comes here about you.'

Joshua laughed. 'Thank you, Elijah, but that is not necessary, all you need to do is tell people to be kind to one another, help one another when needed, yet not in my honour.'

'Fancy a guided tour around Jerusalem?' Elijah asked. 'I can show you what has changed around here since you last visited.'

Joshua nodded and let Elijah guide him out of the temple. Jerusalem was a hive of activity, yet before where there had been poor and sick begging on the streets, there was none. Elijah explained he asks for money on their behalf to heal them and food if they are hungry. He drops anything they need to where they sleep so they do not get hassled by any tourists in the city. Impressed by his good deeds, Joshua carried on listening to Elijah as he pointed out new features.

A group of people coming towards Joshua and Elijah stopped in their tracks and mumbled between themselves as they stared at Joshua.

'Who are they?' Joshua asked Elijah.

'Pharisee that have moved into Jerusalem. They have a good following, yet not as big as yours.' Elijah grinned at Joshua.

The group moved towards Joshua. 'Is that really you? Jesus?' One of the Pharisees asked.

'Yes, it is I.' Joshua replied.

'You need to leave now. Herod has a warrant out for your arrest and his plans are to kill you.'

'Are you friends with Herod?' Joshua asked as he circled the one Pharisee that had moved closest to him.

'I dine with him often, we discuss a lot of matters.' The Pharisee replied raising his chin up to show his importance.

'You give Herod a message from me. I will not shy away from making HIS kingdom a better place for HIS people. I will carry on healing the sick, helping the poor and vulnerable. I will continue this today, tomorrow and the next day. Maybe ask Herod what happens if he kills the son of god, or a prophet? Will the people not rebel?' Joshua raised his eyes at the speechless Pharisees. 'Now if you excuse me, I have work to continue.' He said as he walked away.

'I cannot believe you said that.' Elijah laughed in astonishment as he walked with him. 'I wish I had as much courage as you.'

'It's not courage Elijah, it is speaking the truth. They need to be told. How can they dine and laugh with Herod when they know what he is doing is wrong? I told you the truth and now look at you! If no one enlightens them, how will they know the path they have chosen is not the right one?' Joshua replied as he put his arm around Elijah. 'Now come and show me the best place to get some good wine around here.'

Joshua knew he did not have much time before he was arrested, therefore he travelled around, healing as many as he could. Bumping into a Pharisee one Sunday, they invited him to have an evening meal with them. Deciding he needed some decent food inside him to continue his work, he followed the Pharisee to his grand house. Standing in line for the banquet, Joshua could feel eyes on him. Looking around he saw he was being watched by the servants and other Pharisees that had joined the evening meal. Deciding to ignore them, he moved with the queue and wondered what delicious food was waiting for him at the end of the line.

The man in front of him lent against a pillar as they waited. Beads of sweat dripped down the back of his neck as he clutched his stomach. Knowing this man was in pain rather than hungry, Joshua walked around to face him.

Placing one hand on his shoulder, Joshua asked the man his symptoms.

'My stomach is in agony. It keeps getting bigger. I am hungry yet every time I eat, I throw it all back up again.' The man explained, the pain etched on his flushed face.

'May I?' Joshua asked if he could look at the man's abdomen.

The man nodded and guided Joshua to a quieter part of the house for him to disrobe whilst Joshua examined him.

The Pharisee of the house followed them with a disproving look across his face.

Shaking his head, Joshua knew what the Pharisee's issue was. 'Shall I not heal him because it is a Sunday?' Joshua asked him.

The Pharisee raised his chin in the air and looked away, ignoring Joshua's question.

Examining the man, Joshua could feel he had a blockage in his bowel. Reaching into his leather bag, he pulled out a syringe. Joshua explained to the man he had an obstruction within his digestive system, and he would need to be injected with a laxative as well as some pain relief. Instructing the man, he would need to find a bathroom immediately after the injection as the medication would work quick, yet once he had passed, he would feel great again. The man nodded clearly in pain. Injecting the man, Joshua helped him dress and walked him to the nearest toilet. Waiting for him outside, Joshua could clearly hear the laxative had done its job.

As the man left the bathroom, he saw Joshua stood against a pillar. A huge smile across his face, the man made his way towards Joshua and embraced him. He offered Joshua anything he wanted in repayment. Joshua smiled and asked him to pass on the payment to next person he came across in need in his name. The man nodded enthusiastically and promised he would help more than one person in Jesus's name. Embracing Joshua one last time, he left to re-join the queue, now able to enjoy the delicious food that was on offer, leaving Joshua alone with the Pharisee that still stood staring at him.

'I will not eat where I am not welcome.' Joshua said as he gathered his things to leave.

'No please, wait.' The Pharisee said walking towards Joshua. 'I am not staring because I do not want you here, I am staring to learn from you. You have many followers, loyal followers at that and I wish to know why.'

'I will tell you why.' Joshua said as he walked towards a bench. Sitting down he motioned to the Pharisee to do the same. 'I have followers as I teach them the right path. I teach people to love and help one another. I try to protect them from evil and harm. I heal the poor as well as the rich and do not ask for payment. People from all backgrounds respect what I do, therefore they follow me and help spread the world. Yes, I have great gifts of healing, but I also have a heart. If you plan a banquet, you only invite the rich and the powerful. You seat them in status ranking, the higher the social status, the more honoured the guest is. I do not work like that. The honoured guest at my table would be the person that has given their life to help humanity or that has fought off an illness but continued to care for their family. They are the real heroes of this world and the real ones that need to be honoured.'

The Pharisee stayed silent, contemplating what Joshua has just said to him. 'Would my current Pharisees not turn against me if I did not seat them honourably?' He asked.

'If they turned against you for where you sat them at a banquet, they are no friend of yours. Pick people that would help you in times of need, not times of greed.'

Guests of the Pharisee had begun to filter through to where they sat as they finished their meals. Joshua stood up. 'It was time I left and continued what I need to do on this earth before I am taken away. Make peace with your neighbours, give back to the poor what you have taken away. Your heart will feel light, many will respect you and you will not notice your fellow Pharisee have deserted you.'

Joshua left the Pharisees house and decided to seek out people that had the same mind set as him. The rich had some good ones amongst them, but generally they were arrogant. He needed to be able to enjoy the time he had left on this earth with people that did not look down on him because he preferred to wear common robes.

The weeks passed and Joshua had heard that the search for him was growing. Herod wanted his head on a stick, and they were closing in on Magda and Prisca. Joshua knew how these people worked. They would take Magda and Prisca and hold them hostage until he gave himself up.

Knowing the end was near, he returned to Jerusalem with a few of his friends. Arranging to meet at the temple inside Jerusalem, Joshua could see it had been decorated with beautiful stones, whilst gifts laid on the floor from people with happiness and joy on their faces.

Peter exclaimed in wonderment. 'This is all because of you Jesus.' He said waving his hand towards the temple. 'If it were not for you, the temple would still be in ruins.'

Joshua shook his head. 'I fear this temple will go back to ruins once I have been arrested. A war will come from this. Once I have gone, Herod will persecute those that continue my mission. He will have this city surrounded and the stones will be plucked from the temple and sold to feed the famine after the war. A battle will commence between good and evil. It will take a lot of strength for the people to admit they are still one of my followers. Peter, the guards will be instructed to hunt the closest people to me down. They will throw you into prison for conspiring against the King, your family will turn against you and inform the guards of your whereabouts. All I ask is you never give up on my mission, you continue through, for this is for your children and your children's children, so they will grow up safe and loved.'

Peter nodded at Joshua in agreement.

Looking at Peter and John, he informed them to go to the entry of the city and find a man called Augustus. 'I have already spoken to him about using his guest room for our Passover feast. He will be gathering water at this time. You will know it is him, as he will be carrying a jug of water. Make preparations in his guest room and the rest of us will follow.'

Peter and John walked off leaving just Matthew and Joshua.

'I am glad I have you to myself Jesus, there is something we need to discuss.' Matthew gravely said.

'Go on.' Joshua instructed.

'I have heard word from Herod's guards. One of our own have agreed to hand you over for a large sum of money. Not only has Herod's guards been involved but Leaders of the Jews and Pharisees.'

Joshua sighed. 'I knew this would happen, there is always the one that can be blackmailed by money and the promise of power. This is the reason only you know the location of Magda. Why have the other leaders conspired against me?'

'Do you not want to know who crossed you?' Matthew asked.

'It doesn't matter who crossed me for now. I already have an idea who it is. There seems to be one of my close friends that have started to wear new clothing yet have not visited any villages to be given gifts of these kinds. Am I right?'

Matthew nodded. 'You are correct, it was Judas. The leaders grow fearful of your following as you ask for no payment in return for your healing. They need payments and contributions to keep their temples running.'

'They should have thought about that before they used the payments and donations to buy huge houses and pay for servants.' Joshua grumbled. 'Upon my arrest, please could you inform Magda of Judas' involvement? She will know what to do. Do not mention Judas' traitorous deed to anyone, they need to find out from me.'

Matthew nodded in acknowledgement as Joshua started walking in the direction of Peter and John. He knew Magda would be outraged and her previous words of distrusting Judas echoed in his mind. He would ensure Judas was dealt with, Magda already had plans in place with V.E.L.U.S. to ensure people like Judas would not be able to give up the location of the TT pod and the contents within it.

Chapter 34
Rachel - The Depths of Caroline

Andreas brought the laptop to Rachel exactly when Nick had told her to expect him, along with some cream.

'Nick wanted me to bring this to you.' Andreas advised. 'It will help your wounds heal quicker. Spread only a thin layer, morning and night and you will be able to see the difference.'

Opening the tub of cream, Rachel looked at the green contents curiously.

Andreas laughed at Rachel's expression. 'They used it in Rylitte.' Andreas informed her, as her expression changed from inquisitive to shocked. 'Yes, Rachel, I know everything about Joshua East. My family has been an aid to the East family spanning back generations and we know how important you are to the cause. If you need anything, let me know.' He said smiling at her.

'I heard you were ill the other day, how are you feeling?' Rachel asked.

Andreas smiled at her. 'We both know I was not really ill with food poisoning, we needed to disrupt Caroline's plans, ensure she was no longer in control, yet this did cause unfortunate events. Rodrigo, who was in charge of scrambling the signal from the broach, tried to take his own life yesterday. He had left a note explaining he was unable to live with his failure and Yuri's blood was on his hands. Luckily, we found him before he hung himself and explained she knew the location prior to your arrival.'

'I am not sure I understand why he thought it was his fault Yuri died. I was the one that went outside, and he followed me, if anyone is to blame I am.' Rachel replied.

Andreas sat on the end of Rachel's bed with a grave look on his face. 'Rachel, the person to blame is Caroline. She had the power to not pull the trigger, but she did. She had the power to not pull the knife, but she did. One of her aims was to rid the blood line of Joshua East. Yuri and Stefan are very rarely seen out together, yet she knew they would both be with you, thus it was an opportunity for her. What we have discovered is sombre reading.' Andreas said tapping the laptop. 'It shows her plans and reasons why.'

'I thought no one knew of Yuri? Nick, I mean Stefan to you, said the committee were unaware of his existence.' Rachel said.

Andreas smiled at Rachel. 'It is all here in the laptop.' He said tapping it again. 'Stefan will always be Stefan to me, but I know he is known as Nick elsewhere to keep his identity safe. I will understand whatever name you call him.' Standing up Andreas placed the laptop on Rachel's table. 'It has face recognition when you open it, all instructions are on there. I must go. Stefan is being transported to a safe location with Maria, not in this country to protect him from Caroline. She will be paying top price to have him assassinated and quickly. He should have been moved, yet he wanted to see you awake before he left Cyprus.'

Andreas watched Rachel's face fall as she realised Nick, her safety net, would not be in the country. 'Rachel, you can reach Nick through me, yet I am sure he will still try and call you one way or another. It was not an easy decision to make, having him placed in a safe location, yet we reasoned, his presence could bring more harm to you than good, we also need him alive as much as we need you fighting fit. I will be visiting you daily to answer any questions you may have. There is security surrounding the building and, on this floor, to ensure your safety, as well as that of your brother and sister. The laptop has face recognition, no need for a password. If you need me, I am the only number programmed into this phone, it is secure.' Andreas passed Rachel a mobile telephone. 'I now must leave to oversee Nicks exit, but Rachel.'

'Yes Andreas?'

'You will not recover well if you do not try yourself. Make sure you eat well and do not leave your food.' He said winking at her. 'I find out everything.' Smiling as he left the room.

Feeling somewhat reassured, Rachel looked out the window to see if anyone was patrolling the corridor as Andreas had informed her. The blinds were half closed, obstructing her view to the hallway outside her room. Not able to see any security, she felt she had no choice but to trust Andreas, he was the only one that could protect her now. Opening the laptop, a pair of wireless earphones were placed in the middle with a note wrapped around advising her to use these before opening file 'Project CB5B1'. Putting the earphones in as instructed, she opened the laptop fully. It registered her face immediately and opened to a home screen with a list of files. Seeing a file labelled 5th April, Rachel was tempted to open that one, yet followed the instructions to read Project CB5B1 first.

Clicking on the file, a document opened revealing findings, yet before she had chance to read, a video popped up with a recording of Nick.

'Hi Rach.' Nick's voice came through the earphones. 'The findings go deep, much deeper than we anticipated, and there is a lot of reading involved, yet I wanted to speak to you first. I did not want to leave, especially with you in hospital. I hope Andreas has told you why I had to. I will call you on here when I have got to my location safely and you can always reach me through Andreas. I have known Andreas and his family since I was born, and I trust him with my life. He is one of the good guys. He will be available for you 24/7.' Nicks voice began to stutter. 'I know I have not been honest with you from the start and I have made mistakes which I wish I could go back and rectify, yet I feel like you are my daughter. I have watched you grow and blossom, and …and with Yuri now gone, you and Maria are all I have left in the world. I understand if you do not wish to continue down this path, just like Yuri did not want to, and you may not wish to read the findings of Caroline, yet I urge you to please read 5th April, and you will know why you are so special. Take care, and I look forward until we are reunited again.' The video switched off.

Rachel surprised herself. For the first time on this trip she was not tearful or emotional, she felt level headed, ready to face this head on. She was unsure if it was because Maria had advised she was the only one that could bring Caroline to justice, it could be she wanted to protect Nick as much as he wanted to protect her, or that she was trusted enough to know everything. What she did know, is she would do whatever it takes to bring Caroline to justice and prevent her from retrieving the power source.

Reading the first part of the file on Caroline, it showed she was the leader of Night Wave. The deadliest terrorist group in the world. This had been spurred on by her Mother's side of the family. The ties they had to radical activist parties and the Middle East where incredible. Spanning back years, Caroline's maternal side of the family had worked alongside leaders and terrorists to try and bring the western world to its knees. Once Caroline's Mother had married someone in the committee, the power of the organisation had increased with the confidential information they had access to. Night Wave, terrorists and the leaders had known about the power source for years before they had one of their own on the committee, yet they were unsure of where it was kept safe until a few months ago. This is the closest they had ever been, and Caroline would not go down without a fight. Caroline's determination, wealth and connections were the reason they had selected her as leader of Night Wave. She would bring the western world down. Religion would be abolished as it served no purpose in her new world. Her recruits in Night Wave and allies in leaders and terrorists agreed with her. There would be no religion barring the loyalty to Caroline Bennett and her chosen members. Caroline had planted false information and been in talks with the leaders of the Middle East to gain their confidence, then she had plied them with misleading facts of the committee and what they stood for. Giving them advice on plan of attacks and advising it would not help their countries if they agreed to a truce. The real reason the world was at a constant war was not because of religion, it was because of Caroline and her family. Caroline's Mother had started to sow the seeds of change when she had the access to the information. Taking the successful parts of Joshua's mission and turning it to her advantage to claim the world for her people. Owning sources of news media, Caroline and her family had ensured they all reported on the horrors of the world instead of the good deeds; encouraging riots, turning people against one another through race, religion or gender. Caroline had actively sent her people out, giving them the mission to cause as much disruption as they could. Caroline's power showed no bounds, her payroll showed judges, politicians, and high-ranking officials. Meeting once a month, the recordings attached to the files showed how they brain stormed new ideas to rile up members of the public. Overturning rapists and paedophiles sentences, as they knew the people would take matters into their own hands. Housing them near schools or their victims, to raise more violence and abuse. Caroline had researched on how anger grew more rapidly than harmony. The animalistic nature inside humans, showed how we naturally rose to a defensive stature, rather than resolving conflict and Caroline made sure she probed into our DNA. There was no limit to how low Caroline would stoop to create the world she wanted.

Rachel's eyes opened in shock as she read about Caroline's heritage. She was not Martha's blood line as she had previously claimed, she was a descendant from Judas. A timeline of Martha's descendants had been found within Caroline's database, listing the details of each person that was still alive. Ensuring she killed everyone on Martha and Magda's bloodline was the only way Caroline could keep her ancestors secret.

As Rachel read on, she wondered if callousness was passed down through DNA. Regardless that they were born over two thousand years apart, Caroline seemed to have a lot of Judas' traits.

Caroline's explosive was built and ready to go, it only needed the power source to be as effective as it could. Judas had ensured he had copious amounts of information to pass down through his generations to overturn the following of Jesus. A detailed report of the power source was taken, yet the location of the TT pod and power source had been destroyed by Matthews's successors hundreds of years prior. Knowing Judas' descendants were ready to unleash an inferno to the world, Matthew's family pledged to stop them at all costs, slaying the remaining heirs of Judas to prevent the war they were secretly waging over the years.

Matthew's descendants were unaware they had not completed their promise as Caroline's predecessors changed their names, moved and kept off grid, secretly developing a successful business of weapons manufacturer from the plans Judas had recovered from the TT pod. Keeping the plans safe until they had the resources and technology to build them, the business went from strength to strength, all the while their end plan resting on the source of the power from the TT pod. Judas had never got over the shame and embarrassment that had burdened him. Instead of turning into remorse, it had simmered beneath the surface, converting to anger and resentment. He had ensured his family would wipe out the East's in his name, for his legacy.

The file listed the people Caroline was associated with and the ties her family had, and it was chilling to read.

Everything Caroline was involved in was covered by encrypted messages, deleted files and different names. Bank accounts had been found in different countries across the world.

Nick had decided to fight fire with fire. Instructing his team to infiltrate the dark web they had sourced and paid a hacker. It had been a risk to bring her into the secrets of the committee, but it had paid off. In no time at all, she had managed to find everything related back to Caroline and her family, going back decades. She had managed to retrieve deleted messages and emails. If it had been on any device attached to the internet, this hacker could find it.

Chills ran up Rachel's spine as she featured in the research the hacker had uncovered.

A crew were on standby, ready for when Rachel was captured. The expert team of surgeons were to skin Rachel alive, and place her skin and features on to a mesh organic membrane, covering a bio mechatronic skeleton. They already had enough data from her voice that they could programme into the human robot to imitate her speech, they just needed Rachel. It would take twenty-four hours for the skin to attach to the organic membrane. Once all this had been confirmed and the imitation Rachel was ready to go, Rachel would be put into a vat of acid to melt away and the robotic Rachel would go and retrieve the power source.

Rachel's heart started pounding as she pushed the laptop away. Taking the headphones from her ears, she looked at the clock on the hospital wall. It was 11PM. She could not read anymore this evening, she needed to take her thoughts away from being skinned alive.

As if on cue, a nurse opened the door to her room. 'Just need to check your blood pressure sweetheart.' She said as Rachel shut down the lid of the laptop. Her chatter was a welcome distraction from what she had just read.

Letting her complete her checks, the nurse asked if she would like some crackers and cheese, something light, but to line her stomach. Rachel agreed.

The nurse left the door open and Rachel noticed a man sat behind the nurses' station. Craning her neck to get a better view, the man was dressed in a doctor's uniform, yet something about his stature and continual glancing around, made Rachel feel uneasy. Peering at him, the doctor stood up and stared directly at Rachel. His eyes boring into her as she laid there helpless.

Rachel's heart started to pound as he stood up and reached for something under the desk. Checking around the room for any kind of weapon she could defend herself with, Rachel could only see the laptop within reach. Wincing as she eased herself up, she clasped her hands around the edge of the laptop ready to use if needed. Looking out the door again, the man had disappeared. Rachel began to panic, she knew she was still on Caroline's hit list, yet where was the security she had been promised?

Swinging her legs off the bed, she kept a firm grip on the laptop.

The nurse re-entered the room with the cheese and crackers as promised. 'Where are you off to?' She said as she placed the plate onto the table above Rachel's bed.

Trying to look behind the nurse towards the door, Rachel tried to remain cheerful. 'Just needed to stretch my legs, I have been laid down for too long.' She said whilst craning her neck to view the nurse's station again.

Placing a hand on her arm, the nurse leant in and whispered to her. 'You're safe here Rachel, you can get back into bed.'

Rachel looked at her shocked, she wasn't supposed to know why she was here. Leaning in closer, the nurse whispered into her ear. 'I am Maria's sister. You will come to no harm.'

Rachel was in no mood to trust anyone just yet.

The man dressed as a doctor walked into the room, as Rachel's grip tightened on the laptop.

'Hi, I'm Rick, thought I best introduce myself now you are awake. I have been assigned to your security whilst you are here. We have men patrolling the corridors, yet all dressed incognito. My shift ends in two hours and my colleague Matt will be replacing me. If you ring for the nurse, we will be watching inside the room.' Rick nodded and left the room.

Rachel fell back into the bed with a sigh of relief, she was getting paranoid!

'Come on, let's get you back into bed. I have been given strict orders from Stefan to get you back to your healthy self. Is there anything I can get you?' The nurse said.

Rachel shook her head even though she would have done anything for a cigarette right then. As if reading her mind, the nurse took out a nicotine patch and winked at Rachel. Sticking it on her arm, she whispered. 'This will help until you get out of here.'

Thanking her before she left the room, Rachel tucked into her crackers. Laying back on the bed, she tried to get some sleep, yet curiosity got the better of her.

Opening the laptop back up, she opened the file, 5th April.

Rachel could not believe her eyes what she was reading, she was unsure it was even possible. Shutting the laptop down, there was no questions in her mind. She would move the power source as soon as she was given the word.

Chapter 35
Joshua - The Capture

All of the first members of Joshua's ministry were together again, at last. He looked along the table at them all. They had come a long way since he first landed in Capernaum. Joshua wished Magda and Prisca could be here with them, yet he knew it was too risky. Especially now with the baby born. Magda had given birth to a boy, Joshua Stephen East. He smiled sadly at the thought he would never get to meet his son. Matthew had told him and brought along a device that proudly displayed photos and videos of his new born son. Although they would never meet, he felt extremely lucky he had the technology to see his child before he died.
His eyes glanced at Judas, happily guzzling the wine he had made with the last of the pebbles he had brought with him.
Joshua stood up and cleared his throat as he addressed the twelve. 'I do not have any further wine, therefore please share this out between yourselves equally.' He broke the remaining bread at the table. 'I do not have any further bread, share this out equally amongst yourselves too.'
Smiling at them all, one by one they all beamed back at him. 'I am glad I got to see you all before my impending death. I will certainly be killed once I have been captured.' The table fell deathly silent. 'This is because of one man at this table that has wounded me more than anyone will ever know. You twelve are the ones I poured my trust and vision into, yet one of you have decided to choose greed over our friendship. I know who you are, and you will pay for what you have done.'
The table erupted into outrage, each one of them shouting at Joshua, pledging their allegiance to him and his cause. Joshua held his hand up to silence them. Simon stood up to continue his

speech of his innocence yet, Joshua spoke first. 'Simon your house will be set on fire and your possessions burnt, yet I know you will honour me in everything you do. You will stand by our mission and give strength to the others when they need it most.' He looked at Peter. 'Peter, I know you and I know you will deny knowing me when the war breaks out. You may deny me one, two, three times, yet I know deep down, you will do what is right and carry on just as you know you are supposed to.' Joshua looked at the rest of the table. 'The time has come for you all to carry on what I set out to do. A great war is coming, many wars will follow. We are animals, we are human, and we fight for survival. Do not let others tempt you into a different way of life, we need to change this world for the better. It should not matter where you were born or who to, no person should have to fight for survival. We can do this, yet we can only do this if everyone has the same vision.'

'I have a sword. No one will take me.' Thomas roared ready to fight to the death for his mentor.

'Enough of this talk.' Joshua shouted looking at Thomas in astonishment. 'Let us finish our remaining meal together in peace.'

Joshua looked around the table at his twelve friends, his eyes pausing on Judas. A bead of sweat was slowly making its way down the side of his face as he sipped his wine in thought. The other eleven chattering amongst themselves, yet Judas stayed quiet. Joshua quickly looked away as Judas looked up, as if he felt Joshua's watchful eye upon him. Joshua hoped his little speech would resonate inside Judas, making him see the error of his ways and thinking about the mission and how it would benefit him and his future children. Judas stood up and made his way to the middle of the table. Grabbing the jug, he sloshed the last remaining wine in his wooden goblet and wrapped his arm around Philip. Joshua watched as he raucously laughed and took over the conversation with his brash voice. Shaking his head, Joshua's heart fell. Judas was back to his normal self. For a fleeting moment, Joshua thought he had got through to Judas, yet his speech had not changed anything of what was about to come.

The next day, Joshua was chatting to Matthew when a crowd appeared as if from nowhere, led by Judas. Rolling his eyes, Joshua shot a knowing look at Matthew.

Joshua watched as Judas walked straight at him, no guilt nor regret on his face, just his usual conceited smile.

'Hello Jay, thanks for the meal last night. It was nice to get everyone together again. We haven't done that for ages.' Judas said as he kissed Joshua on the cheek.

'Judas, did you actually think I did not know it was you that told Herod's guards and the Leaders where I was? Your brashness should make me angry, yet it makes me laugh. Magda warned me about you, but I took no notice. I wish I had heeded her words.' Joshua whispered in Judas's ear.

Judas recoiled back. Horror and shame etched on his face whilst the undercover guards and servants proceeded towards Joshua. As he walked backwards, further away from Joshua, Judas stumbled and cried out, alerting the others. Seeing Jesus in trouble, Thomas withdrew his sword and rushed towards Joshua. 'Stay back! Stay away from Jesus.' He cried. 'If you want him, you will have to go through me!' He shouted, swinging his sword near anyone that got close. The group still moved forward trying to dodge Thomas' sword. A servant put his hands up, surrendering to Thomas, trying to make him calm down, inching closer and closer as Thomas wielded his sword. The thud of the servant's ear hitting the ground was heard before the others saw what had happened, Thomas had managed to slice off his left ear.

'Enough.' Joshua shouted. Pulling out some cream and a small pencil like gadget. Joshua reattached the servant's ear.

'Looking at his faithful friends, he smiled. 'I appreciate the gesture, however they are not ever going to stop hunting me down. I do not want any blood shed because of me.'

Holding his arms out, Joshua was arrested and taken to a nearby house of a religious leader. Blindfolded, the guards dragged him, then threw him into a dark room, ripping his bag off him in the process. Asking for his bag as he lay on the cold hard stone floor, the guards stood and laughed.

Picking up Joshua's bag they taunted him with it, before opening it and tipping out the contents.

The sound of vials smashing made Joshua wince. The amount of people he could have helped with that medication now smashed on the ground, made him feel sick.

'Is this what you are after?' One of that guards snarled. 'You can't have it anymore now can you? Not god like when you don't have your bag with you.' They all laughed at him.

'Do you realise how many people I could have healed with all what you have just smashed to the floor?' Joshua cried. 'What if someone you loved and cherished was ill and needed healing. Who would you go to?'

'Not to you!' The guard laughed as he ground his foot onto the smashed objects on the floor.

Joshua put his head in his hands. He knew this was the beginning of the end. He was unsure as to what was going to occur. His Father had warned him, they did not know what would happen when he died. They had never tested it before, never had anything die in the past so they had no idea if the fact he was from the future would affect what happened when he died in the past. Would he be transported back to his original future, and then go to the past like a continual loop? He had never been afraid of dying before, yet now he was uncertain. They had researched and not one person could confirm what happened in the afterlife, even if there was one, yet this was a different situation. He didn't believe in afterlife or heaven and hell, mainly due to his non-religious upbringing from Lamia, although he clung on to the hope there was one now.

A commotion outside, distracted him from his thoughts. Slowly lifting up his blindfold to see if the guards where still watching, Joshua saw there was no one at the door. Pulling himself up, he made his way to the window and pulled back the blackout fabric that was draped over it.

A fire was going in the courtyard of the high priest's house he was in and Joshua could make out figures sat around it. Smiling to himself, he saw a few people he knew. Observing the group, Joshua watched as a servant girl came out of the house and walked towards the group with one of the guards.

'He was with him.' The girl squawked as she pointed at Peter.

'What are you on about?' Peter asked the girl in disgust.

'You were with Jesus, I saw you with him when he was arrested. You are a Galilean through and through, I can tell because of your accent.'

'You are definitely mistaken, I know about Jesus, but I do not know him personally.' Peter said, trying not to meet the girl's eye.

'I know you was with him, I never misplace a face.' The girl twittered on.

'Don't know what she's talking about.' He said looking up at the guard who was now above him breathing hard.

Joshua's heart sank. He knew Peter would do this. He was such a coward at times. Joshua hoped he would keep it together and not tell them about the TT pod and Magda. Too much was at stake for him to be spineless now.

Peter saw movement behind the guard and spotted Joshua watching him. As Peter squinted his eyes focused on Joshua and his face fell as he noticed the bruises and battered face peeping through the window. His expression changing to shock and guilt as he realised Joshua had seen the full conversation between him, the servant girl, and the guard.

The guard moved away, bored of the girl's voice. Peter looked back up at the window were Joshua was. Tears ran down his face as Joshua shook his head at him in disappointment.

'I am sorry.' Mouthed Peter, knowing Joshua had seen it all, yet would not understand. He hoped Joshua would realise how much more use he would be outside of the prison, than in it. He could send a message to Magda and continue to spread the word, yet he knew Joshua would not see it like that.

Letting the blackout fabric fall back across the window, Joshua slid down the wall of the darkened room. He had never felt so alone.

The hours passed and Joshua fell into a fitful sleep. Jolting awake at every little noise. The guards standing duty through the night, stood and laughed each time he jerked awake.

Finally, the morning came, and the guards hoisted him from the dark room and removed his blindfold. The morning sun was bright in his eyes as they dragged him to a cart to be taken to Herod.

The guards batted Joshua's arm down as he tried to shield himself from the early morning sun's rays. His face had swollen more throughout the night, and the bruises across his body had slowly appeared in the last few hours from the guards' beatings. Joshua could only just sit there as each rock they drove over pained his wounds.

Arriving at Herod's, Pilate, the city judge, came down to see him. He was shocked at the wounds Joshua had gained from being captured and alerted Herod immediately.

Joshua was dragged by the guards from the cart into Herod's vast house and seated on the floor.

Herod came flying into the room and demanded who had took it upon themselves to dole out the punishment Joshua had received. As each guard denied physically hurting Joshua, Herod grew bored and dismissed them, leaving Joshua alone with Herod and Pilates.

'Who did this to you?' Herod asked. 'Can you heal yourself?' He questioned.

Joshua groaned as he stood up. 'Herod, it is a pleasure to meet you after all this time, yet please do not pretend you have concern for me. I have heard many times you wish me dead due to the following I have gathered.'

'Jesus, you are mistaken.' Herod laughed. 'I have not asked for your capture, just your audience. I wanted to ask you about your miracles and how they come to be.'

'I have it on good authority you want me arrested and killed due to my miracles.' Joshua said.

'No, no, no.' Herod replied. 'The religious leaders want you killed, that is correct, yet I do not. I have no time for religion. There are too many rules to follow. Yet I would be interested in how you turn water to wine. Now that is a miracle I must see.'

Joshua frowned at Herod. He seemed to be telling the truth, yet Matthew had told him about Herod's plot to kill him.

'I apologise for my direct question, yet I feel I have no choice. You killed my cousin, John the Baptist, how do I know you are not going to do the same to me?' Joshua asked.

'Ahh, you see John's slaying was a request from a beautiful young lady and she would pay me many times over for that wish. If I had the same request for you, I would tell you. I am not in the habit of telling lies to make myself look good. I am the King of these lands, if I want someone dead, I will tell them.'

Joshua continued to frown at Herod.

'Now tell me about the water wine trick.' Herod said excited. 'I have some servants bringing the water to you now and you can show us. I cannot wait.' Herod clapped his hands in excitement at the thought of seeing Joshua turn water into wine.

'I cannot do this.' Joshua explained. 'The guards destroyed my items that helped me create miracles. However, if you let me go, I can try and retrieve these items and show you.'

Herod looked at Joshua. 'No, that will not do. Many have lied to me only to try and take my life once they have gone. The guards advised they did not harm you. I have a feeling that you can turn water into wine you are just refusing to do it because I am your King.'

'Not at all.' Joshua protested. 'I need my items, I can go and get more and come straight back here.'

Herod narrowed his eyes at Joshua. 'I will allow you to go and retrieve more items, however you must be accompanied.'

Joshua closed his eyes and inhaled. He could not lead anyone to the TT pod or to any of his friends. And he would definitely not take them to Magda. 'The items I need are in an incredibly special place and I cannot take anyone with me.'

'I am the ruler of these lands. Nothing is secret from me. You are accompanied or you are tried in the public court.' Herod said.

Joshua exhaled loudly. 'I will have to be tried in the public court.'

'So be it.' Herod replied and started to walk away.

'Herod, please.' Pilate shouted after him. 'This man has done no harm to anyone, he is not starting a rebellion against you. It is only the religious leaders that want him dead through greed. He has helped many people in your kingdom. You cannot try him in a public court full of Pharisees and Jews.'

'He keeps secrets from me in my lands, he will have to go to public court.' Herod replied as he walked away.

Pilates hung his head in front of Joshua. 'Please accept my apologies. I hope the public court will have mercy on you.'

'People are scared of change Pilates. I have learnt that people enjoy the thrill of power, thus my death was written as soon as I tried to treat everyone equally. I am not scared, I just hope my actions will continue to create a more peaceful world.' Joshua replied, as he held his bloodied head up. 'I am ready to face the people that will order my death.'

With a heavy heart, Pilates led Joshua to the public court. The crowd booed when Joshua was brought to them. Holding a hand for silence, Pilates tried to reason with the crowd, explaining the good Joshua had done and will continue to do.

'The rumour's spreading about his rebellion are false. All he wants to do is help the sick and needy. Can you not see he has already been punished for crimes he has not committed?' Pilates shouted as he pointed at Joshua's face.

The crowd where having none of it. 'Crucify him! Crucify him!' They chanted.

Joshua looked at Pilates. 'Do as they say. The rich will not want to lose their power and the leaders will not want to lose their following if I continue my work. If you do not do as they say, they will kill me and then you for defying them.'

'I cannot order you to be killed like a criminal. You have done nothing but good for Herod's people. I would have blood on my hands.' Pilates protested.

'You have no choice. I only ask, you help my people to continue my mission. Spread my word far and wide and encourage the people to help each other.' Joshua asked.

'So be it.' Pilates exclaimed as the crowd went wild at Pilates' decision. Leaning into Joshua's ear he whispered. 'I do not want to live in a place where my religious leaders sentence you to death. I will continue your work Jesus, and find your people.'

'Tell them Joshua sent you. They will understand what that means.' Joshua shouted at Pilates as the guards began to lead him away.

Smiling as the guards dragged him away, Joshua knew Pilates would make good on his promise. He was well connected and if he believed in what Joshua was doing, he would indeed succeed in helping with Joshua's mission.

Keeping him in a holding cell until it was time for the crucifixion, the guards made sure Joshua suffered. Tormenting him they made Joshua walk up and down over sharp stones. 'If you were the King of the Jews, you would be able to heal yourself.' They jeered, laughing as Joshua stumbled. Joshua kept his pain inwards. He knew they would revel in his painful cries and laugh if he begged them for mercy.

Joshua felt another blow to his head from one of the guards, when he heard V.E.L.U.S's voice through his mind.

'Mr East, the V.A.I. is becoming unstable within your ear. Please refrain from anymore damage. Once removed, it cannot be refitted.'

Joshua did not reply to V.E.L.U.S. It did not matter anymore if the V.A.I. stopped working. He would not be needing it where he was going.

Growing bored of Joshua's silence, they dressed him in purple robes and adorned him with a makeshift crown of sharp thorns. The thorns pierced Joshua's skin and dug into his skull as the guard roughly pushed it down on his head. Blood seeped from the puncture wounds as Joshua looked up in silence at the laughing guards. 'Not so royal now are you Jesus!' They tormented.

Taking it in turns to beat Jesus as he sat there motionless, the order came, it was time for him to be led to his death.

As Joshua walked behind the guards, he saw a crowd gather. Pointing towards a huge cross made out of wood, the guards insisted Joshua carry it to his doom.

Groaning as he lifted the cross onto his shoulder and his back, Joshua's wounds that had been inflicted on him previously, began to open. Blood trickled down his face as the cross bounced against the thorns that still adorned his head. Pausing to clutch his now swollen abdomen to try and ease the pain reverberating through his torso, Joshua collapsed under the weight of the wooden object. Slowly getting up, Joshua felt dizzy. The lack of sleep and the pain from the beatings he had been given were rendering him speechless. Breathless he tried to stand up and walk with the wooden cross yet buckled under the weight again.

The guards sneered at him. 'Pretending to be weak will not stop your crucifixion.' They laughed. 'Get up!'

Joshua tried again to stand up with the weight of the wood bearing down on his shoulder. Walking a few paces, he collapsed again under the weight. The guards laughed at him again. 'You do not look much like the son of God. This proves you are a phoney and a crook and deserve to be dead!' They shouted at him.

'I never said I was the son of God.' Joshua panted at them. 'I just wanted to help people. Please give me a few minutes for my strength to return and I will try again.'

One of the guards stared at Joshua. Bending down to his level he looked at his bleeding wounds. Standing up, he shouted at the other guards. 'He is indeed wounded. I am unsure if he will be alive by the time we make it to the skull. Get him help.'

Grabbing a dark-haired man, the guards placed the huge cross onto the man's back. The man buckled under the weight of the gigantic cross yet did as he was told and followed the guards and Joshua towards the base of the hill.

Knowing he would be nailed to the cross, Joshua chuckled to himself. In Lamia's world he would have been nailed to a tree for trying to help the Servians. This world he is going to be nailed to a cross for helping the poor and sick. The thought of there being no point in his mission quickly crossed his mind. Was there any point in trying to change the world? The past seemed no different to the future. Spotting a couple of children by the side of the dirt track as he walked past, Joshua noticed the sadness on their faces as their Mother held them close. There was a point in his mission, those children should never have to watch a man walk to his death.

He looked at the man carrying the cross. 'I am sorry you have been chosen to carry my cross that will display my death to everyone here. I am Jesus and my people will make sure any wounds you acquire will be tended to.'

The man struggled to smile at Joshua whilst carrying the heavy cross. Breathless, he replied. 'I am Simon from Cyrene. I have heard about the wondrous things you have done for everyone. Not just the rich, but for the slaves and poor. This is all wrong. I will make sure my children and their children carry on your story for years to come. You should not have been sentenced to death for doing the right thing for your countrymen.'

'Thank you, Simon.' Joshua smiled at him. 'Your kind words make my impending death easier by knowing my work will continue long after I am gone.'

A large crowd of people had started following Joshua and the two others that were to be executed. Crying and shouting at the guards to stop, Joshua smiled sadly at them all. 'Do not mourn my death, celebrate my life and what I have achieved. Continue my work, help the poor, the sick and the old. Do not turn anyone away because of their skin colour, illness or poverty. Make my death into a celebration of life and how we should live. The world is doomed because of the arrogant, rich and pompous religious leaders that do not know anything of what it is to be like us. Carry on my mission in my name, yet do not create a war where innocent people die.'

Reaching the base of a rocky hill that resembled a skull, the guards halted the precession, telling the prisoners to place their crosses against the rock wall.

More people were starting to join the already large crowd. A mixture of rich and poor.

Joshua thanked Simon and placed his cross against the wall. Leaning against the wooden cross, Joshua watched as the first man was hoisted up by two of the guards, whilst a third hammered nails into his hands and feet. Knowing he was next, he stood there in silence, searching the crowd for a familiar face.

The guards walked across to him, as the wails of the first crucified man, echoed along the rock face. Joshua did not think the pain could get any worse, yet the agony he felt as the weight of his body strained against the nails holding him up, tore through him.

The blood still seeping from his head trickled down his face and covered his eyes blurring his vision. He tried to look for anyone he knew for comfort in these final few minutes yet saw no-one with his vision impaired.

Closing his eyes, he gave in to the pain and let it wash over him. His mind flashed between Magda, his children, his mother, Caelan, Richard, Liz even Jess and then lastly his Father. The tears began to flow, mixing with the blood already on his face, as he thought about his Father and how much this mission meant to him.

'I am sorry I have failed you father.' He whispered with his last breath. 'I hope you know how I fought in your name for this world to be a better place.'

His eyes grew heavy and closed as his mind flitted through memories, good and bad, from this life and the one in Rylitte.

Knowing the end was near, his breathing became laboured. He heard people shouting his name, yet could not react, his body no longer listening to any commands he gave it.

The blackness started to engulf him, the memories displayed in his mind's eye were getting smaller and farther away, when all that was left was darkness.

Joshua's head fell to his chest, as he exhaled his last breath.

Chapter 36
Rachel - The Journey to Retrieve the Power Source

Rachel had healed well, and whilst she had been given excellent care in Cyprus, she felt a lot happier now she was back home in Stanis.
Plenty had happened over the last couple of months, yet the pain of discovering the two children Caroline had captured were not actually her brother and sister, was still raw.
The heart-breaking news had been delivered by Andreas and Nick. As Nick's voice rang out through the blue projection in front of her, whilst Andreas sat by her side, he spoke of how dreadful he felt not being able to tell her in person.
He continued by explaining how a Russian child had been admitted onto the same ward as the two children. The Russian child's parents had stood outside, talking in their native language, when the young boy rushed out, tears running down his cheeks as he stumbled over his words asking them for help to find his family. The two children had begun to talk when they realised they were safe from harm. Swiftly finding a member of the hospital staff to speak in Russian, it was clear these children were not only bewildered by their capture and beatings, but by the strangers talking to them in a language they did not know. Scared and frightened, they had not dared to speak to each other until that day. The children were not even brother and sister. Taken from their parents whilst they holidayed in Egypt, they had not known each other prior to their capture, yet had formed a strong bond with the six-month torture Caroline had subjected them to. Their parents were informed and had caught the first flight to Cyprus to be reunited.

Rachel had watched their reunion from across the hospital corridor. Her smiles were tinged with sadness by her own longing for a family unit.

Trying to clear her mind of the sadness from the children and Yuri's death, she knew she needed to think clearly about the challenges that lay ahead. Today was the 5th of April and there was still a lot that could go wrong.

Most of it had been organised, yet her and Nick still needed to complete the final checks.

The power source had been successfully transported and was now heavily guarded in a maximum secure prison fifty miles from S.U.S. Industries offices. Not that it needed to be guarded. The power source was unmoveable without Rachel's presence.

Nick had ordered tests to be carried out utilising strong and intellectual people to see if they could move it, yet none had been able to. Nick had even drafted in women that looked similar to Rachel to try and move the power source, yet it had stood firm. Even without V.E.L.U.S. as its protector, it had its own security system and was not able to be relocated without Rachel there commanding it to.

Rachel looked out of her front window and could see the Special Forces still guarding her street. To anyone else, they would look like your general public, yet to Rachel's now trained eye, she could spot the little differences.

Not taking any chances, Nick had bought the four houses down her street that were up for sale and moved teams into them for twenty-four-hour protection. Caroline had gone into hiding, untraceable by MI5 and CIA and strangely quiet for the last few months.

Rachel picked up the bag containing her laptop, organiser, and mobile phone. Exiting her house, she entered the car that was waiting for her.

'Good Morning Miss Nichols. Straight to S.U.S. Industries?' The chauffeur enquired.

'Yes please.' Rachel replied. Robert had been her driver since she arrived back in Stanis. He was ex-military, a good friend of Nick's and she felt well protected with him as her driver and the car that followed them behind, yet he was no Yuri. She missed their light-hearted banter. He had only been in her life for a couple of months, yet it felt like longer. Rachel had connected with Yuri like no one else before. He had felt like a brother to her, the closest thing to family she had, her best friend and now with him gone, she felt emptiness like never before. He had been one of the few people that had never let her down, that had put her before himself and protected her, she trusted him and that was no easy feat for Rachel. Rubbing her eyes, she needed to get Yuri out of her head, today was not a day for distractions, she needed to be focused as there would be no room for mistakes.

Arriving at S.U.S. Industries, Robert parked at the back of the building and escorted Rachel in. No matter how many times Rachel heard Robert talk into his wrist confirming Rachel had been safely delivered into the building, it still made her heart hammer with unease.

Walking into the board room, Robert stayed outside whilst she greeted Nick who was sat at the vast oval mahogany table.

Pulling out her laptop and placing it opposite where Nick was sat, she switched it on and looked around the room at the gigantic metallic structure that had been erected. Its square outer shape, with a large, empty circular space in the middle, made it look like abstract art.

'I'll start the checks now.' Rachel said to Nick, tearing her eyes away from the rectangular black metal structure. 'I have gone through the data the original V.E.L.U.S. provided and we are pretty much there.'

Nick nodded. 'Once you finish the first set, let me know.' He said, not taking his eyes off his laptop screen.

'Do you think Caroline has access to the 5th of April file?' Rachel asked, broaching the subject as carefully as she could.

'I thought the same, Rach.' Nick replied.

Rachel looked at him with concern as he typed furiously onto the laptop in front of him. The last few months had aged him dramatically. Gone was the cheeky sparkle in his eyes, replaced with a tired sadness that had seeped into his soul. His once floppy brown hair was now shorter and speckled with grey. His face gaunt with dark rings around his eyes and an unkempt beard. Since Yuri died, Nick no longer took a pride in his appearance, nor thought about the damage he was doing to himself. He needed to grieve but chose to ignore Rachel and Maria when they had voiced their concerns. Nick tried to placate them, advising he would rest once the 5th of April had passed, yet Rachel was unsure he would last out the day. He needed to give himself time to heal, he had lost his son, his only child, it was not something he could sweep under the carpet for another day. She was worried about the damage he was doing to himself.

'We have it covered though if she shows up. Although I am still apprehensive, especially if she gets to you.' Nick grimly replied.

'You do not need to worry about me, the security will have it covered, and even if she does manage to get through, you can be assured, I will not move the power source for her.' Rachel smiled at Nick, yet he did not smile back.

Stopping his typing, Nick looked up at Rachel. 'I am not apprehensive about the power source, I am apprehensive about you.' He said with a touch of anger in his voice, before returning back to his work.

Surprised but slightly comforted at Nick's concern, Rachel changed the subject.

'Do you want a drink?' She asked. 'Coffee? Tea? Water?'

Nick shook his head.

'When was the last time you took a break Nick? How long have you been here?' Rachel said concerned.

'I will have a break when I have finished this.' He forcefully replied.

'I can ask V.E.L.U.S. when you came here and demand you have a break. You will be no good for this afternoon if you are burnt out and not focused. I need the old Nick back, even if it is just for a few hours. Today is too important. I cannot do this without you.' Rachel softly said to Nick as she reached her hand across the table to his.

Pausing his typing, Nick frowned, closed his eyes and inhaled deeply. 'I...I know Rachel. I need to keep myself distracted when I am not doing anything ...I...'

Rachel walked around the table and put her arms around Nick's shoulders. 'I know Nick. I get the flashbacks too.' She comforted him. 'Let's go through the checks together, I'll type whilst you can have a coffee. It will keep your mind on other things, at the same time as having a break.' Nick nodded and wiped the tears that had appeared in his eyes.

Every waking moment felt like his heart had been ripped out. A lump would form in his throat, rendering him unable to speak. He couldn't eat, he couldn't sleep, it evaded him. He spent hours staring at the ceiling and when he finally did manage to get some sleep, Yuri's murder haunted his dreams, jolting him awake for him to relive the realisation his son was dead over and over again.

Yuri was his son and he didn't protect him. He died because of his birth right, the birth right he never wanted to be part of, yet Nick had convinced him to keep involved. Told him he would regret it if he wasn't an S.U.S. Industries employee, even if it was just a driver.

Due to his heritage, Yuri did not have the average childhood. Instead of playing outside, Yuri had self-defence classes, martial arts, tactical intelligence, medic training, weaponry information, the list was endless and the knowledge strictly ingrained. He could not count the amount of times he had sternly said no to Yuri's request to attend birthday parties or school trips. Even a trip to the cinema with friends would have been denied due to his rigorous training. Remembering how the tears had sprung into Yuri's eyes when once again he denied him the freedom to socialise outside of school hours, made Nick deeply regret his parenting. Yuri never complained, only nodded and sadly walked away to his next training session. The pangs he had when he watched Yuri saunter away time and time again, gave way to Nick's justification, Yuri would have the freedom to do what he wanted when he was older. Yet Yuri would never be older, this had been taken away from him. Nick regretted everything he had put Yuri through and for what? All those wasted years, his popular, handsome son could have enjoyed, just for Caroline to shoot him dead. He should have protected his son more, should have been more lenient, let him enjoy his life instead of preparing him to be the next leader of the world, he should have listened to his only child's wishes.

The lump in Nick's throat returned and tears formed in his eyes as the guilt washed over him.

Rachel distracted him by placing a coffee next to his laptop.

'Do you want me to complete on your laptop, or mine?' She asked.

Quickly wiping his eyes and clearing his throat, Nick stood up and stretched. Advising Rachel they would complete the checks on her laptop, he walked around the table with his coffee. He needed to move, he needed to focus.

'How long have you been here Nick?' Rachel asked as she sat down in front of her laptop and booted up the programme.

'I couldn't sleep. I came here around 2am this morning.' He replied whilst taking a drink of his coffee.

Rachel shook her head. 'I know it's easier said than done but you won't be able to function later. Do you want me to get some blankets and you can at least have a nap for an hour?'

Nick shook his head. Rachel narrowed her eyes at him. She would order him to get some sleep this morning whilst she watched. She could not complete this alone.

Checking the metallic frame was all in order, she checked V.E.L.U.S. was online ready for when they got back.

'It's time Nick.' She said to him noticing his skin was now a sicklier ashen grey than before. Frowning at him with concern, she patted his shoulder. 'Nick.' She said more softly this time. 'You do not look well. Did you see the doctor?'

'Yes, he prescribed me some sleeping pills. I tried them, yet they only made me feel drowsy and sick, they did not help with the insomnia.'

'I do not think you should come with me.' Rachel said.

'I am coming …' Nick replied.

'No.' Rachel cut him off. 'You are not coming. You are more of a liability to me like this. If you have not slept, you will not be focused. This is no time for lapses in judgement. We do not know how smoothly the transportation will take.'

'Rachel, I need to be there. You cannot go by yourself.' Nick said holding onto the mahogany table to stop himself from swaying. Feeling slightly dizzy, Nick blinked a couple of times to wake himself up. There was no way Rachel was going on her own. Seeing the concern etched on her face, Nick inhaled deeply and closed his eyes. Opening them he slowly exhaled. 'I am ready to go.' He said slurring his words.

Rachel watched Nick, there was no way he was going with them, his grey tinged face had now turned white, his blood shot eyes looked like they were trying hard to focus on anything. His words slurred and hard to understand. She would have to convince him to stay and try and get some sleep. No way would he be any use this afternoon in his current state.

Watching him carefully, Rachel was about to open her mouth when Nick swayed again. His eyes shot open wide and stared straight at her, before closing quickly.

Rachel reacted and reached forward, grasping onto his arm as he crashed to the floor, yet his dead weight was too heavy for her to soften his landing. Screaming for help, Robert rushed in. Seeing

Nick on the floor, he immediately requested medical assistance, before he rushed to his side and started to check his vital signs.

Rachel stepped back to give Robert more space. Feeling others rush past her towards Nick, she didn't let her eyes leave him for one second. Her hand covering her mouth in shock as she watched Robert perform CPR. Tears began to form as Rachel observed the scene before her.

'What's happening?' Rachel screamed as another person ran past with a defibrillator in his hands. Robert extracted himself from the group working on Nick and took her to one side.

'Nick's heart had stopped. I need you tell me EXACTLY what occurred in the minutes leading up to Nick collapsing.' Robert commanded.

'He...he...' Rachel stumbled as she watched the people surrounding Nick shout 'clear' as they tried to bring him back to life.

'Look at me Rachel, not at what is going on. You need to concentrate. What happened?' Robert demanded.

Looking directly at Robert, Rachel composed herself and relayed the conversation. 'I need him Robert, I… I can't do this without him.'

Paramedics rushed by, as one of the men declared they had found a pulse. Rachel breathed a sigh of relief as she watched the paramedics hook Nick up to different machines. Hoisting him onto a gurney, they began to wheel him out of the boardroom.

Stopping them, Rachel asked the paramedic what they thought had happened.

'90% sure it was a heart attack due to the rhythms on here.' The paramedic replied as he pointed towards the screen of the monitor. 'The reasons obviously are unknown at the moment. We have managed to stabilise Mr East, however we need to get him to a hospital as soon as possible.'

Rachel nodded and let go of the paramedic's arm. She was unaware of how hard she had been squeezing it.

'Miss Nichols.' Robert addressed her. We are twenty minutes behind schedule. 'We need to leave now.'

Rachel's stomach flipped over at the prospect of completing this alone. Thirty minutes previous, she had been adamant she could do this without Nick, she had been prepared to go without him, to bring the power source back here, yet now she knew he would not be here when she returned, she felt over whelmed.

'I...I'm not sure I can do this.' Rachel looked at Robert, her eyes wide with shock and uncertainty.

'Miss Nichols. I have it on good authority you can do this on your own. There will be people with you every step of the way. Do you know what to do when we return? Did Mr East explain the full protocol?'

Rachel nodded.

'Then you will be fine. After you.' Robert waved his arm to motion Rachel to leave.

Taking one step, she turned back round to face Robert. 'I need to let Maria know.'

'We will inform Mrs East. All you need to focus on is retrieving the power source and ensuring everything is ready for 5PM this afternoon. Anything else, delegate to me.' Robert said firmly.

'Will you keep me updated on Nick's progress?' Rachel asked.

Robert nodded and Rachel made her way down the corridor towards the car.

The drive to the maximum-security prison seemed to take forever. The thought of Nick not making it weighed deeply on Rachel's mind.

After what seemed like an eternity, they arrived at the prison. A heavily armoured guard opened the car door and escorted Rachel to the place she last left the power source.

Armed police surrounded her as she walked through each security gate within the building.

Reaching a glass panelled wall, she looked at the power source sat on the table. The small metal box, no bigger than her hand glowed blue around its edges. It still surprised her that something that could fit in her hand, could contain so much power.

As Rachel entered the room, the box glowed more brightly, as if happy to see her. Placing her hand on the metal box, she felt the cool smooth exterior vibrate against her fingertips.

'Release.' She said firmly.

Illegible writings around the box appeared and glowed as it recognised her voice, signally it was ready to be picked up. Carefully placing the box into a leather holdall, she zipped the bag up securely and walked out of the room.

The box was strangely light, no heavier than a feather, though it looked like it was made of metal. While Rachel knew of its robust stature, she still handled it with care, afraid it turned out to be as fragile as it looked. It felt so delicate, yet the tests Nick had ordered had proved it was anything but. Fire, water, bullets and explosives had been tested on it, which had damaged the room, leaving dents and scorch marks on the steel wall interior, yet no harm had come to the power source. No one could move it, nor the table it sat on. The power source seemed indestructible and intelligent.

The power this tiny box contained was scary. She understood why Caroline would want it. Surrounded by all these armed guards and herself kitted out in bullet proof gear, she still felt unsafe whilst the power source was under her supervision. Caroline wanted it, and after everything they had discovered about her, she always got what she wanted.

Exiting the maximum-security prison, Rachel could see the snipers on the roof ready to shoot any unknown in the area. The outside eerily quiet, with only the sound of the gravel crunching under their feet as they walked across the carpark. The guards directed Rachel to a bullet proof van that was to transport them back to S.U.S. Industries office in Stanis, instead of the car she originally arrived in.

Climbing into the back of the van, Robert was by her side. 'You're doing well.' He reassured her. 'Nick would be proud of how confident you are.'

Nodding back, trying to swallow the lump in her throat, she didn't feel very confident, yet she knew she needed to get the power source back to the offices and to the vast contraption erected in the board room.

All of employees that worked within the building, were told there had been a gas leak and they were required to work from home. They were not allowed in the building for at least one week. No one knew what was going to emerge, and they had tried to prepare for every eventuality V.E.L.U.S. could have predicted. The worst being the office would be completely destroyed by the power source once it was attached to the machine.

Knowing she would be full of apprehension for the journey, she asked Robert if he had any news on Nick.

'He is being prepped for surgery. It was a heart attack. His heart has been severely damaged, yet the finest surgeons are being flown to Stanis Hospital as we speak. He will receive the best care and from the report I have been given so far, he will make a full recovery. Make sure he recovers to good news.' Robert smiled at her.

'Not too much pressure then?' Rachel laughed, yet she meant it. The full weight of this was now on her shoulders, she had no one to share it with. No-one else had been privy to the full information of the 5th April. Only partial bits so they could piece it together if needed. Only her and Nick knew the full extent of what needed to be done.

Rachel looked into her bag to check on the power source, even though she knew it would still be there. It vibrated and glowed as she opened the bag. Zipping it back up firmly, Rachel placed the bag on the floor of the van. 'Attach.' She whispered to the power source. Nick's instructions had been clear. Ensure the power source was unable to be taken, even if she was with it. Nick was counting on her to do this alone, therefore she would not vary from the plan. His voice echoed in her thoughts and she closed her eyes, hoping he would be OK.

Rachel heard the screeching of tyres and felt her body fly to the other side of the van, before she registered what was happening. Hitting her head against the metal bars inside the van, she winced at the throbbing pain now pulsating on her forehead. Blood streamed down her faced as she looked at Robert, her eyes wide with shock.

Robert pulled out his earpiece and shouted in frustration. Their lines of communication had been cut. Rachel knew who was behind this, Caroline. Before she could speak to Robert, Rachel felt the van tipping upwards, causing her to fall back onto the metal panel that separated them from the cab. Someone was hoisting the back end of the van up. A grinding noise could be heard as vibrations reverberate through the floor of the vehicle. Someone was trying to cut into the base of the van. Robert stood up, gun in hand, poised, ready for whatever was about to come through.

The metal began to glow as a line formed on the floor of the van. Staring as the line began to get longer, Rachel knew they were cutting around her bag with the power source. Shouting 'release', Rachel picked her bag up and placed it over her shoulder.

'Rachel no, we cannot risk you being taken as well.' Robert shouted at her. 'Put the bag down.'

'No.' Rachel shouted back as the sound of grinding metal stopped. Looking around the van, now eerily silent, Rachel whispered. 'Robert, are there security cameras in here?'

Robert glanced at Rachel and then back at the floor again, a confused look spread over his face. 'What?' He whispered back.
Leaning across to whisper into his ear. 'Are there security cameras in here?'
Robert nodded.
'We know who is doing this and they are watching us. You need to kill the feed to the cameras. We are on our own.'
Robert pursed his lips. Slowly reaching down to his calf, he stealthily removed a small knife and flicked it open behind his back. Inching his way around the van, he cut the wires leading to the cameras.
'Is that all of them?' Rachel asked, her heart pounding.
'Yes. All my communications have been switched off. My mobile signal is blocked. I have no idea what is happening on the outside world. I need to get you out of here.' Robert looked around as if the answer may come to him in the small area of the bullet proof van.
Going into her bag, Rachel pulled out the black shiny comycon. It was the last thing Yuri had given her to keep her safe. Rachel carried it everywhere with her. It reminded her that there was once someone that would do anything to protect her, like a real brother would do.
Pressing the middle, she spoke into it, hoping someone else had one.
'Robert, find a way to get into the cab of the van, you may need to drive us out of here.' Rachel instructed as Robert nodded in acknowledgement.
A thunderous noise was heard as the van rocked slightly.
'Hello, can anybody hear me?' Rachel repeated again as she spoke into the comycon.
'Received. State your name.' Answered back a male voice.
'My name is Rachel Nichols and we are under attack on the outskirts of Stanis. We are carrying precious cargo and need emergency assistance. All lines of communication are out, including satellite signals. Please confirm you have received this message.'
The van rocked again as another explosion was heard.
'Message received Miss Nichols, you are speaking to Field Marshal Sanderson. We have tracked your location with the comycon. We know what you are carrying. Who is with you?' He replied.

Passing the comycon to Robert, he spoke into it. 'This is Agent Robert Ashford, Number 38465294, clearance Alpha Whiskey 48 Sierra Mike. We were travelling in a convoy to the S.U.S. Industries offices in Stanis in operation bluebell. The van is holding well for now, they have not managed to penetrate. I assume the driver is down, yet I have no confirmation. All lines of communication have been cut. We need urgent assistance. Over.'

Rachel looked at the marks on the floor of the van. How much longer would they be safe in this vehicle?

The van rocked again but this time, the explosion was coming from the back doors. Rachel could hear them trying to burn their way through the lock.

Robert was still talking to Field Marshal Sanderson on the Comycon. Seeing a glint of hope in his eyes as he looked her way, Rachel was glad he had hope, although she knew back up would not arrive in time. Turning around, Rachel tried to look through the small solid glass window edged in white metal that displayed the front of the van. The window had limited visibility due to the blood and residue covering it.

The noise at the back of the van was getting louder. 'We need to get into the cab and try and drive this thing ourselves.' Rachel said to Robert. 'Is there anyway of us getting in there?'

Robert shook his head and knocked onto the metal interior. 'It has been made so no one can get in or out. Even with welding materials or explosives, it will still take time to get through this.' He replied.

'We have to at least try and get out of here.' Rachel shouted at him.

'We do not know who, or what, is out there trying to get in. Our safest option is to stay here until back up arrives.' Robert instructed.

'We are just sitting ducks Robert. We both know them doors will come off before anyone arrives to help.' She shouted, pointing at the back doors as the noise stopped. The van now in complete silence, Rachel fixed her eyes towards the rear of the vehicle as the doors flew open.

Two men stood at the back doors all dressed in black, pointing automatic rifles in Rachel and Roberts's direction. Quickly stuffing the comycon into his back pocket before they noticed, Robert held his hands up and addressed the gun men. 'Whatever you want, we do not have and if we did, we do not negotiate with terrorists.' He said firmly.

'That's good, as I do not negotiate either.' Caroline's voice rang out as she appeared at the back of the van and stepped in. 'You are right about one thing. YOU do not have what I need.' She said as she raised her gun and shot Robert straight in the forehead.

Chapter 37
Joshua - The Disappearance

The full crowd stood there in silence as they looked at Joshua, hanging down from the cross. The blood that trickled from his head, hands, and feet, dripped on the floor.
A loud wail was heard as footsteps ran towards Joshua.
It was from Matthew. Kneeling in front of Joshua he touched his forehead to Joshua's feet as he sobbed for the one man that had tried to show the right path to this world.
Turning his head towards the guards, he looked at them in anguish. 'What have you done?' He whispered, as the guards hung their heads in shame.
Standing up, Matthew faced the crowd. Their ashen faces displayed sorrow, yet these people where the ones that caused the death of an innocent man.
'Have you got what you want?' Matthew shouted at them. 'What is it you where accusing this man of? Trying to help the starving and the sick? Bridging the gap between the rich and the poor? Uniting all our nations and religions? Teaching us to help one another in times of need? Because that is all this man had done! Jesus was a miracle sent to us to try and show us the right path, to help humanity unite and thrive. To teach us how to support people when they are down and how they would reciprocate in return. Life can be lonely, it can be hard, it can be scary. This man showed us how to utilise our strengths in aiding others and what joy it can bring. YOU.' Matthew pointed at a Pharisee. 'Why are you here watching?'
The Pharisee stuttered.
'Is it because you cheered for him to be executed and wanted to ensure he was fully dead? Why? Is it because he did what God

told us to do but for free? YOU.' Matthew shouted pointing at a Rabbi. 'Why did you cry out for him to be crucified?'
The Rabbi looked at the floor in shame.
'Were you jealous of the following this man gathered in such a short space of time? You wanted him gone as the donations to your religion had dwindled? Your congregation no longer needed you for support as they could help one another just as God taught us to? Jesus would not want us crying at his death, weeping in sorrow or guilt. If you feel you contributed to the unjustly murder of this man and feel the guilt gnawing away at you, you need to do one thing. That one thing is to carry on Jesus' work. Help one another, not for greed or self-preservation, but for the joy you feel in your heart when you have made that one person's day a little bit easier. Spread the word, make today a celebration of Jesus' life and what he brought to us. Let us not wallow in the death of one of the greatest men that ever came to our cities and our countries, let us learn from him and keep him alive in our hearts and actions.'
The crowd murmured as Matthew turned to face Joshua. 'I am sorry, Jesus.' He whispered as he placed his head on his chest. 'I will devote my life into making sure everyone knows your name and what you did for us.' He wept.
Matthew felt a hand on his shoulder. Turning around he saw a man around the same age as him, dressed in fine clothes, concern etched around his weather-beaten face.
'I did not consent to this.' He said to Matthew. 'I am Joseph from Arimathea, part of the council. I will ensure Jesus has a decent burial. It is the least I can do to apologise on behalf of my fellow council men.'
Matthew nodded and took one step back as Joseph from Arimathea ordered the guards to take Joshua's body down carefully.
The crowd watched solemnly from afar as Joshua's body was carefully wrapped in the best linen. A procession of carts and people followed the body with Matthew and Joseph leading the way to a tomb nearby.
Arriving at a house, not far from skull hill, Joseph advised the tomb was at the rear of the garden. Walking through the garden to where Joseph had directed, Matthew could hear the birds tweeting and feel the sun on his back. The area was serene, peaceful and

calm. Matthew smiled sadly to himself, Joshua would have loved this place.

'I need to send word to his family.' Matthew spoke to Joseph.

'Please go to the house attached to this garden and ask for Bacchus. He will show you were to write a letter.' Joseph instructed Matthew.

He watched Matthew walk slowly and sadly towards the house before he entered the tomb, he had offered for the one they called the son of God, Joshua. The guards, now ashen faced and silent carried Joshua carefully, still wrapped in linen inside the tomb.

'Halt.' Joseph demanded. 'Please take Jesus back out to the cart. The tomb needs to be altered. I will not have our savour of the world scrunched up in an ill-fitting tomb.'

The guards nodded and carefully carried Joshua back outside.

Joseph called out to the crowds that had already formed outside of his garden, asking if anyone was able to make the area bigger. Two slaves raised their hands. The crowd split into two, making way for the slaves to approach Joseph.

'This man helped our Mother when no one else would touch her because we were slaves. Let us craft out the area for the greatest man of our time to lay his head and rest in peace.' The older one offered. Joseph moved out the way to let the two men complete their work.

Laying him carefully in the newly expanded tomb, Joseph smiled sadly at the man that had helped many. News of his abilities and nature had been the talk of many a meeting he had attended. The ones that were scared of his abilities, spun slanderous tales, turning him into an evil villain. Substantiating their stories by explaining Jesus was gaining trust from his followers to brain wash them. Once under his spell, he would lead the people to a rebellion, yet Joseph had doubts. These tales had no witnesses, only hearsay. Asking his own people to conduct a few investigations, he had learnt that whilst Jesus suffered no fools, he would genuinely help people in need regardless of their social status. He was a gift from the creator of this world, and the ones that had caused his death would have to face their punishment in the afterlife.

A few women hovered around the entrance to the tomb. Inviting them in Joseph left to find Matthew.

The darkness had succumbed the sky, signally it was early hours of the morning. Joseph walked slowly, tired and mentally exhausted, it had been a long day for all involved.

As he approached Matthew, Joseph noticed the tears streaming down his eyes as he furiously wrote. These letters would be going to Jesus' most loved, who would be broken by the knowledge of his death. Things needed to change, not just in this city but in the whole country.

'Do you need any assistance?' Joseph asked Matthew.

Matthew shook his head. I am on the last one, I want to sit with Joshua until I am allowed no more. It is Sunday tomorrow. I do not want his name, nor his tomb destroyed by the imbeciles that caused this, just because I am going against Gods will by sitting with a deceased loved one on the Sabbath. I do not have the strength to fight them and advise what they did was against God.' He spoke through his tears.

'Understandable.' Joseph gravely nodded. 'Yet you must get some form of sleep.'

'I will sleep when Jesus is laid to rest.' Matthew instructed and carried on writing.

Leaving Matthew, he went to see the women in Jesus's tomb. The women were from Galilee and were discussing what they needed to gather to spread around Jesus' body. Interrupting them, Joseph advised them all ingredients they needed, would be available in the house. They could take anything they required.

The women left and made their way towards the house. Gathering the herbs and spices they needed, they spoke with Matthew to give him the location where they would be staying and creating the perfumes for Jesus' body.

Thanking them, Matthew stood up and went to join Joseph at Jesus' side. They sat together in the tomb, silently until the sun rose.

Later in the afternoon, Matthew heard rushed footsteps coming towards the tomb. As he looked outside, he could see Magda. Her head wrapped in a scarf, only her tired, sad eyes showing.

'Please tell me it's not true.' Magda asked Matthew. Her eyes filling with tears.

Silently nodding, Matthew held out his arms and put them around Magda to comfort her. 'I promise you, those who caused this will burn in Hell and we will watch them from above. His death will not be in vain. This is just the start of a celebration of his life and what he did for us, all of us.'

Pulling away from Matthew, Magda slowly approach the body laid out in the tomb that was wrapped in linen. Pulling the top part of the cloth away, Magda laid her head on Joshua's chest. 'You were too good for this world.' She whispered. 'I will ensure your legacy lives on in our children and their children, and together, we will make this world a better place. It may take a while, but one day, we shall live as equals. I will forever love you Josh.'

Wrapping him back up, she asked Matthew if anything had been arranged to make their traditional Galilean perfumes for Joshua's' body. Directing her to where the other Galilean women were, Magda left to join them. She would ensure Joshua only had the finest when it came to his burial. She would make it her vocation and her children's vocation to let the world know what happened to Joshua. They would celebrate his death every year, to remind them what he did for them and how he gave his life for them. It would remind them of his mission, how they needed to treat each other as equals and live in harmony, for the good of humanity.

Magda and the other women from Galilee spent the full Sunday preparing the perfumes and spices for Joshua's body. It may have been the Sabbath, the day of rest, yet Magda did not stop until she had finished the most luxurious perfume for her beloved husband.

Returning to the house, near the tomb, Magda sat at the kitchen table and fell asleep.

Awoken by someone gently shaking her shoulders, she heard Martha's voice. 'Mags, it's time.'

'Time for what?' Magda rubbed her bleary eyes as she looked at Martha in confusion. Martha watched as Magda's face crumpled when the realisation of her husband's death came to the forefront of her mind. 'Where are the children?' Magda asked frantically searching the kitchen with her eyes. They were the last part she had of Joshua and she needed to ensure they were safe.

'They are here, at the house. I needed to be here with you Magda, I could not leave you to face this alone. We are in this together.' She said, smiling in sympathy.

Holding her arm, Magda thanked her sister and stood up as her now toddling daughter came running towards her.

'Prisca.' She cried as she scooped her up and snuggled into the crook of her neck. She was the image of Joshua. Squirming to get away from her Mothers stiff grip, Magda sadly put her down.

In the corner of her eye she saw Martha shake her head. 'She is too young to see him. We are only in the garden, she will be safe with our friends.'

Magda nodded sadly as she grabbed the perfume from the wooden table. 'Be good.' She shouted to Prisca, turning her head before her daughter spotted her tears.

The walk through the garden to the tomb seemed to take longer than it was. Knowing this was the last time she would see Joshua before the tomb was sealed and no-one was allowed to enter, Magda's eyes filled with tears once more.

'Someone must already be here.' Martha said as she pointed to the tomb. The huge stone that had secured the doorway to prevent any visitors from entering on the Sabbath, had disappeared.

Walking to the entrance they entered the tomb. Magda and Martha both gasped in shock as the body of Joshua was not there. Only the linen that had covered him remained.

'We need someone, anyone.' Martha cried as Magda remained silent and sat next to the linen. Picking up a piece, she held it close to her. Turning her head to face Martha, her eyes brimming with tears, she shook her head.

'We do not need anyone here. We thought this may have happened with Joshua not being from this world. We need to tell the others.' Magda stood up, a piece of linen still in her hand and hurried out of the tomb towards the house.

Martha ran to catch her up. 'How are you going to explain this?' She asked. 'People will think you are insane with grief if you try to explain who Jesus really is.'

'I am not going to tell them the truth, Martha, yet I will use this moment to carry on Joshua's message to the world. This news will travel fast and help his mission he originally came here for.' Magda replied with a wry smile on her face. 'I cannot dwell on the fact I will never see my husband again, I need to fight for his memory, and his Fathers memory and make this a safer world for his children and yours.'

Martha put a hand on Magda's shoulder to stop her, but she shook it off. 'We need to talk about this.' Martha shouted, yet her words were lost as Magda entered the house.

Taking off her scarf that was wrapped around her head, Magda addressed the men that were in the room. 'Jesus has risen from the dead.'

Gasps were heard around the room as Magda carried on. 'Martha and I have just entered the tomb where Jesus were laid to rest. His body has gone, all that is left behind is the linen. He has not been stolen. Jesus was a gift from God. Our God, and he was betrayed. He has reclaimed Jesus back and Hell will take care of the ones that contributed to his death.'

'Who told you this?' Peter demanded.

Magda's eyes opened up in surprise and shock. Why did they not believe her? They knew of Joshua's miracles, why would they be interrogating his wife?

Martha stepped forward and placed a hand on Magda's shoulders. 'Don't question my grieving sister. She has just lost her husband. We were told by two men at the door of the tomb, who were dressed like angels with rods in their hands. They told us and then disappeared.' Turning to see Magda's grateful smile, she winked back. She was her sister, her twin sister, and she would always be there to back her up, even when she doubted her judgment.

'What a load of shit.' Peter shouted and stormed out of the house towards Joshua's tomb.

Upon entering he sat where the remaining linen laid there with no body.

Hanging his head, tears ran down his cheeks and fell to the dusty floor. 'I just cannot believe this, all of this. He cannot have vanished. His soul may have been taken back to God, yet not his body.'

Magda sat next to him and placed a hand on him for comfort. 'We both know he was not one of us. We need to continue spreading the word and completing his work in his honour.'

Peter nodded with tears in his eyes.

Matthew entered into the tomb, his eyes wide open in surprise. 'I should have stayed with him. I wanted to stay with him, yet I did not want his tomb nor body to be destroyed by the leaders because I was with him on the Sabbath. I could have stopped this.' Matthew broke down into tears.

'No-one could have stopped this.' Magda's voice caught in her throat, as she looked around the crowd of people, Joshua was loved by so many. 'He would have been taken if you were here or not Matthew.'

One by one, people entered the tomb and left after seeing for themselves Joshua's body was gone.

Magda and Martha were sat inside the house as the rest grouped together whispering amongst themselves, still doubting what Magda and Martha had told them.

Visitors from far and wide started to arrive at the tomb as news of his death spread.

Mary came inside and sat next to Magda. Patting her hand, she looked at her with tears in her eyes. 'I do not doubt you for a second. We know where he has gone. To another world, back to where he came from. I know I did not grow him or carry him in my body like his brothers and sisters, yet I felt he was every bit my son. I loved him as if he were mine and I will do anything I can to keep his memory alive and ensure my grandchildren know all about their extraordinary Father.'

Hugging her close, Magda whispered into her ear. 'I will also make sure of this, yet for now we grieve the man we have lost, and for my children that will grow up without a Father. Talk to your family and the others that were close to him. We will have a meeting in one weeks' time, I know exactly how we will carry on Joshua's mission.'

Chapter 38
Rachel - The Metal Contraption

'Rachel, sweetie. I think you have something that I need.' Caroline said, her sadistic smile spreading across her face.

Rachel clutched her bag closer. The power source inside it quivering, as if it knew what was happening.

Walking closer to Rachel, gun still in hand, Caroline raised her eyebrows and smiled at Rachel as she glanced at Roberts dead body on the floor. 'You have certainly changed since the last time I shot someone in front of you.' Caroline laughed. 'Or was you not as close to this driver as you were Yuri?'

Rachel stayed silent, not removing her steely stare from Caroline.

'Just hand it over Rachel. We can work together on this, or I can just take it from you.' Caroline purred, now only inches away from Rachel.

'I thought of you as intelligent Caroline?' Rachel teased. 'We both know it will not work if I am not near it.' She smiled back at Caroline. 'One pull of that trigger, I am gone and so is your access to the power source.'

Caroline's face dropped into a scowl. 'I am getting quite tired of you insulting my intelligence Rachel. I have plans in place. I always get what I want.'

Imitating Caroline, Rachel cocked her head to one side and smiled. 'What like skinning me alive to try and trick the power source into your commands?'

'Someone has been busy.' Caroline smiled as she stalked around Rachel. 'At least you know what is going to happen, it won't come as a shock. I even have a replica V.A.I.. Would you like to see it in action?'

Rachel stayed silent as Caroline shouted for Craig.

A young woman was pulled inside the van. Scared and dishevelled, she was the same height as Rachel.

'Rachel, meet Casey, the new Rachel. Casey here has volunteered to be transformed into you. How wonderful is that? Casey was as sad as we were when the biomechanical skeleton trials did not give the effect we desired. Outraged she was, wasn't you Casey?' Caroline said as she tickled a petrified Casey under the chin. 'She has even had the V.A.I. fitted and can speak just like you. SPEAK.' She commanded to Casey.

'What do you want me to say?' Casey whispered, her head looking down as she was gripped by Caroline's bodyguards.

Roughly pulling her so she was stood next to Rachel, Caroline instructed her to tell the power source to drop to the floor and stay. Rachel felt her bag quiver and drop to the floor taking her with it.

Clapping her hands with glee, Caroline knelt down to Rachel, her evil face blurring the closer she got. 'See, I do not need you, only your skin to be placed on Casey, and that can be easily removed, we have everything ready for your arrival.' She laughed mercilessly.

Instructing her most trusted guard Craig, to remove Rachel with the power source and place them in the waiting vehicle when she gives the signal, Caroline smiled to herself as she walked out of the van. It was nearly time for it all to come together. All the planning, the years of work, the tireless infiltration of the terrorist groups, religious leaders, the committee. Her double life was about to come to an end. Instead, the real Caroline would be able to come out for all to see and bow down to. She would be the ruler of the world. By tomorrow morning, Caroline would wreak havoc on the world. Her heart flipped in excitement as she visualised telling her Mother she had accomplished the mission she had tasked on her. She would be so proud. Reaching to her inside pocket, she pulled out her mobile phone. Scrolling down to her Mother's number, she was excited at the prospect of ringing her, yet nervous too. It had been twenty years since her Mother had last spoken to her, and she had spent the majority of it trying to win back her Mothers approval.

Caroline's Mother, Claudia, had initially disowned Caroline for falling in love with another member of the committee, Frank Raylard. Initially growing close to him to gain information for Claudia's mission, she had started to enjoy their time together. He had shown her love and consideration, supported her in any way he could. Seeing how passionate he was about Joshua's work; Frank had begun to change her way of thinking. Her stomach turned over as the mixture of emotions swirled through her. It felt like a different life, a different world.

'I have not brought you up like this.' Her Mother had spat at her, disgusted after discovering the details of Frank and Caroline's affair. 'You know why you were born, you know what your assignment is. He is the enemy and you have betrayed me, your own Mother. I forbid you from contacting me, until you complete your mission, you have failed me as a daughter. Only contact me when you are worthy to do so.'

Caroline did not even have chance to break off the affair before Frank disappeared. The committee had their full resources set on finding him, yet Caroline knew they never would. She was fully aware her Mother would have had a hand in his disappearance. The years rolled by and no-one found a trace of Frank. His portrait still hung in the offices at Stanis, with a heartfelt message displayed underneath. He was the only person that had ever broke through Caroline's icy walls and melted her heart. Now he was gone, she had not let anyone get as close again.

Claudia's assistant kept Caroline updated on her Mother, passing messages over the years, continually advising how disappointed she was and how the only time Claudia would contemplate a reconciliation, would be in the event Caroline had seized the power source and manage to insert into the weapon of mass destruction. Only when Caroline had the world underneath her control, would Claudia grant her an audience. And now Caroline had succeeded. Her Mother would be so proud, she would reintroduce her into her life and Caroline would be the daughter Claudia had always dreamed of.

Caroline practically skipped out of the van. The joy of being able to speak to her Mother displayed across Caroline's face.

Pressing the call button to her Mother's number, she could hardly contain her excitement as she hopped from foot to foot until it was answered.

The phone rang twice before she heard Claudia's voice loud and clear, yet no words came out of Caroline's mouth. Dropping the phone to the floor, Caroline choked on the blood that was now pouring out of her mouth. Dropping to her knees, Caroline clutched her chest as she struggled to breath.

Collapsing onto her side, Caroline could still hear her Mother's voice projecting out. Spotting the phone on the floor inches away from her, Caroline summoned all her strength and inched along the tarmac, reaching out her arm that was not holding onto her chest, towards her Mother's voice. Her fingertips touching the thin metal casing, Caroline tried to grasp the phone, yet the line went dead. Blood still poured out of Caroline's mouth as she struggled once again, trying to reach it to call her Mother back, yet Caroline managed to push the phone farther out of reach.

Defeated, Caroline stopped moving and stared at the phone. She had almost done it. Her life had been dedicated to her Mother's work, yet this had all been ended by the person she trusted the most. Her glassy eyes moved to look at her killer before she took her last breath.

Craig stood there; his arm still outstretched with the smoke coming from the barrel of the gun as tears streamed down his face. This was his last resort. He had grown close to Caroline, had ensured he was at her beck and call day and night. He had helped her in her mission and knew why she was doing it, yet he could not let her complete this part. His family he held dear would have perished under Caroline's ruling. He knew Caroline's associates would make it their mission to destroy the person that ended Caroline's life, yet he would die with contentment his family would be safe and alive

Rachel watched as the back-up Robert had called fifteen minutes ago, jumped on Craig and brought him down to the ground, kicking the gun away.

Everything happened in slow motion. The sound of the gun shots still ringing in her ears as the soldiers all dressed in black, swarmed inside the van. Rachel had no idea who was who, if they were Caroline's army or Field Marshal Sanderson's.

Ordering the power source to release, Rachel stood up and raised her hands. Keeping her bag close she was roughly escorted to another van, identical to the one she was just in and confronted with Field Marshal Sanderson.

'Sir.' The soldier saluted as he released Rachel from his grip and left the van, shutting the door behind him.

'Miss Nichols. I hate to be direct, yet do you still have the power source?' Field Marshal Sanderson asked Rachel.

Rachel nodded and patted her bag.

Pulling out a radio transmitter, Field Marshal Sanderson uttered commands and the van started moving.

'We need to get you to the office immediately. Anything you need, let me know, I am at your disposal.'

Rachel nodded, too shell shocked to take anything in, yet this was a good thing. She needed to think straight, Nick was not there to guide her, yet at least now she knew there was no Caroline to stop it all going ahead. Looking at her watch that was splattered with blood, she had two hours to ensure everything was set up and ready.

'Call me Charlie.' Field Marshal Sanderson instructed. 'Here.' He said passing her some wipes to clean herself up with. 'Do you need anything?' Rachel shook her head. She couldn't talk about what had happened just yet. It would open a plethora of emotions and right now she needed to concentrate on the task in hand.

Wiping her face of Roberts's blood, she closed her eyes and inhaled deeply. Everything was resting on her and her alone. 'Charlie, when we reach the office, I need a clear pathway. Time is of the essence. I need to get to work attaching the power source to the rigging. I need the room clear of people barring two electrical engineers. I do not need any distractions nor offers of assistance, I will ask for help if I need it. Clear.'

Charlie nodded and used his radio transmitter to bark instructions again.

They arrived at the office and as asked, a clear pathway had been made for Rachel. The streets were clear, and an advisement of a gas leak had been plastered across the venue. The lift was open, ready for her to run inside and get to the seventh floor.

Rachel reached the board room and looked at the huge contraption. Her heart beating, she had no time for doubts, she needed to get the power source in place and ready.

Rachel placed the power source into the metal box next to the machine. Chunky cables ran from the metal box to the contraption, made with materials gathered from the TT pod.

'V.E.L.U.S. is everything in place?' Rachel asked.

'Miss Nichols, all checks have been completed and are waiting for your command.'

Rachel looked at the entrance of the board room. 'Field Marshal Sanderson, I will issue the start up in no less than 3 minutes. If you wish to remove yourself and your men from the building, please order evacuation now.'

'No Miss Nichols, we are in this together.' Charlie walked to the table and sat down next to Rachel. 'If Mr East were here, he would not leave.'

Rachel smiled and mouthed 'thank you' to him.

Placing his hand over Rachel's, he gave it a reassuring squeeze.

'V.E.L.U.S. initiate the start-up sequence.' Rachel instructed.

The metal box that contained the power source glowed blue. White stripes of lightening shot along the outer casing of the huge cables as the power made its way to the metal mechanism in the middle of the boardroom.

Rachel grasped onto Charlies fingers as she watched the large rectangular metal frame, alight with power. The once black frame glowed blue and white as the power surged through it.

A small warm breeze was beginning to blow around the room, moving loose papers and shifting light objects. The empty circular space inside of the metal frame, began to slowly turn different shades of blue and swirl around as if it were made of water. Lightening stemming from the frame flickered across the pool of water as the slow swirling became quicker and faster. The noise in the room began to get louder, until it was almost deafening. The wind swirled around the room blowing anything that was not fixed down into a tiny tornado. Field Marshal Sanderson tugged on Rachel's hand as he manoeuvred her into a safer place, away from the wind.

Holding her tight with his arm around her waist, he held them both close to the fixed metal girder near the window. A loud bang signalled the board room door had slammed shut from the wind. The lightening spreading across the pool inside of the metal frame was getting more frequent and cracking louder with each second that passed.

The room shuddered as the swirling pool inside the metal frame gathered more momentum, swirling faster and faster, until all the different shades of blue blurred together. A loud screeching noise came from the inside of the circle, shattering the windows and covering the boardroom in glass. The middle of the pool started to open up slightly, only giving way to a circle of darkness. The black circle gradually got larger and larger until, a body shot out of the middle of the pool, causing the metal frame to shudder and collapse in on itself. Sparks flew across the room as the power that once surged through the chunky cables to the metal, found itself supplying nothing.

Rachel saw the power source switch itself off and the wind and noise suddenly stopped, rendering the room into silence. Rachel could hear the blood pumping in her ears as she rushed across to where the body had landed.

Bending down, Rachel could see it was a man in his thirties, laid naked on the floor. He was breathing yet unconscious.

'We need medics in here.' Field Marshal Sanderson shouted as the door opened and people rushed in. Rachel looked at the man laid before her. Little did he know how he had shaped the world.

Taking off her jacket, she laid it across him to protect his modesty before the room became filled with people.

His eyes flickered open as she still stared down at him.

The look of confusion on his face said it all as he tried to sit up

'Whoa, lay back down, we need to get you checked out before you move.' She said softly to him.

Reaching out his hand, he touched her face. 'Magda?' He whispered back smiling. 'I thought I would never see you again.'

Chapter 39
United

Rachel paced the hospital corridors. She had never been good at waiting, yet now she was here waiting for information on the two most important people in the world right now.
Nick's operation had been successful, they had fitted a stent in his heart. It had not been confirmed; however, the doctors had a suspicion the heart attack had been brought along by a concoction of drugs. The tests had been fast tracked and the doctor should get the results when Nick came round from the anaesthetic.
Joshua was in an induced coma. He had suffered burns when he came through the portal. V.E.L.U.S.'s calculations were correct. Joshua would indeed return back to the place, same time, and date he had originally left, once he died in the past.
He had no form of protection when he had been transported back. The doctors needed to ensure the burns he acquired, where only superficial and nothing more sinister had occurred. Rachel was confident he would be OK. He called her Magda.
Deciding to sit down, she walked towards Maria, Field Marshal Sanderson and Sandra Callaghan who were all waiting on news for Nick and Joshua.
The doors to the corridor opened and a doctor walked towards them all. Rachel held her breath as she waited for the doctor to speak.
'I am Doctor Wilks, the consultant looking after Mr S East. Mr S East has awoken and is doing well. He needs to rest and recuperate. We have received his blood work back and it seems our theory was correct. A high dosage of methamphetamines, commonly known as crystal meth, where present in his blood stream. Noting his history, we are not concerned he is a user, therefore we have passed this to the police to investigate.' Maria

and Rachel looked at each other shocked at this information, while the doctor continued. 'He has been asking a lot of questions since he came around from surgery, ones we do not know. Is there a Rachel here?'

'Yes, I am Rachel.' She informed the doctor.

The doctor looked at his notes. 'Mr. East has asked for an update on the situation. He is threatening to discharge himself if he is not notified of the outcome.'

Rachel and Maria laughed. It felt like a weight had lifted off their shoulders. Nick was definitely on the way to recovery threatening to discharge himself.

'Maria, his wife, has the answers to all his questions. Along with the authority to make sure he does not discharge himself.' Rachel advised the doctor.

The doctor nodded at Maria. 'Field Marshal Sanderson, I need to speak to you privately.' The doctor motioned for Charlie to follow him.

Rachel stood up. 'If it is about Joshua, you will need to relay the information to myself also.'

Doctor Wilks and Field Marshal Sanderson stopped and turned around to look at Rachel. Field Marshal Sanderson gave the nod of approval and Rachel followed them into a side office.

The doctor sat behind his desk as Rachel and Charlie sat opposite.

'Mr. J East is doing extremely well. We removed his V.A.I. with the instructions you had given and brought him out of his induced coma. His vitals are perfect, and he is sitting up and talking with no adverse effects of the V.A.I. removal. He knows he is no longer in the past; however he has noticed he is not in his future either. We have pacified him for now, however I would recommend someone going to see him shortly to give him some clarity.' The doctor swung the monitor on his computer around. Pointing at the MRI scan, he continued. 'The only defect we have found is Mr. J East's heart is on the wrong side of his body. I have seen this anomaly previously, however due to not having his prior medical history, we cannot determine if this is a defect from birth, or an adverse effect of his time travel. Regardless, this will not hinder his health in any way. Everything is intact, just on the opposite side. His burns are superficial and will heal without any further operations. My only concern is his mental health and what this time travel will do. There are no signs of any contusions to the brain, however, Mr. J East has been through a traumatic ordeal.'

The doctor removed his glasses and placed them on his desk. 'This is something I, nor has anyone in my profession has dealt with before. Mr. J East is coming back to the future he originally left, however from what I can gather, everything he once knew will not be how it was. He has been asking for his wife, Magda, and claims he saw her when he was initially was transported back to this time period. I am not sure if this is a condition from his time travel.'

Rachel shook her head. 'It is not from the time travel. He thinks I am Magda. I look just like his wife, and his wife's twin sister.'

The doctor looked at Rachel and then back at Field Marshal Sanderson. Holding his hands up, he smiled at them both. 'It's been a long day, I am not sure I want to venture further into this, whatever it is.'

'Can we go and see him?' Rachel asked.

The doctor nodded and stood up to lead them to Joshua's room.

Field Marshal Sanderson entered and then Rachel followed.

Joshua was sat up in his bed as the nurse took his blood pressure. Spotting Rachel he looked at her, dressed in jeans and a t-shirt and frowned. As Rachel inched closer, he smiled. 'You're not Magda, are you?' He softly said.

'No, I am not, my name is Rachel.' She replied as she sat on the edge of his bed. 'I am a descendant from Martha. How are you feeling?'

'A bit sore from the burns and a slight headache but apart from that I am good.' Joshua responded not taking his eyes off Rachel. 'You even sound the same.' He said, his eyes boring into her.

'Mr. East. I am Field Marshal Sanderson. I am sure you have a lot of questions. Rachel and I will do our best to answer anything you may need to know. If we do not have the answers, we certainly know the people that do.'

Joshua looked down at his hands. 'I have so many questions, yet there is only one that really matters.'

After a slight pause, Rachel urged him to ask.

'Was my mission a success?' Joshua asked shyly. His cheeks flushed with embarrassment at the question. He felt extremely arrogant even asking it. Of course, they only knew him due to V.E.L.U.S. and any archives they would have found. He started to apologise for even asking when Rachel and Field Sanderson Marshal started laughing.

'Was your mission a success?' Rachel looked at him. 'You have no idea how successful your mission was. The full world knows who you are and still knows who you are over two thousand years later. Everyone knows when your birthday is and celebrates it. We mourn and rejoice your death every year. Millions of people talk about you every day and you are a part of a majority of the earth's population daily routine. There is still evil in the world and that is being fought daily. At one time in history, nearly every person followed your way of thinking and the world was a happy place for a while, yet the world is beginning to turn into a darker place yet again. The gap between rich and poor, races and religion are growing larger by the day, fueled by hatred and anger. Everyone is looking out for themselves and not for each other. Money is the driving force of the world, without it, you are left to rot and there are only a few decent people out there that help the ones in the gutter. I am ashamed to admit, I have thought only of myself at times and unfortunately others suffered because of my choice.' Rachel choked back the tears as she thought of Yuri.

'It wasn't your fault Rachel.' She felt Field Marshal Sanderson's hand on her shoulder. 'It was not her fault.' He said again speaking directly to a startled Joshua.

'I know evil when I see it, and that is not you Rachel.' Joshua said smiling at her. 'Is the TT pod still in action?'

Rachel smiled at him. 'Yes and V.E.L.U.S. is still very much with us.'

A huge smile spread across Joshua's face. 'My mission was not just to teach people how to help one another, it was about giving people hope that there is something out there looking after them in their darkest days. Giving them something to hold on to, and speak to when they are alone and suffering, building a community where everyone is accepted. I know I have a lot to catch up with, yet I think I may have an idea on how to stop the darkness spreading across the world again.' He said as he placed his hand on top of Rachel's.

They both gasped as they felt the spark of electricity run between them. Joshua looked deep into Rachel's eyes and pulled his hand away.

She was the image of Magda, and of Jess, yet she was neither of them. He knew he needed to steer clear of her, he would be mistaking her for Magda too much, yet deep down he knew she was the only person he trusted right now and the only person he would be able to count on to complete his mission of peace on earth.

To Be Continued ....

Printed in Great Britain
by Amazon